ADDRESSED TO GRETA

ADDRESSED TO GRETA

Fiona Sussman

BATEMAN
BOOKS

Typographical design © David Bateman Ltd, 2020

Published in 2020 by David Bateman Ltd,
Unit 2/5 Workspace Drive, Hobsonville,
Auckland 0618, New Zealand
www.batemanbooks.co.nz
ISBN: 978-1-98-853860-0

A catalogue record for this book is available
from the National Library of New Zealand.

Cover design: Keely O'Shannessy
Printed in China by Everbest Printing Co. Ltd

To Luigi

'This above all: to thine own self be true
And it must follow, as night the day
Thou canst not then be false to any man.'
— Shakespeare, *Hamlet,* Act I, scene iii

CHAPTER 1

'Good on you, love,' the old fellow said, his Adam's apple tracking up and down his bristly neck. 'Bloody nuisance, pukekos.'

Greta blushed. 'I didn't mean to kill it,' she said, horrified that he thought the act deliberate. 'I swerved too late and—'

'A modest hero, too.' The man gave a gruff chuckle and tossed the dead bird headfirst into the bin. 'I keep a tally of my roadkill. Bonus points for possums. I'm into double digits this month.'

Greta started to cry. It was the stress of having driven through the suburbs with a dead bird wedged under her fender. Of having had to stop and ask for help removing it. Of being judged to be a person who killed pukekos . . . for sport.

The man blinked. Clicked his dentures. Shifted his weight from side to side.

But Greta could not stop crying.

The poor, bewildered chap. He'd probably grown up on a farm somewhere and believed animals were not something to get sentimental about.

She apologised. Waved away her tears. Thanked him through strings of snot.

What she really wanted to do was retrieve the pukeko. Take it home and bury it at the bottom of her garden. Give it a proper farewell. But she couldn't. What would the man think? She'd asked for his help. Furthermore, she was no good with gore.

She considered retracing her route to search for any chicks she might have left orphaned under a garden hedge or in some roadside ditch. But it was late, the traffic was terrible and she had to get to work.

Later, when she trawled through the day, it would be this that bothered her the most. Her inability to act in synchrony with her heart. As if by asking for the man's help she'd signed up to his values.

1

She climbed back into her car and pulled her door shut, then opened it again to release her trapped skirt.

The man was still standing in the forecourt, his mouth slightly open, as if he'd got stuck trying to process what had just transpired.

Greta turned the key in the ignition. Too far — the teeth-tingling noise alerting everyone in the fuel station that there was an incompetent driver in their midst.

She felt herself flush; forced a laugh; gesticulated through the windscreen to make light of her clumsiness.

Then she started the car, put her foot flat, stalled twice, and lurched onto the road to resume her journey.

The incident had gatecrashed her morning, setting the tone for the rest of the day. When she'd woken in her small stucco villa, stripes of April sunlight falling across her bed, there'd been nothing to suggest anything other than the rubber-stamp usual. A dew-damp *Herald* poking out from under the clumps of agapanthus, tossed there by Dylan, the careless paperboy. Marilyn Monroe, all cluck and squawk, on the back deck, demanding to be fed. The spitting Moka pot spraying freckles of espresso across her hotplate. Sparrows agitating. Breakfast TV exaggerating. This was the constancy that ordered her days, her weeks and months, routine stretching across her life like weed mat, keeping all chance at bay. Well, almost all.

It had been different for a brief pocket of time. Two years. More like two-and-a-half. But that period was now just a crumpled cluster of memories concertinaed against the rest of her thirty-something years.

Thirty-something. Not owning up to her age was a habit Greta had acquired after a childhood of forever being propelled into the following year by her mother.

'Seven-year-old girls are not afraid of the dark.'
Greta was six.

'Just being a teenager does not give you carte blanche to be insolent.'
Greta was twelve.

What had a pukeko been doing in the middle of a suburban Auckland street, anyway? It was not, after all, some countryside lane. If only she hadn't been forced to turn into Bardia Street, the incident would never have happened. But there'd been an accident on Lake Road and a diversion was in place.

Greta edged slowly forward through the shopping precinct. She was definitely going to be late for work. She chewed her lip and tried focussing on her pelvic floor exercises.

She'd been 'holding' for the count of three when something caught her eye. She leaned over the steering wheel to take a better look. There was a woman standing on a stepladder in a store window, taping a large red sign to the glass. *Business for Sale.*

Greta's breathing picked up, the idea growing instantly full and round in her head, like one of those tiny toy capsules which, when tossed into a basinful of water, burst open and unfold into some fabulous, spongy sea-creature — a red octopus, green seahorse, a purple puffer fish.

Already she could envision herself standing behind an old-fashioned cash register in *The Dainty Spork*. She loved that word. Spork. The way it sounded. The cleverness of combining two words in one — spoon and fork. The shop would be a destination to satisfy both the stomach and the soul. A place where cake would be sold by the slice, so that even patrons who were single were catered for; no pressure to buy a cake fit for a family or big group of friends. There'd be Sachertorte, chocolate-mint sponge, and walnut-and-coffee gâteau. Cakes soaked in citrus syrup. Lemon meringue pies piled high. Even a simple sultana loaf. She'd have glass domes set out on a rustic farmhouse table to display the day's delights, and the air would be infused with caramelised sugar, heilala vanilla, and poached Black Doris plums. There'd be a bookshelf stocked with baking books, a giant blackboard scribbled with quotations, and curled up in the sunshine, blissfully unfazed by some prodding little customer, would be the shop's mascot — an English bulldog replete with polka-dot kerchief and shop-appropriate name. Raisin, Coconut, or Caramel perhaps.

Greta sighed, the fantasy instantly fading. She was getting older and reality was far quicker to douse her dreams. She'd grown resigned to the fact that there was no link between her aspirations and ambitions, and the tarmac of life as it unfolded. '*No expectation, no disappointment*' had been her mother's mantra. It served Greta well too.

An ambulance siren exploded her reverie. She glanced at her watch: 8.43am. She'd never get to work on time, let alone early. Orders would have piled up in her absence, and the thought of beginning a new week on the back foot . . .

Organisation was the scaffolding on which Greta hung her days, tidy lines and measured minutes the leash she secured to the capriciousness of human existence. She sent out invoices as orders came in, packed her lunchbox every evening, wrote Christmas cards in September, and renewed her car licence a month before the due date. Trying to stay ahead of the game was an all-consuming task. Like weeding a garden, it was a job which could never be signed off. Despite her best efforts, a prevailing sense of unease threaded through her days, a sense of unfinished business ever eroding her calm. And now, after a week away from work, she couldn't imagine what mayhem lay in wait.

She wiped her palms on her skirt and wondered why she'd agreed to take a week off from work to housesit for her former neighbours, Lorraine and Rory, while they holidayed in Hawaii. Greta never took time off, except for statutory days when the shop was shut, preferring instead to stockpile leave in case she needed a significant chunk for an emergency. *'Being prepared for a rainy day'* was how her mother used to phrase it. Since childhood, Greta had fretted about rainy days.

To be fair, she did give thorough consideration to all the implications of housesitting before acquiescing. Including the need to hire an automatic chicken feeder for Marilyn Monroe, place the delivery of her newspaper and post on hold, forego the fourth session of council-run composting classes at the local community hall, and apply for annual leave from the shop. She'd never applied for leave before.

In the end it was her fear of losing Lorraine's friendship which overrode the inconvenience of it all. And, once she'd committed herself, Greta did experience a brief frisson of excitement at the thought of the impending adventure.

It didn't last. As the spectre of disruption loomed, Greta found herself wishing she'd had the gumption to say no.

The traffic came to an abrupt halt, catapulting her up against her car horn. It usually offered only a pitiful mewl, but today managed a full-bodied blast.

The man in the car ahead shot Greta a furious glance in his rear-view mirror, then stuck his head out the window.

'What? You want me to fly?'

She waved her hands apologetically.

'Fucking insect!' he bellowed, ducking back inside.

People in the street turned and stared. A woman pushing a pram shook her ponytail. A cyclist thumped his fist on her roof. 'Patience!'

Greta felt a flush move up her body like a Mexican wave. She glanced in the mirror. Her face was a hot, ripe red.

Insect? The word had felled her like a boxer's left hook. A grub of a word hollowing her out and confirming what she already knew, that she was small, insignificant, a nobody. A nobody who drove a small blue hatchback with a dent in the driver's door.

The dent was courtesy of Dylan, the paperboy, who'd cycled into her parked car while texting. It was too big for the Ding Man to smooth out, and too small a depression to justify Greta losing her no-claims bonus. So, it had remained. The thing was, a dented door carried connotations, instantly dropping a driver several rungs down the ladder of respectability. This day of all days Greta wished her door had been dent-free.

As the queue of cars began to move, she eased to the left into a loading zone and switched off the engine. Her heart was thumping in her throat and her breath was a tense trill. She knew what Judy, her therapist, would say. 'Something so small should not impact on your equanimity, Greta.' But 'should' was a fine word indeed. Like her blue hatchback, it took very little to dent Greta's tin-thin self-esteem.

She tried repeating out loud the cognitive reinforcements Judy had gone over with her so many times before, each mantra worth at least fifty dollars when one took into account the cost of a single therapy session. However, the expensive little words didn't stand a chance against the barrage of negative thoughts now assailing her. Finally, she fumbled in the glove box for the small blue bottle she kept there and placed a few drops of Rescue Remedy under her tongue. Then she closed her eyes and tried to focus on her breathing . . . Easier said than done with a passing street sweeper's bristles rotating in a completely different rhythm to her metered inhalations.

CHAPTER 2

By the time Greta arrived at Blue Sun Spas, Pools and Pipes she was over an hour late for work and her boss was pacing the shop floor. For more than twenty years Greta had been the first on site to open up, except for the time she'd suffered a gangrenous appendix and been rushed to North Shore Hospital.

'I thought something terrible had happened!' Jud Rutland growled. 'I do wish you'd carry a mobile phone. For situations such as this. It is the twenty-first century, after all.'

Greta didn't like the idea of a mobile phone. She was suspicious enough of microwave ovens, let alone carrying some small radioactive device on her person. It didn't fit with her ethos anyway, of celebrating nature, preserving the planet, limiting the constraints that came with being a slave to technology.

Some years back, when her dementing mother had started wandering the streets and Greta needed to be easily contactable, she'd succumbed to societal pressure and bought one. However, she kept forgetting to charge the blessed thing. It was probably now in some bottom drawer, its long-dead display clouded by dust.

'I'm terribly sorry, Jud. The traffic. It was beyond my control.'

Punctuality was something Greta prided herself on. It was part of the rigid framework she applied to her life. Losing control was what she feared the most. In fact, the only recurring dream she ever had was of being inside an elevator as it plunged down its shaft.

Judy had suggested that perhaps the randomness of significant life events in Greta's early childhood had made her this way.

'I'll work through lunch,' Greta said, hurrying to her desk. The answering machine was already flashing *Full*.

Her boss waved his hand in protestation. 'Don't be silly, girl! Catch your breath. Make yourself a cup of tea or something. I could even be persuaded to have one.'

In February it had been twenty-two years since she'd arrived fresh-faced from school to work for Jud's father. Greta suspected that Rutland Senior had offered her the job more as a favour to her mother, with whom he'd been having an affair. Part of a guilt package designed to appease, when he told her mother he was in fact married and would not be leaving his wife.

Greta had harboured career notions loftier than working in a pool chemicals shop. 'I'm going to be famous,' she'd told the careers counsellor at Takapuna Grammar. When Wimbledon was being broadcast, Greta was going to become a famous tennis player, for days afterwards practising against the garage wall to roars of adoration from the centre-court crowd. Then, after seeing her first musical, Greta decided she was going to be the next Libby Morris, her name spelt out in Broadway lights. And when she was given a book of magician's tricks for her birthday, she again re-envisaged herself, this time releasing white doves from a tall black hat.

Despite the variance in her aspirations, there was always one common denominator — an impressed, bewildered, and adoring crowd. Being extraordinary and being seen were recurring themes in her dreams.

When Greta took the job at the pool shop, she reasoned it would just be a stopgap until she was free to pursue her own ambitions. Her mother needed the additional income; a self-employed seamstress did not draw a good wage, especially when the well-heeled housewives of the northern suburbs were forever bartering her down.

Greta sighed as she thought back to those early days behind the shop counter, padded shoulders and a Princess Di hairstyle lending her at least the illusion of importance. In retrospect, her frizzy brown hair, solid limbs, and oversized feet were at odds with the sleek Sloane Ranger look.

For a while she held on to the belief that a different life was waiting for her around the corner — a life which would propel her out of the mundane into a world of colour and adventure. Yet as the years wore on and the bills kept coming, her designs grew less grand and the gap between her aspirations and reality increasingly unbridgeable. The longer she remained in the small shop steeped in the nostril-singeing smell of chlorine, the harder it became to contemplate leaving. She even stopped trying to force her hair *this* way, when it always ended up going *that* way.

And now, in 2017, at the age of thirty-something, her dreams, like her ovaries, had shrunk down to fit within the small cubicle of space housing her desk, telephone and few photographs. She didn't even put aside paper any longer for her maybe-one-day children, something she'd done for years in preparation for the global paper shortage after too many trees had been cut down.

To be fair, it hadn't been all bad. Courtesy of the company, Greta enjoyed the latest model spa pool on the deck of her rented Devonport home. It featured twenty-six hydrotherapy jets, two recliners with padded headrests, an LED mood-lighting programme, ultra-quiet jet pump, and a Scandinavian-Spruce finish. Enjoying a spa after work was one of Greta's few indulgences. Chocolate and cake were, of course, her others.

However, the biggest boon to come out of her years of service to pools was Walter. Walter had walked into the shop and into her life one overcast October morning — tall and tanned, with a languid voice and an easy, crumpled smile, his grey-green eyes like giant lily pads floating beneath soft hoods of skin.

Greta glanced at the clock above her desk, her hand hovering over the ringing telephone. Her first day back at work had been a massive clean-up exercise, just as she'd feared it would be, and she was weary. Too tight to employ an agency temp in her absence, Jud had cobbled together the unlikeliest of cover for her five days away — his wife, Charlene, and their bottle-orange daughter, Tiffany. In just five days Greta's sanctified space and filing system had been completely disrupted and her keyboard encrusted with doughnut sugar.

There was an abrupt *click* as the answer phone was activated, followed almost immediately by the drone of a dial tone.

Greta chewed her lip. She should have picked up. Technically the shop was open for another seven minutes. Now she would never know who'd called, and it might have been important.

As she bent down to retrieve her handbag from under the desk, the ringing began again.

She lunged for the receiver. 'Blue Sun Spas, Pools and Pipes. You're speaking with Greta.'

'Miss Jellings?'

'Yes?' It was always a surprise, and a little terrifying, to be the intended recipient of a call.

'I am calling from the chambers of Parse and French.'

Chambers. Greta's mouth prickled and her mind started scurrying down several different alleyways, all of which involved wrongdoing on her part.

'You are a hard person to get hold of, Miss Jellings,' said the woman on the other end of the line, her husky voice edged with reprimand. 'I've been trying to contact you for some time.'

Greta hated the way people referred to her as *Miss*; it felt like a pointed reminder of her single status. Men were simply *Mr* regardless of whether they were married or not. No exposure required.

It was not as if she was single by choice. She would have given her eyeteeth to have a man in her life. Although how her life would look with a man in it was beyond the reaches of her imagination.

'I'm so sorry,' Greta began. 'I . . . you see . . . I don't usually take time off. But Lorraine and Rory, they're my neighbours, or rather used to be, until—'

'Miss Jellings, I'm ringing on behalf of Angus French, the lawyer acting for Walter Haywood's estate.'

Walter. Greta closed her eyes. She hadn't heard his name spoken out loud for over eight months. She wanted to run away from it and also straight towards it.

'Mr French wondered if you would be able come into his office to attend to some rather important paperwork.'

'Unfortunately, I . . . well, it's just that—'

'It shouldn't take long. How about one lunch hour next week? Tuesday perhaps?'

'Uh, Tuesday should be fine.'

Now her entire week would be hijacked by worry. She should never have picked up.

After Walter came into her life, Greta had changed. In so many ways. In every way, really. He used to call her his little lancewood, likening her to the small New Zealand tree, which, he explained, underwent such a radical transformation that for a long time the young and mature trees were believed to be entirely different species.

Months had now elapsed. Eight months. And Walter's words, which had once wooed her out of her very complicated head, were so soft they were almost inaudible. Just whispers, memories, make-believe.

The blueprint laid down in her early life could not be so easily altered. What she'd taken to be change in the two years she'd known Walter was really just veneer. She was still the same puny person.

In her darkest moments, Greta wished she'd never met him. It was harder to have tasted a different reality, glimpsed some other life — a life which now served simply as a taunt and tease. A brutal yardstick against which to measure the rest of her existence. A dissatisfactionometer.

6th October 2014, the day she met Walter, had begun like any other at the shop. Large order in from the public baths, a frustrated Coatesville customer complaining about his pea-soup pool, flowers for Jud's wife selected and delivered.

'Excuse me?'

Greta looks up, expecting to see the shiny-faced Taiwanese man who hurries from place to place in his courier-red van. She keeps a stash of caramel clusters in her top drawer just for him. But it is not the kindly courier. Instead, a man in long khaki shorts and a sky-blue shirt, sleeves rolled to his elbows, is looking at her from under a fringe of messy blond hair, with the same head-tilted shyness as Prince William.

Any man taller than Greta's 'big-boned' six-foot frame has her immediate attention.

'Walter Haywood! Well I never,' Greta's boss bellows from the back of the shop as he scuttles over to greet the newcomer.

'Jud Rutland?' The man's voice is Alan-Rickman deep. 'It has been a long time,'

'Too right,' Rutland stutters. 'Year thirteen, eh? Year bloody thirteen.'

The man is at least two heads taller than Greta's boss, and his reserved manner in complete contrast to the excitable Rutland's.

'So, tell me, Walt, where have you been all my life?' says an over-animated Jud.

The man gives a self-deprecating shrug. 'Long story. I just recently moved back to Auckland to manage a private estate out west.'

'Moved back?'

'From New York.' He includes Greta in his gaze.

'New York!' Jud says, his lower jaw protruding in an excited tic. 'So, what, you got tired of those brash Yankees?'

'Pretty neat bunch of people, actually.'

Rutland pulls in his chin and nods earnestly.

'Well, what can we do for you? But, hey, before we get to that, how about a bite of lunch first? I was just about to head out. Be great to catch up properly. Reminisce about good old Grammar days.'

'Uh . . . sure.'

'Excellent! Excellent! Now, where's my wallet?'

Rutland makes a show of patting his pockets. It is a ritual Greta has witnessed a few times before.

'No worries. I've got mine,' says the visitor. He puts his hand out to Greta. 'I'm Walter, by the way.'

His grip is strong and warm.

Greta makes a weird grunting noise. Her face feels very hot.

'Are you joining us?'

She shakes her head. Moves her hands randomly.

'Someone's got to man the fort,' Rutland says, giving her a vaudeville wink. 'Or should I say, woman the fort. Gotta be careful what one says these days.' Then he ushers his friend out of the shop.

Greta watches as they disappear down the road, her boss's short legs working twice as fast as his friend's long lollop.

There is something very likeable about Walter Haywood. Very likeable indeed.

Feeling the prick of tears now, Greta squeezed the bridge of her nose with her forefingers.

Outside, a wintry evening was collapsing in on the day. Wind slapped rain against the glass, streetlamps carved jagged lines of light across the dusk, umbrellas tugged and bobbed. People were heading home to dinner, family, loved ones.

She put her handbag back under her desk. She might as well stay late and prepare the next day's orders.

CHAPTER 3

Walter was a regular face in the shop that summer. As head gardener for a twelve-hectare estate boasting two swimming pools, a sauna and spa, he was frequently dropping in to get water samples tested or to collect more chemicals.

'Looks like bagmoth,' he says to Greta one Thursday morning, as he examines the cutting she's brought in from her garden. Walter's hands have remnants of dirt embedded in the creases of his sun-weathered skin, but his nails are immaculate, blunt white lines. Greta always takes note of a man's fingernails.

He points at the cocoon embedded with plant matter. 'The silk pouch is a giveaway.'

She peers closer, pulling a face.

'You can use some natural organic spray,' he says. 'Pyrethrum should do it. I'll bring some in next time, if you like.'

The two talked gardening whenever Walter dropped by, plants proving the perfect intermediary. When Greta was focused on the name of some flower or the growing habits of a shrub, her awkward self-consciousness magically faded.

Walter, like Nora, Greta's late mother, had green fingers. (Since Greta was six, her mother had insisted on being called Nora. Not Mama, or Mother, or Mum. Only Nora.)

And like Nora, Walter knew the Latin names for plants. *Pelargonium peltatum, Pittosporum tenuifolium,* and *Viola cornuta* spilt from his mouth with matter-of-fact ease. There was nothing pretentious about it though; Walter appeared entirely comfortable in his own skin.

They were talking mass planting when he first invited her over.

'Clustering a single species can create real drama in a garden,' he says,

while signing for an order of muriatic acid. 'We've just created a bed of yellow irises. It's pretty striking. Like a living Monet.'

'Gee whiz!'

Greta cringes as the dated exclamation slips out.

'Please take a photo. A photo would be really very great!'

'Really very great, hey?' he says with a playful wink. 'Better still, come see for yourself.' He scratches his shoulder with his pen. 'What about Saturday? We can have a picnic.'

Greta could still recall how her vision had blurred and the room listed. She hadn't seen it coming. Didn't believe it possible.

Nora used to say there was *'a lid for every can',* but Greta had long given up trying to find a soulmate. Right from schooldays she'd known she was different. Not one of the popular kids who effortlessly acquired friends like charms on a bracelet, she'd been left to navigate the lonely periphery, spending most lunchtimes with Cyril Denopoulos, (and sometimes Claudia Peplinksi, when Claudia had had a falling out with Sandy Rogers). Of course, rescuing Cyril's shorts from the girls' toilets had done little to help Greta's bid for inclusion into the cool club.

By all accounts, Greta lacked another crucial qualifying criterion — the ability to make small talk. It wasn't as if she didn't try. However, it was a vicious cycle; the harder she tried, the more contrived and silly her efforts sounded.

'It's really groovy hanging loose with you,' had dangled in space like a pair of ugly grey bloomers left out on the line for everyone to ridicule.

'Do you want to come over to my house? We could watch the video of Charles and Diana's wedding.' That the video was over a decade old and the couple no longer joined in blissful union had somehow eluded the teenage Greta.

'If you don't know what to say,' Nora once suggested, *'ask people about themselves. Show an interest in their world. People love to talk about themselves.'*

Greta had tried that too, interrogating one fellow so enthusiastically about his new car that he'd asked if she was hoping to buy it off him.

Another problem, or so she'd been told, was her tendency to take people too literally. There was the time Nora connived to get Greta together with the hardware-store assistant's sixteen-year-old son. He arrived on the doorstep one humid afternoon dressed in tight jeans, black pointy boots, and a leather jacket, and asked if Greta would like to go to *Grease* with him. She said no, because she thought he was asking her to go to the other side of the world with him.

Judy, Greta's therapist, had laughed uproariously when Greta shared this anecdote. '*Oh Greta,*' she'd said, once she regained her composure, '*you're so sweet.*'

But Greta couldn't help it; that was just the way her mind worked. Of course the boy would not have asked her to go with him to Athens or Corfu! Greta could see how funny that was now, but obvious was obvious only in retrospect.

With Walter, however, it had been effortless from the start, as if all the awkward preliminaries had been dealt with on some previous occasion. As if she'd finally found the missing foot of a comfy pair of slippers. And as he drew her into his leafy green world, her insecurities started to miraculously evaporate.

Much later, Greta would try to understand what it was about Walter that had made him so easy to be around.

His height?

It was definitely easier to talk to a man who didn't leave her feeling like Gulliver.

The absence of judgement?

After years of practice, Greta was hardwired to pick up on the slightest smirk, folded lip, or mocking lilt. In Walter, though, she found a willingness to look beyond her ineptitude. Even an obliviousness to it. That he himself had first-hand knowledge of living on the fringe might have explained his easy empathy.

Their shared love of Nature?

Yes.

His easy-going demeanour?

Certainly. Walter's relaxed manner was contagious and quick to quiet the ever-critical policeman who ruled Greta's thoughts.

It was only much later that she came to realise she was not the only one to benefit from the relationship; Walter also derived comfort and safety from their connection.

She still held in her head every detail of that first picnic.

The air is a screech of cicadas carried on a poplar-leaf breeze, the sky its best summer blue. Walter shakes out a creased tablecloth and lays it in the shade of a giant chestnut tree.

She hovers.

'*Find a comfy spot,' he says.*

It feels too familiar to sit cross-legged on the ground, so she perches on her knees as he unpacks the cardboard box he's carried from his cottage.

Soft white-bread sandwiches. White bread! Hard-boiled eggs. Baby tomatoes. Black figs. (Expensive at this time of year.) Poppy-seed friands.

'*Chips!' she cries, when he pulls out a packet of Salt and Vinegar chips. 'This feels like a* Famous Five *picnic.'*

He laughs. 'I guess we could be on Billycock Hill.'

'*Yes, we could!' she says, sitting back on her bottom and crossing her legs. 'I was always ravenous by the end of any one of their adventures. Potted meat, jam tarts, homemade ginger beer.'*

Walter pours elderflower cordial into two hand-painted mugs. 'For me it was Charlie and The Chocolate Factory. *I'm still in search of Fudgemellow Delight.*

She likes the way he says Fudgemellow Delight with a slight American twang.

'*And a peach as juicy as the one in* James and the Giant—'

She falters. Blinks away the image of her father. 'Now I always make a point of reading with a snack in easy reach. Peanut butter on toast, my preference.'

'*Sounds like we both love our food.'*

'*And books,' Greta says quickly, ticking off another ideal-man quality. Not that she is putting Walter to the test. But there are some basic prerequisites for any prospective partner.*

Prospective partner? Ha! She is getting ahead of herself. It is just that this is the first date she's been on in years. And so far, unbelievably, it is going well. Extraordinarily well.

'*What's your favourite book?' she asks, delighted she can unapologetically embrace her nerdiness.*

'*I don't think I have one favourite,' he says, picking up a sandwich and taking a bite.*

15

*He chews, taking his time. 'I enjoy Annie Proulx. Vikram Seth . . .
Tuck in Greta. We have to put a dent in this — it's just you and me
today.'*

*Greta takes a chip. 'I love chips,' she says, chewing carefully so as not
to make too loud a crunching sound.*

'What's your favourite?' he asks.

*'Sour cream and chives. Not that I eat junk food very often. Ever, really.
The only time I got to eat chips at school was when Cyril Denopoulos
and I swapped lunches.'*

Why is she talking about school? She is nearly forty years old.

*She feels the rush of blood to her face. 'I wasn't criticising your choice
of food. This is all amazing. It's just that—' And she is off. On a roll.
Sabotaging the moment with her ineptitude.*

*Walter nods. 'The very fact that chips are junk food only adds to their
appeal, don't you think? Sort of forbidden fruit. But you still haven't told
me your favourite book.'*

*'Gorillas in the Mist,' Greta says as automatically as her favourite
chip flavour.*

'About that conservationist, isn't it?'

*'Yes, Dian Fossey,' Greta says breathlessly. 'It's about her life and
the work she did in Africa with the gorillas. An incredible story. Heartbreaking. I cry every time.'*

'How often have you read it?'

*Greta blushes. 'About once a year. You should. I can lend it to you—'
She stops. She does not like lending out books; it is like loaning out a
member of one's family. 'You'll find it in the library too, if that's easier.'*

'So you prefer true stories?'

*She shakes her head. 'To be honest, I mostly read fiction. But that book,
for a number of reasons, means a lot to me.'*

Walter waits.

She looks away. Chews her lip. 'May I have a fig?'

*She can't, or rather shouldn't, share anything too personal on a first
date; she doesn't want to scare him off.*

*The afternoon disappears as they talk about books and birds and the
endangered blue whale. Self-service supermarket checkouts. Eating with
chopsticks. The art of making a good omelette too. Talking has never
been so easy.*

Greta keeps waiting for reality to barge in. It doesn't. And when she gets home later that day she floats through her house, taking down all the pieces of paper pinned to her walls and stuck to her mirrors — the quotations, inspirations and magazine-wise words, which have only ever temporarily assuaged, their power lost long before the sun has bleached their print and curled their corners.

'Happiness is like a butterfly: the more you chase it, the more it will elude you.' — HENRY DAVID THOREAU

'A journey of a thousand miles begins with a single step.' — LAO TZU

'Better a little which is well done, than a great deal imperfectly.' — PLATO

CHAPTER 4

Greta arrived at the offices of Parse and French just before one. Already unnerved from the drive over the Harbour Bridge — dark semi-circles of perspiration blooming under her arms — she was out of breath by the time she'd walked the four-and-a-half blocks from her parked car to the lawyer's office.

Ponsonby, a trendy inner-city suburb of cafes, pedigreed pooches and svelte apartments, was like an ant nest — it never slowed. This was a place unconcerned with the mundaneness of work, mortgages, renewal of motor-vehicle licences, or roof repairs. Rather, the steady supply of Prosecco, dermal fillers, and café lattes was what kept this part of town pumping. Greta felt entirely out of place as she hurried down the glamorous avenue in her sensible sandals and bargain-bin sunglasses.

The address directed her to an old brick building with an ancient, cage-like lift and graffitied lobby walls. Graffiti seemed oddly unbefitting of the neighbourhood, as did the dank-smelling stairwell.

She opted for the stairs, despite her blistering heels. Only recently she'd read about a woman's skeleton being discovered in some rarely used elevator many months after the lift had apparently broken down.

The letter **P** was missing from the frosted-glass door on the third floor, leaving just **ARSE & FRENCH** to indicate that Greta had arrived at the correct destination.

She made sure her blouse buttons were done up, checked her breath in cupped hands, then clasped the door handle.

The door didn't budge.

She tried again.

It was definitely locked.

Of all the scenarios she'd entertained over the previous week, a locked office was not one of them. Had the entire exercise been for nought?

18

Lunch hour was the time the woman had proposed. One o'clock surely fitted the brief.

As she looked up and down the dingy corridor lined with its threadbare runner, her gaze met the bulging black eye of a security camera. She looked quickly away. To be caught staring at a security camera implied guilt. And then trying to look innocent, which of course she was, only made her look shiftier. It was a scenario she wrestled with every Friday when she stood in the queue for the bank teller.

She considered leaving a note. But what would she say?

Greta was here.1pm.

She certainly would not include her surname. She was in the habit of revealing too much about herself, as if to convince people of her legitimacy. But she knew nothing about this Angus French. He might be some scammer for all she knew.

She chided herself for not having found out more about the purpose of the appointment. It was the mention of Walter that had thrown her. She'd lost all focus after that.

Pondering her predicament, Greta spotted a tarnished brass button hiding in the dark doorframe. She pushed it. A bicycle-bell-ring rang out. Greta had expected something more expensive sounding, but then again, nothing about the premises was in keeping with her expectations so far.

A loud buzzer invited her in.

Panicking, she pushed open the door before the buzzing stopped and found herself in a dimly lit rectangle of room dominated by a sun-bleached wooden desk.

A water cooler slouched lopsidedly in the corner, one of its support feet missing.

Greta recoiled — there was a fishy whiff to the place — then stepped gingerly into the room.

Opposite, on the far wall, was a window so dulled by dust it afforded very little natural light. A rubber plant hung limply from the ceiling in a frayed macramé hanger. Off to her right stood a single classroom chair, and to her left, a faux-leather sofa. Towers of boxes stood stacked against one wall, surnames scribbled on the sides in a rudimentary filing system of sorts — *Johnson v Stokes. Reeves v Worthington, Tabak Holdings Ltd.* The office definitely did not match the tone of the receptionist who'd called.

'Hellooo,' Greta called out, feeling increasingly uneasy.

Was this a hoax? Or worse. She hadn't told anyone of her whereabouts. All she'd said to Jud was that she'd be taking her full lunch hour for an appointment in town.

As she moved into the room she tripped over a half-eaten bowl of cat food.

So that was what she could smell.

Just as she was about to retreat, a woman with big hair and a tight teal skirt burst in through a side-door.

'Miss Jellings, darling, you made it. So sorry to keep you waiting.' She flashed Greta a geranium-red smile. 'I was just in the WC.'

She extended a hand in greeting. 'I'm Cassandra. Angus's PA.'

Cassandra's hands were thick and broad, and her fingernails were perfectly painted in the same colour as her lipstick.

Greta folded her own gnawed fingernails into her palm.

'I didn't have an opportunity,' she began, trying to sound assured, but her breathlessness sabotaging any attempt at authority. 'I didn't get to ask you over the phone what this is all about.'

'Angus won't be long,' Cassandra said, with a dismissive toss of her head more in keeping with her telephone manner. 'He'll explain it all, I'm sure. Take a seat in the meantime, hon.'

Greta regretted choosing the sofa as she sank down further than she'd bargained for. She hauled herself out of the dip, yanked down her skirt, and repositioned herself on the edge of the seat, tucking her feet to one side to minimise their conspicuous size.

'Can I get you a tea or coffee while you're waiting?'

She would have killed for a cup of tea — a strong brew of Orange Pekoe with a dash of trim milk and half-a-teaspoon of sugar. But trying to cope with drinking something in a foreign setting when she needed to keep her wits about her meant she was forced to decline.

She picked up a magazine from the small stack on the side table. Surprisingly, it was a recent release, unlike the out-of-date magazines at her doctor's, with features on Jennifer Aniston and Brad Pitt's upcoming nuptials, and all the recipes missing.

Ten Risky Ways to Excite Your Lover.

Greta felt herself flush. She glanced up to see if Cassandra had noticed, then hastily turned the page.

Audi R8 — The Businesswoman's Car
Romances to Read Over the Summer
Bronzing Lotions Put to the Test
Fashion Forward. Gaunt models with death-dark eye sockets, blank stares and hollowed-out cheeks.

Suddenly an image of Walter was in her head. His sunken temples, where the robustness of health had melted away. The scaffolding of his cheekbones, all angles and emptiness. The bossing of his forehead, nature's proportions so cruelly disrupted.

'Ms Jellings.'

Greta looked up, momentarily disoriented.

An imposing man with a heavy jowl and bushy black eyebrows was standing in the middle of the room.

'Angus French,' he said, in a soft voice incongruous with his large physique. 'Good to finally meet you.'

Greta wished she'd been reading a more serious magazine, even though the man's navy suit looked a little tired and his tie had been loosened over an undone top button.

'I feel we already know each other,' he said with a generous smile. 'Walter spoke a lot about you.'

Nothing coherent came out of Greta's mouth.

French led the way down the corridor into a small, windowless office even more cluttered than the one they'd just left. He moved some papers off a chair and invited her to sit down, then took up the seat opposite.

'So,' he said, leaning back in his chair, 'Greta Jellings.'

Her eyes widened. She crossed and then uncrossed her legs.

French smiled and rubbed his palms together, as if contemplating something mischievous.

'I don't mean to be rude,' Greta blurted out, her tone coming as a surprise even to her. 'But I don't have very long. I'm expected back at work by two.'

'Of course,' he said, bouncing forward and flipping open the folder in front of him. 'Sorry for the delay, but these things always take time.' He scanned a piece of paper. 'Eight months is actually pretty good, considering. Some estates can take up to two years to wind up.'

Estates?

'There's been of a bit of a delay in contacting you. Walter's will posed a few problems. I'm hopeful we've managed to address most of them.'

Walter's will?

'Greta. Can I call you Greta?'

It felt too familiar, but she could hardly say no.

She nodded.

'Greta, Walter has left you something.'

Her innards started to wobble. Hearing Walter's name out loud again was putting flesh back on his bones.

'And you'll be glad to know,' French continued. 'It's not Mitsy and Delores.'

Greta burst out laughing — an embarrassing, tension-releasing guffaw, followed by a loud 'whoop'. Mitsy and Delores had been Walter's pet rats. Greta loved animals — they were so much easier than humans. But she had not been able to feel any affection for Walter's two rodents.

Mortified by her outburst, Greta cleared her throat and arranged a frown, trying to lend her expression the gravity such a conversation demanded. The man had just made mention of Walter's will.

Walter's will. It had never even crossed her mind. It was, after all, none of her business. The final sorting of Walter's belongings had been left to his estranged sister, Clare, as was only right and proper.

Saying that, just recently Greta had found herself wishing she had some physical reminder of him. A small token to touch and treasure. Some concrete proof of their past. Though she'd never dared ask anyone in case they interpreted her motivations as mercenary.

Angus French pulled something from the file.

'Walter left you this.'

Greta stared.

He was holding a cerulean blue envelope, addressed in Walter's beautiful cursive hand to *Greta Jellings*.

CHAPTER 5

Greta stared at the envelope in Angus's hands, her stomach a whorl of bumble bees. She'd seen envelopes like it many times before — identical, brightly coloured ones had found their way into her childhood, arriving in the letterbox every few months to liven up the brown-paper world she lived in with Nora.

She couldn't bring herself to take it. As a six-year-old, her excitement was always quickly extinguished with Nora tossing the mysterious letters unopened into the bin.

Memories came tumbling back.

One particular envelope, a vivid orange one, had driven Nora to tears. After that, Greta found herself hating the coloured cards every time they appeared, for intruding on her mother's calm. For days afterwards, she'd dash outside to intercept the postman before he could deliver another dose of sadness. However, over time, the gap between letters grew so long that Greta had forgotten all about them by the time the next one turned up.

Once, she managed to retrieve an unopened envelope from the bottom of the bin.

Slipping it under her t-shirt, she heads for her hideout behind the feijoa hedge, where she sits cross-legged on the cool, damp earth, her breathing tremulous and her hands shaking as she inspects her haul. A hydrangea-mauve envelope, the colour of her mother's favourite flowers.

The handwriting is very untidy. Mrs Mansfield would never approve.

'Gr-et-a Je-ll-ings,' she reads out loud.

It is addressed to her!

Grinding her teeth with excitement, Greta examines it more closely. The stamp, positioned askew, is long and narrow, with the picture of a dark-skinned man in a shiny suit, playing a brass instrument.

She runs her fingers around the stamp's serrated border. Someone, somewhere, had licked the back of it, before securing it to the top right-hand corner of the envelope. She lifts the letter to her nose, hungry for a clue, but all she can discern is the smell of mandarin peels from the rubbish bin, and a little of the postman's perished-leather satchel.

There is a smudged word in the centre of the postmark.

York.

Her chest thumps with excitement. A letter from York, wherever that might be.

Greta starts to slide her finger under the flap.

'Gretaaa!' Nora's voice rings out across the garden.

Quickly Greta slips the envelope under her waistband.

'There you are, my girl. I've been looking for you everywhere. What on earth are you doing back here?'

'Nothing,' Greta says, jumping up.

As she does so, the envelope falls out from under her skirt and lands with a soft thwip *on the ground in front of them.*

Mother and daughter stare at it as if it is a hand grenade, then Nora's expression grows dark and thunderous.

'Don't let me catch you meddling with one of these ever again,' she shouts, walloping Greta with her fluffy grey slipper. 'Do you hear me, Greta Jellings? Never!'

And so the coloured envelopes continue to wield mystery, misery, and a little magic, over Greta's childhood, until she and her mother move to a smaller rental and the letters finally stop coming.

Since reading her mother's diary, Greta's pain had been as acute as ever. It was the thought of her father waiting in some far-away place for a reply to even just one of his letters. A reply that would never come.

That Greta had been complicit in this silence, albeit unwittingly, was excruciating. And with that pain came an overwhelming sense of loss — of letters unopened, words unread, sentiments unacknowledged. Anger too. At Nora, for robbing Greta of her father.

Now she was staring at a similar envelope in Angus French's hand. This time, a letter from Walter.

There were tufts of black hair sprouting from the backs of Angus's fingers. Greta found this oddly comforting. She too suffered from hairy digits (toes in her case) and had made the mistake of shaving them only once.

'Aren't you going to take it?'

She closed her hand hesitantly around the rectangle of colour.

It didn't implode.

'Don't feel you have to open it now,' he said reassuringly. 'Read it in your own time.'

Relief washed over Greta. She'd lost her mooring. Was being swept out to sea. She needed to regain control.

She slipped the envelope into her handbag and stood up. 'Thank you, Mr French.'

'Angus, please,' he said with a kind smile. 'Let's regroup sometime later in the week, shall we?'

Greta swallowed. 'Is that really necessary, Mr French? I mean, Angus. Aren't we all done now?'

'There's more to discuss, Greta,' he said, coming out from behind his desk. 'And the sooner we do it, the better. From a legal perspective, at least.' He rested his hand on her elbow. 'See Cassandra about an appointment on your way out.'

Greta walked through the door, past Cassandra's empty desk, down the three flights of stairs and out into the afternoon.

The light was squint-bright, the road noise too loud, the footpath too busy.

She looked at her watch. She had less than ten minutes to get back to the shop.

CHAPTER 6

By the time Greta got home from work that evening she was exhausted, her mind a figure-of-eight around which her thoughts had careened all afternoon. Even Jud had noticed.

'Everything hunky-dory, Greta?'

No, everything was not hunky-dory. What a fortnight it had been, her strange housesitting experience just the first in a series of unsettling events.

Lorraine and Rory's new house was situated on the outskirts of Warkworth and nothing like their previous 1900s Devonport villa with its rambling roses and hedge of French lavender. Greta had felt the first drag of disappointment driving up their driveway, as a huge house — all angles, reflective glass, and cold cubes of concrete — interposed itself between her and her friends of the last nine years. That her favourite couple had moved from their characterful Devonport home to this modern mammoth was both alarming and disconcerting. As if they'd switched from being vegetarians to meat-eaters overnight.

As for the garden . . . 'structural statement planting' was how Lorraine had described the bleak mosaic of mesh baskets filled with rocks, the Jurassic-Park succulents and clustered bamboo sentries.

Greta found herself wondering whether she'd perhaps not known her friends as well as she thought she did. It was a disquieting realisation.

The house was indeed unlike anything she'd stepped into before, with breathtaking views over Kaipara Harbour, sharp modern furniture and an emperor-sized bed. Even the en-suite, a vast space with oversized taupe tiles and automated taps, was bigger than Greta's lounge and dining room put together. Yet while the house left her in awe, she couldn't wait for her week there to end. She didn't even unpack properly, her bags a sort of reassurance that her stay was temporary.

To Greta's relief, Lorraine had left a comprehensive list of telephone numbers, alarm codes and highlighted directives, including instructions on how to turn on the television.

How to turn on the television? Greta was somewhat affronted by this, until she discovered that turning on the TV was no simple task; it involved three different remote controls — devices which also operated the heat pump, surround sound and outdoor speakers.

She watched television only once during her stay. As she sat in front of the six-o'clock news on her first night in the house, she might as well have been in the midst of the warzone being reported on. The temperature in the room soared to that of the Syrian Desert (heat pump on high), sniper fire echoed from every corner of the lounge (surround sound activated), and distorted strains of *Ground Control to Major Tom* blasted from the pool house (outdoor speakers engaged). Two cups of camomile tea did little to settle her.

Many would have eagerly swapped places with her. Greta felt guilty about that. And yet, living in Lorraine and Rory's house was like living inside a glossy housing catalogue devoid of soul or story. Worst of all was the complete absence of books. There was not a single earmarked paperback beside the bed, or tome of recipes in the kitchen. And no novella in the bathroom to help with a long sit-in. The only book Greta did find buried in a bottom drawer was *The Life-Changing Magic of Tidying Up*.

Digital devices might occasionally summon a cast of characters, be that Magwitch, Harry Potter or Pooh, but their presence would be limited. Then they'd probably be deleted like old blankets taken to the tip, their smell and itch and warmth lost forever.

The absence of books left Greta on edge all week. Books had been one of the few constants in her life, sharing her journey like a motley mix of passengers in a railway carriage, each with its own distinctive smell and heft and story. Every milestone in her life was yoked to some volume: *The Wind in The Willows* the weeks she'd languished in bed with measles; *Nancy Drew* that sublime summer at Rings Beach on her one and only family holiday; *James and the Giant Peach* the week her father left and never came back. (Greta still couldn't eat a peach without her chest feeling brick-heavy with despair.) And of course, *The Secret Life of Bees* the week Walter . . . the week Walter died.

27

If the housesitting experience had caused a small earthquake in Greta's world, then the aftershocks kept coming well after she returned home. Someone had called her an insect. Her filing system at the shop had been completely disrupted. And now, to top it all, there was a mysterious letter in her handbag. An unopened letter from Walter!

She brewed herself a proper pot of tea. The no-name teabags at the shop were a poor excuse for the real thing. Just leaf dust really. But even a well-drawn cup of Orange Pekoe couldn't work its magic.

She sat at the kitchen table eyeing her handbag as if it were a dead mouse some stray cat had dragged in.

The letter was an unexpected gift. Yes, a gift. One last conversation with Walter she never dreamed she would have. A sort of resurrection.

Then again, words written by someone now deceased did not constitute a conversation. Her late mother's diary, a case in point. While it had finally afforded Greta some explanation, it provided no opportunity for her to respond. Her resentment and sense of betrayal had to be left unarticulated. Her guilt and despair too.

No, a letter from the grave was not a conversation, but a unilateral declaration. An unfair tipping of power in favour of the deceased. A loose end, which would flap forever in a timeless breeze.

What worried Greta most about the letter was the possibility that Walter's words would paint over the picture she held of him in her head. If he remodelled the past, she'd be left with nothing.

She was desperate to see inside, but also filled with fear. Perhaps it was better to throw away the letter still sealed. To read Walter's letter would be to make its contents real.

Loud knocking at the front door brought her to her senses. She peered down the dimly lit hallway. A woman's slight frame was silhouetted behind the leadlight panes.

Greta opened the door and was met by an outstretched hand — a ballerina-slender hand.

'Hiya, I'm Holly,' said a young woman dressed in floppy floral pants and a shapeless green jumper. 'Your new neighbour.'

Greta opened the door a little wider. 'Hello.'

The newcomer — despite her casual, almost slovenly, attire — was, well there was no other word for it, beautiful. Utterly and effortlessly beautiful. High forehead, ski-ramp nose, large brown eyes. A handful of waist. Languid limbs. Ideal height. (Almost certainly 5ft 7.) And perfect-sized feet. (Probably size 6.)

The woman was as delicate as a praying mantis. Greta felt like a giant huhu beetle in comparison.

There was that insect image rearing its head again!

'I moved in a few weeks ago,' said the woman, swinging her head in the direction of the boundary fence. Her craze of sandy spirals shuddered and settled. 'I've popped round a few times to introduce myself, but always seem to miss you. So, when I saw your lights on this evening, I thought, Holly, get over there, girl.'

Greta opened her mouth.

'Not a bad time, I hope?' The outdoor light was bouncing off the woman's forehead, lending her skin a pearly glow.

'I've been away,' Greta said, her words coming out abruptly. She hadn't meant them to.

Her new neighbour's smile shrunk. 'Ah, that would explain it.'

There was an uncomfortable pause. Greta did not invite Holly in. She couldn't face trying to make conversation. The inevitable fumbling, falling over herself, blushing. What's more, her kitchen was a mess. If she were going to invite her new neighbour in, the place would need to be perfect. Vacuumed, baking in the tins, Nora's china out. Spontaneous arrangements were just too stressful.

How she wished Lorraine and Rory hadn't moved. They at least knew her, understood her, liked her. No effort or introduction required. What's more, Lorraine had cellulite.

The young woman passed Greta a torn corner of the local gazette on which she'd scribbled a telephone number. 'Here's my mobile if you ever need to get hold of me.'

Greta stared at the piece of paper.

'By the way, don't be fazed if you hear a bit of whining. I've got a puppy. Mario.' She gave a little laugh. 'He shouldn't give you any trouble though; the property is fully fenced.'

'A puppy?' Greta rubbed her forehead. 'You know I have a chicken?'

'A chicken?'

'Yes. Marilyn Monroe.'

'Marilyn Monroe!' Holly grinned. 'Maybe Marilyn and Mario can be friends.'

Greta's eyes narrowed, her mind navigating a scene in which her hen tore terrified around the garden.

The woman stepped backwards. 'I didn't catch your name.'

'Greta.'

'Don't hear that very often. Is it Swiss?'

'Actually,' Greta said, opening the door a little wider, 'it comes from the Greek, *Margarites*. Though some sources suggest it's of German origin. *Margarethe*. Hard to know which is accurate. Both have links to the name Margaret.' Greta's eyes started tearing. It always happened when she was speaking earnestly about anything. 'Greta means pearl,' she continued. 'You know, like the pearl you find in an oyster, not the knitting stitch.' She swallowed loudly. 'Have you heard of Greta Garbo?'

The girl scrunched up her eyes.

'A stunning actress from the twenties. I was named after her. Not that I'm saying I'm stunning.' Greta felt her face grow hotter. 'It was just a name my parents liked. My father, actually. He loved all those early movies. Nora not as much. Nora was my mother. She preferred to be called Nora, after . . . look at me, I'm rambling.'

The woman smiled, but Greta knew that sort of smile. A you-are-a-bit-weird smile.

'I better get going,' Holly said. 'See you round then, Greta of the Greeks.'

'Yes. See you.'

Greta shut the door, leant back against the glass panes, and closed her eyes. She'd done it again, made an utter fool of herself. And worse, she'd watched herself do it, unable to temper her performance.

'Greta of the Greeks,' she said, as she sloped down the corridor.

She switched on the bedroom light and sank onto the stool in front of her dressing table. Her mother had bought the Baroque-style chair at a garage sale when Greta was about fifteen. The teenager had been less than impressed by the low-slung seat with puckered mustard fabric, and she let her mother know so. Now she felt guilty about her petulance all over again.

Nora, however, had remained undeterred by her daughter's disapproval and set about sanding, varnishing and reupholstering the stool, the end-product nothing short of splendid. Greta never did admit her change of heart though. That bothered her a lot of late, especially since the vintage chair was now her favourite piece of furniture.

Leaning forward, she inspected her face in the mirror. The humid evening air had frizzed her fringe and dulled the auburn highlights in her hair. Her eyebrows needed plucking, and the eczema above her top lip was a raw red.

She pulled the skin under her jaw taut, then let it go again with a sigh.

Opening the top drawer of her dressing table, she rummaged through the motley mix of cosmetics covered in a film of blusher dust.

She shoved the drawer closed. It jammed in its frame.

As she wrestled with it, a small gold compact was dislodged from beneath the other paraphernalia. Greta picked it up, her breathing tremulous, and ran her fingers around the circumference of the gold lid, then over the bevelled initials.

N J.

Nora Jellings.

A strangled cry escaped her mouth. In her mind's eye she could see Nora patting on powder with the small disc of sponge, her tall frame elegantly angled towards the mirror. How Greta used to love watching her mother transform her morning face. The practised sweep of Nora's hand as she applied eyeliner to accentuate her large grey eyes. The muted red she coloured her lips, painting them methodically from outside in. The way she ran her fingers through her closely cropped hair to give it height, and pulled at single strands to camouflage her prominent widow's peak. And the way, when she'd finished, she sat back, her neck long, her demeanour determined. Nora Jellings never let her appearance slip. Not once. No matter what life hurled at her.

Greta pushed in the protruding pin and the case sprung open into two perfect halves — a small mirror on one side, a discoloured circle of sponge on the other.

With shaking hands she dabbed the sponge onto the excavated cake of powder, then applied it in rapid-fire pats.

Nature was not symmetrical. Greta knew that. But the truth of this seemed more pronounced in her; her left eye was significantly smaller than her right, and the regrowth of her left eyebrow, for some reason far less vigorous than its companion.

She reappraised her appearance.

No pearly glow, though her freckles did look less like fly spots now.

She glanced down at her feet. Her big boat feet. There were parts of her body not even make-up could improve.

As she dabbed the sponge above her top lip, trying to camouflage her eczema, Greta caught a whiff of linen, oranges and dressmaker chalk.

Her heart hiccoughed.

She pressed the sponge to her nose and inhaled. It had been nearly five years since her mother had passed. Even Nora's clothes had lost their signature smell. Yet the little compact had somehow managed to secure Nora's scent.

Greta snapped the lid shut. She couldn't risk diluting her newfound treasure. Then she dropped her head into her hands and started to sob.

CHAPTER 7

As night fell around the ankles of a new day, Greta picked up her letter opener and ran it under the envelope seal. It had been a long eight hours. She hadn't slept a wink.

Carefully she withdrew the letter and unfolded it, her eyes taking a moment to focus. The handwriting, as on the envelope, was familiar.

Grets,

It feels odd writing this, with the knowledge you'll only read it some-time in the future. As if I'm preparing a time capsule for later discovery, or tossing a message-in-a-bottle overboard. At least I know you will receive it — Angus is utterly reliable, the very best of friends.

Greta pulled her night shawl tighter and moved the envelope slowly down the page, as if watching a scary movie from behind the comfort of a cushion.

Who would have thought that the act of writing could be so bloody tiring? But this body of mine is packing up. Finally.

Greta swallowed.

God knows we've had our fair share of false forecasts. D-days have come and gone. I've learnt to live on death row. You too. Though never once have you let it derail your care. Thank you.

A tear spilled onto her cheek.

This endless limbo almost became permanent. I started to believe finite was forever. A bit like unpacked boxes left in a hallway long enough to start owning the space.

This time, though, it's for real. There's a surety in my bones, a change in my breathing. I know.

Greta's mind navigated the long linoleum corridors, Walter's bile-yellow face, chemo-knotted veins, his sagging mandible slung from tired tendons. Yes, she'd walked with him to the edge several times.

How cruel life could be. To survive the diagnosis of HIV, remain robust on antiretroviral therapy, and then succumb to liver cancer.

She looked out of her bedroom window. A kingfisher was perched on the telephone line, its blue body silhouetted against the blushing dawn sky.

I've never been a tidy person, but I don't need to tell you that.

Greta's throat tightened around a circle of emptiness. Walter's untidiness had driven her crazy. The way he washed his dishes only when all the clean crockery had run out. The way he let his hair grow far too unruly before visiting the barber. Mitsy and Delores, his beloved pet rats, who had free reign of his house.

I feel a compulsion to align all the elements of my life. One final tidy-up before I shut the door.

'At last!' I hear you say.

It's a basic human instinct, I guess. The same sort which must drive a mother to prepare a nest for her young.

His reference to a mother nesting speared Greta in the ribs. Of late any mention of children did it.

Greta adored children. Their honesty and energy. Their irreverence, openness and imagination. However, that particular age doctors always bandied about, was nigh. With no suitor in sight and Greta not far from forty, her ship was getting ready to sail, and then her application to motherhood would be permanently denied.

As far as possessions go, it's been relatively easy. I don't own many things.

Walter's cottage had been sparse yet tastefully decorated. A harlequin set of second-hand chairs around a refectory table. Two 1970s Deco-scalloped couches. A rustic Kilim rug. Turkish table lamp. An appliance-free kitchen. A bicycle, not a car. An open hearth for heating.

But then those weird anomalies. A William Kentridge original hanging on his lounge wall. A William Kentridge original! And a vinyl collection that took up an entire room. The most expensive turntable money could buy . . .

At first Greta was shocked by these small touches of excess — inexplicable extravagances in an otherwise restrained life. They didn't match with who she thought Walter was, or perhaps who she wanted him to be.

When she got to know him better, though, they started to make sense. Walter did not fit into any particular box. He was custom-made, his sometimes paradoxical ways of being simply an alignment of his priorities and passions. He was indulgent when it came to music, travel and food; yet more careful with his coins when it came to 'less important' things such as cars, clothes, haircuts. There was a refreshing honesty about that. About leading a life that was true to himself and not the madding crowd.

And anyway, I want to leave you with more than an artefact, Grets. Something more than the sum of its parts.

Grets. She smiled and leant back against her pillows. What had she been so anxious about? The letter was all Walter. Familiar, comfortable, and comforting. He hadn't tampered with the image she held in her head. No, he had simply reaffirmed it. All the conversations she'd had with herself now seemed so silly.

So, what had he left her?

She felt like a child playing pass the parcel. The music had stopped and it was her turn to rip off the wrapper.

A few of his vinyl records perhaps? How great that would be!

Then again, records were artefacts . . . although music wasn't. And music was definitely greater than the sum of its parts. If she got the chance to pick, she'd go for his Johnny Cash album. She knew the words of 'I Walk the Line'. All of them.

Who would have thought? Greta, the person who always got song lyrics wrong. Even Christmas carols. She was still mortified when she thought about the time Jud had corrected her rendition of 'Silent Night' one Christmas party. He laughed so hard he'd popped two shirt buttons.

It wasn't her fault she'd come to music late. A loud silence had hung over much of her childhood, pierced only by the intermittent whirr and drill of her mother's Singer sewing machine. Nora had considered music too frivolous for the weightiness of the world. A distorter of the truth, a Pied Piper high, and not to be trusted.

Yet at the back of this silence, stashed in the dark recesses of Greta's mind, behind many other childhood memories, was one standout musical moment.

Five-year-old Greta stands at the kitchen door in her pyjamas watching her parents dance to a tune, her mother laughing and laughing as Victor Jellings spins his wife around the room.

Walter exploded the silence Greta had lived with for so long, with Bach, Aretha Franklin, Edith Piaf. Rodriguez. The Beetles. Leonard Cohen . . . How Walter loved his music, and how Greta grew to love it too.

Perhaps, she thought excitedly, he'd left her his Pink Triangle Tarantella turntable? Now that would be something.

She stopped herself. Coveting the possessions of a dead person was not an admirable trait. She'd be grateful for anything. Anything.

So, Grets, I have decided to leave you—

A flash of colour spun past her bedroom window. Probably a rosella. The colourful birds were frequent visitors to her garden.

—an adventure.

An adventure? Greta swallowed.

A clump of dirt hit the glass.

She leapt out of bed and ran over to the window.

There was a dog in her garden! A brindle puppy digging up her flowerbed.

'Hey! Stop that right now!' she shouted, struggling with the window latch.

The hound, oblivious to her ranting, began yanking at the fairy-lights cable.

Greta grabbed her dressing gown, raced down the hallway and out into her garden.

'Shoo! Get! Get off!' she cried, throwing one of her slippers in the dog's direction. It missed.

Her second slipper was more successful.

The boxer jerked its head back, tucked in its small stump of tail, and made for the fence.

Greta looked around. Clods of mud and crushed blooms lay strewn across the lawn. Her string of fairy lights had been pulled so tightly around the elm's trunk that most of the coloured bulbs had been crushed. There were muddy paw prints across the front deck . . .

'Blasted dog!'

The situation called for a word with more muscle, but Greta could not bring herself to swear. *Swearing is unbefitting of a female, Greta.* Nora needed ever only wash Greta's mouth out once with soap.

Greta got down on her hands and knees and began replanting the uprooted marigolds. Suddenly she froze, blood draining from her face, and cast about frantically. Then she was clambering to get up, her hands and knees covered in mud.

It had been inevitable. Just a matter of time. She should have been more forceful with her new neighbour. Checked the perimeter fence. Secured Marilyn Monroe's space.

Greta swayed woozily. Marilyn Monroe was everything to her. Everything! Since the day the bedraggled Leghorn had landed uninvited on the back lawn, she'd proved the most faithful of friends. There to welcome Greta each day as she pulled into the driveway. There to listen to Greta's work woes, head cocked to one side. A supreme television companion too, watching whatever Greta chose so long as she could do so from the comfort of her lap. And always the most appreciative of audiences when Greta auditioned in the lounge for *Stars in Their Eyes*.

Greta had nurtured the stray chicken back to plump, precocious health, naming her after the American movie star because of the way the hen dipped her head and puffed out her plumage, white dress billowing in the breeze.

Of course, Marilyn Monroe became the butt of many jokes.

'There's only one place for a chicken,' Rory once teased. 'And that's in the roasting tray.'

Lorraine had reprimanded her husband for his insensitivity, but only two weeks later had made a joke about Greta keeping company with 'the fowlest of friends'.

Even Walter took to calling Marilyn Monroe 'The Diva of Devonport'.

However, Greta had ignored them all. Keeping a hen in the suburbs might have been a little unusual, but it wasn't as if she was sheltering an anaconda or bearded dragon. Nor two rats, for that matter.

Marilyn Monroe had chosen her and that was all that mattered. What's more, Greta admired the hen — she knew her mind. In fact, Greta was a little envious of Marilyn's take-no-prisoners approach to life.

An indignant *cluck* brought Greta to her senses.

She looked up.

Perched on a branch above her was Marilyn Monroe. And, as if in reprimand, the bird released a massive chalky poop, which narrowly missed Greta and landed with a *splat* on the paving below.

CHAPTER 8

'Greta, I've received a call from Derrick Cumberland,' Jud Rutland said, putting his head around her cubicle door. 'Apparently you sent over a box of twenty-micron filters instead of the one-micron ones he ordered.'

'Did I?' Greta said absently.

Her boss stood over her desk. 'That's the third complaint I've received today.' He sounded irritable. 'Don is still waiting on his Aqua Safe order, and a woman by the name of Sandra Kelman says you promised to email her the details of our UV controllers, but nothing has come through yet.'

Greta focused on the hair poking out of Jud's ears like clumps of tussock grass. She wondered why Charlene never attended to them.

'For some reason I'm also getting all your calls.'

Greta felt herself flush. She shot a glance at the dislocated receiver.

Jud followed her gaze. 'You . . . left the phone off the hook? What in heaven's name is going on, Greta? This is unlike you. Very unlike you.'

'I'm sorry, Jud. I really am,' she said, tears welling. 'I've just had a lot on my mind of late and I can't seem to think straight. I didn't sleep a wink last night. The neighbour's dog dug up my garden. I haven't had a chance to speak with the owners yet, and—'

'Greta,' Jud said, flicking his thumb against his forefinger. 'Whatever is going on in your personal life right now is starting to affect your work.'

He perched on the edge of her desk. He was too close. His new eau de cologne, a confusion of Nordic pine and Christmas spice, was overpowering.

'I'm not an unreasonable guy, but—'

Greta was doing everything in her power not to cry. It wasn't working.

Jud looked away. Tears were in the too-hard basket.

'Right, then,' he said, standing up. 'Let's leave it at that. A bad day.' He hovered for a moment, fiddling with his tie, then turned and walked out.

'Just sort these issues out,' he said, without looking back. 'And for goodness' sake, put the phone back on the hook.'

Greta looked around her small space. The demo model of a PH pump. The yellowing diagram of Giardia and Cryptosporidium cysts pinned to her corkboard. The curled corners of fluorescent Post-it Notes. Rolls of bubble wrap. Shelves of lever-arch files. The shredder. And the desk calendar — an annual gift from the local undertakers, each month featuring a different style of casket against some country-side backdrop.

She lifted the lever under her seat. Her chair dropped a few inches.

She lowered it. The chair sprang back up.

Lifted the lever . . . lowered it . . .

What an incurable romantic Walter had been, right to the very end.

An all-expenses-paid holiday of indeterminate duration.

His letter was like a pocketful of glitter. A Catherine Wheel spraying silver stars across the night sky.

An opportunity for you to step away from the world you know. Have a go at some other life. Try out one, or two, or even three of your dreams. I've seen you get so excited talking about Dian Fossey, chocolate ganache, palazzo pants . . . I don't see the same spark in your eyes when you talk about the shop.

You've been a responsible daughter, a responsible employee, an all-round responsible human being. I don't want you to one day be a responsible corpse.

A shiver ran up Greta's legs.

Forgive the dark humour. I'm a bit preoccupied with death right now.

What I know is this, Grets — sometimes it's only by leaving something behind that you learn whether you really want it or not. An informed decision, weighed up against other experiences. Not a life lived by default.

His words were convincing. Almost persuasive. But there was no way. No way. She couldn't. Shouldn't. She had obligations. Responsibilities. Yes, responsibilities. She was not ashamed to use that perfectly respectable word. Rent to pay. The power and water bill. A rainy day to prepare for.

She wiped the smudge of fingerprints off the credit-card machine, dusted between the grooves on her keyboard, and pushed down the paper in the wastepaper bin. Nothing good came of dreaming. Nothing.

She wished she could be brave. She did. But she'd been like this for so long, ruled by ritual. She couldn't remember how to take a risk even if she wanted to.

According to Judy, the cocoon of safety Greta had constructed around herself was her way of dealing with an uncertain world. '*The routine you impose on your days is an attempt to order the unpredictability and muddle of human existence.*'

And what was so wrong with that? It worked.

Greta blotted her cheeks with a tissue, careful not to stretch the delicate skin around her eyes. She didn't want premature wrinkles. It was time to deal with this unsolicited interruption in her life and move on. She would make an appointment to see Angus French later in the week.

By the time Greta arrived home from work that evening, she'd forgotten all about her garden, and it came as a nasty surprise to discover the mayhem all over again.

She'd left a note in her new neighbour's letterbox that morning, which meant she now had to confront her in person. Greta squirmed at the thought.

Perhaps she'd overreacted. The dog was a puppy after all, and the affected flowerbed small. She could easily purchase more potted colour. In fact, there was a special on at the nursery — five punnets of impatiens for the price of four. As for the fairy lights, they were into their fifth season and due for replacement anyway.

Marilyn Monroe scurried across the garden to greet her.

'Hope you've had a better day than me, Miss Marilyn,' Greta said, crouching down on her haunches.

The spry hen cocked her head to one side, her comb falling across one eye like a slipped fascinator. Most chickens' combs stood upright. In every other way, though, Marilyn Monroe was a very robust bird.

Greta pulled out a half-eaten muesli bar from her pocket and crumbled it onto the grass.

Her hen made a few approving clucks and set about demolishing the treat.

Greta shuddered as she reflected on the events of that morning and what it would have been like to find a trail of feathers leading to a limp, mauled Marilyn. There was no avoiding it; she had to confront her neighbours. Holly would need to keep her puppy restrained. The woman could not simply waft through life on the breeze of her beauty.

Greta bit her lip, chiding herself for the uncharitable thought. Jealousy was an unflattering emotion. She could do better.

Her mouth was dry and the vessels in her neck pulsated as she unlatched her neighbours' gate and made her way up the paved path.

The evening sky was fading and the air was filled with the sweet scent of daphne. Baskets of violas hung from the villa's eaves. An old bench nestled in the brick alcove beside the pizza oven. A birdbath had been positioned beneath the Japanese maple, and a small marble Buddha now sat beside the fishpond.

Greta was surprised. She would never have picked Holly for a gardener.

She paused at the front door and took a deep breath. The bristles of the doormat were stiff and the WELCOME still a bold black. She quickly stepped off it, not wanting her big feet to be the first to sully it.

No sooner had she rung the doorbell than from around the corner of the house bounded the offending Mario, all wagging rump and drooling jowls.

He dropped a tennis ball at Greta's feet and nudged her leg with his muzzle, smearing grit-laden saliva over her pantyhose.

'No. Off you go,' she said, trying to sound stern.

Mario picked up the ball and dropped it again.

'I said no.'

The door opened.

Greta coloured. It was not a good feeling being caught reprimanding someone's puppy. A very cute puppy at that.

Holly was dressed in faded denim dungarees and a peasant-style blouse, and her hair had been pulled back into a loose knot.

'Greta!' she said, her face collapsing. 'I'm so sorry. I can't tell you how—'

'I—'

'Come in, come in,' Holly said, pulling Greta through the front door.

Greta ducked. She knew how low-slung the beams were.

'I feel so bad about your garden. No, Mario! Outside. You're in the dogbox, mate.'

She led Greta into the lounge.

Greta gasped. How different the room looked from when Lorraine and Rory had lived there. The carpets had been lifted and the floorboards sanded back and varnished. Two calico-covered couches were scattered with lime-green linen cushions. Wild grasses filled a rustic pottery jug. There was a purple yoga mat laid out on the floor.

'It all looks so . . . different,' she stuttered. 'Such a change from Lorraine's antiques and Persian rugs.'

'I found the hole Mario must have squeezed through,' Holly blurted. 'Cheeky fella. I've done a temporary fix, but I'll sort out something more permanent on the weekend.'

Greta nodded, still taking the room in.

'Can I get you a drink, Grets? A kombucha or iced tea perhaps?'

Grets. Only Walter had ever called her that.

'Oh, I don't want to be any trouble. Only if you're having something. Nothing alcoholic though.' She felt embarrassed bringing up alcohol when Holly hadn't even mentioned it.

She looked about the bright, airy room. The blood pounding in her temples settled to a dull throb.

Holly returned with two tall glasses dripping with condensation.

Greta peered into hers. There were mint leaves embedded in the ice cubes.

'What a clever idea,' she said, taking a gulp. 'The mint leaves, I mean.' Then she burst into tears.

Holly peered into her own glass, as if the reason for Greta's distress could be found there.

Greta shook her head.

'I really feel terrible about your garden,' Holly said, leading Greta to the couch. 'I'm going to go to the nursery first thing on the weekend and—'

Greta waved her hands in a confusing tangle. 'No, it's not that. Not that at all.' She knew her face would soon be all blotchy and her eyes rimmed with smudged mascara.

It was Holly's kindness coming on the back of such an unpleasant fortnight that had done it. She'd been betrayed by Lorraine and Rory and their soulless monstrosity. Killed a pukeko. Been called an insect. Made a multitude of mistakes at work. Let her boss down. Her flowerbed was a mess. Her life was a mess. And . . . and her Walter, who was dead and buried, was inviting her to do the impossible.

'You don't need to go buying more plants,' Greta finally managed, dragging a string of snot across her face. 'I've just had a lot happening lately, that's all.' She started to sob again. 'I'm so embarrassed.'

Holly put both arms around Greta. Her skin was soft and she smelt of summer holidays — coconut, sun cream, the ocean.

Greta realised how devoid of touch her life was. In an increasingly cautious society, touch had largely become the prerogative of lovers and parents and pets.

'Will you stay for some supper? It's just minestrone.'

'Oh, I couldn—'

'Think of it as a peace offering.'

Greta hadn't eaten all day — her Wednesday cheese-and-chutney sandwiches on wholemeal bread were still untouched in her lunchbox. It had been the stress of the morning, and Walter's words about trying out a different life, that had hijacked her appetite. A bowl of minestrone was just what she felt like.

'Only if it's no trouble. Really. I wasn't expecting to be fed.' Greta blushed. 'Fed is not really the right word. Makes me sound like . . . what I mean is, well, I didn't intend to come over here at dinnertime hoping for something. It's just happened tha—'

Holly signalled for Greta to follow her into the kitchen, a room Greta knew well. She and Lorraine had shared a fair few cups of tea in it over the years.

Just thinking about Lorraine left Greta feeling hurt and confused all over again. The change in their friendship . . .

No expectation, no disappointment.

Perhaps Greta's standards were too high.

'It's my mum's recipe,' Holly said taking the lid off a large pot. 'First time I'm trying it out.'

She placed a bowl in front of Greta, then removed a baguette from the oven and dropped it onto the tablecloth.

'Break off a piece, but careful, it's hot.'

The casualness of putting bread straight on the table, without even a bread board, bothered Greta. As for breaking off a piece . . . that felt far too familiar.

She slunk down in her chair, trying to minimise her height.

'Wine?'

'Oh, not in the middle of the week.'

Wine had the effect of loosening Greta's guy ropes. After a glass or two her thoughts inevitably became less predictable. Even rebellious. It was easier to maintain control when sober.

'Mid-week or not, I think you deserve a glass after Mario's exploits.'

'Alright, just a little then,' Greta said, drawing her thumb and forefinger together.

Greta took a spoonful of soup. It was rather bland and the vegetables not diced finely enough. She was relieved. At least Holly wasn't an amazing cook to boot.

'So is there a Mr Jellings? Or a Mrs Jellings?'

Greta broke into a hot red blush. 'Oh, gosh no! I'm not like that.'

She sounded judgemental. She hadn't meant to.

'I mean, I'm not averse to it—'

That didn't come out right either.

Greta took a gulp of wine.

'Sorry. I'm a bit of a sticky beak,' Holly said, resecuring her hair. 'Feel free to tell me to butt out of your business.'

'There was someone,' Greta said quickly, chasing a small circle of pasta through the soup. 'But he died.'

'Oh, no!'

'He had AIDS. It was complicated. He was a friend more than—'

Holly's eyes sprung wider.

Why did Greta have to go and tell her new neighbour about this? There was no need to share such an intimate detail of her life with an almost stranger and risk sabotaging the chance of friendship. But it was always the same. Like target attraction. The thing she most wanted to avoid divulging was what she wound up blurting out first.

'That would have been hard.'

It was the way Holly said it, without exclamation or artifice, that gave Greta the confidence to continue.

'He was gay, you see.' Greta looked up. 'I didn't realise for some time. Fell head over heels in love with him. I can be pretty stupid, that way.'

44

'I don't think it's stupid to fall in love.'

Greta broke off a piece of bread, scattering crumbs over the table. 'What a mess I'm making. I—'

'When did he die?'

'Eight months ago.'

Holly nodded.

'But he's back again, toying with my head.'

Her neighbour took a swig of wine and leant forward. 'What do you mean, back?'

'He left me something in his will. I'm terrified of it. Don't want it. Really, I don't. But I wouldn't want to offend him either. I know he's dead. Still. You know what I mean? I don't want to offend his memory. Or disappoint. It's just that I can't. He thinks I can, but I'm not that sort of person. Strong. I'm not a very strong person, Holly.'

'What has he left you?'

'It's hard to explain. A sort of holiday.'

Holly opened both her hands in exclamation. 'He's left you a holiday and you don't want to take it? Are you unwell, woman?'

Greta burst out laughing. It was the brash casualness of Holly's words.

Holly joined in and soon tears were streaming down both their faces like a pair of giggling schoolgirls.

'You don't understand,' Greta said, finally catching her breath. 'What he's suggesting. He wants me to leave my life behind. Head away to some mystery destinations. No specified timeframe. Sort of freewheeling, if you will.'

'Holy shit!'

'Exactly! Holy sh—. The thing is, I'm no freewheeler.'

'How well did he know you?'

Greta took two spoonfuls of soup in quick succession, the second one missing her mouth. Minestrone trickled down her chin.

'Oh, you know,' she said, shrugging.

Better than anyone scrolled through her head.

She dabbed her chin. 'He was my best friend.'

'Then maybe you have to trust that he wouldn't have given you something he didn't think you could handle.'

Greta started shaking her head. She did not need Holly taking Walter's side.

'I can't. My job for one. I've been there twenty-two years. That's gold-watch territory. Not that I'm materialistic or anything.'

'Twenty-two years, Greta! Nobody should be in the same job for twenty-two years.'

Greta faltered. Suddenly what had seemed like a sterling record now sounded more like a prison sentence.

'Then there's the question of Marilyn Monroe. Who will look after her? She relies on me. We're like this.' Greta put two fingers together.

'My friend Donna lives on a dairy farm. I'm sure she'd be happy to have your hen.'

Greta stood up and took her dish over to the sink.

'Sometimes you just have to give over to the universe, Grets, and trust what it brings you.'

Greta stared at the sink, the drain with its crisscrossing strips of stainless steel, the grey rubber plug . . . *Sometimes you just have to give over to the universe and trust what it brings you.*

Later she made her way back home, a full moon softening the night. Even the dug-up flowerbed looked less severe cast in its cool platinum glow.

CHAPTER 9

Greta slept fitfully, the full moon toying with her dreams. She woke with a start, hungry for air.

2.12am.

She sat up and turned on the light, hoping to chase away the worries that seemed to wedge themselves with such ease between sleep and wakefulness.

That Holly's persuasive words had seen her even consider Walt's proposition was terrifying. When Greta first read Walter's letter, she'd known there was no way, absolutely no way, she would, or could, pursue the ludicrous, albeit very generous invitation. But here she was at two in the morning sitting on the fence. In fact, even leaning more towards the idea than away from it!

How well did he know you, Grets? Better than anyone.

Greta doesn't hear him come in, the vacuum cleaner and her sobs loud in her ears.

'*So, it's cleaning that's keeping you from answering your phone.*'

She spins round. 'Walt!'

'*On a Saturday too. Shame on you!*'

She's been getting better about relaxing on weekends, but cleaning is still her go-to whenever she gets stressed. The purpose of it seems to soothe her.

'*You haven't been putting haemorrhoid cream under your eyes again, have you?*' *he asks with a cheeky smile, deftly sidestepping the elephant in the room.*

She laughs. Laughs, even though she's been crying all morning. But that's Walt.

'*I should never have told you,*' *she says, blowing her nose. In a moment of over-sharing, she'd told him about trying to shrink the bags under her eyes with haemorrhoid cream.*

'I was going to ask if you wanted to come for a ride to Te Hana Nursery,' he says. 'But on second thoughts, I see that an op shop crawl is what's called for.'

One of Greta's favourite pastimes is to wander through second-hand stores in search of a bargain. Some of her best buys have come from op shops. The Le Creuset casserole dish, her navy jumper with strawberry motifs, the Moka pot . . . Though never shoes. She's never found shoes to fit.

And Walt is the perfect shopping companion. Honest to a fault.

'That dress makes you look like you belong to some religious cult.'

'No, you do not want that hanging on your wall. Next thing you'll be buying a set of ceramic geese.'

'In that you look like a film star, Greta Jellings.'

So, they spend the rest of the morning meandering through op shops. And later, when she feels stronger, she tells him about finding her mother's diaries and the secrets she's discovered between the fine, gold-edged pages.

Walter listens. It is what he does so well. And it is better than any advice. Listening at least lifts some of her burden.

Greta slipped on her dressing gown and padded through to the kitchen to prepare herself a glass of warm milk. She stirred in a spoonful of honey. Then another. She was in need of sugar and she was right out of chocolate.

It wasn't rocket science. Everything was telling her to stay. The security of her job. Her flawless history at the shop. The familiarity of the work, with very few surprises or unknowns. She didn't have to prove herself to anyone in HR. Wasn't obliged to share her desk with some gum-chewing office gossip. Nor be answerable to a micromanaging boss. (Online poker mostly kept Jud out of her hair.) She lived in the quaintest of cottages, in a much-sought-after suburb. Her landlady hadn't put the rent up in years, despite frequently threatening to do so, and even allowed Greta to house her spa pool on the property. As for Marilyn Monroe . . . Greta was a responsible pet owner, not some fair-weather friend. What would Marilyn think if Greta abandoned her at the first offer of a free holiday? All of this added up to certainty, consistency, security. You could not put a price on that.

The only time she'd ever thrown caution to the wind in the name of fun had ended badly. Very badly. Going away to Taupo with the Denopoulos family had proved the wrong thing to do. Swimming in the icy blue lake, eating baklava for lunch, playing war in the garden, and being allowed to stay up late to read *James and the Giant Peach* were all very well. But when Greta got back home her father was gone.

The lesson she learnt at the tender age of six was that it was safest to keep what was dear to her in plain sight, safest to lead a sensible life, and not one defined by the pursuit of pleasure. This was a lesson Nora had reinforced many times over the years, drumming into Greta the importance of being grateful for what she had, rather than dreaming about what she did not.

Greta finished her milk and stood up. It was clear what she had to do. She would call Angus French first thing in the morning.

She turned off the light and stood for a moment in the moonlit kitchen.

Her friendship with Walter had been like living under a moonbeam, the incredible two years immersing her existence in silver-blue magic. With Walter she'd glimpsed some other life. Some other Greta. His letter had reminded her of that.

Her thoughts turned to her father. To his unopened letters. What might they have said? Would he too have offered to fit her with wings?

She would never know.

She walked back to her bedroom, past all the books she owned, stacked floor to ceiling on shelves lining the narrow strip of passageway.

That her father's letters had landed in the bin was irrevocable. But for Walter's words to land in the bin too, would that not be unforgivable?

'Yes,' grunted Paddington Bear.

'Yes,' cried Thing One and Thing Two.

'Yes,' nodded Madeline and Nancy Drew and Amelia Bedelia.

'Yes,' whispered Dian Fossey.

CHAPTER 10

'You've read Walter's letter,' Angus French said slowly.

Greta fidgeted with her handbag strap. She envied the lawyer's steady, measured manner. How she wished she could be so assured as to never feel hurried. To feel comfortable occupying space and time in another person's day, be that a friend, stranger or someone of note.

'It was a very Walter thing to do, wasn't it?' Angus said.

'Oh yes.' Her words pushed past a gulp of air. 'It was.'

French looked down at his hands. 'Walter was the most generous of people.'

Greta thought she detected a hint of tenderness beneath his tempered demeanour. She wondered whether Angus and Walter had ever been . . . together.

'I keep checking to see that I haven't missed a similar such letter addressed to me,' he said, giving a booming laugh.

Greta pulled her mouth wide in awkwardness. 'I could, I mean you could . . .'

He waved away her discomfort. 'Only joking. Only joking. You clearly had a special place in Walter's heart.'

Greta's skin rose into goosebumps.

'Right then, Greta Jellings. What is it to be?'

'I, well . . .'

It had been her new neighbour's words which helped turn the tide.

Sometimes you just have to give over to the universe, Grets, and trust what it brings you.

Greta was conflicted about metaphysical stuff. '*Thinking positive thoughts will not pay for the power,*' had been a well-worn Nora line. But Greta was tired, her defences down, and Holly's words had offered some respite from all the conversations she'd been having in her head.

She wondered how Angus could work in an office without windows.
'Yes. I mean, I do.'

French laughed. 'I'm not asking you to marry me.'

Heat surged into Greta's face. 'No! No! What I wanted to say was that I'll do it. Take up Walter's offer, that is.'

French slapped the desk with his hand. 'Good on you, Greta! Good — on — you. Who wouldn't grab such an opportunity with both hands, eh? Who wouldn't?'

She laughed nervously.

'This calls for a toast.' He yanked opened the bottom drawer of his desk and pulled out a squat whisky bottle and three black mugs, which, judging by the fingerprints all over them, had not seen the inside of a dishwasher in a very long time.

'Walter did like his whisky,' he said, pouring three generous measures.

Greta glanced at her watch. It was just after midday. What's more, she didn't drink whisky.

Angus lumbered over to the door. 'Cassandra!'

A few moments later, his secretary appeared in the doorway dressed in a long orange kaftan, hooped earrings and gold platform shoes.

'You called?' she purred.

'Greta and I are about to celebrate some good news. Care for a nip?'

'What sort of question is that?' Cassandra said, pulling up a chair and folding her legs elegantly to one side. Greta was transfixed by Cassandra's amazing shoes. Also her pose. The way she tucked her legs to one side. It reminded Greta of something. Of someone . . .

An image popped into her head of her father perched on their corduroy couch, legs positioned, not rugby wide, but neatly to one side.

'What are we celebrating?'

Angus looked to Greta to elaborate.

'I've been left some money in a will and—' What else was there to say?

'To Walter,' said Angus, lifting his glass in a toast.

Not wanting to be impolite, Greta took a sip.

Fumes surged up her nose. Then she was coughing and spluttering and stumbling around the office, her whole being in full whisky revolt.

Cassandra patted her on the back, while Angus darted to the water cooler.

'Thank you,' Greta said, wiping her eyes and taking a gulp of tepid water.

It soothed instantly, despite tasting of every day it had spent inside the dusty glass dome.

She cleared her throat, pulled the hem of her skirt straight, and sat down. 'I'm not a big drinker.'

'I never would have guessed,' said Cassandra.

'Right now, where were we?' Angus said.

'You'd been left some money in a will,' Cassandra prompted, turning to Greta with a Roger-Moore raised eyebrow.

Greta nodded, closing her mouth to suppress another cough.

'That's fabulous, darling!' Cassandra said, when Greta added nothing new.

'Money, but not in the conventional sense,' added Angus.

Greta wiped her mouth on her arm. 'Yes. I mean, I've been left a holiday.'

'Nice.'

'A holiday with a difference,' Angus said.

'Yes, with a difference.'

Cassandra rolled her eyes. 'Oh, for goodness' sake, you two. Spit it out! This is like trying to squeeze wine out of a raisin.'

Angus chortled. 'An all-expenses-paid holiday of indeterminate length.' He raised his forefinger. 'But, and this is where it gets interesting, only if Greta adheres to the itinerary Walter has planned for her.'

'Now that is some condition,' Cassandra said, clicking her long red nails together. 'Just hope you aren't headed for somewhere like the Sinai Desert, or Kazakhstan.'

Greta shot Angus a horrified glance. She hadn't given the destinations much thought.

Angus shook his head. 'I am sure that it will be an itinerary to be envious of. Each destination will only be revealed on the eve of Greta's next port of call.'

'Well, well, well,' Cassandra said, putting down her glass. 'That's a will with a twist, if ever I heard one. Sort of like *The Amazing Race*.'

Hearing the details articulated out loud made it sound so much more daunting. The bequest represented everything that frightened Greta — relinquishing control, uncertainty, newness.

Distracted, she took a swig from her mug — the whisky one, instead of the water one.

Balking at this second insult, her body sent amber liquor spraying everywhere.

'Oh, my goodness! So sorry. I'm so sorry.' She dabbed desperately at Cassandra's kaftan.

'Honey, if you'd wanted to fondle my breasts you should have just said so.'

Greta retracted her hand in horror, her face no doubt the darkest shade of crimson.

Cassandra gave a throaty chuckle. 'Do not let this woman near any more of your Glenfiddich, Angus.'

Greta willed the floor to open up. She'd lost any semblance of dignity and was behaving like a compete buffoon.

Every additional second in the room was torture. She should change her mind. Escape. Never see these people again.

But could she? As kindly as Angus appeared, Greta suspected he was not one to brook indecision easily. And as if reading her mind, he proceeded to clear a space on his desk.

'To business then.'

I want to leave you something which satisfies.

Travel. Greta had barely travelled over the harbour bridge, let alone further afield.

You're a supremely sensible woman, Grets. Not used to spoiling yourself. Always putting others first. I hope this will free you, for a time at least, from that conveyer belt of commitments.

Conveyer belt of commitments had a wearying ring to it.

I'm not being unreasonable. I know you'd rather have the cash in hand, but all that would happen is it would find its way into your rainy day fund, and you'd keep working for jolly Jud Rutland in that awful pool chemicals shop. Life is short. I know.

So, this was Walter's way of forcing her out of her comfort zone.

I've included a deadline, because I know you too well, Greta Jellings.

She would be obliged to embark on the adventure within three months. If she did not take up the offer in that time, the money would go instead to a charity Walter had nominated.

Angus will be managing it all from his end. Any glitches or dramas, he'll sort them out, so don't fret. And yes, I've paid him a retainer. You will not be inconveniencing him.

Angus winked at her.

But where did he get the money for such a gesture. He was a gardener.'

Angus leant back in his chair, as if pondering how much to reveal.

'Walter came from a very wealthy family,' he said finally. 'Though, as you may know, he was estranged from his parents. His mother passed away some time back, however his father died unexpectedly just a couple of months before Walter himself succumbed. No will was found, meaning his father died intestate. Because of this, Walter and his sister, the closest living relatives, automatically became equal beneficiaries.'

Walter had barely spoken about his family. Greta knew he'd lost contact with his sister, but always assumed his parents to be dead.

'It is somewhat surprising that such an astute businessman did not leave a will,' Angus added. 'Perhaps he could not conceive of parting with his wealth even in death,' he said wryly. 'Had he left a will, I very much doubt Walter would have inherited a single penny.'

Greta chewed her thumbnail.

'So, my dear,' Angus said, handing her a pen, 'the time has come to commit.'

Greta ran her tongue under her top lip as she tried to order her thoughts; they felt stretched like a cassette tape left too long in a sun-baked car.

She didn't even have a passport.

'Greta?'

She'd need to give her landlady notice. Valenka would be devastated. Greta had been renting the Devonport villa for going on eleven years.

And her furniture? That would have to be put in storage.

As for her car, she couldn't get rid of it; to replace it would cost a fortune. Perhaps Lorraine and Rory would keep it on bricks for her. They certainly had enough garages at their new place.

'What about my spa pool?' she blurted out. 'It's fitted at the home I rent. If I give up the house, what will happen to it?'

'Don't let these logistical issues bother you,' Angus said, draining his drink. 'I'm here to facilitate all that.'

She looked at the fountain pen in his hand. She'd never done anything so rash or reckless before. Not everyone was made for adventure.

She shook her head. 'I'm sorry Angus, but—'

'*'Tis but a banging of the door behind you,*' he said, '*a blithesome step forward, and you are out of the old life and into the new!*'

Greta's entire body tingled.

'*The Wind in The Willows!*' she cried, the quote instantly unlatching a door in her head.

Memories tumbled in. Memories, which had been buried for so long under years of Nora words.

Her father is reading to her about Mole and Ratty and Badger and Toad. Then it's morning and she leans over the side of her bed in search of the note he will have left.

There, scrawled on colourful card, a line from the chapter they'd read the night before.

'Take the Adventure, heed the call, now ere the irrevocable moment passes!'

Sometimes the words are hard to understand, but every day a different note, a different quote. Some small treasure. Some amazing truth.

The power of Kenneth Grahame's words. The fun of her father. The feeling that anything is possible — the biggest dreams, the best dress.

She'd forgotten that feeling. She'd forgotten him.

Angus sneezed, snapping her out of her daydream.

'I should mention,' he said, pulling a crumpled handkerchief from his pocket. 'Walter was concerned that his sister Clare might scuttle his plans and contest their father's will.'

Greta frowned.

'Though, to date, I've received no indication that this will happen.'

Greta quickly took the pen and proceeded to sign her name with a clammy but determined flourish.

CHAPTER 11

The morning after making her momentous decision, Greta awoke to the thud of realisation dropping like an anchor to the bottom of her belly. What had she done? She was about to be catapulted out of the life she knew. The existence she'd led for so long seemed, on reflection, to be entirely satisfactory. Entirely satisfactory. But it was too late. She'd allowed herself to be swayed. Had only herself to blame for signing up to this ludicrous notion. She could just imagine what her mother's reaction would have been, Nora's disappointment summed up in one pithy summation: '*The grass is always greener on the other side, Greta. Always greener.*'

Three months was not a long time considering everything Greta had to achieve. Just ninety days to tie up all the loose ends of her life and prepare for . . . for what? For anything and everything. How could she prepare for that?

She started compiling lists which challenged her from the refrigerator, bellowed from her bedside, and glowered at her from the back of the bathroom door. At least on a list, tasks were tethered to some tangible, audited reality. But left in her head, they would grow rampant, like weeds in a hothouse.

For a while the lists became endpoints in themselves. Greta wrote a job down, categorised it, prioritised it, revised it, then perhaps demoted it, her mind lost in the assignment of it all.

Find caregiver for Marilyn Monroe
Apply for passport
See GP for vaccinations and travel meds
Request final power and water bill
Put post on holiday hold
Cancel newspaper

Contact Valenka re tenancy
Give notice at work (**Delay as long as possible**)

Six weeks into her three-month amnesty, Greta suffered her first full-blown panic attack. It was when Jud suggested they trial a new computer system in the shop later in the year. Greta was not going to be at the shop later in the year.

She booked an emergency therapy session with Judy.

'You're revving in neutral,' her therapist counselled, as Greta sat limp and exhausted in the green felt chair.

'But—'

'The lists give you the illusion of action, when in reality they've simply become distractors, aiding and abetting your tendency to procrastinate. It's time to turn your intentions into achievements.'

Making the first phone call to her landlady came as a relief, like landing in the water after hours of trying to avoid capsizing a craft. And once in the water, there was nothing to do but swim.

An advert for Greta's home appeared in the local gazette just a few days later. Greta almost reapplied for it.

Characterful, one-bedroom cottage in Devonport. Small, well-kept garden. Vegetable patch. Five-minute walk to beach. Long-term tenancy preferable.

Enquiries to Valenka Sokolov.

Greta wanted to add that the kitchen was filled with all-day sunshine and the windowsill lined with potted herbs. There were the prettiest coral curtains in her bedroom (she'd hemmed them herself) and a vintage front door with stained-glass panels. Fairy lights added a bit of magic to the elm tree every evening, and . . .

The property was not hers to describe. Not hers.

The advertisement rammed Greta up against reality. She'd made her decision. The world was moving on. There was nothing to do but swim.

The one task she delayed doing for as long as possible was giving her notice at work. She owed Jud sufficient time to find a replacement. However, the notion of giving up her job was the most daunting thing being asked of her. Her job was the last guy rope holding her up. Working in a pool chemicals shop might not have been her career of choice, but it defined her. Gave her purpose. It was the backdrop against which her weekends were positioned. The reason her bank balance was topped up fortnightly. It was as reflex and necessary as breathing.

Jud looked up from his desk and scratched his ear irritably.

'You look busy. I'll come back later, shall I?' she said, reversing out of his office.

He rubbed his nose. 'It's fine. Come in. Sit down. Just the accountants giving me a bloody headache. What do I pay these people for?'

Greta wasn't certain if the question was rhetorical.

'Doing your tax returns. Balancing your profits. And losses, of course. Salaries. Working out—'

'What is it, Greta? Can't you see I'm busy?'

'Yes. Sorry. The thing is . . . well, Jud, I need to tell you something.'

Time slowed. She felt like the foreman of a jury, about to pass the death sentence on her boss. Jud could be annoying at times. Infuriating, in fact. But Jud was Jud. A constant in her life over the past two-and-a-bit decades. Even the fact that he never plucked the hairs in his ears was, in an odd way, reassuring.

'Mmh,' he said, eyeing the spreadsheet in front of him.

'I've got some bad news, I'm afraid.'

He looked up.

'It is with deepest regret that I must tender my resignation.'

Tender my resignation? How ridiculous she sounded. But that was the wording recommended in *Top Tips for Landing and Leaving a Job*, which she'd found in the library. Perhaps with Jud she needed to use a more direct, casual approach.

'I'm leaving. The shop. Going away. On an adventure. To . . . well, I don't know yet. Walter's arranged it. I'm really sorry for the inconvenience. I really am.' Greta burst into tears. 'I hate to let you down, I—'

'You want another holiday?'

'Oh no. This is, well, more permanent. Final. For good. Over rover.'

Jud's eyes widened. His left cheek twitched. He opened his mouth. Closed it. Frowned.

'You're leaving?'

She nodded, her face distorting in apology. 'I'm so sorry. It's just . . .'

'I don't know what to say, Greta. Just don't know what to say. This comes as a complete shock. Out of the blue like this. Have you been unhappy here?'

58

She shook her head vehemently.

Jud put a hand to his left shoulder, then his throat.

Greta shifted uneasily.

He pulled open his desk drawer and rummaged through it.

Greta had heard of rage attacks — an unexpected disappointment triggering murderous intent in an otherwise sane individual.

Jud did not pull a gun from his drawer.

No, he was holding his nitroglycerin spray.

He lifted it to his mouth and gave two sharp squirts under his tongue.

Blood drained from Greta's face as newspaper headlines scrolled through her head.

Selfish shop assistant gives long-time boss heart attack.

Owner of pool shop dies as employee deserts him for a holiday.

'Should I call an ambulance?'

He shook his head. Put up his hand. 'Just give me a moment.'

A cup of tea seemed to settle him. And later, Greta wondered whether Jud had in fact needed his medication after all. She'd seen him use it to great effect the time Mrs Gladwell, a tricky client, had threatened to take him to court.

As she drove home that evening she replayed the events of the day over and over. Giving notice had gone worse than she could ever have imagined. Though what had she been hoping for? '*Of course, my dear. See it as a sabbatical. This is not about what I want, Greta, but what you need. We'll keep the position open for you.*'

Jud's demeanour had devastated her. He'd looked so wounded, so betrayed, as they locked up that night. Twenty-two years of working together wiped out with just a few words. There was no coming back from that.

And yet, threading through Greta's guilt, was something else too. A skein of excitement? She'd done the unthinkable, the inconceivable, the impossible. On her own. Walter would have been proud.

CHAPTER 12

Three days out from her departure, Greta stood watering her garden as if nothing had changed, when everything had. Everything! In less than seventy-two hours the garden would no longer be hers. The garden, and so much else. And all in the name of a holiday.

Holiday? The word was entirely unsuitable, doing nothing to convey the momentousness of what Walter had invited her to do. She was about to embark on a journey into the unknown, challenging years of Nora doctrine. How *foolhardy* she was, giving in to *such selfish tendencies. Only disaster* would come of it.

For as long as Greta could remember, her mother's words had underpinned her every thought and regulated her every day, grounding her in unembellished reality.

It is the first Easter Greta will have without her father.

'We mustn't forget to put out a carrot for the Easter Bunny,' she says as she sits at the dinner table, working her way through a copse of Brussels sprouts.

Nora puts down her fork. 'Greta,' she says in a tone, which always means something serious. 'I don't have carrots to spare.'

Greta is gripped by panic.

'But we have to! He'll be hungry! And how will I know where to look for my Easter eggs, if he can't leave a trail?'

Nora shakes her head. 'Sorry, Greta, but it's time you knew. There is no Easter bunny. It's just a silly story made up by shopkeepers to get parents to buy expensive Easter eggs for their children. It's a naughty lie.'

Greta gulps. There is no bunny. There is no bunny. The words travel quickly around her head, snuffing out any sparks of excitement in their way.

'Come now, my girl. It's nothing to cry about,' her mother says briskly.

'I've bought us a large slab of chocolate for tomorrow. And let me tell you, there's a lot more chocolate in a slab than some hollow egg. And for a lot less money.'

Greta never questioned the veracity of her mother's take on the world. Had Nora told her the sky was about to fall in, Greta would have believed her. There was a security in that, in trusting a parent so absolutely. For a child anyway. But Nora's influence had extended well beyond Greta's childhood. That financial constraints prevented Greta from leaving her mother's home at an appropriate age meant the Nora-Greta status quo remained unchallenged for years. And by the time Greta did finally move out, the paths of thought had been so well worn that Greta could no longer distinguish which were Nora's and which her own.

'How's it all going there, Grets?'

She swung round. Holly was peering over the back fence.

'Not long now. Exciting!'

Holly had taken to calling Greta *Grets*, and to dropping round uninvited.

Greta was not a fan of spontaneous drop-ins, not even from her lovely new neighbour. She'd taken to parking at the end of the street, just so that Holly would not know she was home. Then later, under cover of darkness, she'd slip out of the house and move her car into the garage.

When Holly asked one day why she kept parking at the end of the road, Greta was forced to make some convoluted excuse about her car having water-cooling problems and the mechanic suggesting she keep it in the open air for a while after driving it.

It wasn't that Greta didn't like Holly. On the contrary, she did. A lot. Holly had an infectious energy about her. An easy laugh. An unaffected authenticity. But the more Greta was drawn to her, the more Greta also pulled away.

Judy once suggested that Greta's fear of friendships, or any relationship, for that matter, was founded on her belief that she'd driven her father away. 'Deep down, you still believe that he left because of something you did.'

Greta closed her eyes. How many nights had she lain awake as a six-year-old trying to pinpoint what she'd done wrong? If she hadn't gone

61

away with the Denopoulos family to Taupō. If she hadn't answered back when her mother scolded her about licking the peanut-butter knife. If she hadn't been *'such a boisterous child'*, her parents wouldn't have had all those loud-whisper fights about how to manage her.

'New relationships usher in the fear that you will chase away the people you care about most. So you try to maintain a distance from the start. It's easier that way. Easier than negotiating the pain of loss.'

'All good, thank you. Holly,' Greta said, yanking at the hosepipe. 'Yes, just three days. Can't quite believe it.'

'You sure you are okay, Grets? You look awful.'

Greta looked away. She wanted to say that she was exhausted and frazzled and frightened. That she had worked through all her lists and now there was nothing standing between her and the big unknown. She wanted to let it all out, but she was at least ten years Holly's senior and 'the adult' in this equation. She had to behave appropriately. Holly clearly imagined Greta to be someone else. It was just a matter of time before she realised her mistake and registered her disappointment.

'Hang fire a mo,' Holly said, darting back to her house.

A few moments later she returned bearing a bottle of cloudy yellow liquor.

'I've just made a new batch of kombucha. You should be looking after yourself in preparation for a long-haul flight. Travel can take it out of you.'

'Long-haul.' The word sent a new wave of nervous energy careening through Greta. She still didn't know her first destination.

Holly passed over the bottle. 'And remember, Grets, time to give over to the universe.'

Later Greta drank the concoction in one go. It tasted like a mix of vinegar and drain cleaner. She belched all night, but by the next morning felt a lot better. Kombucha had clearly done the trick.

As she did her ablutions, she scrutinised the last of the lists. Every point now had a line through it:

Jud had interviewed four applicants for Greta's job and finally filled the position.

Valenka had secured a new tenant.

Donna, a friend of Holly's, had agreed to look after Marilyn Monroe on her farm in the Waikato.

Greta had attended the travel clinic and been vaccinated against every disease known to mankind.

Her passport had been delivered by courier post. (A bewildered, double-chinned Greta now her official face for the next ten years.)

And the first instruction pack from Angus was due to be delivered the following day.

It was indeed time to give over to the universe. Greta had come too far down the track to turn back now. And as her apprehension and the belching subsided, a small space opened up in her head. A space, which slowly started to fizz and bubble with anticipation. She'd forgotten what excitement felt like, having learnt so long ago to guard against it. *'The higher your hopes, Greta, the further the fall.'*

Her mother had not been wrong. Rebecca Wilkinson's ninth birthday party was a case in point.

The promise of a clown, helium balloons, Mrs Wilkinson's homemade peppermint slice. Rebecca's present wrapped and ready on the kitchen table for over a week.

But on the day, Greta wakes covered in small, itchy blisters.

'Chickenpox,' Nora declares with an executioner's solemnity.

It takes some time for Greta to feel kindly towards chickens after that.

Then there is the time she is invited to be flower girl at the wedding of one of Nora's clients. Nora sews both the wedding gown and Greta's dress — a taffeta creation with an oyster satin bow and pouch for carrying confetti. But one week out from the big day, the groom gets cold feet. Apparently this is not something a pair of warm socks can fix. And that is that — Greta's dress sold to recover costs.

There is also the occasion she is due to sing in school assembly . . . and the Christmas her mother promises her a budgie . . . and Walter.

So, even as the hour of her departure drew near, Greta kept her newfound excitement tightly harnessed, just in case something intervened to ruin it all.

CHAPTER 13

On the eve of the big day, Greta sat in her lounge surrounded by boxes. It no longer looked like her lounge, the space already disowning her. Yet she was the one who'd decided to leave. She was doing the disowning, wasn't she?

That morning she'd dropped off Marilyn Monroe at Holly's friend's farm. She hadn't hung around, despite the woman inviting her in for a cup of tea. Greta handed over the cage and left, crying all the way back to Auckland, before heading on up to Warkworth to drop her car at Lorraine and Rory's. She timed her arrival to coincide with Lorraine's Pilates class in a bid to avoid too many prying questions.

Rory gave Greta a lift to the intercity bus station, rambling on during the seven-minute journey about the challenges of rural life. Only as Greta was getting out of his car, did he toss a question her way. 'How long we keeping the hatchback for?'

And now here she was, in her soon-to-be-someone-else's house, upended like a tree in the storm.

The busyness and forward motion of the preceding days had kept the sediment from settling. But now, with nothing more to do but wait, the enormity of her decision dawned. Even though her relationships with Jud, Lorraine and Rory, Valenka, the courier driver, postie, and paperboy all lacked depth, they existed. Filled gaps. Insulated her life. Without them, and without her job, who was she?

She picked up the envelope Angus had delivered on his way home from work. It was addressed to her in Walter's unmistakeable script.

Greta

My City

'Here goes,' she said to herself, carefully running her forefinger under the flap. The envelope tore, the tear extending through the letter inside.

Another bad omen. The previous day a black balloon from some liquor store's birthday display had bounced across her path.

So, you've probably guessed where you're headed...

Drum roll.

Actually, it should come as no surprise. I've harped on about it long enough.

Yup. The Big Apple.

More than just the place, though, it's the people I want you to experience. New Yorkers are a crazy, eclectic mix of humans revelling in their uniqueness and point of difference.

The norm casts such a long shadow, Grets. I know. I lived within its gloom for a long time. It was only in New York that I first felt the sun. The city holds so many different stories. Mine is there too. The place gave me the confidence to be me. I tried on a fair few Walters before I found the one that fitted. I hope you get to try on some different Gretas too. And have fun doing it. No one is watching, Grets. No one is watching.

She could almost see him unconsciously rubbing his hairline as he talked, his mouth pulling into an easy smile, his deep voice shaping generous words.

You'll be staying for just over a week. A taster really. But it can be full on for a first-timer. I don't want to overwhelm you.

She sat back. New York! The name conjured up gangsters, Broadway, the Bronx. Margarine yellow taxis, private investigators sitting slouched in their cars drinking countless cups of coffee, detectives chucking half-eaten hotdogs in the bin. (The waste, even if it was just in the movies, had always bothered her.)

The Twin Towers.

Walter.

How frustrated he used to get over her *preconceived* notions about America. '*Just misconceptions fuelled by Hollywood.*'

He'd promised to take her there one day, to the city where his life had begun again, and where it would also begin to end.

'*It's a city like no other, Grets. An unstoppable stream of diversity, energy, creativity, culture.*'

Greta sighed. Couldn't he have started her off somewhere a bit closer to home. A bit tamer too? Australia perhaps?

On second thoughts, New Zealand's trans-Tasman neighbour was no tamer. While it didn't boast the same eye-watering gun-licence statistics as the States, it had pythons, the huntsman spider and box jellyfish!

You'll be staying in a hotel in Manhattan.

Manhattan. A small smile tugged at Greta's lips. It sounded so sophisticated.

All that was left to do was have one final spa before it became the prerogative of some stranger. She shuddered at the thought.

Greta pulled on her old turquoise swimming togs and turned side-on to the mirror. The fabric hung baggily around her dinner-plate bottom, and because of her long torso, just covered her breasts. She felt a prick of panic. Wearing togs had always been a private affair, but now that she was going travelling. . . At least her first port of call was not some tropical island.

She sucked in her belly, lengthened her neck, and pushed up her breasts.

'I'm going to Manhattan,' she said in a posh accent that did not sound quite American, nor from anywhere recognisable. 'Man-hatt-an.'

CHAPTER 14

'Welcome on board, Ms Jellings. My name is Nigel. A glass of champagne for you?'

'How much is it?' Greta asked, eyeing the silver tray.

'Beg you pardon, ma'am?'

Greta took out her purse.

The businessman seated beside Greta let out a snort of laughter.

'Oh, no charge,' Nigel said, waving a hand in horror. 'All part of the service.'

Greta hesitated. According to Nora, there was no such thing as a free lunch. '*There are always hidden costs, Greta. Always.*'

Realising she must have made some sort of faux pas, Greta grabbed a glass of bubbles, her swiftness translating into more of an act of desperation, than conviction. It was hard knowing how to behave when life kept presenting new challenges.

Greta sat back to inspect the wonder of her cubicle, including her very own television screen.

She pushed the button and the monitor was instantly illuminated.

Welcome Greta.

A personalised welcome! She cast about excitedly. This was more special than she could have ever imagined.

A flight attendant with an impossibly tiny waist, petite feet and hair pulled back in a classic chignon, leant over Greta. She smelt of sweet peas and sophistication.

'Can I put that in the overhead locker for you?'

'Oh no, I'm fine, thank you,' Greta said, wrapping her arms around her handbag. Angus had warned of pickpockets and the importance of keeping an eye on her belongings at all times.

'I will need to put it out of the way for take-off,' said the woman through a fixed smile. 'But don't worry, I'll retrieve it for you as soon as we're in the air.'

Reluctantly Greta handed it over.

'Quite a heavy little number,' muttered the hostess as she lifted it above her head.

Well, Greta had prepared for all eventualities. She was embarking on a twenty-hour trip, after all. She'd packed the latest Liane Moriarty novel, and Anna Karenina (if she needed to impress); a couple of hardboiled eggs in case she got hungry; a spare pair of clean knickers in the event of finding herself on a paramedic's stretcher; an atomiser of Evian water, as per the guide-book recommendations; a miniature tube of insect repellent; a box of aspirin; a whistle . . .

'I nearly brought my mother's crocodile-skin handbag, which is heavy even when empty,' Greta confided in the air hostess. 'She bought it at an op shop many moons ago for just seven dollars.'

The woman arranged a fresh smile.

'Quite a find really. Or so my mother thought.' Greta leant forward and lowered her voice. 'That was until one of her sewing clients explained the reason for its heft.'

The hostess glanced over Greta's shoulder, indicating to the couple behind that she'd be with them in just a moment.

'It had been made from the crocodile's tail pelt and not the soft belly skin usually used for high-end products.'

The hostess raised her eyebrows and glided away.

'A bargain indeed,' Greta said to no one in particular. 'My poor mother had bought a lemon.'

Greta had vacillated for some time about whether or not to bring the bag, which was a very tangible reminder of her late mother. Her hesitation was borne out of her confusion and conflicted feelings towards Nora. Feelings that had become more pronounced after reading Nora's diaries. She'd finally decided in favour of the bag, reasoning this was no time to break from the security of her mother's doctrines, just as she was about to embark on a daunting adventure. Without Nora's words, Greta was nothing.

It was Holly however, who put an end to Greta's dilemma. 'I'm sure you can't travel with crocodile-skin products unless you have some sort of special permit.'

Just the thought of unwittingly breaking any laws left Greta hyper-ventilating. And so the handbag had been left behind.

'Crew, please arm the doors.'

Greta clasped both armrests. 'Here we go.'

The man beside her did not look up from his laptop. He had office-sallow skin, a closely cropped beard and steel grey hair. Oddly, his eyebrows were a serious brown, as if they'd been stuck onto his face as an afterthought.

Greta was reminded of the card game she used to play as a child. Every player was dealt ten cards, each card displaying some unique facial feature — a nose, ears, eyes, a chin . . . The winner of the game was the player who could compile the most plausible looking person from the cards they'd been dealt. Judging was subjective of course, and inevitably ended in tears. The irony was that there would have been no dispute about Greta's fellow passenger; his eyebrows definitely did not look like they belonged to him.

'*All phones and electronic devices must now be turned to flight mode and safely stowed.*'

He continued on his laptop.

Greta caught the eye of the attendant at the front of the cabin and tilted her head towards the offending passenger. The woman did not pick up on Greta's signals, so she gave an exaggerated wink and repeated her head-tilting manoeuvre. The hostess's cheeks pinked and she looked away quickly.

Realising she was going to have to take the matter into her own hands, Greta nudged her neighbour.

'Sorry, sir, but I think you might want to switch that off. Aviation rules and all.' She shrugged, trying to soften her message. 'Better to be safe than sorry. I'm told the waves can interfere with the electronics of the plane and we don't want that.'

She was glad she'd done the research. At least she was talking from a position of knowledge.

The man glared at her, before pulling down the lid of his laptop.

'*Take note of your nearest exit.*'

Greta craned her neck. One . . . two . . . three rows away.

'*In the event oxygen is required, a mask will—*'

As each safety manoeuvre was demonstrated, Greta rehearsed it

— deep-vein-thrombosis-prevention exercises, brace position, retrieval of lifejacket.

She was pulling the lifejacket over her head when the Audrey Hepburn hostess hurried up to her and offered to put it away again.

The man beside Greta summoned the woman closer.

'Yes, Mr Price?'

He whispered something in her ear.

'I'm very sorry, sir,' she said, drawing back. 'Unfortunately there are no spare seats. The flight is full.'

Greta leant in. 'If you're unhappy with your seat, we can swap. I don't mind if I'm beside a window or not. In fact,' she dropped her voice, 'I have IBS.' Then she mouthed *Irritable Bowel Syndrome*. 'When it's playing up, I need to use the you-know-what quite frequently.' She rolled her eyes. 'It's been much better since I started taking peppermint oil, so fingers crossed. Anyway, what I'm saying is that swapping seats might work well for me too.'

The passenger and hostess looked at each other, then back at Greta.

'It's fine,' the man said, his eyes wide with exasperation.

The plane started taxiing down the runway.

Greta expected to feel more frightened. The previous night had offered up a carnival of nightmares — a jammed parachute, freefalling through the sky, leeches in some jungle, Jud dumping a wheelbarrow of unpaid invoices on her desk.

The champagne must have been working its magic.

The engines roared, built to a crescendo, then Greta was forced back in her seat as the plane started to pick up speed.

She sucked in a stuttering breath as strips of grass, beacons and houses hurtled past.

The cabin tilted.

'Woah!' Then they were airborne. 'Woah! Woah!'

Her neighbour turned sharply.

'Sorry,' Greta said, feeling a blush envelop her. 'It's just, well, I cannot believe I'm actually flying.'

The man's expression softened. 'First time?'

She nodded vigorously. 'Yours too?'

He snorted. 'Done this a few times, you could say.' He stretched out his hand. 'Duncan. Duncan Price.'

'I don't mean to be rude, Duncan, but I can't really shake your hand right now.' She was too busy gripping the armrests.

Her neighbour was dressed quite trendily for his age, in a silver fox, Richard Gere, sort of way. Black polo jumper, chino trousers, taupe suede shoes. He wore a gold signet ring studded with diamonds on his left pinkie finger and a big-faced gold watch on his wrist.

Ask people about themselves. Ask people about themselves.

'Are you holidaying?' Greta said, forcing herself to talk, when all she really wanted to do was focus on not falling out of the sky.

'Business.'

'Oh right.'

Another long pause.

'What sort of business?'

The plane started levelling out.

'Chocolate.'

'Chocolate?!' Greta released the armrests and swung one leg over the other, momentarily forgetting about dying, or the need to keep her oversized feet hidden. 'That must be the best job ever.'

Duncan Price shrugged. 'Has its moments,' he said, hauling out his laptop again.

'I have to ask—'

He turned warily.

'Do you get free chocolate bars at work?'

His face sprung into a smile. He looked much nicer when he wasn't frowning.

'I guess I can have chocolate whenever I want,' he said, as if the idea had just occurred to him.

He started scrolling down a spreadsheet.

'I get work perks too,' Greta said, straightening. 'Fifty percent off any pool chemicals. And—' She took a breath for maximum effect. 'A twenty-six-jet spa pool installed at my house.'

Her neighbour did not comment. Hopefully he did not think she was gloating. She wasn't. Well, maybe a little.

'It's not actually my house,' she said, trying to temper the brag. 'I rent. Or rather, did rent. Anyway, that was when I was working at Blue Sun Spas, Pools and Pipes. My landlady is going to keep the spa pool at the house until I get back.'

The man's brow furrowed again.

'But chocolate,' Greta said quickly, anxious not to lose their tenuous connection. 'Now that would be my dream job. Honestly. Chocolate whenever I wanted. Imagine.'

'It's not all a party,' Price said, still focused on his screen.

Greta felt deflated by his dourness.

'Every job has drudgery,' she said, channelling Nora. 'It's invoicing for me. I hate, hate, hate it.'

Price's fingers glided impressively over his keyboard. Greta was more a two-finger typist, but a fast one at that.

'You must get a thrill from producing something that makes other people so happy.'

He looked up again.

She was talking too much. Being overfamiliar. It was lack of sleep, compounded by champagne on an empty stomach. Nerves too. Trying to make a good impression, sound intelligent . . .

She thought back to Mrs Shriver's comments in her Year 6 school report.

Greta needs to give the other students an opportunity to say their lines. She is in the habit of ad-libbing on stage when another student is supposed to be talking.

The thing was that Greta was always anxious her fellow players had forgotten what they were meant to say. Spaces were frightening. Pauses between people. It was easier to keep the momentum going.

Duncan Price stared past her.

'Sorry, I'm interrupting.'

'No. It's fine,' he said, making proper eye contact for the first time.

Greta was encouraged.

'I don't know where I'd be on a slow day without two squares of dark chocolate. Seventy-percent cocoa, at least. You're in the business of saving lives, Mr Price. Chocolate has brought me back from the brink many a time.'

He laughed again.

'Have you had a chance to look at the menu yet?' It was Nigel.

'Sorry, we've been too busy talking,' Greta said, tilting her head to her neighbour. She looked down the menu. 'Wowee! Ricotta cakes with drunken raspberries.'

'That's for breakfast after we've transited through Sydney,' Nigel said, directing her to the correct meal. 'Tonight we have poached salmon on cress with a balsamic vinaigrette. Sirloin steak, potato rosti and asparagus spears. Or a vegetable stack with spicy peanut dressing.'

'Is it, you know, also on the house?' Greta asked, embarrassed at having to raise the question of money again. 'Otherwise,' she said, dropping her voice, 'I have boiled eggs in my bag.'

Nigel's eyes widened. He kept his arms by his side, while moving his hands in a sort of emphatic sign language.

'Then yes to it all, thank you. I'm not a fussy eater. Nora saw to that. She could never understand why parents prepared different meals for their children. I was no chicken-nugget child. No sir. I guess it paid off. I should say that Nora was my mother. It can get confusing. She preferred me to call her by her first name.'

'Just to clarify,' Nigel said slowly. 'The madam would like the salmon, the steak, *and* the vegetable stack?'

She nodded. All this talk about food was making her hungry.

Nigel shook out a white napkin with an extravagant flourish and laid it over her tray table. Then he set out the cutlery.

Greta fingered the chunky pieces of metal. They were fridge-cold and all the more luxurious because of it.

'I feel like a queen!' she said, sinking back in her chair.

Nigel shivered with delight. 'We aim to please.'

Just when Greta thought she could eat no more, he wheeled a cheese trolley down the aisle.

Cheese was another of Greta's weaknesses, especially a sharp, crumbly blue. Though she rarely had it in the house; it was too expensive.

'Could I ask you to please wrap up a wedge of the blue for me? I'll stash it in my seat pocket for later.'

Be Prepared had been Baden Powell's motto. Nora's too. Thinking about it, the two had had a lot in common — discipline, dedication to work, a strong moral code. Nora just didn't wear a uniform.

After dinner, Nigel helped Greta work the entertainment system, then she settled back to enjoy *The Shawshank Redemption* — a favourite. She preferred watching films she'd seen before; the territory was already chartered, the trajectory unchanged, and the outcome a comfortable certainty.

She was sobbing quietly when her neighbour tapped her on the arm. She spun round.

'You alright?' Duncan Price mouthed.

Greta nodded, wiping her nose on her sleeve. 'Tom Hanks is broadcasting the duet from *The Marriage of Figaro* to the other prisoners. I—'

Price's mouth was moving.

'What?'

He put a finger to his lips.

She flushed and quickly removed her headphones.

'Tim Robbins. Not Tom Hanks.'

'Right. Yes. Thank you. I'm not very good at remembering actors' names.'

It bothered her that she had such a poor recall for names. She'd read several books on the topic and tried various aids to improve her memory, but with only limited success. The problem was that when introduced to someone, she was so busy thinking about not making a fool of herself, all else fell away.

She'd tried the trick of repeating a person's name as often as possible after being introduced to 'create new neural pathways', but gave up because it seemed to make people uncomfortable. 'Nice to meet you, Barbara. So tell me, Barbara, what do you do? Gosh, Barbara, how interesting.'

Another ploy was to create an association with the new person's name, as a sort of prompt. This was not all it was cracked up to be either. Rena Dankworth was a case in point. The woman was an infrequent customer at the shop, popping in perhaps three times a year at most. She was a lovely lady with a soft lisp and fine tremor, and someone Greta was loath to ever offend. Yet for some reason, she could never remember the woman's name. After drawing a blank on several embarrassing occasions, she decided to create an *aide-memoire*; picturing Rena driving a Renault.

Some months later, as she'd hoped, she retrieved the French car association immediately. The trouble was, Greta couldn't remember *which* French car. After an awkward pause, Greta settled on Peugeot.

'And how are you today, Peugo?' she mumbled.

Rena Dankworth must have gone elsewhere for her pool chemicals after that, because Greta didn't see her in the shop again. The irony was that Greta could now remember the woman's name without any difficulty at all.

After *The Shawshank Redemption* had finished, Greta padded along the darkened aisle to the toilet, the blackness of her route broken up by the occasional square of blue light.

There was something comforting about being inside a warm cocoon of sleeping people, coasting above her life and all its attendant worries.

The toilet cubicle was very tight and the noise of the engines magnified ten-fold inside it, so much so that Greta felt as if she'd stepped into a separate pod of the craft, which might at any moment detach from the mother ship. As for peeing under pressure in a claustrophobic space . . . She contemplated leaving the door ajar. This was not feasible, so she decided to leave it unlocked. This also proved a no-goer, because the booth remained shrouded in darkness until the door had been bolted. Greta reluctantly secured the bolt. Immediately, the room was doused in unforgiving white light.

A pale, wide-eyed Greta looked back at her, her blow-dried hair already haloed by frizz. Mirrors were such a disappointment.

This was no time to linger on appearances. Greta hovered over the toilet seat, her mouth dry, her thighs shaking, and did her ablutions. However, the challenges kept coming. Whoever had designed the space seemed to have done so with the express purpose of prolonging the agony of it all.

Greta waved her hands under the tap. Nothing.

Depressed one lever. It lowered the plug.

She tried another. A thin trickle of water finally flowed.

She lifted her hand off the lever to wash her hands. The stream stopped.

Washing her hands became a futile exercise of trying to get them under the water fast enough before the stream stopped running. In the end, she was forced to wash one hand at a time, while depressing the lever with the other.

Rubbing the fingers of one hand against each other proved no easy task, the challenge heightened when she mistakenly used hand lotion instead of soap.

Finally, she pulled out what she thought was a paper handtowel, only to discover she was holding a sheet of baking-paper in the shape of a toilet seat.

She cast around for the flush button.

Who on earth decided to hide the flush button behind the lifted toilet lid?

The bowl let out an almighty bellow.

Greta grabbed the handrail to avoid being sucked down the wind tunnel and pitched into space, then flung open the cubicle door and burst out into the corridor. She would not be using the toilet again, not if her bladder was about to burst.

CHAPTER 15

Greta stirred. It was the aroma of pork sausages that woke her. She opened her eyes. Nothing felt familiar.

Then she remembered.

Delight and dread landed in her belly. This was no dream.

She pulled up the shutter and an oval of light poured over her. It felt different from the sunshine that reached the ground. Almost celestial. It left her feeling weightless and oddly euphoric. She peered out the window. Pasted onto the corridor of blue sky was a frieze of toothpaste-white clouds.

'Morning, Ms Jellings,' Nigel said, handing her a steaming hot flannel with a pair of silver tongs. 'Trust you slept well.'

'Like a log, thank you, Nigel.'

'When you're ready, I'll make up your bed, so that you can have some breakfast.'

She sat up and looked across at her neighbour. It felt oddly intimate waking up beside a stranger.

Duncan Price was in the same position he'd been in when she fell asleep — hunched over his laptop. However, he was now dressed in a charcoal suit and tie. She'd have expected a chocolatier to have more Willy-Wonka colour and charisma.

Greta ran her fingers through her hair and sprayed Evian mist over her face, the spray's reach further than she'd expected.

Duncan Price swung round.

'Oops,' she said, with an embarrassed giggle. 'These things are . . . sorry.'

Price wiped his laptop screen with his sleeve.

'You're in the office early,' she said, trying to move the moment on. He seemed to be the sort of guy who got annoyed by too much fuss.

He nodded, the gesture double-chinned and restrained.

'Did you sleep well?' she asked

'Not bad.'

She tried to imagine what sort of life Duncan Price led outside the flying metal box. He wore a wedding band and there was a photograph of two teenage children on his screensaver, but he didn't look very happy, his clipped demeanour permeating all his interactions, even when business was not on the agenda.

Sitting next to him left her feeling uncomfortable and on edge. In an odd way, he reminded Greta of herself. Someone who dealt with life as if it were a serious chore.

She turned quickly away from this thought. It came encumbered with lost opportunities, wasted years, passionless performance . . .

Greta had always been in awe of the Duncans of this world — rich people whose affluence automatically endowed them with intelligence and achievement. She felt like a dent-in-the-car-door sort of person when around them. A silly intrusion in their very important lives. And yet, sitting beside Duncan Price for longer than a brief meeting had tempered her reverence just a little. Like her, the businessman was obliged to fasten his seatbelt, use the toilet, and rely on the pilot to get him to his destination.

She thought back to the patients she'd met in Walter's oncology ward. A hospital gown was a great leveller, stripping a person of props — the gold watch, officer pips, fashion labels. Under every grey gown was just a body. Two arms, two legs, a derriere. What distinguished someone under such circumstances was their character. And how they treated others.

The plane, which only an hour earlier had been a safe, dark nest, was now a bullet of noise and activity. Trolleys clattered, babies cried and overhead lockers were clicked open, then banged shut. Passengers edged past each other with toiletry bags stowed under their arms, and staff strode down aisles, handing out arrival documentation and collecting headphones. Greta felt the familiar twist of apprehension.

The plane began its slow descent and soon they were enveloped in a thick wad of cloud. Instead of acting as a buffer, the clouds seemed to provoke the plane to roil and shudder. Then it bounced in the sky.

Greta screamed and flung her head onto her knees. Well, she didn't quite reach her knees. She wished she'd been more diligent about doing her stretches.

'No need for that,' said her neighbour. 'A bit of turbulence, that's all.'

Greta remained clasping her calves. She'd be the judge of what was necessary, thank you very much.

She started counting back from a hundred, but had to begin again with every judder and jerk. She was down to thirty-seven when Nigel tapped her on the shoulder. She looked up warily.

'It's all fine, Ms Jellings. Really.'

People were staring. She felt foolish, but still afraid. The impossibility of keeping a massive metal tube moving through the sky . . .

The plane rocked again. 'Ooh no, I don't like this, Nigel!'

'I've been flying for nineteen years,' he said, leaning over and taking her hand, 'and I'm still here to tell the tale.'

'Sorry. I feel so stupid. But . . . here we go again.' She fought back tears.

'Don't apologise,' he said, waving his forefinger back and forth. 'The way I like to look at it is that the world needs both those who take risks and those focused on preserving life. One is charged with our progress, the other with our survival. The world needs people like you.'

Greta had never thought of it that way before. For the first time ever her anxieties did not feel such a burden, Nigel's words as valuable as anything Judy had proffered in therapy.

Twenty minutes later they landed at JFK airport.

Greta breathed. She'd survived. Overcome her first hurdle.

First hurdle. The word instantly sobered her. This was no time to rest on her laurels.

She undid her safety belt and emptied the seat pocket of her belongings.

Someone tapped her on the shoulder. She looked round. It was Duncan Price, black briefcase in hand.

'It's been a pleasure, Greta.'

Greta's eyes widened, her thoughts suddenly scrambled. Of all the things for the man to say! He'd barely spoken to her all flight. Not asked her a single thing about herself. He was probably just glad to be rid of her.

'You know, I'm a little envious of you,' he said, looking down at his feet.

Greta swallowed. 'I am very fortunate, I know,' she blurted out. 'Being flown Business Class and all. And a fully paid holiday—'

'No. It's not that. I envy that you get excited about such things. Things that even my kids have become blasé about. I envy you that.'

She opened her mouth. Nothing came out. His words almost felt like a compliment.

Price handed her his business card. 'Happy to show you round my factory if ever you're passing through.'

The queue started to move. 'Free chocolate bar included.'

Then he was walking towards the exit.

Greta looked down at the embossed card in her hand.

DUNCAN PRICE
CEO PRICE CHOCOLATES

CHAPTER 16

Greta joined the queue of people snaking across the vast JFK concourse. Bleary-eyed travellers, crying kids, businessmen and backpackers, all waiting to be processed at the grand gates of America.

Progress was slow and Greta was starting to feel peckish. It would have been suppertime in New Zealand, and even though she'd had breakfast on the plane, it didn't count for much when pitted against the power of habit.

She opened her handbag and pulled out a tiny Tupperware.

As she peeled off the lid there was a rush of eggy odour. Thankfully, she'd already peeled the eggs at home. It would have been a nightmare trying to deal with little bits of shell and egg membrane in the customs concourse.

People turned and stared. She hadn't fully thought through the issues around eating a boiled egg in public.

In a bid to get rid of the offending item as quickly as possible, she stuffed the whole egg into her mouth. In retrospect, this was an unwise move. It sucked up all the moisture in her mouth, and when she tried to swallow, lodged halfway down her gullet. Greta gagged, elongated her neck in a chicken-like manoeuvre, tried swallowing again. But the egg remained stuck behind her sternum.

She was so preoccupied with her dilemma, that she did not notice the queue melting away in front of her, and just as she was casting around for a water dispenser, she was called to the counter.

The customs officer eyed her over thick-rimmed spectacles more suited to The Cold War.

Greta smiled too widely. 'Morning,' she managed, her voice sounding oddly like a chipmunk's. It was the egg effect, compounded by nerves.

The woman with blue lapels and a shiny brass badge flicked pointedly through Greta's passport. 'This a new document?'

'Brand new,' Greta said, her nervous chatter kicking in. 'Your stamp will be the very first, in fact. It only came through two weeks ago. Which was a relief, because at one point—' She swallowed hard to prevent an eggy uprising. 'I thought it was going to get to me too late, and that would have been crushing, because I'd built myself up to—'

'What is the purpose of your visit?'

Greta felt herself flush. She hated the way she reddened at the most inopportune times. This was a serious setting and blushing would surely cast her in the crimson light of suspicion.

Judy had once tried to pinpoint the cause for Greta's tendency to colour. And why she always felt guilty and anxious in the face of an authority figure?

'Low self-esteem, perhaps. When your father left, you felt responsible. Guilty, even though you didn't know what you'd done to drive him away. You grew up thinking you were a bad person. It didn't help that your mother used to say people would think differently of you if they only knew what you were really like.'

Greta could still remember the day almost thirty-three years earlier when she'd returned from Taupō to find her father gone.

Breathless and excited, she runs into her house. She has so much to tell about her weekend away.

Hearing the sound of sobbing, she bursts through the kitchen door. Her mother is bent over the kitchen table, still in her dressing gown, making an awful moaning sound.

'Mama?'

'Mama!'

Her mother swings round, her hair wild, like a windswept haystack, her eyes red and puffy. There is a letter in her hand.

'Greta,' she says, in a strange, strangled voice. 'You're home early.'

Greta remains at the door, as if by stepping into the kitchen she will be contaminated by the sorrow and thereby make it real.

'What's wrong, Mama?'

Though her mother is looking at her, her eyes seem to be taking in a different scene.

'Nothing. Everything is fine,' she says, wiping her nose on her dressing-gown sleeve.

'But Mama—'

'Did you have a good time?'

Nodding slowly. 'I brought you a present.'

Greta pulls out a smooth white pebble. 'From a lake as big as the ocean.'

Her mother is now standing. She stares at Greta's gift.

'We had competitions to see who could skim their pebble the furthest. Mr Denopoulos won every time. I brought a pebble home for Papa too.'

Her mother's face twists and contorts, as if someone has just put a megaphone to her ear.

'He's had to go away, Greta. It's just you and me now.'

The way her mother says it — just you and me now — tells Greta more than she ever wants to know.

She starts to cry. 'He didn't say goodbye.'

'That's enough now. Go and put your bag in your room. I'll help you unpack later.'

And just like that her mama loses her softness, her laughter, her music. As if someone crept into their house while Greta was away and turned her mother to stone.

By the next morning, all traces of her father have vanished, as if his entire existence has been a fiction. A space yawns in the wardrobe where his suits had hung, the only thing left is the pomander she'd made him for Christmas — a shrivelled navel orange studded with cloves and suspended from a maroon velvet ribbon. Two toothbrushes stand to attention in the blue bathroom mug, not three. There is no ashtray in the lounge, nor dented brass tobacco tin on the bedside table. Photo albums are missing photographs, like an orchestra robbed of instruments. Books slope sideways on the shelf where her father's collection of glossy theatre programmes had lived . . .

One has been overlooked! Evita is still wedged between two shelves. Greta manages to extract the bent brochure and hide it under her bed.

She didn't know it then, but it would become her only tangible record of Before.

Greta pointed to the scrawl on the Arrivals document, her writing extending beyond the purpose-of-visit box.

'You see, I was gifted a holiday by Walter who is, or rather was, a very dear friend.'

She always struggled to describe their relationship. 'Friend' did not feel full enough, yet there was no word to adequately describe a person who occupied so much of her heart. The man she'd been in love with both before and even after she'd learnt he was gay. The most special of people, against whom all others were measured.

'Liver cancer,' she continued, words rushing out of her mouth. 'It's more common in people with . . . with . . .' Even in her nervous state, when she was usually compelled to share too much, Greta knew that HIV was not a good word to introduce into this conversation. 'Anyway, he died last year. Eight months ago. And—'

'Office two,' the woman said, waving a hand in the direction of a corridor to the right.

'Office to . . .?'

'Go to office two,' the woman said brusquely.

Greta's gaze followed the woman's finger. 'Oh, the number *two*! Now I understand. I thought at first you meant *to*, as in office *to* the left, or office *to* the right, or office *to* get a stamp. But what you meant was *two*, as in one, *two*, three, four.'

The door with a giant number two painted on it in green was in the opposite direction to the route most other processed passengers were taking.

'Right you are then,' she said, trying to sound chipper. She reached for her passport.

'Stand back from the counter.'

'But my passport.'

'Stand back.'

Greta stepped back, her thighs starting to tremble. 'My passport.'

'That is not your concern.'

'I don't mean to argue, but it is. Really, it is my concern.'

'The document will follow duly.'

'Duly?'

'Move along now, ma'am, or I'll have to call Security.'

The word 'Security' pierced Greta like a sewing-machine needle. She hurried down the corridor in question, her vision blurring. Best city indeed!

Outside office two, Greta blotted her eyes, took a deep breath, then slowly depressed the handle. The door swung open with the speed of

84

someone assisting on the other side, and she lurched into the room and up against a large uniformed man who smelt of rancid sweat and cigarette smoke.

She glanced down. Black belly hairs were bursting through a gap between his shirt buttons, and there was a gun on his hip. A gun!

Greta started to pant. She'd expected some small office, but instead was standing in a space the size of a school hall. Row upon row of chairs faced the long counter upfront, behind which roved two uniformed officers.

The belly-hair man handed Greta a card with the number eighteen on it.

'Take a seat till your number is called.'

She nodded and slipped into the back row like a schoolgirl arriving late for assembly.

A tiny woman was standing up front, her back to the rest of the room. She had a cream scarf wrapped loosely around her neck, despite the heat, and a thin black ponytail, which reached right down to her bottom.

'How many months?' barked a female officer.

'Three,' came the barely decipherable answer.

'Ma'am, you are *not* three months pregnant. May I remind you it is an offence to tell mistruths. We can have the gestation of your foetus assessed by a medical professional. Now, were you planning to birth your child in the United States of America?'

'No, no. I am just visit my friend. Like I say. Holiday.'

A Hispanic-looking man stood up.

'Sit down,' bellowed the man with a gun on his hip.

'But suh—'

'Sit down!'

'Yes, suh.'

The scene felt surreal, as if Greta had stepped onto the set of some movie. Surely all she had to do was step out again and she'd be back in her lounge in Devonport.

She blew into cupped hands; her breath smelt of egg.

Her fingers were clumsy with fear as she rummaged in her bag for a mint. Coming to America had been a bad idea. A very bad idea. So much for her *misconceptions about New York being fuelled by Hollywood!*

She thought back to Leila, her mother's intrepid spinster friend who'd spent years travelling the world. The eighty-five-year-old would regale an enthralled Greta about her past adventures. One of her accounts was imprinted on Greta's memory — the time Leila as a young woman unwittingly left an immersion heater on in her hotel room in Turkey and the entire building burnt down. Leila was arrested for arson. On the day of her hearing she shared the courtroom with a handful of other 'criminals'. The man one ahead of her was found guilty of stealing a loaf of bread and sentenced to have a hand chopped off.

'And I'm thinking,' says Leila, her eyes melodramatically wide, 'burning down an entire hotel must surely count for two hands, or a foot.'

Only a last-minute intervention by the New Zealand embassy got Leila a reprieve.

The image Greta had held in her head ever since was of Leila walking around with two pale stumps where her hands should have been. The story now seemed terrifyingly pertinent.

Finally, after waiting for well over an hour, Greta's number was called. *'Eighteen.'*

Greta jumped up and hurried to the front, her size ten-and-a-half sneakers squealing on the polished linoleum.

'Greta Jellings?' a female officer said in a slow drawl.

She nodded nervously.

'Speak up.'

'Yes, your honour.' Why on earth had she said 'your honour'?

'Have you ever entered the United States of America before?'

'No. This is my very first time here. In fact, first time venturing beyond New Zealand. Which is where I was born and have lived my whole life. I'm not a traveller. It's just that I was gifted—' Her words unspooled like fishing reel.

'Yes or no.'

'No. No, I have not.'

'Have you ever entered the United States of America illegally?' the other official asked, scrutinising Greta's passport under a giant magnifying glass.

'No,' Greta said, her cheeks hot. 'Never.' She hated herself for blushing right now.

The woman glanced at her side-on. 'Ever falsified a travel document?'

'No!' Greta cast around to check that there was no unobtrusive television camera filming her for some border-security programme.

'Been refused entry into the United States of America?'

86

'Please. I don't unders—'

'Ever been convicted of a criminal offence?'

Greta's blush drained away. Of course she had never been convicted of a criminal offence. Who did these people think they were, these bullies?

'Ever used banned substances?'

'Traded in narcotics?'

'Been refused entry into a country besides America?'

As the interrogation continued, Greta's ire grew. This was totally unacceptable.

And then, without even tapering to a close, it was over.

'You may go,' said one of the women, handing Greta back her passport.

Greta stood trapped in disbelief. One incorrect move and they'd likely mow her down with a machine gun.

'You mean go, as in go?'

The official gave a tight nod.

'But . . . I don't understand. Can you tell me what the problem was? I mean, will this happen again at the next border?'

The woman dismissed her with the sweep of a hand.

'*Nineteen.*'

Greta turned. A woman in a hijab was scurrying towards the counter. Their eyes met, the woman's were dark pools of fear and uncertainty.

Greta tilted her head. Tried to smile. She wanted to stay and offer this scared stranger her support, but she knew that doing so would only aggravate both their situations. She hurried from the room.

In the corridor she leant against the cold cream wall and sank to the ground. The source of her tears was not distress, but anger. How dare they treat her in such a manner? Be so arrogant and entitled. It made a mockery of all the guidebooks and airline posters inviting her to the Statue of Liberty's fair shores. And what of Americans who travelled abroad? Did they not expect courtesy and ease of passage on their travels? Countries had borders to guard and security to uphold, yet laws could, and should, be implemented with respect and civility. In the end everyone was simply a citizen of the world.

An awful image popped into her head of *that* terrible day. She scrunched up her eyes, trying to block it out.

Relentless knocking on her door.

'*Greta Jellings?*'

'Yes.'

A young policeman standing in the dim light of dawn, uneasy with the news.

'I'm here about Walter Haywood.'

'What's happened? Is he alright?'

'You are down as his next of kin.'

Walter had given her name as next of kin. Next of kin! In amongst the horror of that morning, the intimacy and comfort of being notified as if she were family.

'I'm afraid Mr Haywood was attacked last night while leaving a bar. He has sustained serious injuries.'

'Attacked? No! Is he—? Why? How? What happened?'

'Preliminary enquiries suggest it was an attack sparked by his sexual orientation. A homophobic attack.'

Greta can't speak. She feels dizzy.

'He's in Intensive Care. His condition is stable.'

Walter doesn't look like Walter. His distorted face, purple panda eyes, missing front tooth. He's hooked up to medical machines by myriad wires and plastic pipes. He looks so small in the big hospital bed, as if he's been punctured and most of Walter has leaked out.

Greta covers her mouth to hide her horror. Tears run down her cheeks.

'Walt.'

He turns his head. Blinks. As he tries to smile, his lower lip splits.

Instinctively she puts her hand to it.

His eyes search hers; the whites are clouded with blood.

She knows that he knows that she knows.

Such a brutal attack is hard enough to bear. But to be set upon by three thugs just for being someone who loves in a different way . . . the thought is unbearable. Walter is a good person. A good person.

What is it about man's intolerance to difference, Greta wonders? Hatred for what is foreign, be that the colour of a man's skin, his religion or the way he loves?

Loves. Walter had been out searching for love. And even though Greta understands this at a cerebral level, it is still painful to acknowledge that her love is not enough. It never will be. Walter needs what she cannot offer.

He reaches for her hand.

She takes it carefully, cradling his pale fingers in her palm. And after a time lets her thumb draw small circles over his bruised and broken skin.

It takes him months to recover. Though never completely. He is more of a dotted line after that. A sketch. A faded diagram.

No, Greta had no cause for complaint; she was a white Western woman. But for the woman in the hijab, for Walter, for the thousands of others who didn't fit the prescribed mould, life was surely much harder. This was no time to feel sorry for herself.

Sobered by the thought, and spotting another lapelled official walking down the corridor in her direction, Greta stood up. Loitering outside office two was not wise. She smoothed her blouse, blew her nose and headed for the luggage-collection hall. Oddly, she felt good about herself. Something inside the room had galvanised her. She was Greta Jellings. She would not be bullied. Not even by some US official with a gun on their person.

Her resolve was short-lived. The luggage hall was teeming with people.

Her breathing picked up. If she went missing in this noisy, anonymous crowd, would anyone even miss her? There were no threads anchoring her to another person's life.

She searched the carousels for her flight number. It had been almost two hours since she'd landed and it appeared that luggage from later flights was circling. She hadn't even begun her holiday and already her luggage was lost.

She turned round and round in the midst of the mayhem, like a child separated from its parents at a fair.

'You need help, miss?'

A stooped Afro-American man with rheumy eyes was standing beside her.

'My bag,' Greta said, her voice shaking. 'It's . . . I can't find it. I don't know what—' She stopped, remembering Angus's caution about strangers.

'Why, see over there. That's the Lost Luggage Counter. They'll help you, for sure.'

'Thank you. Thank you very much.'

'Now you have a good day then, won't you.'

True enough, at the counter, Greta spied her leopard-print suitcase, already labelled with an orange sticker and tucked into a cubbyhole.

She felt somewhat self-conscious about claiming it. She was not a leopard-print sort of person. It carried connotations out of keeping with her personality. But the suitcase had been on special and she couldn't justify wasting Walter's money on something as trivial as a bag. The leopard-print luggage would serve its purpose just fine.

Greta wheeled her trolley through a crowd of expectant faces, scrutinising the whiteboard signs.

Mr And Mrs Denver
Sally Bunting
Welcome home Dad!
Extreme Adventures

She felt as if she too were holding up a sign: *Single. Thirty-nine. Travelling alone.*

She scanned the throng of people for a smirk, pointed finger, for whispers behind cupped hands. But instead, she spotted two women kissing passionately in the middle of the concourse, an elderly man in a wheelchair talking to a teddy bear, and a youngster with fluoro-pink hair munching on some fries.

They smelt good. She inhaled deeply and pushed her trolley towards the exit. It was official; she had entered the United States of America.

The previous week America had been just a word on a piece of paper, now it was gun real. And yet, the milestone had so quickly lost its lustre. She'd been gone from New Zealand less than twenty-four hours and already wished she'd never embarked on this ludicrous adventure. She wanted to be back home with Marilyn Monroe, Lorraine and Rory. Even Jud.

Would Jud consider having her back, she wondered? They had ended on good terms once he'd got over the shock and inconvenience of her announcement. He'd even said some nice things about her at the little party they'd held at the shop on her last day. The replacement, a dumpy woman called Sandra, was there too. Greta should have felt kindly towards her, though she couldn't help feeling as if they were in competing camps. Would Sandra outshine her?

The undertakers from next door had been invited to boost numbers. Greta would have preferred it if the staff from Caroline's Cakes had been included instead.

Jud's wife Charlene brought in several plates of sushi, and some barbecued chicken wings. (Greta did not hold this against her, even though Charlene would have known about Marilyn Monroe.)

As a parting gift, Jud gave Greta a voucher for a body massage. She'd never had a massage before, and hoped she would never have to endure one again. It was excruciating being nearly naked in front of a stranger, her broad back, non-existent bottom, cellulite and huge feet on display. She spent half the massage with her face forced through a toilet-seat-shaped headrest, saliva pooling in her cheeks. Then there was all the wriggling and giggling and involuntarily kicking out when her feet were being massaged. But despite Greta's antics, the woman had persisted, as if ticklish feet were simply a temporary phenomenon to be massaged out.

Stepping from the airport building, Greta was hit by a thick, foreign heat. She followed signs to a caterpillar of yellow cabs creeping along the kerb, and joined the line of people waiting, a line diminishing as fast as it formed. Never before had Greta wished for a queue's progress to be slower.

Ahead of her stood a young couple in their early twenties. The guy, dressed nattily in a tartan shirt and two-tone trainers, ran his finger casually up and down the girl's bare arm. Greta felt a spear of envy at their comfortable connectedness. Then they were climbing into a cab and Greta's last buffer had disappeared. Nothing but a taxi ride stood between her and New York City.

Anxiety bore into her belly. She glanced at the cab next in line. The driver's eyes were close-set and his face tapered to a pencil-sharp chin. Her mind spun to the movie, *The Bone Collector*. She would not be getting into his cab. Next thing he'd be torturing her in the underground sewers of the city.

What to do? She could pretend to have misplaced her purse and suggest the people behind go ahead. But they were a family of five with a mountain of luggage and likely to need a larger vehicle.

She looked back at the cab earmarked for her. The driver looked no less menacing than he had seconds earlier. This was no time to procrastinate. There was only one thing to be done.

She shot forward after the young couple and grabbed their closing cab door.

The young guy released the door handle, his expression all surprise.

'Excuse me.' Greta leant into the car. 'Sorry. But would you mind if I shared your ride?'

'Oi! Wait on line!' shouted a man in a fluorescent yellow vest. 'There's a cab back here for you.'

'Please?' Greta implored.

The cab driver heaved himself out of his seat and leant across the roof of his vehicle. 'We don't share no fares, lady.'

'But, I'm . . . I'm new to New York and—'

'Nah. We don't roll like that.'

'It's okay. It's okay,' said the young man inside. 'I'll cover her ride.'

There was a pause, and before the driver could object, Greta squeezed herself in beside the couple.

'Thank you. Thank you so much.'

'I gotta be frank with you,' said the cabbie climbing back into his car and peering into the back seat. 'I am not happy about this. No, I'm not.'

Greta pointed apologetically to her bags still on the kerb.

'Now I seen it all,' he said, shaking his head, as he climbed out again.

There was a strong earthy smell in the car of day-old clothes and tobacco. Greta glanced side-on at her fellow passengers. The young man had a generous, boyish face.

'Where you from?' he asked politely.

'New Zealand.'

'New Zealand!' the couple and the driver exclaimed in unison, as if being from New Zealand explained everything.

'Last month I gave a ride to that Jackson dude,' the driver piped up, starting the engine. 'Ya know, *Lord of the Rings*. One cool guy, I can tell you. His limo didn't show, so he took a ride with me. Can you imagine? Quiet, mind you. Reluctant to talk, if ya know what I mean. I had to ask all the questions. You come from near where the movie was shot?'

Greta had no idea where *Lord of the Rings* had been filmed. She hadn't even seen the movies. Coming from New Zealand had won her a second chance with these people and she'd just blown it. What sort of New Zealander had not seen *Lord of the Rings*? She felt like a fraud.

The taxi pulled out into the road.

'I've taken a bunch of famous people in my cab,' the cabbie went on, apparently unfazed by her lack of cinematic knowledge. 'You got no idea. See in that folder back there. Yup, in the backseat pocket. Pictures of all the highfliers who've taken a ride in Jimmy Capolsky's cab.'

The file was poking out of the pocket in front of her fellow passengers, who made no attempt to retrieve it. Greta did not feel comfortable to reach across them.

'So, where you headed, young lady?' The driver asked, turning round.

No one replied. They were looking at her.

'Me?'

'Nah, the Queen of England!'

It felt good to be called a young lady, though Greta did wish the driver would keep his eyes on the road and not keep turning around to talk. They were navigating a frenetic tangle of freeways.

She unfolded the piece of paper crumpled in her fist and read out Angus's scrawl. 'Manhattan. Upper East Side.'

'Upper East Side!' the cabbie said with a chuckle. He eyeballed the young man beside Greta in his rear-view mirror. 'How you feel about that, sir? Paying for the fare of this lady going to the Upper East Side?'

The tartan guy didn't answer, but the atmosphere in the backseat felt suddenly frosty.

The driver refused to let it rest. 'A Brooklyn boy financing a fare to the Upper Eastside. Now that's one for my folder.'

'Oh, I really don't expect you to pay. I—'

'Where on Upper East Side?'

Greta looked at the piece of paper again. 'Madison Avenue. The Carlyle Hotel.'

'The Carlyle! Well, of course you are.'

'Do you know it?' Greta asked anxiously. 'The area. I mean, is it safe?'

The driver slapped his steering wheel and let out a half-exclamation, half-chortle.

'You could say that. Now who've I dropped there of late? Let me see, just the other day the guy with a scar down his cheek from that new Netflix series. Name escapes me. Anyway, guess who was arriving as we pulled in? None other than George Clooney. The man himself.' He scratched behind his ear. 'I got me some fierce tips I have, dropping people at the Carlyle.'

Tips. Greta couldn't remember what the guidebook had said about tipping. She didn't have much change, other than the few notes Angus had given to get her going. The rest was on her credit card.

'Ya know Princess Diana once stayed at The Carlyle.'

'Princess Diana!' Greta sucked in a whistling breath.

'She did indeed.' The driver pulled his shoulders back. 'All the presidents too. Johnson. JFK. The lot. Marilyn Monroe was rumoured to have visited JFK's suite there on more than one occasion. Used some secret passages.' He tapped his nose. 'It is what it is.'

Marilyn Monroe. Greta's chest tightened. Her dear hen would be convinced she'd been deserted. She was no fool. She wouldn't have been hoodwinked for one minute by the huge slice of watermelon Greta had given her before dropping her off at the farm.

There was a blast from a car horn and the cabbie swerved to avoid another cab. Greta fell across her neighbour's lap.

'Sorry. I'm so sorry.'

'Keep ya hat on, Henry!' shouted the cabbie out his window.

Then a siren sounded and a disk of red and blue lights started flashing on the roof of the cab they'd just swerved to avoid.

'See that!' spluttered the driver excitedly. 'An undercover cab.'

The couple beside her were staring at their phones, oblivious to the drama unfolding on the freeway.

It was hot and stuffy inside the car. Eventually Greta plucked up the courage to wind down her window a fraction. A warm breeze blew in. Horns blasted. A reversing truck beeped. There was the strong smell of rotting garbage, and an acrid odour of exhaust fumes. Something burnt-sugar sweet too.

Building, upon building, upon brown-brick building, blocking out the blue. So many people too. A schoolgirl with bright green hair. A man bent crooked, his matted beard reaching down to his navel. Two old ladies in identical polka-dot pantyhose. A cluster of policemen gazing up a tree. A girl in a graduation gown with a tiara on her head. A guitar player. A tramp. A bed out on the sidewalk. A bed! Newspaper stands. Shop mannequins. A man with a black hat, beard and ringlets.

'Here we are then,' the cabbie said, pulling up alongside a scalloped awning.

A doorman approached the car.

The driver pressed his meter.

$52.

He turned to face his passengers. 'So, who's getting the fare?'

'Me,' Greta said, hurriedly hauling out her purse. The doorman had already opened her door.

She pulled out a note and scrutinised it for its denomination. $100. What change should she ask for?

The pause felt too long, her hesitation awkward. She didn't want to look stingy, especially since she'd been the one to gatecrash the ride. She was representing New Zealand. Had to make a good impression.

'Keep the change,' she said, leaning through the gap in the glass partition.

She'd always wanted to say that line, and it was as satisfying as she'd imagined it would be.

The cab driver's eyes grew round. 'Why thank you, ma'am. Hope the rest of your day turns out just beautiful. And remember, you been for a ride in Jimmy Caplosky's cab.'

CHAPTER 17

Greta caught a hint of bergamot as the woman behind the dark wooden counter handed over a key card.

'We hope your stay with us will be an enjoyable one, Miss Jellings.'

Greta glanced at herself in the mirror opposite. Her clothes were creased, her hair flicking up instead of curving down, and she smelt of twenty-plus aircraft hours. She was a dirty smudge on this very grand establishment.

'This way, ma'am.'

Greta scuttled after the concierge.

The cool, uncluttered chic of the lobby was a welcome relief from the sweltering New York afternoon. Long cream tiles bordered a black marble floor. Two palms in giant pots stood sentry at a doorway, framed by sumptuous swathes of velvet. The high ceiling led the eye to one simple chandelier. A mustard couch had been discreetly positioned beneath a long bevelled mirror. Library lamps cast unobtrusive glows. Were Cleopatra to have stepped into the room, Greta would not have been the least bit surprised.

The elevator doors parted and out bounded a beagle, followed by a man in a faded blue tracksuit.

Greta was incredulous. A dog. A man in a tracksuit. In a place like this!

'Afternoon, Mr Christie,' said the concierge. 'Lovely day for a walk.'

'Indeed, Solomon.' The man tipped his head at Greta. 'Cooper, heel!'

'Which floor?' asked the operator.

'Fourth floor for the lady, please Bernie.'

The doors slid closed and the lift began an almost imperceptible ascent. Greta hated elevators. The shudder and jerk. The claustrophobia. The awkwardness. Though this was as comfortable a ride as she'd ever experienced.

'Fine day,' said the operator, his back to her and his face pressed up against the control panel like a schoolboy made to face the wall.

'Oh, it is. Yes. A fine day.'

They drew to a cushioned stop. 'Here we are.' The doors opened. 'Have a good day, ma'am.'

Greta hesitated, before stepping out into the quiet corridor, her footsteps instantly absorbed by a luxuriously thick carpet.

'Right opposite,' said the operator, pointing to her room number.

'So it is.' She blushed, as if she should have been familiar with the layout.

She decided to wait until the lift doors had closed, before attempting to use her key card.

Scan. Wait for green light. Depress door handle. Push.

There was clearly a trick to the timing, and it took several goes for her to get in.

Once inside she closed the door, bolted it, secured both the latch and security chain, and then turned around.

'Oh my!' If this was a hotel room, then her Devonport home was a . . . hut. No, a shack.

She was standing in a parquet-floored entrance hall, the sophisticated space slightly cheapened by her tacky leopard-print bags already on the luggage carrier.

In front of her was the entrance to a lounge — the room complete with Chesterfield suite, magenta-rich scatter cushions, antique writing desk and a stocked bookshelf. There was even a bowl of fresh fruit on the coffee table.

Greta pinched off a grape, then quickly put it back in the bowl.

Off to her right was a bedroom decorated in sage green and salmon. She ran her hands over the velveteen headboard. All her life she'd wanted a bolstered bedhead.

The bathroom, decorated in classic black and white tiles, boasted an enormous bath and shower.

Greta peered at the row of tiny tubes evenly spaced on a floating glass shelf. Face cream, shampoo, conditioner, body milk. She fingered each in turn, their small size delighting her in a dollhouse sort of way. How she'd love to take them back home to put on display in her own bathroom.

Home. Her own bathroom. She closed her eyes. She no longer had a home. Nor her own bathroom.

There was a kitchenette too, an umbrella cupboard, a . . . that was all. All, as in an awful lot.

She perched on the edge of the bed, careful not to crease the cover, and performed some alternate-nostril breathing — a technique the yoga instructor on Breakfast TV had suggested to help settle a racing heart.

There had obviously been an error; the suite was probably meant for some actor or prestigious politician. She would call Reception presently. But first she was going to indulge herself for a few fabulous minutes.

Slipping off her 10.5 (UK) sneakers — sneakers were always a size bigger than a person's actual shoe size — she sank her bunioned toes into the carpet.

Release and freedom spread up her body like an expansive sigh.

That was shoes for you. An item of clothing, which, for most people anyway, covered only a small part of the body, yet still had so much to say. More than a jacket or handbag or hat. A pair of shoes could transform a person from plodder to powerhouse, builder to ballerina, from a woman to a lady. The reverse was true too; oh, the disaster of an unsuitable pair. Then there was that indescribable relief when taking off a pair after a long day, the freedom quite out of proportion to the offending footwear.

Greta's eyes settled on a small white box with a brown velveteen bow on the bedside table. Shaking it gently, she caught the unmistakeable whiff of cacao — sixty-five per cent at least. She untied the bow and eased off the seal. There, nestling in a sleeve of white tissue paper, were two perfectly imperfect chocolate truffles. She inhaled, vacuuming up some chocolate dust onto the tip of her nose.

It took all her willpower to reseal the box. Chocolate was one of Greta's great pleasures — chocolate and cake — her day-to-day happiness definitely determined by the presence or absence of either. Even her recollections of people and places were filtered according to whether cake or chocolate had been involved.

There was the time Norbert Green brought an Easter egg to school for her. *Greta is dizzy with delight — a sign the other kids take to mean she and Norbert are fresh. And in her happy, post-chocolate haze Greta does almost agree to be Norbert's squeeze. But then his schoolboy smell breaks through.*

Chocolate had also played a part in cementing her friendship with Lorraine. Her former neighbour always had a bowl of Cadbury's Favourites in her lounge for visitors.

Then there was Caroline's Cakes just two doors down from the pool shop. On the last Friday of every month Greta bought their 6-inch chocolate-fudge cake (the only flavour to come in a small size). After cutting it into twelve, she'd wrap up and freeze the individual slices, which were then rationed out over the following month.

As the 12th of February drew near each year, Greta would gaze longingly at the splendid creations on display, ever hopeful Jud might order one of the big ones, such as the 11-inch carrot-and-caramel cake, for her birthday tea.

'I don't know why I always think your birthday is on the 18th,' was his standard line, despite twenty-two years of heavy hints. 'Was planning to get you something from that cake shop. Never mind, we can still have a little party. I think there are some coconut cookies left in the biscuit tin.'

But as far as Greta (and Julia Child) was concerned, a party without cake was just a meeting.

'Reception, how may I help?'

'It's Greta Jellings here. I was just checking . . . I think there's been some mistake with my room allocation.'

'Is there a problem with the suite, ma'am?'

'Oh, not at all. It's enormous, you see, and I'm—'

'It is the suite booked under you name. Would you prefer a different outlook?'

'No, no. Everything is just perfect. Thank you.'

Greta replaced the receiver and remained sitting for several minutes, before carefully putting the cushions to one side, folding back the bedspread, and allowing herself to fall back gently onto the bed.

'Just perfect.'

She should have been over the moon. And she was. Sort of. She just couldn't get past the feeling that she didn't deserve all this. That she was going to get into trouble for indulging in such extravagance. She hadn't earned it.

'There are so many better ways to spend this money, Greta. Children are starving, while you live it up like some socialite.'

Greta put her hands over her ears to block out Nora's admonitions.

What she needed was a strong cup of tea. Tea was her go-to for most troublesome situations. A sure way to restore perspective.

She slipped her feet into the white waffle slippers provided, her heels hanging over the backs (well, the hotel wasn't obliged to cater for giants) and padded through to the kitchenette. There were bottles of wine in the cupboard. An array of miniature spirits too. And an entire shelf of snacks. Packets of pistachios, salted crisps, a slab of chocolate . . . However, minibars were off limit.

'Nothing short of highway robbery,' says Nora, as they settle into the tiny motel unit.

The rare weekend away has come about because of a wedding dress Nora has sewn. The accommodation is courtesy of the bride.

Unable to resist the novelty of a minibar, ten-year-old Greta squirrels away a packet of Twisties, which she later eats behind a locked bathroom door. They are delicious, but in retrospect, not worth it. Nora contests the addition to the bill the following morning, making a huge hoo-hah of the fact that she and her daughter have not consumed a single item from the minibar.

It proves an important lesson for Greta. Indulgence always comes at a price.

She never does own up to her indiscretion. She means to, once her mother has simmered down. Only it becomes harder and harder with Nora relaying the story to each of her sewing clients.

The lie still bothered Greta all these years later. Nora would know now, of course, in an all-seeing kind of way, and the thought left Greta somewhat uncomfortable.

'Reception.'

'Sorry. Greta Jellings again. I'm struggling to find the teabags.' She gave an embarrassed grunt. 'They're probably staring me in the face.'

'I'll get a tray sent up right away. Your preference of tea, ma'am?'

'Oh, that's really not necessary. I wouldn't want to trouble you.'

'It's no trouble, Ms Jellings. Kettles are not provided in the suites.'

Not provided? Now that took the biscuit! Everything Greta could ever want, and more, except for a good cup of char.

Ten minutes later the doorbell rang.

Greta unbolted, unchained and unlatched the door, to find a little woman with crow-black hair bearing a silver tray.

100

'Your tea, madam.'

Greta stood aside as the maid, with a well-camouflaged limp, glided in. Everything in the hotel, including the staff, moved with unobtrusive ease.

'Thank you, Carmila' Greta said, scrutinising the woman's brass name badge. 'Am I looking forward to this!'

The woman handed Greta the docket to sign.

Greta squinted at the piece of paper. $16. Sixteen dollars for a cup of tea!

She could have bought three boxes of teabags for the price. It was nothing short of highway robbery.

The maid stood waiting.

Greta scribbled her name on the docket, then traced over her signature again, trying to tidy her G and S.

'Thank you.'

Carmila remained where she was.

Greta smiled.

Carmila smiled.

Greta smiled more widely.

Was she supposed to give permission for the maid to leave? Say something like 'dismissed' or 'at ease'?

Then it dawned on her. 'Oh! Just a minute,' she said, darting into the bedroom.

All she had in her purse were the big denomination notes from Angus, less the one she'd used for the cab.

She pulled out another hundred-dollar bill, then stopped. No, she should not be tipping Carmila one hundred dollars for a cup of tea, which had already cost sixteen dollars. The entire trip still stretched ahead of her. She couldn't use up all her spending money in the first week.

She cast around the room. What could she give instead?

The bathroom miniatures? No, they were too special.

The truffles? No.

Bathroom miniatures.

Truffles.

She picked up the small white box. She could always buy more chocolate.

'I'm so sorry,' she said emerging from the bedroom. 'I'm afraid I don't have any cash on me.'

Carmila's eyes narrowed.

Greta clumsily shoved the box of chocolates into the woman's hand.

'Oh no, is fine,' said Carmila in surprise. She handed Greta back the box. 'You have a good day, madam. You nice lady.' Then she scurried from the room.

CHAPTER 18

Greta was woken by a loud ringing sound. She opened her eyes. Her cheek was wet with drool. Another ring pierced the fug. Her surrounds came slowly into focus.

Tea tray at her feet. Grapes cascading over the edge of a fruit bowl. Crimson scatter cushions . . . New York!

She sat up and rubbed her eyes. The light outside had been diluted either by dusk or dawn.

Consulting her watch only added to Greta's confusion; it was still on New Zealand time.

Then the front door to her suite was opening.

Greta leapt off the couch. She'd forgotten to bolt it again after the tea had been delivered.

Carmila's face appeared, her eyes stretching wide with surprise. 'Oh, very sorry. Very sorry. No one answer. I am think the room is empty.'

'That's alright,' Greta said, trying to steady her voice. 'Just got a bit of a fright.' She forced a laugh.

'I do turndown. Is okay?'

Greta nodded. She didn't know what turndown meant, so pretended to busy herself while Carmila disappeared into the bedroom.

Once the maid had left, Greta retraced her steps.

The drapes in the bedroom had been drawn, confirming it was indeed evening. The bedcover had been folded further back, and the bedside lamps switched on. A linen napkin lay on the floor beside the bed, something Carmila must have dropped in her hurry. There was also a brand new, sealed box of truffles on the bedside table.

Greta immediately opened it and popped a chocolate in her mouth.

What to do next?

She contemplated drawing a bath, ordering room service, then watching some American television. Just the thought of room service sent a ripple of excitement through her. She'd only ever seen such luxury on the silver screen: a waiter sporting pristine white gloves pushes a trolley along hotel corridor, replete with red rose, bottle of bubbly and large silver cloche. But this time Greta would be the one to lift the cloche.

She perused the menu, settling on a Waldorf salad, sautéed Dover sole, and chocolate bavarois to finish.

As she picked up the phone to dial the kitchen, an annoying voice began chirruping in her head. *Walter did not fly you halfway across the world for you to fritter away your time inside a hotel room.*

She thought back to the Australian sitcom, *Kath and Kim*. Kath and her husband Kel would take their weeklong annual vacation at the local airport. They'd book into the airport hotel, shop at the airport shops, and eat in the airport food hall, without ever leaving the country. Greta had laughed uproariously at the time. Now the scenario did not seem so silly.

Walter had told her to *have fun*. Those were his words. And TV and room service *were* fun.

She sighed and replaced the receiver. She owed it to him to explore New York properly, the city on which he had felt free to write his own story.

It was hard to believe he'd ever been anything other than the calm, self-assured man she'd come to know, and yet a few times he'd hinted at something darker in his past. It had unsettled her, the suggestion of sadness. It didn't fit with whom she believed him to be.

She thought back to the time they'd gone to see *Amy*, a film about the singer Amy Winehouse.

Halfway through the screening Greta becomes aware of Walter shuddering beside her. She takes a quick peek; he is crying silently. The emotion surprises her; she hasn't seen him cry before. And yet it is also entirely in keeping with who he is — a kind, sensitive person.

'Mind if we skip grabbing a bite tonight,' he says after, his face pale in the dim light of the lobby. He looks oddly defeated.

'Of course. Not that hungry myself,' she says, blustering over her disappointment. She'd been thinking about pumpkin-sage-and-blue-cheese pizza all afternoon.

In the car, he sits motionless in the driver's seat. The space between them feels confusing.

The story of Amy Winehouse's life was tragic, but Walter is so robust; nothing dents his steadiness and quiet calm.

Perhaps, she thinks, his mood has nothing to do with the movie, but more with her. Perhaps she has unwittingly upset him?

'You all right, Walt? If I've offended you, I—?'

'What a crazy old world this is.'

How to respond to that?

He stares straight ahead. 'Parents can really mess up a kid's life.'

So it is about the movie.

'I guess they just do their best,' she says, surprised at her own equanimity; she hasn't been feeling very charitable towards Nora of late.

'Sometimes that isn't good enough.'

Walter's almost anger catches her by surprise.

'There's really only one thing a parent needs to get right,' he says. 'Just one thing. Yet so many get it so wrong!'

Had Nora got it wrong too, Greta wonders?

'A parent should be the person to give a kid space and permission to be the best he or she can be.' He flicks the steering wheel absentmindedly. 'But instead, how many overlay their own dreams and expectations and insecurities on to their impressionable little people. What a legacy to leave a kid — the weight of an adult's flaws and prejudices and missed opportunities. The weight of inadequacy.'

A thought flies into Greta's head as fast as a tiny fantail swooping through the bush. She catches it for a second, then quickly lets it go. What might she have been like without the weight of Nora's words?

'Everyone needs someone on the sidelines. A person who, despite everything, says, "I believe in you". It should be a mother or a father. But even a teacher or a friend.'

Yes, thinks Greta, or a friend. Walter had arrived on the sideline to cheer her on. For some inexplicable reason he believes in her.

What had his childhood been like? He never speaks about his family. She doesn't want to pry. He seems such a together person.

The more she thinks about it the more she realises that his observations are likely just an intelligent response to a sad movie. Nothing more.

But now, as she revisited that night, she saw that Walter had been trying to tell her something. She'd missed a crucial cue in their friendship. She owed it to him to discover his full story. New York was the perfect place to start. She needed to understand what the city had offered him, which New Zealand had denied.

Greta languished in a chin-high bubble bath, after succumbing to one of the bathroom miniatures. (She was banking on them being replenished at the next turndown service.) Then she got dressed to go out. Her little black dress was something she'd bought when Walter was alive; the only outfit in her luggage suitable for cocktail hour.

She pulled back her shoulders. It looked good on her, even if she said so herself. But as her eyes travelled down her reflection, her satisfaction evaporated. Her flat black shoes were an ugly full stop at the end of a long, clumsy sentence. But nothing could be done about that.

To think her feet still bothered her after all these years. The thing was, age did not automatically usher in acceptance. Just the week prior, one of the tellers at the bank — a man in his fifties — had had orthodontic braces fitted. The poor fellow had more wire in his mouth than a switchboard. And while Greta couldn't imagine it being a very good idea to move teeth around the mouth at his age, she admired him for having the resolve to attend to something which had clearly bothered him for the best part of half a century. Big feet, however, could not be so easily remedied. If only fitting them with braces for a year could solve their size. As for the choice of footwear available to a person with super-sized feet . . .

She was getting distracted.

An evening out in New York! What a terrifying thought.

It was Walter's words which finally pushed her out the door. *No one is watching, Grets. No one is watching.*

The lift operators had changed over, and a man by the name of Noah was now at the helm. Noah, with slicked-back hair, a boxer's nose and a broad accent.

Like his colleague, he too positioned himself with his back to Greta and his face just centimetres from the control panel.

The stance left Greta uneasy. She wondered if it was a required code of conduct.

'Enjoy your evening, ma'am,' he said, as they reached the ground floor. 'It's a fine night out there.'

'Would you be so kind as to point me in the direction of Bemelmans

Bar.' She said the word bar as quietly as she could. Would he think less of her for asking for directions to a bar?

'Right, and right again. You can't miss it.'

Greta had only been to such an establishment once before in her life. For Jud's fortieth. Bars were intimidating, tawdry places and best avoided. However, it was the information pack in her hotel suite, which had convinced her to visit Bemelmans. That it was also situated within the hotel made her first solo outing less daunting.

Apparently the place had been named after Ludwig Bemelmans, creator of the classic Madeline books. Greta needed to read no further.

The legendary capers of the plucky French girl had been amongst Greta's favourite childhood reads. How she'd idolised the cheeky lass who, despite her diminutive stature, had been daring and determined, and oh so mischievous, doing everything Greta was never allowed to do.

She was not afraid
of mice —
she loved winter,
snow, and ice.
To the tiger in the zoo
Madeline just said,
'Pooh-pooh.'

Madeline's exploits had vicariously afforded Greta the adventures absent from her own regimented childhood.

It was only after reading her mother's diaries, and with Judy's sage spin on things, that Greta had come to understand better the possible reasons for her harsh upbringing. Nora's severity had likely been born out of her determination to raise a respectable child in what had been thoroughly unrespectable circumstances.

Greta hovered at the entrance to the bar — a room extravagant with detail. Even the glow from the table lamps dotted around the room felt rich and substantial. The description in the hotel folder had been gloriously accurate: '*Chocolate-brown leather banquettes, nickel-trimmed black glass tabletops, a dramatic black granite bar and a 24-carat gold leaf-covered ceiling.*'

Greta felt a rush of childish glee as she stepped into the quirky room, Madeline holding her hand. The murals, painted by Bemelmans himself, depicted Madeline and her eleven boarding-school buddies in Central Park, alongside a variety of fantastical scenes. There were cigar-smoking rabbits and a handbag-clutching giraffe. Animals in high heels, a businessman in a cage, and even a rabbit with a rifle.

The adult world came back into focus. Seated at a gleaming Steinway grand piano was a man playing jazz, his body following his long fingers in a rhythmic sway.

A waiter with white gloves, black tie and tomato-red jacket approached.

'Evening, ma'am. Are you meeting someone this evening?'

Greta blushed. 'No. Not meeting anyone. I was just—' She wanted to leave. This had been a bad idea.

The waiter's expression remained genial. 'Would the madam like to sit at a table or the bar?'

Leaving was not an option.

At the bar, Greta would be obliged to speak to the bartender, though at least, she'd be less conspicuous. At a table, her solitude would be more apparent, but she'd not have to engage with strangers.

'A table please.'

'Right you are.'

She followed him to a small table nestled in the corner.

'Best seat in the house,' he said, winking at her.

Greta sank onto the leather banquette, positioned to offer an uninterrupted view of the piano.

'Now, what can I be getting for the madam to drink?'

Greta could feel another blush brewing. Blasted blushes!

'Oh anything,' she blurted out. 'Whatever you're having.'

He chuckled. 'Good one.'

How foolish she sounded. Thankfully, the man thought she was pulling his leg.

'Our special tonight is a Red Velvet cocktail. It comprises a shot of rye whisky, spiced plum syrup, egg white, a dash of fresh lemon juice and a sprinkling of bee pollen.'

It sounded simply delicious.

'I, I—' Greta shrugged her shoulders. She shouldn't have come.

'But,' the waiter said, lifting a white-gloved forefinger. 'I recommend a Kir Royale for the lady — champagne with a measure of cassis. Sophisticated, yet delightfully unpretentious.'

Sophisticated, yet delightfully unpretentious. He was describing the drink, yet it felt as if he was paying her the compliment.

'And will the madam be eating?'

Greta could have eaten an elephant she was so hungry. However, the thought of having to make another decision, and then negotiate a meal in front of strangers.

'We have a New York Reuben,' her ally continued, expertly taking charge. 'Corned Beef on toasted Rye, with Swiss cheese, sauerkraut and our signature tomato remoulade. I can personally recommend them. And very New York for a visitor, if I might be so presumptuous.'

Greta could have kissed the man.

She looked cautiously around the room as she waited for her order to arrive. The cosy alcoves were populated mostly by couples and the occasional bigger group. There were some solitary patrons too.

Her toes loosened against the walls of her plain black shoes.

'Your Kir Royale, ma'am.'

'Oh my!' The cocktail looked like a lava lamp with small violet bubbles rising to the surface.

The first sip was sublime. And the Reuben utterly delicious too.

She was busy trying to lick her fingers inconspicuously when the barman came over to collect her plate.

Greta's pulse quickened at the thought of him removing her props.

'Another Kir Royale?'

She usually never drank more than one glass of alcohol on a night, and only on weekends. Medical research indicated the importance of alcohol-free days.

'Had a good evening, ma'am?' Noah asked, as she stepped into the elevator just after eleven.

'It was wonderful, Noah. Just wonderful. You see, I've read the entire Madeline series. They're about this little French girl who stays in a Catholic boarding school and—'

'Yes. My daughters love them too.'

Greta bit her lip. She'd made a snap judgment about the man operating the elevator. How arrogant of her.

'Interesting fact,' Noah said, lifting a forefinger. 'Mr. Bemelmans did not take payment for the paintings in the bar. No ma'am. Instead, he asked for a suite right here at the Carlyle as payment. I believe he and his family lived upstairs for one-and-a-half years.'

'One-and-a-half years!'

'We have permanent residents who've stayed a lot longer than that.'

Greta tried to visualise the suite upstairs as her permanent abode.

The lift doors closed and Noah took up his position at the control panel, his face again pressed to the wall.

'Noah, may I ask you a question?'

'Of course, ma'am.'

She hesitated. Paused too long. The space felt suddenly serious.

'Do you know where I can buy . . . shoes? Nice shoes.'

'Why, there are more shoe shops in the city than crosswalks,' he said, sounding relieved. 'It just depends on your budget.'

'Not just any shoes,' Greta added. 'You see, I have, well, I have rather big feet.'

Noah did not turn around, the consummate gentleman that he was.

'It's impossible to find attractive shoes my size. I'm a nine-and-a-half in regular shoes.' Then, more softly, 'ten-and-a-half in sneakers.'

To his credit, Noah kept his eyes on the brass plate in front of him.

He nodded slowly.

'I'm a lost cause, I know.'

He cleared his throat. 'No offence meant, ma'am, but a cousin of mine, she has the self-same challenge, and she buys all her footwear from . . . from a cross-dressing shop.'

'A cross-dressing shop?'

'As I said, ma'am, no offence. But with them catering for bigger-sized feet and all. My cousin has found some fine footwear there.'

Then it dawned! Greta was mortified, her face on fire. On no account would she be shopping in such a store. She hoped she hadn't given Noah any reason to think she was, well . . .

The lift doors opened. She stepped out, her feet leading the charge.

'Thank you,' she said quickly.

'Have a good night, ma'am,' Noah said, glancing down for just a second.

CHAPTER 19

Greta slept soundly her first night in New York. The combined effect of sensational sheets — a thread count surely in the thousands — goose-down pillows, and three Kir Royales. Yet despite an uninterrupted night, she awoke with a gravel-grinding headache.

Her first thought was that she was suffering from some life-threatening condition. Meningitis perhaps. Or a leaking cerebral aneurysm. However, after Googling the most common causes for a headache on the courtesy iPad, she settled for a hangover.

A hangover! She felt rather chuffed with the diagnosis. Her very first hangover ever.

She looked at her watch. 8.50am. She was meant to meet Frank Buchanan in the lobby in less than ten minutes.

Frank and I go a long way back. He'll look after you.

Greta felt conflicted about this. Having someone look out for her in the daunting metropolis of New York was a comforting thought. But then there was the stress of having to engage with a stranger. And a good friend of Walter's, no less. She didn't want to prove a disappointment.

She swallowed two paracetamol, gargled with mouthwash and tied the laces of her chunky khaki numbers. They were a cross between a trainer and a hiking boot — ugly to begin with, before adding her size into the mix. But they were comfortable, and she anticipated she'd be spending a good part of the day on her feet.

Already seven minutes late for her rendezvous, she shut her hotel door and headed down the fire escape, two steps at a time.

'Greta?' A short, balding man moved across the lobby towards her.

Her heart sank. Short people only added to her awkwardness. *You can't help being a big-boned girl,* was all Nora had ever offered.

As he got closer, Greta saw that the man had a diamond stud buried in his left eyebrow. Her skin prickled at the thought of how it had been inserted. She'd given up on getting her own ears pierced after the jeweller marked a dot on each of her earlobes, before stepping backwards. Greta had bolted, thinking he was going to aim from a distance. She still had visions of a stray stud embedded in her forehead.

'Frank?'

'Welcome to New York,' he said, looking down at her feet. A bemused grin spread across his face. 'I see you're ready for some serious action.'

Sometimes Greta wished her face were a permanent red. It would be easier than coping with the endless fluctuation in hue.

'Had breakfast yet?' he asked, ushering her through the lobby towards the revolving door.

She shook her head. Too vigorously. The paracetamol had yet to kick in, and it felt like there were cannon balls rolling around inside her skull.

'Me neither and I'm famished. Let's do the diner thing, alright? Give you the authentic Manhattan experience.'

'That sounds very good, thank you,' she said, taking one step for his every two.

She was relieved food was also a priority for Frank. Food was one of the main reasons Greta rarely accepted invitations to stay with people. If a host's food focus was different to hers, the stay could be very miserable indeed.

Greta's first weekend away from home had been with Lucinda Argent's family.

The Argents didn't believe in lunch, a discovery Greta only made when they were already three hours north of Auckland and it was too late to turn back.

A savvier Greta did her research the next time she was invited away, this time by Cyril Denopoulos. Lunches would most definitely be on the menu, Cyril's mother reassured. In fact, they proved to be a highlight of the three-day trip to Taupō. However, all the moussaka and halva and baklava were not worth it when pitched against a lifetime without her father.

As Greta hurried after Frank, she passed two women chatting in the lobby. It was the brunette's shoes that caught Greta's eye. A fantastic pair of electric blue heels.

At the revolving door Greta hesitated — she hated the spinning contraptions, as she did most modes of pedestrian transport. Escalators in shopping centres were the worst, especially when a queue of people was building behind her.

She darted into the segment of space between two walls of glass and shuffled forwards until she was delivered onto the street.

Her relief was shortlived. Her heart hiccoughed when she spotted a posse of photographers on the sidewalk, their long lenses all trained on her.

She wrapped an arm across her face and hurried blindly after Frank. She did not want to be unwittingly caught in some celebrity shot. Especially not in her big brown shoes.

There were no bursts of flashlight, nor whirr of any cameras.

'Wonder who they're waiting for?' Frank said.

Then the hotel doors were spinning again and the brunette, all long legs and dazzling blue shoes, strutted out towards a waiting limousine.

The cameras went crazy.

'Victoria, this way! This way!'

'Lovely day, isn't it, Victoria?'

'Hey, Victoria!'

Greta pulled at Frank's shirt. 'It's Victoria Beck-ham!' Never before had she been so close to someone so famous.

Victoria's blunt bob, satin suit, lip gloss and limo, were silvered in successive bursts of flashlight. Then the long black car with darkened windows was pulling away from the kerb and the photographers immediately started to disperse.

The solidness of life came back into focus. An overflowing stainless-steel dustbin. The empty, watermarked vases in a florist's window. A dust-dull sparrow. Rows of burglar-proof spikes. Greta's big brown shoes.

She felt strangely flat. As if she'd veered close to something golden but had missed the opportunity it presented. Someone braver might have introduced themselves. Asked for an autograph. Basked momentarily in the glamour and shine.

'Rubbing shoulders with the rich and famous, hey?' Frank said, breaking into her moroseness. 'Ever the romantic, our Walter, booking the Carlyle for you,' he said, shaking his head and laughing. 'C'mon, let's grab something to eat.'

Walter had indeed been a hopeless romantic. A Peter Pan sort of person. It was the little things in his life, the detail, which spoke of his love for the quixotic. The champagne-coupe tower at his Christmas party. The white fantail pigeons in his garden. The gas lantern he lit every night for atmosphere. Walter. Dear, dreamy Walter.

If Greta was grounded in the mundane and practical, then Walter had been bewitched by the extraordinary. Life for him was less about daily drudgery, than about music, movies, the magical. Even in his day job, digging and weeding and planting and pruning were all secondary to the art of a garden, the aesthetic. His dreams were grand, and ordinary tasks simply the means to a stage-production finish.

It had taken Greta some time to realise who Walter reminded her of. And when she did, it then seemed so utterly obvious. Walter reminded her of her father in his excitement and fascination for the fabulous. No doubt Nora would not have approved of Walter either, had she been alive to meet him.

Breakfast was a few blocks away, in a diner that looked every bit the set for an American police procedural. High-seated booths with maroon banquettes lined one side of the room, a long counter the other. There was even a waistcoated Italian waiter with a pencil tucked behind his ear. And in the booth directly behind Frank, sat three men in CIA-serious suits, coiled wires spiralling down their necks.

Misconceptions fuelled by Hollywood indeed!

Greta stared at the menu, waiting for Frank to take the lead. To her delight he ordered hotcakes, giving her permission to order them too.

They did not disappoint. She could easily have demolished the entire stack of pillowy discs drenched in maple syrup, but was careful to temper her enthusiasm. She didn't want him thinking her a glutton. First impressions were so important.

'Mind if I finish those?' he asked, pulling her plate over to him.

'Of course. Delicious. Just too full,' she said, making a slicing movement across her neck.

Greta was surprised and relieved by the lack of awkward preliminaries with Frank, as if they'd begun mid-reel. It was a comfortable place to begin.

'Now, Greta,' he said, wiping his mouth on the square of serviette he'd tucked into his collar. 'I'm at your disposal for the week. I have a few things in mind, but really the next seven days are about what you want to do.'

She shifted in her seat. Frank looked like a busy man. He had an air of distraction about him.

'That's very kind of you. Thank you. I just hope I'm not inconveniencing you too much. You must be very busy.'

He held up a hand. 'No apologies. Anyone who was a friend of Walter is a friend of mine.'

His no-nonsense directness was unnerving.

'How do you know Walter?

The tense of her own question threw her. Walter was dead. Gone. No longer. Eleven months almost to the day. It was the letters that had done it. Confused her, written as they were in the present tense.

Reading his words had brought back all the pain, pain she thought she'd managed to bury.

She and Walter had squashed a lifetime into their two-year friendship; the bond further deepened by the intimacy that came with his cancer. His illness had not been pretty or manicured or carefully choreographed. It had stripped away the superfluous and laid him bare. That Greta had still been invited to hang around. . . Friendship didn't get any deeper than that.

'More coffee?' Frank asked, signalling to the waiter.

She shook her head. She would have loved another cup, but did not want to take advantage of Frank's hospitality; she wasn't sure who would be paying.

The waiter topped up Frank's cup from a squat glass jug. On the side of it, in peeling print, were the words *Bottomless Cup*. So, she could have had another cup after all.

'Walt arrived in New York with nothing,' Frank said, rubbing his brown beard.

She wondered how men could go bald, yet still have so much facial hair.

'Nothing but a dream. A dream to live when everything in his world was willing him to die.'

The words caught Greta by surprise. They didn't feel like they belonged to Frank. There was a sensitivity and depth beneath his brusque, matter-of-fact manner.

'When Walter applied for a job at our firm, he'd already been in the city for some months.'

'As a landscaper?'

Greta wondered what opportunities would be available for a gardener in the concrete jungle that was New York.

Frank looked somewhat nonplussed. 'No. As a junior architect.'

'Architect?'

'Yup. He was not long out of architecture school. We were looking to expand our firm and take on some young blood.'

Greta felt as if she'd been punched in the stomach.

'Oh right,' she said quickly, trying to conceal the fact that she had not been privy to this vital piece of information about Walter's life. Walter, an architect?

It was as if she'd just learned that he'd had an affair, though this was not a good analogy, since she and Walter had been friends, not lovers.

Her mind circled Frank's words, trying to find some safe place to settle. A truth suddenly an untruth.

She scrolled back, trying to reinterpret the time she'd known Walter. His sense of aesthetic and design. His mathematical logic. Being an architect made sense.

'A respectable enough profession for his parents,' Frank continued. 'But as we both know, Walter really wanted to go to drama school.'

Greta nodded, her nod now also a lie.

Perhaps Frank saw her confusion, because he elaborated. 'He'd always given in to what his parents wanted. Gone to football matches, or, what do you call it, rugby? Drank beer, dated glamorous girls, attended college.'

Tears prickled. Greta opened her eyes wide, focusing on the stud embedded in Frank's eyebrow.

He sniggered. 'Walter would tell the story of how his father bought him a rifle for his twenty-first birthday.' He shook his head. 'A rifle for Walt, can you imagine! And paid for a hunting trip to Africa for after he'd graduated.'

A rifle. A hunting trip. Walter? Greta felt as if they were talking about two different people. Maybe there had been some mix up.

Frank gulped his coffee.

She clenched her teeth. She couldn't help herself. She hated the sound of people swallowing loudly.

'He went through the whole palaver of getting a gun license, but far as I know, never took the damn thing out of the safe. Not once.'

Greta succumbed to the newness of this information. They were journeying backwards beyond what she had always considered the beginning. Of course, she'd understood that Walter had lived a life before they met. But Frank was teasing out dimensions beyond anything she'd held in her head, or ever imagined.

Anger and fear surged through her. Walter had lied to her. And not just about one small aspect of his life. About a significant part of his back story. It was frightening to realise that the one thing she'd held to be most real, had not in fact been real after all. Her hands were shaking. She had to keep it together.

'As you know, Walter never got to drama school, despite the fact that at twenty-two he had the lead role in a performance which showed no sign of drawing to close.'

Greta anticipated what was coming next. She screwed up her eyes, as if to hold it at bay. But she couldn't. She was back on North Head catching her breath on a knoll between the battlements.

Walter sinks down beside her, his cheeks pinched-pink, his smile unfettered, his chest heaving from the run.

'One evening it did,' Frank continued. 'End, that is. Like a spring mechanism wound too tightly, Walter suddenly snapped. Handed his parents his degree and told them he had no plans to practice as an architect. Use a rifle. Or marry. Ever.'

Greta nodded, Frank's story now at last in keeping with the memory playing in her head.

'I used to come here as a child,' Walter says, looking out over the ocean. 'Play hide and seek in the battlements with my sister, Clare. I haven't been here in years.' He is still out of breath, his cheeks collapsing sinkholes every time he draws in air.

'You're unfit, Walter,' Greta says, wagging her finger. 'I beat you by a whole heap.'

His face drops.

'Don't look so hurt, silly,' she says poking him in the ribs. 'I'm just teasing!'

He lies back on the grass.

Then she says it, the words coming out on their own, surprising her too.

'Walter, I think I love you.'

He smiles widely, 'I love you too, Grets,' and punches her hand play-fully. 'BFFs.'

'No, Walter,' she says more urgently. 'Not BFFs. I mean, I love you.'

Where has this confidence come from? The confidence to say such things!

She knows the answer.

From him. Walter.

In just the few months she's known him, she has felt herself begin to change. Even in her own mind, Greta Jellings is becoming a less hazy image.

Walter frowns, his face blotchy where circles of colour have been sucked from his cheeks. His eyes widen. He sits up, searching for words.

'Grets, you know I'm gay.'

She is stunned. Those words. The terror they instil in her. She'd let down her defences. What a fool! What a fool she's been.

Nora would have known. She would have. How often would she say, with such derision in her voice, that she could 'pick a gay from a mile away'?

Greta has been so stupid to declare her love first and risk all her self-respect.

No expectation, no disappointment. No expectation, no disappointment.

'All his parents' anxieties were realised in that small word,' Frank said, breaking through her thoughts. 'The cheek of it, his father told him, attaching such a hideous meaning to what had previously been a wholesome, happy word. *Faggot*, he told his son, at least had the guttural ugliness suited to such an appalling persuasion.'

Greta closed her eyes.

'Walt's mother must have reflected on the day she found him in her high-heeled shoes. Her son's easy tears. Artistic flare. His tendency to be bullied.'

Frank fingered his chin. 'His father will have recalled how he'd once come upon his teenage son singing along to the score from *The Sound of Music*. How Walter had winced when they'd driven over a possum. How he was always sick before rugby practice.'

Frank paused.

The blood was pounding in Greta's temples.

'Walter's father slapped him across the face, told him that he was no son of his, and kicked him out. Out of the house. Out of the family.'

Greta couldn't bear it. She wanted to hit Frank for telling her this. Wanted to rewind time, scoop Walter up, cradle him.

'Walter drove around all night, before finally parking near a beach at dawn. A beach where the sand is apparently black?'

Greta nodded. The volcanic sands on the West coast of Auckland. Probably Piha. But Frank's interest in the specifics irritated her. Whether the sand was black or blond was irrelevant when pitched against the weight of this story.

'He connected a piece of hosepipe to his exhaust.'

Greta put her hands over her ears. Tears spilled onto her cheeks.

'I should stop?'

Greta shook her head. 'I need to know. I just wish he'd told me himself.'

'I think Walt wanted to leave that part of his life behind.'

The explanation did not wash. How could Greta have believed that Walter was the most honest, authentic human she'd ever met? That their friendship was free of secrets?

'He obviously didn't succeed in killing himself,' she said, forcing the story forward.

'A young girl out for a morning jog found him not yet pinked by carbon monoxide.'

The waiter topped up Frank's cup again. Greta turned to the wall to hide her tears.

'The hospital contacted his family, but no one visited. Not even his sister.'

Greta wanted to scream, the pain inside flaying her. The pain of having Walter's true story denied her until now. The pain of the story. The pain of it being shared by some stranger.

'So when he was discharged, he packed his bags, withdrew his savings, and booked a ticket to New York.'

Greta blew her nose.

'Why New York?'

'Oh honey,' Frank said putting on a very camp accent, 'he'd heard the rumour. New York was where all the homos hung out.'

CHAPTER 20

Greta followed Frank out of the diner in a daze. The day was no different. Two strangers had shared breakfast. And yet, everything had changed. Everything. The street was dingier, the pavement dirtier.

Frank suggested a walk in Central Park. Greta was reluctant. A walk without a destination seemed pointless — they would simply be marking time. What's more, Central Park was dangerous. People got mugged there. And Frank did not exactly look the tough type, his beard the most robust bit about him.

He laughed at her concerns. 'You New Zealanders are really quaint.'

Quaint! Greta gave a little laugh, but when the pedestrian light changed, she stomped across Fifth Avenue.

The cloud cover had burnt off and it was already too warm for even a light cardigan. At the entrance to the park a man trailing a pack of dogs overtook them. Greta counted seven, and not one was straining on its leash or barking.

'We gonna do jus' two loops today, guys,' the man said to his canine crew. 'Unless we meet up with Benji, then we'll— Oh! Hey! There he is. Yo, Benji!'

Greta followed his gaze. Another man with a similar number of hounds was disappearing down a paved pathway. Was it an American thing to own so many dogs?

Frank answered her bewildered stare. 'They're dog walkers. You have them in New Zealand, right?'

'Dog walkers? You mean someone walks your dog for you?' Greta was incredulous. 'Now that takes outsourcing to a whole new level.'

'The city is full of apartments,' Frank said, a little defensively. 'People can't keep their pets cooped up all day. They pay for someone to walk them while they're at work. Happy dog. Happy owner.'

Greta was secretly impressed, though she wasn't going to admit it. Being called quaint still stung. In fact, she had a good mind to tell Frank that in New Zealand percolated coffee was passé, and that flat whites and cappuccinos were the order of the day.

Frank slowed to a seemingly aimless meander. It took more energy matching this pace than his earlier urgency.

Gradually the greenery and sunshine grew more pronounced, and Greta eased into the openness, marvelling at this immense green lung in the middle of high-rise Manhattan. The vast stretches of lawn. Trees casting generous canopies of shade. The waterways and footpaths. A circuit around which joggers ran in a dedicated direction. She spotted a family picnicking on the periphery of a softball game, and three jazz musicians jamming. Street artists displayed their craft, two toddlers licked their melting ice creams, lovers held hands. A student lay asleep on the grass, a textbook sheltering her face from the sun.

Since their earlier conversation, Greta had been locked inside her head, but now the knots started to slacken slightly. It was something about the greenness and the space. Like a big sigh, the park breathed out. Gardens were so calming, so restorative. No wonder Walter had loved being a gardener.

She caught herself. Ha! Did she really know anything about what Walter had loved? Frank's revelations had hurt. There were important parts of Walter's past she'd known nothing about. Nothing!

But was she being hypocritical? Everyone had secrets. Greta too. She'd never told Walter how her mind played tricks on her. How she sometimes got trapped in the most ludicrous circles of thought and could only release her mind by performing seemingly random actions — clicking her fingers, blinking in bursts, alternating the red and white pegs on her washing line. No one knew. Some things could not be shared.

But still. Walter knew everything else about her life. Everything. There was a code of disclosure proportional to the depth of a relationship. Clearly she'd believed the two of them were closer than they actually were.

He'd trained as an architect.

It was as if she'd just learnt that his real name was Roger.

And he'd been estranged from his parents.

All this time she'd thought they were dead.

Thinking back though, she couldn't remember if Walter had explicitly lied about this, or simply omitted the information. Was it she who'd joined the dots and formulated her own truth?

But the bit that hurt the most was learning Walter had once tried to take his own life. That he'd suffered alone. She hadn't known him then, so couldn't have done anything about it. But still . . . Still. She wished he'd been able to tell her.

This new information had punctured the perfect image Greta held in her head of Walter. Perfect, flawless Walter.

And then it dawned. Just as the words 'perfect' and 'flawless' were forming. Perhaps the fault lay at Greta's own door. She was the one who'd put him up on a pedestal. The one who couldn't conceive of him having any shortcomings. She hadn't given him the room to be honest.

Now the Amy Winehouse movie evening made sense. Walter had been trying to tell her. Trying to tell her more about *his* life.

A ringing bicycle bell pulled Greta back to the present. They'd covered quite a distance in silence. It occurred to Greta that Frank would think her very rude. He wasn't obliged to show her the city. He owed her nothing.

'It's incredible they've managed to preserve a bit of the countryside in the heart of all these high-rises,' she said, making an effort to engage.

'Oh, this wasn't here before,' Frank said. 'All eight hundred acres of the park is manmade. Rock blasted away and soil trucked in.'

Strains of jazz wove around their conversation. They'd looped back towards the trio of musicians. As they grew closer they stopped to listen.

The saxophonist, a short man with greying sideburns and a bulbous nose was dressed in a red satin suit. On someone else it might have looked garish, but on him, well, he owned it. Like his instrument, the musician oozed individuality and sass.

'You got to be pretty brave to wear such a brightly coloured suit,' Greta said.

Frank looked at her quizzically.

She laughed and shrugged her shoulders.

The saxophonist bent forward stiffly, blowing soul into his score. Then he tilted backwards, lifting his instrument to the sky. Shards of sunlight glinted off the big brass tube. There was no discernable division between where his fingers ended and where the keys began.

Greta loved the sound of the saxophone, and not just because Walter had introduced her to it, along with his love of jazz. Playing a saxophone made a statement of sorts. It was as much about the player as the instrument itself. A declaration of self-assurance.

An image flashed into her mind, but it disappeared as quickly, like a subliminal advertisement.

She tried to pull it back into view. A memory, hoarded for years, had risen to the space just below her consciousness. She couldn't reach it. It was like a word just on the tip of her tongue.

So much had happened in her head over the previous twenty-four hours; her mind felt like an archaeological dig.

Clearly encouraged by her enthusiasm for Central Park, Frank suggested another walk. 'One with a difference.'

Greta hesitated. 'I'm not very fit, Frank.' Exercise was something she'd never had the inclination to pursue.

'It's completely flat,' he assured her. 'We'll take the subway downtown to save your feet.'

She chewed her lip. Any mention of her feet, even such a vague reference, left her uncomfortable. The word carried connotations. As did the word 'subway', which was already conjuring up claustrophobia, carnage, a terrorist attack.

'The subway sounds scary,' she said with forced light-heartedness. She knew she was being a ninny, but everything felt frightening. New York had ripped off her trainer wheels, and it was terrifying navigating all this newness.

Greta is an adventurous child. Eager to explore.

That she still recalled Mrs Mansfield's perfect cursive comments on her primer one report card was nothing short of tragic. How could she be hanging onto words from a primer one schoolteacher? Did she really believe that who she was at six had any bearing on who she was now? Ha! She was not that child any longer. She was a timid, insignificant, thirty-nine-year-old nobody.

'I like that Mandela quote,' Frank said as they walked towards the mouth of a subway station. 'You know, the one about a brave man still being afraid, but having the courage to conquer his fear.'

The words caught Greta by surprise. She felt something inside her shift slightly, like an unexpected alignment of numbers on a combination lock. She'd always had a penchant for pithy sayings, for words married together wisely, which could capture some essential aspect of the human condition.

123

Frank's air of distraction was deceiving. He was more perceptive than she'd given him credit for.

'All okay?' he asked. 'You're very quiet.'

'Yes, yes. Just jetlagged. Whew! Sorry.'

They descended into the earth down a narrow flight of stairs. A warm wind howled up the hole, carrying with it the stench of disinfectant. A violin screeched. An accordion moaned. People scurried back and forth like ants.

They joined a rapidly dwindling queue. Greta scanned her ticket, then stopped. Someone pushed her from behind.

'Go lady, go!'

She forced the turnstile forward.

'C'mon, let's get this train,' Frank said, grabbing her elbow.

Please stand clear of the closing doors. Please stand clear of the closing doors. Please—

Greta stalled.

Frank yanked her into a car as the doors slid shut.

'That was close,' he said, his cheeks coloured by the sprint. 'Not the time to hesitate.'

She was laughing like a child. From her belly. It was a good feeling.

He pointed to a vacant seat. She sank into it, her calves burning.

The car was almost full. She crossed her legs to the side, placing one foot carefully behind the other. Then she uncrossed them and crossed them the other way.

A bride was standing barefoot in the middle of the car, her arms looped around the central pole, a bouquet of crushed white roses hanging limply from one hand. She appeared oblivious to an insect buzzing in the twist of her veil.

Greta looked around for the groom. No one in the carriage seemed to fit the bill.

The hem of the woman's gown was rimmed with dirt. Greta felt a swell of sadness seeing this.

Diagonally opposite Greta sat a woman dressed in jeans and a white T-shirt with a flawless caramel-coloured complexion and a shaved scalp speckled with pinpricks of new growth. She wore no makeup or jewellery, and her sneakers were unisex. A tan leather briefcase rested on her lap, its corners worn, the handle darkened by use. There was an enviable authenticity about her. A freedom from stereotypical trappings.

Greta decided the woman was probably a writer. Perhaps a part-time lecturer too. She loved imagining people's lives. It was almost as satisfying as looking into a stranger's lit window at dusk.

As the train slowed for the next station, an elderly man stood up and shuffled unsteadily towards the door. The fabric of his pants, which were belted just below his nipple line, fell in two beige pleats to the floor. When he turned, Greta saw that he had a large square of gauze taped to his cheek.

'Is this Seventy-second?' he asked, turning to a youngster.

The kid had earbuds in and a skateboard tucked under his arm. He pulled out one bud. 'What? Seventy-second? No way, man. This is Fiftieth commin up.'

The old man's head was a constant tremble. 'No. I don't mean—' He put a hand to his head as if to steady his thoughts. 'I mean Seventy-second.'

A crowd of commuters bunched around the door as the train came to a halt.

The skateboard kid shook his head.

The old man's eyes were bouncing around the approaching platform searching for somewhere familiar to land. 'Murdoch said Seventy-second.'

The doors opened. People surged forward. The old man stumbled. The kid caught him and hauled him back. 'This is not where you wanna get off, sir.'

'Yes, I must,' the man said, getting agitated. 'Murdoch said Seventy-seven. I mean second.'

'We passed Seventy-second some stations back.'

A dark stain had bloomed on the old man's trousers and was leaching in a long dark line to a puddle at his shoes. He started to whimper.

People stepped back into each other, lifting their bags off the floor to avoid the stream of urine now trickling down the car.

'He's lost,' said the kid.

'I think he's confused.'

'Come sit down, sir. What's your name?'

'Ask him his address.'

'Yes, get his address.'

'Watch out, ma'am. The puddle.'

'Sir, where do you live?'

'Laurie. Laurie Platz.'

A mother with a baby in a papoose leaned over him. 'Laurie, where do you live?'

'Has he got some ID?' suggested the skateboard kid as the train started to move again. 'A wallet, or something.'

'Not my wallet. Help! Somebody help!' screamed the old man.

'Fuck you!'

The white t-shirt woman put her hand on the skateboarder's arm. 'Don't take it personally, son. He's confused.'

'Not that confused that he don't recognise a black face,' said the kid, plugging in his earbuds again and moving to the back of the car.

'Nobody's going to rob you, sir,' Frank said slowly.

The man looked at Frank suspiciously. 'Who're you?'

'I'll get off with him at the next station,' volunteered the woman with the baby. 'I can take him to the station office.'

'You sure? Looks like you got your hands full already.'

She nodded and looped an arm through the old man's. 'You come with me, Laurie.'

The old man stood next to her obediently and began pulling funny faces at the baby.

People moved back to their seats with a smile, a shrug, a whispered comment. No longer strangers.

Greta felt strangely satisfied.

At the next station, Laurie and the woman got off and new commuters climbed into the car, unwittingly walking through the old man's wee.

Greta shook out the pins and needles in her fingers. It was good to be above ground again.

'You made it,' Frank said dryly.

She felt silly, but also pleased with herself. She'd survived the subway.

'Sorry, I'm a bit slow,' she wheezed, as they started to climb another set of stairs, this time above street level.

'It'll be worth it. You'll see.'

Ever since coming last in cross-country at school, Greta had had an aversion to exercise. Most of the ill-fated race she'd been second from the back, then just before the finish line Claudia Peplinksi overtook her. Greta reran that race many times in her head. The thing was, no one ever remembered who came second-to-last in anything, only who came last. There were likely still people who found themselves reminiscing about the poor puce-faced Jellings girl.

Greta stopped at the top of the third flight of stairs, her chest tight and burning.

'Woah!' Her gaze followed a thread of greenery unspooling between offices, old warehouses and tenement blocks. A path of shrubs and trees, and flowering weeds, winding through the sky.

'Impressive huh?' said Frank, as if he'd created it himself. 'It's called the High Line. An abandoned railway turned into one stellar garden path.'

There were views of the Hudson, the New York skyline, the Empire State Building.

'Back in the day, the railway moved goods between the Meatpacking District and Chelsea. Having it above street level was a way of avoiding the congestion below.'

They wandered along a boardwalk lined with sculptures, sunloungers, and edgy street art.

'When the line fell into disuse in the late seventies early eighties, people began pushing for it to be demolished.'

Frank stopped, turning to look at her, his eyes bright.

'But something astonishing was happening up here. Grasses and weeds had seeded the space and were softening the rusted steel and ugly angles.' He was nodding enthusiastically, as if he were the one being told the story.

'Two locals spotted the potential to transform the track into a public park.' He turned in a circle, as if seeing it all for the first time. 'This was their vision.'

Greta was starting to understand why Walter had loved New York. It was like nothing she'd experienced before. The ingenuity, chutzpah, the confidence. A Ludwig Bemelmans kind of place.

'Don't be completely beguiled by it,' Frank cautioned, as they sat on a bench, pondering a massive mural on an old tenement block. 'There's another side to this city. It has many faces.'

Yes, Greta thought. Life was complex. People too.

Try on some different Gretas.

She smiled.

Frank pulled out a crumpled brown packet and offered her a large purple candy.

She parked the boiled sweet in her cheek, letting the odd flavour leak slowly into her mouth. It reminded her of the grape-flavoured bubble gum of her childhood.

'Our Walt experienced all New York had to offer. The good, the bad and the downright ugly.'

Our Walt. She wondered . . .

'So, you're also an architect?' she asked, trying to divert Frank from delving into darker territory. She wasn't ready to hear more. Didn't trust herself.

He nodded. 'I work for a small group of architects in SoHo. We're mainly into renovating derelict warehouses. Turning them into trendy loft apartments. That sort of thing.' He glanced at his phone. 'We're small. Only three of us. Walter was the fourth,' he said, now texting as he talked. 'Pretty timid guy when we first met. As skinny as an eel, with a personality which didn't exactly jump out at you.'

Greta forced a laugh, though immediately regretted doing so; her politeness making her complicit in Frank's assessment of Walter.

'And the weird way he spoke.' Frank sniggered. 'Everything sounded like a question.' He nudged her, including her in his mockery of the New Zealand accent.

'I thought you said that he told his parents he would never work as an architect.'

'Walt had been trying to make it as an actor here for some months before he succumbed to his qualifications. He and a thousand other wannabes trying to break onto Broadway.' He shook his head. 'By the time Walt came to us, he'd worked every job under the sun to keep the wolf from the door. Waited tables. Shovelled shit. Sold roses in restaurants. You know, those annoying kids who interrupt your dinner to ask if you'd like to buy a rose for the lady.'

Greta pretended she knew what he was on about. She didn't go to restaurants, except for the shop's annual Christmas do. And that was never at a proper restaurant, but rather some all-you-can-eat buffet house. She did once take herself to a local bistro after reading a wonderful write-up in the newspaper, but spent the entire evening staring at the same page of her book. She didn't dare order a glass of wine either, even though French food demanded it. Ordering alcohol on your own required confidence (or a persuasive Carlyle barman).

'Walt used to make us laugh recounting his flower-selling exploits.' Frank chuckled. 'One time a guy asked Walt to give a rose to every lady at the table. Walt couldn't believe his luck; it was a big group.'

Frank grinned, as if watching the scene on replay.

'So, he proceeds to hand out about a dozen or so roses. Then all of a sudden everyone at the table is laughing.'

Greta frowned.

'You see, all the women he'd given a rose to were actually men dressed in drag.'

Greta put a hand to her mouth.

'You can imagine how delighted they were that Walter had been duped. And Walt was of course thrilled to have sold his entire allocation of flowers. Winners all round.'

Frank crunched a candy between his teeth. The skin behind Greta's ears tingled. She could almost feel the cold plastic covering of Dr Robotham's dental chair and hear the cat-fighting whine of his drill.

'We had to practically extract a portfolio from him,' Frank continued. 'Pretty shy about coming forward was young Walt. But hey, we were not expecting what he showed us. No, we were not! It was something special, let me tell you. His drawings got him the job, just like that,' Frank said, clicking his fingers.

Greta felt her chest swell, as if she were the one who'd been paid the compliment.

'And you'd never have guessed from his drawings that he hadn't chosen the profession. I mean he left his heart on every page.'

Greta felt as if she'd peered through a small crack in a wall and a giant hole was opening up.

'I just . . . I just can't understand why he never told me.' She put her fist to her mouth to stop the sob that wanted out. 'It's so confusing. So hurtful. It's like learning that you've only read half of your favourite book.'

Frank looked at her, his focus unsettling.

'Sometimes, when you decide to leave part of your life behind, it's easier to make a clean cut. Like amputating a gangrenous limb. Either you keep nibbling away with a scalpel just above the line of black, or you make a definitive decision and sever the leg higher up.'

Greta started subtracting sevens from a hundred to distract her mind from the extremely gory image.

'You knew Walter. He wasn't one to draw attention to himself,' said Frank. 'I suspect sending you here to New York was his way of— Look, he wouldn't have arranged for you to meet me, if he didn't want you to find out about his past.'

Yes, that made sense. And yet . . .

'He told *you* everything,' she said. 'About his parents. His twenty-first. His attempt to take his life. Why couldn't he share that with me?'

Frank tilted his head to one side, as if conceding her point.

'It can happen,' he said slowly, 'that two people find themselves suffering some trauma simultaneously. A time when both their lives are laid bare. The pain they share creates a bond between them, not dissimilar to that between soldiers trying to survive in the trenches.' He sighed. 'Walter and I—'

Frank's words were drowned out by a throng of teenage schoolkids bunching around their bench.

'Who can tell me about this one?' asked the teacher pointing to the kaleidoscopic mural on the wall of the tenement building opposite.

'The artist is Kobra,' said a pale, freckly lad.

'Way to go, Ethan. You're college ready,' teased a bigger boy.

The group laughed.

'Correct,' said the teacher. 'Eduardo Kobra. A Brazilian street artist.'

'Isn't it based on the famous VJ-day kiss in Times Square?' piped up a girl.

'Very good, Linda.'

'Seriously cosmic,' said another.

Greta was impatient for the youngsters to pass. Finally, they moved on.

Frank stood up. She wanted him to stay seated. Wanted to pick up where they'd left off.

'So, Walter came to work for you?' she prompted.

'He did,' Frank said, beckoning her with his finger. 'Let's keep moving.'

She followed reluctantly.

'Walt was the best decision we ever made,' Frank continued. 'Clients loved him. His push for simplicity. The way he let materials speak for themselves.' He popped another candy in his mouth. 'His work was understated. Know what I'm saying?'

She nodded. Walter's modesty was intoxicating.

'Not out there like us New Yorkers.'

She laughed loudly, then caught herself. 'I wasn't laughing because I agree with you,' she said quickly. 'I mean, I don't think Americans are loud—'

'When we stopped trying to turn Walt into another one of us, we began to appreciate what he brought to the table.'

Greta wondered about Frank. About his history. She couldn't quite work him out. There was a brittleness to him. A cynicism around the edges. And then, small pockets of unexpected tenderness.

'Time for some lunch,' he said, picking up the pace. 'Let's head uptown to Zabar's. Best cheese blintzes in the whole city.'

Cheese blintzes. Greta didn't know what they were, but just the sound of the word *blintze* was appetising.

A little girl's head of tight black curls appeared and then disappeared in a stretch of waist-high cornflowers, as she struggled to balance on a segment of rusted track.

'Then I'll leave you to do your own thing,' said Frank. 'You'll have had enough of me by then.'

Greta shook her head. She definitely did not want to be left to do her own thing. Not in New York.

'I have to go in to work for a bit.'

'Yes. Of course. Sorry.'

'Greta,' Frank said, turning to face her. 'Stop apologising. It can't be good for you.'

'Oh, I know. I'm sorry. I mean—'

They both burst out laughing. As they did so, the small girl's smile vanished and she ran back to her mother.

'You were doing very well,' Greta said quickly.

The girl peeked out from behind her mother's skirt.

Frank had walked on ahead. He turned, waiting for Greta to catch up. He looked almost annoyed.

'Sorry. I know you're short of time. It's just I think she thought we were laughing at her, and—'

'Tomorrow we'll do the galleries.'

'Right,' Greta said, uncertain of what she'd done wrong.

'And then I've got tickets for the ballet on Wednesday.'

'The ballet!'

Since Greta was small she had dreamed of going to the ballet.

CHAPTER 21

Frank pulled open the door of the delicatessen and an aroma of cured meats, ripe cheeses and freshly baked bread assailed them. Strings of sausages hung from hooks. Rotisserie chickens spun slowly in big ovens. Wicker baskets swayed in the burst of breeze.

They eased past a long central table around which patrons were perched, and joined a line of those waiting to be served by one of the white-coated assistants bustling behind the counter.

Greta peered into the cabinets at the enormous rounds of cheese and buckets brimming with olives, artichokes and roasted red peppers. There was a caviar corner, a platter of pickled herring, a bowl of creamy lobster salad. Yolk-golden loaves twisted into plaits. Poppy-seed pastries. Slices of pastrami. A side of rare roast beef. The selection was overwhelming.

There could be no dawdling — New York was an impatient place — so Greta settled on a sweet cheese blintze and a smoked-salmon bagel. Then they squeezed into a vacant space at the table.

Greta began on the blintze. As a child she was never allowed dessert until she'd finished her dinner, which was especially challenging when said dinner was fish pie.

She now added blintzes to her list of favourite foods. The pocket of crepe crammed with warm, sweet curd was nothing short of sublime.

She smiled when she thought about all the New Zealand snacks she'd packed for the trip — the muesli bars, dried fruit sticks, the crackers.

Frank glanced at his mobile. 'Gotta go, I'm afraid,' he said, pushing back his chair and packing away the rest of his pastrami sandwich.

Greta jumped up.

He put a hand on her shoulder. 'Stay. Finish your lunch. We'll catch up again tomorrow.'

'Tomorrow? But how will I get back to the hotel?'

Frank rattled off directions to the nearest subway, jotting down a few crucial key words on the back of her serviette, then hurried away.

Greta sank back into her seat. She'd lost her appetite, the warmth and insouciance of the previous hour draining quickly away.

'You will eat the sour cream?'

It was an old woman seated on Greta's left, her sparse grey hair concreted into airy waves above her scalp.

Greta shook her head.

'Mind if I am?'

'You want my sour cream?'

'It is my weakness,' said the woman in a Russian, or perhaps Polish, accent, reaching across Greta for the pottle. She smelt of mothballs and mouldy bread.

Greta glanced at the old woman sidelong as she scooped up sour cream with her forefinger. A clump landed on her already stained blouse.

'Oy vey!' she said, lifting her crooked palms to the heavens. 'You have a napkin?'

'I'm afraid it's been used.'

'Is fine. Is fine,' said the woman, swatting away Greta's concern and making a grab for Greta's napkin.

Greta couldn't believe the audacity. Old age was not a free pass to behave badly! She retrieved the scrunched-up serviette and smoothed it out. Frank's instructions were just legible.

She pushed back her stool, then stopped. As long as she remained in the deli, she didn't have to face the subway on her own.

'You not eat that also?' The woman was pointing at Greta's half-eaten bagel.

'Help yourself,' Greta said curtly. The woman had thick limbs and a big bust. She did not look underfed.

'Thank you, my love,' the woman said breaking off a small piece of the bagel and pushing the rest back to Greta.

'Have more. Really,' Greta said, suddenly ashamed at her mean-spiritedness.

But the woman was busy rummaging inside her large canvas bag.

Greta wished she'd not been so uncharitable. Her mood had nothing to do with the poor woman. It was just the prospect of navigating New York streets on her own that had thrown her into a state.

The old lady slumped back in her chair, her face collapsing. 'Felix,' she moaned quietly. 'Felix.'

'Is everything alright?'

The woman looked into Greta's eyes, then put a finger to her lips. With her other hand she beckoned Greta closer.

Greta peered into the bag.

A tatty maroon purse. Roll of Triple-X mints. A dog-eared Mills & Boon . . .

Greta gasped.

The woman grabbed her arm. 'Shhhhh, or they will kick me out!'

'But there's a *mouse* in your handbag!'

The only reason Greta hadn't screamed was all the months of practice she'd had tolerating Mitsy and Delores, Walter's pet rats.

The old woman scooped up the tiny creature and cradled it under the table, stroking its disease-dull coat.

'Is Felix's last day,' she said slowly, a tear driving a furrow through her caked foundation. 'We go now to the vet. I stop here for one final treat. Is Felix's favourite place, but he won't even eat!'

'I'm so sorry.'

'I do just like Dr Koplin say. Put steroid on two time every day. Then yesterday Felix he begin to—' She sucked in a stuttering breath. 'His nose, it begin to be bleeding. Dr Koplin say it is time.'

Greta felt like the meanest person in the world. How could she have been so horrible?

'Felix has a special friend in you,' Greta said, patting her neighbour's arm.

The woman tipped her head to one side in a gesture of self-deprecation. 'Is me who am having a special friend.'

When they parted, Rosa and Felix were headed for the veterinary clinic, and Greta, the nearest subway station. But her heart was not thumping in her chest any more and her mouth was no longer dry. She looked at the notes Frank had scribbled on her napkin, now smudged by sour cream, and she knew that making her way back to the hotel would be no real hardship at all.

CHAPTER 22

As a rule, Greta avoided art galleries. They were daunting places poised to expose her ignorance. However, the Guggenheim gallery got to her before she had time to mount a defence. It was the beauty of the building that first bewitched her. Like an upended spiral shell, the coil of concrete expanded into the sky.

She looked into the void around which the gallery twisted. At the top, a domed skylight suffused the space with warmth and light.

She and Frank climbed to the top, which was the bottom of the shell, then meandered down the ramp, perusing the artworks displayed on the one continuous curve of wall.

'That's a Picasso,' Greta blurted out, finally recognising a piece. A print of *Le Moulin de la Galette* had hung in her primary school hall. She'd spent many an assembly daydreaming herself into Paris's glamorous, top-hat world.

Frank was neither impressed nor unimpressed. Occasionally he shared his thoughts about some painting, but in a way that was simple and unpretentious. Gradually Greta's mind loosened and her fear of appearing foolish fell away. She found herself starting to recognise artists' familiar traits — Modigliani's elongated faces, Gauguin's countryside colours, the multiple plains of a classic Picasso portrait.

'I can't stand Monet,' Frank said, as they shared a blueberry muffin in the gallery cafe. 'All those pastel shades. Not my thing.'

Greta was stunned. She loved Monet. What's more, he was one of the great masters. Who was Frank to question such brilliance?

'Art is like wine,' he went on, his mouth full of muffin. 'No point drinking something you don't like just because others say it's good.'

A crumb landed on Greta's arm. Frank flicked it off.

'Sure, one's preferences might change with time, but life's too short to force something on oneself just because others say so. Fuck the connoisseurs.'

Greta glanced around to see if anyone had heard. The two women at the next table remained deep in conversation.

There was a bombastic confidence to New Yorkers Greta had not encountered before. It was confronting, but also appealing, that bold sense of self. Even the street-sleepers had it. The guy playing his accordion in the subway had refused an encore. 'Come back tomorrow if you like it so much, love. I'm done now.'

As for Greta Jellings. Who was she? That depended on who was asking. She was an amalgamation of who her mother, her boss, and her few friends had wanted her to be.

After the Guggenheim Gallery, Frank took her to the Metropolitan Museum of Modern Art. If Greta's soul had been loosened of its limitations at the Guggenheim, at The Met it found wings. The distance between herself and the art, a space usually cluttered with expectation and apprehension, fell away. Installations drew her in, closing the gap between seeing and being. Her favourite — if a favourite were possible — was the Tiffany stained-glass display. She'd not seen anything so exquisite before. That Louis Comfort Tiffany had first been a painter before turning to glassmaking and jewellery design, made perfect sense; every window and lampshade, tumbler and vase, was like a painted canvas, with depth and texture. There was opalescent glass, folded glass, glass which had been creased and draped like a doily. There were magnolias, irises, wisteria ... Greta tried at first to tie the beauty down with descriptions, but soon stopped trying and simply gave over to the emotions the pieces evoked.

When she and Frank finally emerged from the gallery, sections of the museum remained unexplored. It had been a long day and blisters were bulging on her heels; she'd worn her black flats on the off chance of another Victoria Beckham encounter. However, her mind felt refreshed. Like a powerful meditation, the art had drawn her outside of her head.

'I'll collect you around five tomorrow afternoon' Frank said, as they sheltered from a passing shower under the Carlyle's canopy. 'We're having dinner at the Lincoln Centre, before seeing *Giselle*.'

Greta avoided Frank's eyes.

'Catch you then,' he said, hailing a cab.

'Frank?'

He turned.

'I'm sorry, I really am, but I'm going to have to give the ballet a miss.'

Frank raised an eyebrow, then flung his head back and laughed. 'Very good, Greta. You nearly had me.'

She grimaced. 'No, I . . . it's just that I'm not feeling very well. I think I'm coming down with something.'

'Shit!'

Greta stepped back, her hand covering her mouth as if she'd been the one to swear.

'You should have told me earlier.'

If there was any concern in Frank's voice, it was buried deep beneath his obvious annoyance.

'I could try to get you in to see my doctor, but it's late and . . . what are you feeling?'

She shook her head. 'It's probably just some twenty-four-hour bug.'

Frank waved away the taxi and started scrolling through his contacts on his phone.

'Please don't worry. Honestly. I'm sorry. I'll pay for my ticket.'

'Do you feel fluey? Queasy? Is it your gut?'

'Well, I . . .' It was pointless. She was a hopeless liar. 'Frank, the thing is, I don't have any decent shoes to wear to the ballet.'

'You what?'

Greta stretched her eyes wide, trying to hold back tears.

'You serious?'

She blinked.

'Greta, you're in New York! Shoe stores are a dime a dozen. You've got the whole day to shop tomorrow.'

She shook her head. Pointed at her feet. 'Look!'

Frank's dark eyebrows pulled together. She wondered if he plucked them or had just been blessed with a great shape.

'Well-dressed women don't have feet this size. I can't go to the ballet in trainers, or in these!'

Frank looked from her flat black shoes to her face and back to her feet.

'Greta, you can go to the ballet in your bathing suit if you want.'

Greta imagined the scene — the crowd parting as she slunk ahead in her baggy, turquoise togs.

Frank started to smile. She clenched her jaw. She'd never forgive him if he burst out laughing.

He looked at his watch. 'C'mon then,' he said, grabbing her hand.

'What? Where are we going?'

'To get the lady some shoes, of course!'

It was dark by the time they left a fourth store, empty-handed. The owner followed them out and began rolling down his shopfront shutter. There were no more options for the night. Even Frank's optimism had waned.

'Your dad must have had pretty impressive bits. Just saying,' Frank said, shaking his head. 'You know what they say about big feet.'

Greta felt her face colour. 'I would rather not be the butt of such crass jokes.'

'Better to laugh than cry about it,' Frank said, unapologetically.

'Do you know what the elevator man suggested?' Greta said, holding onto her indignation. 'He suggested I go to a shop for people who, you know, dress in drag. Can you imagine?'

Frank paused, then punched the air. 'Fantastic!'

'What do you mean?' She was panicking now.

'I'll be here first thing tomorrow.'

'But Frank . . .?'

'No ifs or buts, Miss Jellings. Tomorrow we are going to buy you a perfect pair of shoes for the ballet.'

CHAPTER 23

Greta pulled up her raincoat hood before shadowing Frank into Sassy & Sensual. Her humiliation would be off the charts if someone she knew spotted her there. It didn't bear thinking about. And while she appreciated that this was unlikely, what with her being in New York and everything, it remained a possibility. After all, she'd once bumped into Mr Meyers, her school principal, in Orewa. Greta remembered being aghast at seeing him in a supermarket aisle, let alone so far out of town.

A statuesque woman tucked into a tight red dress with a beaded bodice approached them. She was already tall, before adding stilettoes into the mix. Around her neck hung a string of Jacqueline Kennedy pearls. Greta loved pearls.

'Morning,' she crooned. 'And how may I help you two beautiful people?' Her voice reminded Greta of Cassandra, Angus's PA.

'We're after shoes,' Frank said stepping aside to expose Greta. 'For the ballet.'

'Ballet slippers?' the woman said, blinking slowly.

Greta looked enviously at the woman's long lashes. Despite applying castor oil to her own eyelids every night in a bid to promote lash growth — some magazine pro tip — Greta's lashes remained sparse and toothpick straight.

'A pair of heels to wear to the ballet,' Frank explained.

'I'm with you, I'm with you,' the woman said, ushering them to the back of the store. 'What size, love?'

'Oh, not for me,' Frank said with a chuckle. 'For this young lady.'

The woman's cat-green eyes widened. She looked Greta up and down. 'Impressive.'

Greta felt the blood draining from her cheeks. The scale of her embarrassment was beyond blushing. Fainting felt more appropriate.

'No, I'm not a . . . that sort of . . . you see . . .'

A grin tugged at the corners of Frank's mouth. He did not help her out.

The woman directed Greta to a throne-like chair upholstered in purple velvet.

'We'll measure you up,' she said, kneeling down in front of Greta and eyeing Greta's khaki trainers as if they were pig's trotters.

'Let's get these off,' she said, gingerly untying Greta's laces and lifting out her right foot.

It felt a very intimate thing to do. Greta blushed.

'What lovely slender feet you have.'

Sparks arced across Greta's body. No one had ever called her feet lovely before.

'Such a shame to keep them locked away in these . . . clodhoppers.'

Greta didn't flinch. She was still basking in the very best of compliments.

As directed, she stood up and placed her foot on the cold metal measuring device. It was worse than standing on the scales in front of her doctor.

The woman slid the crossbar towards Greta's big toe.

Greta squinted, terrified that by some stroke of fate, her feet had grown bigger since she'd last looked. She'd read somewhere that one of the first signs of acromegaly was when an adult's feet started to increase in size.

'Size ten,' the woman announced. 'Lucky you. We have a large selection in that size.'

Greta blanched. 'Ten? You sure? I'm normally nine-and-a-half. Only ten-plus in sneakers'

'US sizing?'

'Silly me. I forgot, I'm in America. But that still doesn't make sense. I'm an eleven and a half or twelve, US.'

The woman remeasured Greta's foot. 'Ten it is, honey.'

Greta felt a surge of excitement. Were her feet actually smaller than she'd—'

'Ten, men's size,' Frank interjected, quashing Greta's blissful disbelief.

'What colour, what style, love?'

Greta shrugged. She'd never had a choice before. 'Black, I guess.'

'You're new to this, aren't you?' The woman patted Greta's knee. 'Leave it to me.' Then she disappeared through a door at the back of the shop, her hips undulating slowly under the red silk.

Frank's phone started ringing in his pocket. He excused himself and headed outside.

Greta stared hard at the floor. If she couldn't see people on the street, they couldn't see her.

After what felt like forever, she slowly lifted her eyes and glanced furtively around the shop. The mauve-walled space was cluttered with clothing racks, glass cabinets, mannequins and busts. One rack was crammed with dress-up costumes — bright yellow booty shorts for 'Beach Patrol', a white apron and little black dress for the 'Sexy Maid', a hat for a 'Smooth Sergeant'. There were boxes of hip boosters, padded girdles with buttock inserts, and a pair of panties with female genitalia in detailed relief.

She blushed and looked down.

Her eyes crept back up.

A cabinet of costume jewellery, a leather-clad mannequin, rows of wigs — blunt bob, girl-next-door, auburn curls.

Auburn curls.

Greta again felt a cold twist of recognition. She closed her eyes trying to capture and banish a thought at the same time.

The brass bell above the door clanged. She swung round, expecting to see Frank. Instead, a sandy-haired man was standing in the doorway, a navy-blue suit hanging limply off his apologetic frame.

A surge of heat enveloped Greta. It was like bumping into another client in her therapist's waiting room.

She was contemplating how to make her escape when he greeted her, trapping her with politeness.

'Hi.' He sounded hoarse.

She gave a silly wave.

The man closed the door and moved into the shop with self-conscious woodenness.

'Be right with you,' called the shopkeeper from the back, her intrusion temporarily mediating the awkwardness.

The man tilted his eyebrows towards Greta in a gesture of collusion. His eyes had a pained patina. He fingered the Cindy-Crawford mole above his top lip. He had bony digits, but perfect file-rounded fingernails.

Victor Jellings turns the page and carries on reading. Greta loves her father's long fingers and file-rounded fingernails. The way they lift the corner of a page and glide from right to left, carrying the page with them.

Later, when she is reading the same story to her dolls, making up the words she doesn't know, she imitates her father's mannerisms, using the same flourish and sweep as she turns the page.

'Here we go then,' said the owner, emerging from the back room, behind a tower of boxes. 'Shoes for the ballet.'

She lowered them and looked around. 'I could have sworn I heard someone come in.'

Greta pointed to a clothing rack, just as the newcomer emerged from behind it.

'Leonard! How lovely to see you. And yes, everything has arrived.'

The man's expression loosened.

'Let me just get this lovely lady underway, then I'll be right with you. You'll want to be trying it all on, I'm guessing?'

He gave a barely perceptible nod.

Greta looked down at the boxes. Eight boxes. Eight! She would not allow herself to get excited. The number of boxes was never an indication of the pairs that would fit.

As she lifted off the first lid, she gasped. Lying in a bed of pastel pink tissue paper was a pair of black velvet courts with specks of glitter scattered over the vamp.

'They're beautiful!' she said, stroking the air above them. 'But they'll never—'

The woman handed Greta a shoehorn. 'Have a play. See what suits. I'm just going to help Leonard here. We've got lots more where those came from.'

Greta braced for disappointment as she prepared to force her foot into the shoe. Her pulse picked up.

It slid in with Cinderella ease.

She felt woozy.

They were a little tight at the toe, but nothing she couldn't tolerate.

She put on the left shoe, her apprehension ratcheting up again, as if the right fitting was a fluke. Then she stood up slowly and teetered towards the mirror. She was wearing slacks, a raincoat (hood still up) and the most perfect pair of shoes she'd ever laid eyes on.

She walked back to her seat, then towards the mirror again. She turned to the right. To the left. Finally, she sat down, her legs trembling. All the years of pain. The teases. The taunts.

'Here comes Gulliver Girl. Out of the way or she'll squash you.'

'At least people know you're coming before you round a corner.'

'Hey, Puss in Ginormous Boots.'

Her super-sized school shoes were made all the more conspicuous by the white socks Nora crocheted for her. All Greta ever wanted was a pair of regular polyester socks from the uniform shop.

'You're just a big-boned girl,' Nora had reassured her, as if being called an ugly stepsister were a compliment.

Throughout her childhood, whenever life came at her too hard, Greta retreated into the world of shoes. She'd spend hours sketching fancy footwear, then fall headlong into the stories she'd created on the page.

Now she twisted the skin on her wrist till tiny bloodspots verified her reality.

'How're you going?' asked the assistant, holding an auburn wig and long sequined gown.

Greta took a moment to remember where she was.

'They're perfect,' she said, her bottom lip quivering.

'You're easy to please.' The woman passed the dress and wig through a gap in the change-room curtain. 'What are the others like?'

'Oh, I've still got to try them. Sorry.'

'No hurry, honey.'

Greta was trying on a pair of red wedges when Frank returned.

'Any luck?'

'Five pairs so far, and each as beautiful as the next,' she said breathlessly, 'Thank you, Frank. Thank you so much.'

'Finally!' he said, throwing open his hands.

'The hard bit will be deciding which ones to take and which to leave behind.' The squirrel in Greta was already battling with Nora's parsimony.

'Doesn't sound like a problem to me.' He glanced at his watch.

Greta felt instantly guilty for seeming to complain when there was nothing to complain about. 'If you need to get back to the office, you can leave me here. I'll be fine.'

'You sure?'

His retort sobered her delirium. She'd been hasty. Caught on a shoe high. She'd prefer it if he stuck around.

'Right then. See you about five.' And with that, he was gone.

She should have learnt by now that with Frank there was no ritual of politeness. Every word carried its designated weight and was not a code for something else. Yes meant yes. No meant no.

She turned back to the boxes. It felt reckless to take any more than a single pair.

'I'm ready when you are,' she finally called out in the direction of the change room. Two figures were still silhouetted behind the curtain.

'Just a moment,' called out the assistant. Then in a more muted voice, 'There you go, Leticia. Just gorgeous.'

Greta thought she could hear someone sobbing.

'I'd cry too if I looked so sensational. A brand new beginning, love.'

'Thank you.' The small hoarse voice again.

The assistant swept into the room. 'So, what's it to be?'

Greta placed four boxes on the counter.

The woman lifted each lid and nodded with approval. 'Black suede courts, 1960's sling-backs, and oh, I just love these red wedges. A real theatre-red, isn't it?'

'The charcoal flats too,' Greta said quickly, as if the woman's failure to acknowledge them would prevent their purchase.

Four pairs of shoes. Greta wondered how she would ever reconcile this indulgence with her philosophy of frugalness. She kept expecting shame to accost her, but the guillotine of reproach did not drop down as she handed over her credit card. Shoes were in a special category, beyond the reach of remorse.

The assistant handed her two shiny shopping bags. 'Enjoy the ballet, darling. I'm so envious.'

At the door, Greta turned to check that she hadn't left anything behind.

As she did so, she saw a hand draw back the dressing-room curtain and out stepped a woman with a mane of auburn curls, slinky, sequined frock and navy stilettoes. The woman turned, tentatively sweeping her hair back over her shoulder.

Greta stared at the small dark mole above her lip.

'Oh, you look . . . you look amazing!' she said.

The woman beamed, her eyes shining with tears under the bright store lights.

CHAPTER 24

Greta had been ready for over an hour when Frank arrived to collect her. Instead of waiting in her room, she'd decided to wait downstairs in the lobby on the glamorous mustard couch, her legs angled neatly to one side. She tried not to look down at her feet too often; but whenever she did, a shower of magic crackled over her.

Then Frank was walking into the hotel, clean-shaven and dashingly dressed, a glossy cummerbund packaging his torso rather pleasantly.

Greta had always liked the look of a man in uniform. Black tie was not bad either. Not bad at all.

She leapt up, straightened her dress, and started towards him.

The catwalk gait was harder to master than it looked. She chewed her lip, her arms flying out to steady herself.

'Great shoes,' Frank said, taking her arm.

She lurched forward.

He caught her. 'Not so fast. We're in plenty of time.'

As they pulled up to the Lincoln Center, a fountain in the forecourt sent a plume of water into the dusk sky. When it subsided, Greta gasped; the opera house coming into full view. Five elongated arches invited the eye into a wonderland.

She even forgot about her high heels as she stepped into the Metropolitan Opera House, the cantilevered staircase sweeping her gaze, along with a tide of elegant patrons, upwards. Crystal chandeliers sprayed light through the space like tiny silver explosions. Two Chagall murals framed the pavilion. A crimson carpet softened all sound.

Time slowed. Tiny details came into focus. An emerald brooch in the shape of a frog pinned to a woman's velvet wrap. A child dressed in a pink tutu, talking breathlessly to a lady leaning on a tortoiseshell walking stick. An usher assisting a woman with giant lampshade-like earrings. Two men waving excitedly over the crowd. Glossy programme paper. A whiff of floral fragrance. The hum of anticipation rising off the crowd like steam.

Then a gong was struck.

·'Better get to our seats,' Greta said, breaking into a wobble walk.

An usher led them into the auditorium.

'Oh my goodness!' Greta cried, turning full circle to take in the balconies stacked above her, the gold-leafed dome, the cinch and drape of sumptuous silk curtains.

'I feel like the luckiest person in the whole world!'

Frank chuckled. 'If only Walter could have seen you right now.'

When they'd found their seats, Greta opened the programme, but there were too many other distractions.

Frank pulled something out of his breast pocket. Her eyes narrowed. He was holding an envelope.

'I've been instructed to give you this tonight.'

Greta came crashing back to earth. The next leg of the itinerary was not due to be revealed for a couple of days yet.

'Aren't you going to take it?'

She folded her fingers around the navy envelope with silver writing.

Navy and silver matched the occasion perfectly.

Suddenly she was desperate to see what was inside. Was there time to make a dash to the toilet?

She looked along the row. It had already filled up. No way could she contemplate getting past all those people. Not in her high heels.

She slipped the envelope into her handbag.

The lights started to dim, and darkness enveloped the hall. Then the stage curtains were being drawn back.

Greta lowered her handbag to her feet, her toes tingling with excitement.

A ballerina had appeared on stage, trapped in a circle of white light.

Music rose from the orchestra pit, soft at first, then louder, and the dancer came to life.

Five-year-old Greta opens the jewellery box her parents have given her for her fifth birthday. The inside is marshmallow pink. And there, in front of a small oval mirror, is the tiniest of ballerinas. Her father winds up the box, and, to Greta's delight, the ballerina starts to spin.

146

As that ballerina now pirouetted across the stage, Greta flicked her temple to be sure she was actually seated in the Metropolitan Opera House. But soon her smarting skin, and even the splendid venue, disappeared as she climbed into Giselle's enchanting world. The precision and patter of satin feet, the tulle tutus sighing over every échappé, the stirring music, the story . . .

Sitting in her seat, Greta managed to mimic Giselle's proud neck and defiant collarbones. She moved her hands in small tight movements on her lap. An anguished extension of the wrist. A recoiling elbow of sorrow . . . *Giselle* was, after all, a tale of unrequited love.

She stands at the barre behind Rosemary and in front of Danielle.

Mrs Keegan calls out, 'Tendu front. Tendu side. Tendu back. Grande Battemente front.'

The class point their toes to the front, the side, the back.

How Greta loves these afternoons.

She only gets to go to the 'frightfully expensive lessons', because Mrs Keegan is one of her mother's dressmaking clients and so the lessons are free.

One day she eavesdrops at the sewing-room door as the two women talk about the upcoming concert. It will be Greta's first time appearing on stage. She hasn't been able to sleep with excitement since the rehearsals began. She will need a new pair of ballet slippers and a pastel blue tutu for the performance.

'Between you and me, Nora,' Mrs Keegan says, 'if the cost is going to stretch you, I'd just tell her that you can't afford them this year. I mean, if I felt that she was going to . . . well, how do I put it? Some girls are just not built to be ballerinas.'

Greta carries that sentence through her childhood like a dead bird around her neck. 'Some girls are just not built to be ballerinas.' It is the word 'built' that gets to her. As if she is some unsightly house, and her feet the solid concrete slabs out front.

She never makes it onto points. Not proper ones anyway. But in her bedroom she'd bends back the fronts of her slippers and tries to balance on the tips of her toes, ribbon offcuts wound tightly around her calves.

And then the curtain was coming down.

People stood, stamped their feet. 'Bravo! Bravo!'

Even Greta felt free to shout out, her voice anonymously joining the others. *No one is watching. No one is watching.*

The lights in the auditorium came up. Flowers were flung. The conductor held his baton to his chest and bowed. The company curtseyed. And for the briefest moment Greta was a seven-year-old ballerina in pink satin slippers and a pale blue tutu, curtseying to the crowd.

Back in her hotel, Greta spun round and round the suite, finally falling back on her bed, exhausted. She hadn't felt so happy in a long time.

Perhaps a little extravagance was not always a bad thing. Not if it sent a person soaring. Not if it spoke to someone's soul.

She lay on her back in a pleasant daze until a thought hauled her back. The letter.

She sat up, grabbed her handbag and pulled out the navy envelope with shiny silver writing.

Greta
'Glitter'
By now your jetlag will hopefully have cleared and the city will be starting to make more sense. Are you enjoying yourself?

I am butting in on your day not to tell you about your next destination — that will come in another letter. No, this is to tell you what I haven't had the courage to say before. I apologise for hiding behind the safety of death to say it now.

Greta swallowed.

The thing is, having one's end in sight sort of clarifies the mind. Focuses it. What's annoying is acquiring this insight only now, when it would have been far more useful at the beginning of my journey. It's like being given a route map upon arrival at one's final destination.

Anyway, if I can't share my newly gathered wisdom with you, it will disappear into the dust and then what will have been the point of it?

I'd like to believe that in a few days, or weeks if I'm lucky, I will not be snuffed out, but continue to exist, if only in echoes. It certainly won't be through any offspring.

Must be my ego talking, but the alternative, nothingness, is really quite frightening.

I used to wonder what it would be like to have children. I'd have liked

148

to have been a father, but never allowed my mind to go too far down that track. It was the challenges that I, by being me, would have introduced into their lives. One day it might be different for others.

Anyway, it's not like I am some all-seeing sage, Grets. God knows I've made enough stuff-ups. But for what it's worth, here goes.

Greta chewed her thumbnail, bracing for what was about to be hurled her way.

Glitter is important.

She read the line again.

Glitter is important. Ha! Was that not the conclusion she'd just reached after her experience at the ballet?

What I'm trying to say is that I think you've let your life be stripped of magic. I've watched you move through it in survival mode, each day ticked off, accomplished.

She frowned.

Life should be more. I think you already know that. I've spied a hunger in you. Remember the bookshop job?

Her chest rose and fell.

'What's this?' Walter picks up the newspaper she's left open on her kitchen table.

'Oh nothing,' she says, trying to take it off him.

He swings it out of her reach and begins to read the advertisement circled in red.

Position: Manager of village bookstore. Suited to
someone who loves books, reads widely and—

'Give that here!'

'Option to have a share in the business.'

'Walter, give it back.'

He lowers it. 'So . . . looking for a new job, are we?'

'Don't be silly,' she says irritably. 'Anyway, the salary is a lot less than I'm getting.'

'Ah, so you've enquired about it.'

She feels herself blushing.

'It was just a stupid flight of fancy,' she says quickly.' And it's none of your business.'

'I could see you running a bookshop,' he says with a smile. 'You'd be great. You're always recommending books you think I'd enjoy. And you're usually spot-on.'

She falters. Shakes her head. Folds away the paper and puts it in the bin. 'Coffee?'

But I'm getting side-tracked. I was talking about magic. Hence the Business Class flights, the Carlyle, the glamour of the ballet. It's not to squander cash, but because I want you to feel the fun of the frivolous, of doing things not necessarily sensible or practical or advised, but which speak to a place deep within you. I call it the fairy-tale factor.

No way can a kid spend eight hours a day in a classroom without some time on the seesaw or swings. A beggar might occasionally blow his takings on the biggest burger or a pack of cigarettes. A boy who dreams of one day being a chef might save his pocket money for that gourmet pie in the bakery window. The human soul needs magic every now and then.

So, leave your guilt at the door and give yourself permission to indulge Greta. Be a bit selfish.

That word — selfish — it's like a rock-filled sack on a mule's back. Our parents and teachers were the first to instil in us the dangers of self-indulgence. But the truth is, you need to attend to yourself as much as to anyone else. It's only when the balance gets distorted that things go awry.

So, for now, for this trip at least, put Greta up there alongside all the other people you strive to gratify, and satisfy her a little too.

Walt x

Greta lay back on the bed and closed her eyes. She'd read the letter three times, maybe four, and the words had started to settle more comfortably in her head.

She felt a spike of satisfaction knowing that even before Walter's words of advice, she'd bought herself four pairs of shoes. And not the most practical ones either.

The strange thing was, what impacted her most about his letter was not so much the explicit message, but rather the unwitting one. Behind the words she spied a man with his own doubts and fears. A man who'd apparently only gained certain insights towards the end of his life. Someone who'd also once felt bad about wanting things for himself. Whose parents had instilled in him that dreaded G word. Guilt.

It was as if he was wanting off the pedestal. As if he wanted her to see him as more ordinary. More human. More like her.

And as she drifted off to sleep that night, Greta felt in some way the echoes of their friendship deepen.

CHAPTER 25

Greta awoke on her seventh day in the Big Apple knowing that, by the end of the day, she'd know where she was headed next.

She tried to quash the flicker of panic the thought ignited. She was just getting used to the city. No longer did she feel as if she were sitting too close to some giant cinema screen. New York had begun to shrink to something more manageable. The Carlyle. Noah and Bernie. Carmila. The subway station on Seventy-seventh. The logical layout — streets east to west, avenues north to south. Central Park. Bodegas stocking everything she'd expect for a convenience store, plus so much more — drain plungers, a prayer book, frozen calamari! The coffee shop down the road which served wedges of the best lemon drizzle cake ever. She'd bought two slices every day — one to accompany her afternoon cup of tea, the other for the pockmarked teen who laid out his bedroll in the florist's doorway each evening.

Frank laughed when she told him that she was getting to grips with the place.

'Sorry to burst your bubble, but you haven't even scratched the surface of the city.'

Visiting the 9/11 Memorial was Frank's idea. She wasn't keen. He remained firm.

The footprints of the two towers were immense, the walls deep, the pools at the bottom very far down. Looking over the edge, Greta felt an overwhelming sense of emptiness. She breathed it in, the void expanding within her. This was a record of reduction. Man sunk to his lowest.

She traced one of the names engraved on the bronze ledge. One life. Another. And another.

'My wife worked on the fifty-third floor.'

Frank's words swung into Greta like a body at the gallows. She opened her hands, lifted them, dropped them back down by her sides. She couldn't find suitable words.

He nodded. 'Yeah, life's a bitch.'

Suddenly Frank made sense. His pace. His candour. The occasional silhouette of sensitivity and emotion.

'I'm so sorry, Frank.'

'Simone had a soft spot for Walt,' he said, smiling. 'She was always happy to have him and Woody over for a meal.'

Woody? Who was Woody? But it would have been insensitive to switch focus.

'Simone. That's a lovely name.'

'French. She worked for the French Embassy.' His voice wavered. 'She was carrying our first child.'

Greta was felled by this further confidence. It felt too enormous for their very new friendship, and she entirely ill-equipped to receive it.

They sat down on a block of polished concrete. This time she didn't rush to fill the space.

She thought about the small child balancing on the tracks of the High Line and Frank hurrying irritably on. She thought about his reference to two soldiers trying to survive in the trenches, bonded by trauma.

Frank's posture slackened, his robustness melting. He looked smaller and vulnerable. She rested a hand on his. He didn't pull away.

The clamour and colour of the city receded. The sound of cascading water grew louder. Dappled light trickled through the trees.

The silence between them became easier. For the first time in so long Greta felt necessary and needed, and comfortable with her conduct. Perhaps her foreignness had given Frank the safety to share his most private grief with her.

As they looked across the concourse, she noticed one tree in the grove was different from the rest. It had darker foliage and an odd-shaped trunk with branches emerging from a disfigured, bulbous bit. A metal barrier surrounded the tree.

'What's special about that one?'

Frank looked up. 'It's a Callery Pear. We call it the Survivor Tree.'

'The Survivor Tree?'

'It was found in the rubble after 9/11, its roots ripped and limbs scorched. Bar one, that is. One branch was still intact. Someone took the tree to a nursery in the Bronx, where they nurtured it back to health. In 2010 it was replanted here again.'

Greta's skin prickled.

Frank smiled. An open generous smile. 'The best time to visit is April when it's covered in white blossom.'

'Please tell me more about Walter.' Time was running out. That evening they were going to see *Beautiful*, the Carole King musical on Broadway, and then the next day she'd be preparing to get on a plane. Her hands started to tremble. There was still so much she didn't know. Where was Walter's favourite restaurant? Who was Woody? What did Walter's office look like?

The sun moved across the sky, toying with the shadows. Some shrunk, others swelled, some simply slipped away. People came and went, and Greta and Frank spoke about the man whose friendship they'd both treasured.

On the way back to her hotel, Frank took her past Walter and Woody's former brownstone apartment in Greenwich Village. Though they couldn't go inside, Greta found herself imagining the two men climbing the short flight of stairs from the tree-lined avenue to their door with its shiny brass knocker. They'd just popped out to the bodega and were carrying groceries. Once inside, Walter appeared in the front room, lifting the large sash window to invite in a balmy afternoon. What was for dinner, Greta wondered? Walt's famous eggplant curry? Or perhaps it was Woody's turn to cook. Did their fingers fit when they held hands? Did their lips fit when they kissed?

Greta stood on the steps. Held the cool, wrought iron railing . . .

Back in her suite at the Carlyle, she sat on the sofa willing tears to come. They wouldn't. Her grief remained trapped in her chest.

In a way, she was relieved. The mind was clever how it protected itself from implosion. It would be safest to let the sadness leak out over time.

Finally, she picked up the bulky, brown envelope the concierge had handed to her at the front desk and slid her finger under the flap.

Inside, along with a typed itinerary from Angus and airline tickets, was another Walter envelope.

Greta
<u>*Food and Family*</u>

Family? The word jarred. Greta was the only Jellings left. An entry in Nora's diary on March 4th, 2006 erased all hope of Greta ever finding her father alive. Three words — *Victor died today* — had filled Greta with grief and anger. The loss of her father was finally complete, and Nora guilty as charged.

> *Cooking is like love. It should be entered into with abandon or*
> *not at all. — Harriet van Horne*

My dear Grets,
Time is up in New York. Pretty amazing place, hey?
That casual, chatty tone, as if Walter were sitting opposite her.
And yes, there is much, much more to see. But for your first visit, it's
probably enough.
For your first visit. There was a confidence in those words, a certainty that shrunk the gap between what was only for dreaming and what was still possible. One phrase was already lifting the curtain on a new view.
I hope Frank has been a good host. His bark is worse than his bite.
Does he still chain-suck those awful boiled sweets with a synthetic
grape flavour?
She laughed.
His drawers at work were filled with them. It used to drive me crazy
the way he crunched them. He's probably got a set of falsies by now.
Anyway, to your next destination . . .
Can you tell I'm enjoying this?
Next is a place to explore food and family.
That word again. Greta had no family. No parents. No partner. No child, or sibling, or cousin.
This destination is a thank you for every meal you've cooked for me,
the most challenging of patients.
She chewed the inside of her cheek.
Despite my illness forever changing the goalposts, you've remained
undeterred. Though the drugs play noughts and crosses with my appetite
and tamper with my tastebuds, still you fill my bowls and stock my fridge.
One day I love lemons, the next I can't abide them, yet you never give in.

155

A tear spilt onto her cheek.

*And let me tell you, your food never seems like invalid's fare,
not even the broths and custards. Not when served on Nora's fine bone
china. There's something about eating jelly set in a proper mould,
and drinking freshly squeezed orange juice from a thin-rimmed glass.
Thank you.*

The print blurred as Walter's words filled holes in Greta's heart.

*By the way, that liquorice sorbet (I know I only managed a mouthful)
was pure joy on a day when everything else felt furry and smelt of
sadness. I felt like a prince when the rest of the world was treating me
like a pauper.*

So much had changed, thought Greta, and yet still the stigma stayed.
Those infected with HIV remained lepers of the western world, even if
the ostracism was more carefully camouflaged. Behind closed doors souls
were still cast out, sheets burned, and handshakes scrubbed and scrubbed.
Fear was such a rampant, indiscriminate weed.

The irony was that Walter didn't die from the virus. Miraculous new
medicines had kept it quiescent. For him, and many others, it became a
chronic condition, not a death sentence.

In the end it was liver cancer which they stamped on his exit pass,
the incidence apparently higher in those infected with the virus.

*So now it's your chance to cook, Grets. With abandon. (I was going to
say gay abandon. Ha!)*

*Anyway, I want you to cook not for something, or someone, but just
because. I've asked Angus to book you in to a couple of classes at a top
London cooking school.*

A cooking school! London!

Greta clapped her hands.

Now, as they say, 'food tastes better when you eat it with family'.

That word again, standing in relief to her orphanness.

*I remember you telling me that once, when you were very young, Nora
alluded to having a sister.*

Greta's heart whooped and dived. She could remember it well — being
held up in comparison to imaginary cousins.

'*You can be sure my sister's children would never give her the grief you
give me, Greta Jellings.*'

'*You don't even have a sister.*'

Nora's face colours and contorts, leaving Greta both thrilled and devastated by the effectiveness of her jibe.

She isn't smacked, or even sent to her bedroom. Her mother just walks out in a daze, back to her sewing room. And with each whirring hour Greta hates herself a little bit more.

I can confirm, God still willing, that thanks to Angus's incredible detective work, Nora did indeed have a sister, who is alive and well and living in a rest home in Kent. Enclosed are her details if you would like to make contact with her.

Greta stared at the paper, incredulous. How many surprises could one person cope with?

'I have an aunt?' she whispered after a time. 'I have an aunt.'

Aunt was such an odd-sounding word, as if part of it had been amputated. It evoked images of austerity, spinsterhood, funereal-black. Yet now, looking at it on the page, Greta thought it was the most beautiful word she'd ever seen.

She held the letter to her chest. 'Thank you, Walter.'

Suddenly, waiting twenty-four hours to catch the next plane felt far too long.

CHAPTER 26

Greta got little sleep that last night in New York. She was buzzing from the heart-bursting happiness of Carole King's music, the colour and energy of Times Square, the knowledge that she and her aunt formed a family.

She looked back into her hotel suite one last time, then pulled the door closed.

Carmila was in the corridor, hidden behind the linen trolley.

Greta lunged forward and kissed her on the cheek.

The maid stood very still, hands by her side, her eyes wide.

Greta decided to kiss her other cheek too, to make it look more like a European goodbye. But as Greta leant forward, Carmila leant back. Then Carmila leant forward, and Greta back.

'I am going to miss you,' Greta said, her face hot, her thoughts scrambled. 'You've completely ruined me. I mean, who's going to leave chocolates beside my pillow now?'

Carmila pulled her apron straight. 'You come back to Carlyle, yes?'

Greta shrugged. 'You never know.'

'You can get for me autograph for Russell Crowe?'

'Russell Crowe?'

'Ho, he very sexy man, no?' Carmila moved her eyebrows up and down. 'You can send to Carmila Martinez, c/o Carlyle.'

'But Russell Crowe lives in Australia. That's not my country. The two should never be confused. New Zealand is here,' Greta said pointing to an imaginary map on the wall, 'and Australia here. Very different. See. This country has snakes and spiders. Dangerous. New Zealand, none of that. We also created the pavlova, although the Australians say otherwise.'

Carmila was mouthing Greta's rapid words.

'What say I send you a picture of Sam Neill instead?'

158

Carmila's face dropped. 'Sameal? I not know him.'

'Look, he's a different sort of handsome,' Greta said. 'Quite lean and rangy, but with a great sense of humour. He was in a movie called *Hunt for the Wilderpeople*. A fantastic film, if you get a chance to see it. There's this bit where the kid says *Shit just got real*.'

Greta blushed. Even though she was repeating a line from the film, it felt awkward to use a profanity. 'Excuse my French, but it was such a funny mo—'

Carmila was fidgeting.

'I'd better get going,' Greta said quickly. She cast her eye longingly at the linen trolley — there was an entire tray of chocolate boxes on the top shelf.

'One thing I've been meaning to ask you all week,' she said as she eyed the sheets and towels one shelf down. 'You keep leaving a white napkin on the floor beside my bed at turndown service. I don't understand.'

Carmila frowned as she processed Greta's words, then she let out a roaring smoker's cackle. She pulled a hanky out of her bra and wiped her eyes.

'Is so the madam not have to put her foot on the carpet when she get out of bed.'

Greta shook her head in disbelief. The habits of the rich and famous.

She was delighted that it was Noah on duty for her final elevator ride. He was standing in his usual position, soldier straight, face centimetres from the control panel. His constancy had been a comfort and anchor in the craziness of her week in New York. The bookends to her days. All of a sudden she wanted to stay in this safe space forever. She didn't want the doors to open on a new unknown.

One last elevator ride with Noah in a week that had been full of firsts. The last time she'd see this kindly man, who'd help solve her lifelong shoe problem. Their lives had brushed briefly against one another and her orbit had surely been altered as a result.

'Noah' she said, her voice losing its volume. 'It's only because of you that, for the first time in my life, I'm wearing such stylish shoes!'

Her vision blurred as she admired her red platforms.

'I can't really explain what this means to me. All I can say is thank you. Thank you so very much.'

He turned his head almost imperceptibly to the right, and she saw that a smile had softened his serious expression.

'Why, it's been my absolute pleasure, ma'am.'

In that moment Greta could have kissed him.

But then her imagination took over. Noah gulping in horror. Pressing the alarm. Security waiting to frogmarch her from the building as cameras flashed. And Noah, blameless in this all, fired on the spot . . .

The lift doors opened. Greta hurried out. Turned. Blushed. Gave Noah a little wave. Then headed over to Reception.

The woman at the front desk took Greta's key card, proffering a perfect smile — not too warm, not too cool, just right.

'Your taxi should be here shortly,' she said. 'If you'd like to take a seat in the lobby, I'll notify you when it arrives.'

Greta started towards the mustard couch, then stopped. Was she a man or mouse? Worse still, was she an insect? (That word was still hanging around in her head.) She turned back to the counter. She would not rest easy if she didn't. This was her last chance.

She held a finger up in the air. 'One thing,' she said, her voice starting to quiver. 'Could you please pass on a message to Management for me?'

A man glanced up from his computer at the other end of the counter.

Greta twisted a strand of hair around her finger.

'In this day and age, demanding such a rigid code of behaviour from your elevator staff reflects rather badly on your hotel.' She gulped. 'There is surely no need for the operators to stand with their faces pressed to the lift wall, in order, I'm assuming, to make themselves less obtrusive.'

Her voice hit a squeak-high note. She knew her face would be schoolgirl red.

'Permitting staff to engage with patrons in a more informal manner would not erode standards.' She was on a roll. 'But rather, afford them the dignity they deserve, irrespective of their station in life. This is the twenty-first century after all.'

The two people behind the desk stared, their mouths agape.

'Anyway,' Greta said quickly, with a weak smile. 'Thanks again for a lovely stay.'

As she turned to walk away, her heels spun on the highly polished floor, making her exit more dramatic than she'd intended. It was however, supremely satisfying to act in synchrony with her heart. To call something out and not endorse it with silence.

Her heart was still thumping in her chest as she made her way outside to wait for the taxi. She could not sit on the mustard couch now. It was one thing to speak her mind, quite another to retain composure in the wake of it.

She felt both pleased with herself and churned. She hated making a scene. Hated the thought of anyone disliking her. The Carlyle was a truly wonderful hotel. However, someone needed to challenge the relics of colonial conduct.

She looked at her watch, a familiar loop of disquiet lassoing her. Frank was late and her taxi was due any minute. Where on earth was he?

She scanned the street in both directions. She could not possibly leave without saying goodbye, yet neither could she risk missing her flight.

A yellow cab turned into the street, slowed, and pulled up beside the kerb. The doorman leant forward to open the back door.

'JFK,' he said to the driver.

Greta cast a frantic last glance up the street. There, about a block away, was Frank.

She waved wildly and tapped her watch.

'You leaving already?' he said, out of breath by the time he reached her. 'Your flight's only this evening.'

'I have to be at the airport at least three hours before departure for security checks. And it's important to leave a buffer for unexpected eventualities. Anyway, you said you'd be here an hour ago.'

'I got waylaid at work. We've still got time for a coffee.'

'I don't like to rush, Frank, I'm so sorr—' She stopped herself. No apologies.

He smiled. 'I guess this is goodbye then.'

Greta's throat prickled. It had been a week like no other, a week she could not pin down with words. The city had lent an authenticity and congruency to Walter's biography. And, in its daring brashness and boldness, had afforded her the opportunity to risk reinventing herself.

Frank stretched out a hand. She wanted to pull him into a jumper-warm hug, but that wasn't him. Maybe it never had been, or perhaps he'd ring-fenced his vulnerability some years back.

He handed her a small brown paper bag and a folder. 'For the plane.'

She peered into the folder. It was full of photographs.

'Photos of some of the warehouse conversions Walt did. It'll give you an idea of how talented he was.'

'Oh, Frank!' The rustic beams, floating staircases, skylights, exposed brick walls . . .

'Look at them for the plane. You'll have more time.'

As the taxi pulled away from the kerb, Greta peered into the brown paper bag.

Inside was a handful of boiled sweets. Giant, grape-purple gobstoppers.

CHAPTER 27

The flight to London was uneventful. Greta now knew what to expect. The entertainment system, meals, take-off, the toilet. She was surprised by how familiar it all felt already.

She thought back to a therapy session where she'd bemoaned her lack of sophistication and worldliness.

'Sometimes I feel like a naïve fool.'

'Worldliness is only an experience away,' Judy had counselled. *'There's no magic to it. Trainee surgeons have a mantra: See one, do one, teach one. It can be that easy.'*

Yes, Greta thought. Perhaps it can.

Her first impressions of London were through a Caribbean cabbie's eyes.

'*When a man is tired of London, he's tired of life.* Not my words, love. Some famous fella's.'

Greta was struggling to make the shift in accent, attitude, and setting. Once upon a time a person would have travelled between continents by boat, the passage taking three to four weeks, the time affording an opportunity to round off the old and prepare for the new. Yet only eight hours earlier she'd been in America. New York was still a fray of loose ribbons flapping in her mind. She was being driven past Piccadilly Circus, but her head was still in Times Square.

It was Woody she couldn't get out of her mind. Here she was calling him by name as if she'd actually known him, as if she'd met Walter's longstanding lover. Yet Frank's words had been so vivid, his descriptions so detailed, she felt as if she'd watched Walter and Woody's New York life together unfold in front of her.

She ached imagining what the men had gone through when, eighteen months into their relationship, Woody had succumbed to meningitis.

That would have been frightening enough, but then, in amongst the spinal-fluid microscopy, renal function tests, blood gases and full blood count, another result. HIV-positive.

'AIDS was an unknown quantity,' Frank had told her, as they sat in the sun at the Ground Zero memorial. 'With cases multiplying at a plague-terrifying rate, it was a time of mass hysteria. Moral outrage. Ostracism. Those in government turned a blind eye. "They brought this on themselves." "The Lord's condemnation." "A disease sent to right the moral wrongs." You can just imagine.'

He told her how some doctors and nurses even refused to treat the infected. 'Dying men were deserted in hospital beds, their food trays dropped at the door.'

Greta couldn't fathom that. Medicine was meant to be above prejudice.

'The mentality was simply to keep apart and contain, not find a cure. It was only when the gay community started educating itself about the baffling disease that research was finally forced forward.'

And to think she'd believed that those in science and medicine worked for the greater good of all. Ha!

'April 19, 1987 changed the world's perception of HIV forever,' Frank continued. 'You were barely out of nappies.'

Greta does the math. 'I was nine,' she says a little indignantly. For once she wants to be thought of as older.

'It was the day Princess Diana shook hands with an AIDS patient.' Frank paused. 'She wasn't even wearing gloves. Can you imagine? A member of the British royal family no less, making skin contact with the dreaded disease. It was unimaginable, the impact of that handshake. Changed things for all the Woodys and Walters of the world.'

As grateful as Greta was for Frank's revelations, his rationalisations about why Walter had not shared significant bits of his biography with her still did not fully appease. She couldn't move beyond the hurt of having been denied his story in his own words. Friend to trusted friend.

'Bloody kids done this,' the London cabbie said, popping Greta back into Britain. He was pointing to a vandalised bus stop, shattered glass scattered over the pavement. 'Back in the day they'd have had their arses whipped. Now they just get a slap on the wrist with a wet bus ticket.'

Greta gazed out the window.

London looked different. Felt different. The shiny black cabs, rosy-cheeked buses, the soft hues of sandstone. Even the dawn was a more polite pink. If New York was the cabaret girl, then London was the lady.

Greta felt a dull ache in her belly. She missed the blue-grey-greens of Auckland. The ocean. The morning mist. She missed the familiarity of road signs. Takapuna. Belmont. Browns Bay. The casualness of class. The newsreaders on Breakfast TV . . . She had never credited her country with having any particular defining characteristics. In fact, she'd never really queried the maps that positioned New Zealand at the bottom of the world, or, worse still, left it off altogether. Yet now, sitting in the back of a London cab, she recognised for the first time the uniqueness of her small country. New Zealand's quirkiness was a treasure. A treasure she was hankering for.

Greta often wondered why Walter had come back to New Zealand after living for so long in New York. When they'd first met, he'd been back just a few months, though had remained vague about his reasons for returning. Now she knew more.

'*Woody succumbed to full-blown AIDS eight years after he was diagnosed. By this time, Walt was HIV-positive too. Fortunately for him, though, he had time on his side. The virus, unlike in Woody's case, remained quiescent long enough for him to see new treatments developed.*

It was only when Walter was diagnosed with liver cancer in 2012, some twenty-seven years after landing in New York, that his homing instinct kicked in.'

Was that the natural circle of life, Greta wondered? To return to the start in preparation for the end.

'Where's home for you?' Greta asked Baba Achong, reading the taxi-driver's identification card displayed on the dashboard.

'London, love.'

Greta's face felt instantly hot. 'Sorry, what I meant was—'

The driver chuckled. 'I know. I know. I don't look like no Londoner.'

'It's just . . . your complexion—' She stopped; she could feel herself heading into excruciating territory. 'I'm sorry, what I meant—'

'Don't mind me, love,' said the cabbie, winking at her in his rear-view mirror. 'Just taking the piss. To answer your question, I hail from tropical Trinidad.'

Greta nodded vigorously.

'Do you miss it?'

'I been back. Had a damn fine holiday there too. Where you born is always home, right? But it's not all sunshine and cocktails; there are a hell of a lot of people there with nothing but an empty belly. Anyway, no point looking back. Don't have no reverse gear.' He gave a hearty chuckle.

Greta couldn't imagine moving countries. A holiday was hard enough.

'I got mates whose old folk moved here sixty-odd years back, when it was no fun to be dark-skinned, I can tell you.' He rubbed his left ear. The top third was missing. Greta visualised a gruesome scene involving balaclava-clad men, dingy alleyways and a rusty razor blade.

'But they survived. Had to. No point living in remember-when land. You gotta make your own nirvana.'

Baba pointed out a chateau-style building. 'They do a damn fine high tea at the Ritz. Something special, I can tell you.'

Greta was relieved she was not staying there. Her small hotel, just around the corner, was much less ostentatious. That the carpets were a tad tired and the wooden counters worn pleased her. The realness of it. As much as she'd enjoyed her stay in New York, the perfection and opulence of The Carlyle had left Greta a little on edge. She was more at ease in a place that had flaws.

She collapsed onto the bed. Her body clock was completely confused. New York was sixteen hours behind Auckland, London five hours in front of New York. And she hadn't slept a wink on the flight over.

She drew the curtains. The bedside lamp cast a grey glow over what would be her home for the next ten days. Bed, mirror, telephone, TV, faux-leather folder, tea-box, kettle. Thank goodness for the tea-worshipping British.

According to Angus's instructions, she'd be on her own in London. No Frank to hold her hand, just the names of people to call on if she got into trouble.

She looked in the mirror. The space between her eyebrows was puckered and her mouth pulled tight. Her New-York-acquired confidence had apparently been just one-layer thick and was already lifting at the corners.

She made herself a cup of camomile tea, then climbed into bed, sleep dropping over her like a blackout blind.

She awoke hours later, her right arm numb and her pillow damp with drool, sharp white light slicing the brown drapes in two. London was clamouring for her attention.

She rolled over.

If she kept the curtains closed, the day's seal would remain unbroken. It was the thought of the effort required to push through the foreignness once again. She didn't know if she had it in her.

She gave an odd barking whimper and pulled the blankets over her head. But crying without a witness felt rather futile.

It wasn't as if she was not used to being on her own. Her existence in Auckland was largely solitary. But there, the familiarity of life served as a sort of friend — her home, Marilyn Monroe, the routine of her job. Stripped of these, and in a strange city, the absences were overwhelming. She was lonely.

Lonely. That word made her feel like defective goods.

She shut her eyes and drifted back to sleep, her dreams tangling with the fug of sporadic wakefulness. Mice scurrying up a skyscraper. A tsunami of shoes — sequined stilettoes, pink clogs, Lilliputian slippers. A cabaret of drag queens singing too softly. Louder! Brochures for the London Eye, Madam Tussauds and Buckingham Palace raining down from the sky. Nora. *I told you so, Greta.'* And Victor, his image confoundingly clear — his fine nose, freckles (she used to count them as a kid), his cola-dark eyes, broad hands, beautifully-kept fingernails. It had been decades since she'd seen her father so clearly.

By late that afternoon Greta had eaten everything in the minibar — the chocolate bars, crisps, nuts and packets of processed cheese. It was the first time she'd ever let herself go like this. But it was when she started to unscrew the second dinky bottle of sauvignon blanc that she knew a monster had escaped its box.

'If you ever find yourself feeling really low, pick up the phone and call someone,' Judy had once advised.

Who could she call? And what would she say? She was on an all-expenses-paid holiday. So, she was a little bit homesick. Not even she could feel sorry for herself.

However, if she were honest, something much bigger was bothering her. Something more than a mere pang of homesickness. It was the realisation that she could at any time call a halt to this fanciful experiment and go home. Angus had been very clear that there was *always an out available.*

167

It was this that frightened her. The temptation to restore the status quo and return to a life that was safe and certain.

She'd already searched for flights online; there was an Air NZ flight leaving the next day. All she had to do was let Angus know and he'd make it happen. That simple.

Things would be a bit different for a while. She'd have to find a new place to rent. A new job too. Though there was the possibility Jud would take her back. She'd be willing to job-share with Sandra if she had to.

People might look at her askance for a time, but it would surely come as no great surprise that she hadn't had the metal to see the trip out.

She dialled Angus.

No reply.

She dialled again. And again. She had to talk to someone.

Should she try Frank, she wondered? Her time with him had been short. Too short to now burden him with the responsibilities of friendship.

Lorraine and Rory maybe? Lorraine would listen. It was just that Greta felt oddly distanced from her former neighbour. She'd hoped her friend would have made more of an effort to keep in touch after their move. Of course, she and Rory had been busy with their new house, and then their holiday in Hawaii . . .

There was Judy. But she was paid to listen. And she never picked up during consultation hours.

Holly? Greta had known Holly for less than ten weeks before leaving on the trip. She wasn't even her neighbour any longer. Some stranger was now living in Greta's house, paying Valenka rent, fiddling with the temperamental stove, picking the huge lemons in the backyard and using Greta's spa. Greta grimaced at the thought of some other person's heat-pinked body immersed in her pristine waters.

What's more, Holly was over a decade Greta's junior and very hip. On paper a long-term friendship looked unlikely. And yet, Greta had felt the skeins of something meaningful draw around them in the weeks before her departure.

She picked up the phone and dialled.

A crackling pause was followed by a trill of beeps, then ringing.

'*Hi—*'

Greta clenched her toes.

'—*you've reached Holly's house. Sorry I can't come to the phone. Please leave your name and number*—'

As she listened to Holly's bright voice, she was visualising the answer machine sitting on the narrow console table in the hallway.

'—*after the beep and I'll get back to you as soon as I can.*'

'Uh, hi Holly . . . it's Greta. I . . . sorry.' She hated talking to machines — her foolish fumbles on record. 'I'm no good with answer-phones. Ha! Always feel so stupid. But look, I know they're practical and stuff like that. So, it's not a criticism. Just . . . anyway . . . look I was calling to see how Marilyn Monroe was. My chicken. Of course you know who Marilyn Monroe is, stupid! Me, that is. I mean, I'm stupid. Anyway, look, I was wondering whether you'd heard from Donna about how—'

'Helloo?' A sleep-creased voice.

Greta paused, perplexed.

'Hello?'

It was Holly. She sounded groggy.

Greta's mouth went dry. She had not given any thought to the time difference. She should hang up immediately. But the idea of being alone again with just her thoughts for company kept her holding on. 'I'm so sorry. I've woken you, haven't I?'

'Greta? Is that you? Where are you?'

'I feel terrible. Hang up. I can call another time.'

'It's fine. Fine. Is everythi— all right?' It was a bad line. 'Are you still in —York?'

York?

Greta put a hand to her mouth as a missing piece of puzzle fell into place. She was back behind the feijoa bush, inspecting the smudged postmark of the envelope in her hands. The one from York.

Had her father been sending her letters, not from York, but New York?

Greta tried to steady her voice. 'I'm in London now.'

'London! Ooh, I'm so envious.'

'Is Marilyn Monroe alright?'

'Yes. Yes. I spoke with Donna a couple of days ago. She's apparently one happy hen. Don't give her a second thought. She didn't eat much the first few days, but has settled into farm life and is being lavished with attention. Apparently she loves marshmallows. Pink ones in particular.'

169

Greta closed her eyes. Marilyn Monroe was fine. She wanted her to be fine. Though a small part of her also wanted her hen to be pining for her. What if Marilyn Monroe preferred Donna?

'How's the trip going?' Holly asked, stifling a yawn.

'Oh, great. You know. Really great. New York was amazing, and now I'm in London and—' Tears spilled onto Greta's cheeks.

'Grets, you okay?'

'Oh yes, yes. Sorry. I've just got a bit of a cold. I feel so bad having woken you. Please go back to sleep.'

'Poor you. Hey, I keep thinking how brave you are riding off into the sunset all on your own, no idea where you're headed. You rock, girl.'

Brave. That was the last thing Greta was. She felt like a fraud.

She blew her nose.

'I've told everyone in my office your amazing story.'

Greta felt a twist of anxiety. People knowing about her. Strangers. Thinking she was something she was not. *'If people only knew what you were really like.'* Nora's words rung in her ears.

'We all wish Walter had been our friend too.' A Holly laugh, warm and bubbly. 'Hey,' she said in a loud whisper. 'You won't believe our new neighbour. A crusty old guy who sells stamps on the Internet. He's as sour as a mouthful of vinegar and hasn't mown the lawn since you left.'

Greta smiled.

'When you've finished gallivanting, perhaps we can stage a coup and get you back next door.'

'That would be . . . would be . . . yes! I'd like that. Look I better go. I'm really sorry for disturbing you.'

'Send an email,' said Holly, her energy and vigour rushing down the line. 'Or a postcard, if that's easier.'

'One thing,' Greta said quickly. 'Don't let Donna give Marilyn Monroe any more marshmallows. They can't be good for her. She might choke.'

Afterwards, Greta replayed the conversation over and over in her head. Then she got up and pulled open the heavy brown drapes. The evening sky was a glorious whorl of mauve.

CHAPTER 28

As a child Greta hated kippers — the hair-thin bones, slippery skin, their sunbed-orange colour. Not to mention the smell that permeated Nora's kitchen for hours after breakfast. Only one thing was worse — the tripe her mother boiled up once a year.

'It might be considered poor man's food, but cooked correctly, with onions, is better than any restaurant fare.'

Greta wasn't sure how Nora knew that because they never went to restaurants.

Smell aside, it was the little facecloth filaments of flesh that did it. Greta only lifted the lid on her mother's tripe pot once.

Ha! And here she was, years later, sitting in a sunny breakfast conservatory in London eating kippers and savouring the salty fillets between bites of buttered brown toast and mouthfuls of tea. That Nora had hailed from Britain made perfect sense. Eating the meal felt familiar. Funny, how food could do that. Hold in its flavours the DNA of a childhood, a person, a nation.

Seated one table along from Greta, and separated from her by a planter box, was a large woman with heavily pencilled eyebrows and a helmet of fluoro-pink hair. Her stubby fingers were bedecked with rings.

She caught Greta's eye through the fern fronds.

'Sun's shining,' she said in a jazz-deep voice. 'Too bad for those of us who have to spend the day indoors working.'

Greta lifted her palms to the sky. 'I know.'

Why had she said that? It implied she was also going to be indoors all day.

'So, it's work for you too then?' said the woman.

Greta nodded half-heartedly. She had to. Otherwise she'd have made a lie of her first comment.

'I'm at a conference all week,' said the woman with a sigh. 'But I'm taking Friday off, come hell or high water. Going to find myself a beach and soak up some of this sunshine.'

Greta smiled in support. The woman had the paleness of someone who spent too much time indoors, a serpent tattoo disappearing down her very white cleavage.

'Do you—' the woman began.

'What's your conference about?' Greta interrupted, anxious to avoid being quizzed about her fictitious commitments.

The woman took a mouthful of Danish pastry. 'Advances in embalming techniques.'

Greta lowered her fork.

'Annual Morticians and Undertakers Conference.'

Greta pushed the last piece of kipper to the side of her plate and put her knife and fork together.

'We're meant to alternate who attends, but this is my fifth year in a row. The boss is always too busy to attend herself. That's what she says. Me, I think there's something else going on. Agoraphobia. Enochlophobia. Maybe panophobia. Otherwise she's just been dealing with the dead for too long.'

Greta shifted in her seat.

'And you?' asked the woman.

Greta wiped her mouth with the thick linen serviette.

'What line of work are you in?'

'Oh, nothing as exotic,' she mumbled. The woman clearly knew a lot about phobias and was probably analysing Greta as they spoke.

Greta pushed back her chair. 'Sorry. I'd better be getting on or I'm going to be late.'

The woman gave a boisterous laugh. 'The mention of morticians. A guaranteed conversation killer.'

Greta felt herself blush. 'No, no.' She hovered behind her chair. 'It's just that I have to be somewhere by—' She looked at her watch for a clue. 'By nine-thirty.'

The woman gave a knowing smile. She had a gold crown on one of her eyeteeth. She stretched a stubby arm through the fern fronds. 'Muriel. Muriel Maloney.'

Greta shook the woman's hand, but did not proffer her name.

An hour later she was on a train to Kent.

She'd rung the rest home the previous evening to confirm that Elma Bird was indeed still a resident there. The nurse who answered put her on hold for a very long time, during which Greta's hopes had looped and dived. Eventually, someone else came on the line and explained the confusion. Elma was a resident, however most staff knew her as Mimi.

Relieved that she had not been robbed of her only family member before even meeting her, Greta planned the route to the rest home, packed a small daypack, and laid out her striped blouse and fitted green skirt for the morning. She'd wear walking shoes for the train, but carry the slingbacks in her daypack. It was important to make a good first impression. Life was not a rehearsal.

Catching the underground proved as trying as it had in New York — tides of humans, precipice-steep escalators, icy tunnels. However, her anxiety felt a little less acute than it had in America. She survived two line changes and the hugeness of Charing Cross Station.

One minute, blackness was rushing past her window; the next, the train had burst into the day. Rusted metal pipes, broken bricks and derelict warehouses interposed themselves between her and the summer blue sky. A woman in a red dressing gown was sitting in a wheelbarrow in her allotment, smoking a cigarette. Two boys teetered on a bicycle, the smaller one balancing on the handlebars. A yellow dog lay in a death-distorted pose beside the tracks.

As the tatty outskirts of the city receded, the scenery started to change. Greta's window captured green fields, hedgerows, stonewalls and steeples. Trees splayed cosmic shafts of sunlight. A blue tit perched on a power line. A lake reflected the black and white geometry of a Tudor home. And gradually, the angst she'd felt in the city started to fade.

She was dozing when she heard the approaching refreshment trolley. Her brain was tuned to tea, like Captain Haddock's to whisky.

She'd have a cup of Earl Grey please, and a slice of fruitcake.

'Where you from?' asked the bespectacled young man, as he poured boiling water into a Styrofoam cup.

'New Zealand.'

'Great accent.'

Greta felt herself flush. She'd never thought of her accent as great before. Other accents always sounded more interesting and alluring. She couldn't even discern her own.

'Where you headed?'

'Sevenoaks.'

'Excellent place,' he said, with the air of an English aristocrat. 'Dates back to the thirteenth century.'

'The thirteenth century!' There was a safety in that sort of history, humans enduring through the ages.

'The oaks still exist, though they're not the originals.'

The fellow sounded disconcertingly learned for someone serving tea on a train.

He passed her a cup, the teabag still floating inside. Nothing annoyed Greta more. Leaving the bag in meant the tea would stew, but if she tried to fish it out, she'd burn her fingers and be left with a soggy sack of tealeaves to get rid of.

'Thanks to a massive storm and vandals, the trees have been replaced a fair few times,' continued the boy, oblivious to her conundrum. 'There are now eight oaks bordering the Vine cricket grounds. I guess the additional one is future-proofing.'

'So, I'm actually headed for Eightoaks?' Greta said, with a giggle.

The boy looked at her, his face deadpan.

She shifted in her seat. 'You know, because there are now eight oak trees, so they can't really call it Seven . . .' She petered out.

He handed her a slice of fruitcake wrapped in cling film. She'd had her eye on a different piece — one with more glacé cherries — however, didn't feel she could ask to swap.

'You know a lot about the place,' she said, trying to revive their conversation.

'Any food or beverages?' the boy asked a couple across the aisle.

Greta wondered what she could have done differently. Conversations could be unfathomably hard.

The fruitcake was a little on the dry side, though still satisfying when washed down with milky tea.

Doors sprung open in her head.

She is sitting at the kitchen table, a glass of milk and wedge of fruitcake in front of her.

Nora baked a fruitcake every Sunday evening and stored it for the week in the dented Dairy Milk tin. The number of sewing jobs the previous week determined how much fruit made it into the cake. Some weeks, only raisins speckled the loaf. Other times, there were sultanas and glacé cherries too. Regardless, there was always a slice of cake waiting for Greta when she got home from school.

She eats alone in the kitchen, before seeking out her mother in the sewing room at the end of the passage — the room that buzzes and whirrs, and is home to a scary, bald mannequin.

There she finds Nora bent over her Singer sewing machine, forcing fabric into the path of the furious needle.

'Hello Greta. You had a good day?' she asks, a pin between her teeth.

This gives Greta the heebie-jeebies. What if her mother coughs or sneezes and accidentally swallows the pin?

'Made any new friends?'

Greta shrugs.

She lingers for a few long minutes before escaping the unpleasant little room where crumbs and muddy shoes and boisterous girls are forbidden.

As the train swayed from side to side, Greta reflected on those afternoons. Was her mother's daily gesture more than mere nourishment? Perhaps, in a world where love had been so fickle for Nora, the constancy of cake was her way of saying to Greta what she couldn't articulate out loud.

This was a bittersweet epiphany.

Sevenoaks was a quaint town with cobbled streets, redbrick buildings, dormer windows and shingle rooves. Petunias tumbled from lamppost baskets; pub patrons lounged in sunny courtyards; a bakery window boasted Sally Lunns, Jammie Dodgers, and meringues the size of cricket balls. There were Eccles cakes too. Eccles cakes! Greta bought two to take to her aunt.

She had an aunt! For most of the morning she'd been focused on getting to her destination, but now, as she followed the stationmaster's directions to the rest home — *'Just a ten minute walk, love'* — fresh worries gnawed at her. More than meeting a new family member, she would be meeting Nora's sister.

She turned into a tree-lined avenue and scanned the dwellings for a building resembling a rest home. She hated the term. To rest was an appealing pastime only because it was so elusive. But to find yourself in a home where that was all that was on offer . . .

Greta had fought hard to keep her mother at home. However, Nora's midnight wanderings, stovetop fires and unlicensed escapades onto State Highway 1 had finally forced her hand.

She stopped in the street. Shut her eyes. Tried to imagine a peaceful garden, trickling stream, daisy-dotted lawn. However, panic kept intruding. She opened her eyes, swung around, and started to walk back in the direction of the station.

Her relationship with Nora had been complicated. Even more so since Nora had passed. Greta now swung between love for her late mother and violent eruptions of resentment. Her newly discovered aunt would no doubt cast Nora in a new light, and Greta wasn't sure she could cope with any more surprises. Her mother's diary had been enough. In the wake of Frank's revelations about Walter, there seemed to be fewer and fewer certainties against which Greta could stake her life.

She hadn't known until a few days ago that Elma Bird even existed. Perhaps she should leave it that way. Walter might have meant well, but what did he really know? He'd been estranged from his own parents. Just because he'd tracked her aunt down didn't mean she was obliged to meet her. What would be the result of one random meeting anyway, other than to unsettle everyone involved? Nora had told Greta nothing about her sister; she must have had her reasons. To meet Elma now would feel like going behind her mother's back.

'Here again so soon?' said the stationmaster, a gaunt man with spikes of grey hair poking out from under his hat.

'Oh, she wasn't . . . I mean . . . she was there, but asleep.' Greta said, dragging one of her shoes back and forth, trying to rid it of a blob of chewing gum. 'She'd just taken her medication. Makes her very drowsy. A side-effect, you know. An unwanted side-effect.' She was a terrible fibber. 'But thank you for your directions. Spot on. I found the place no trouble at all. You must know the town like the back of your hand.'

She sat down on the bench.

'That's a silly expression, isn't it?' she continued, unable to halt the verbal deluge. 'I mean I don't know if I'd recognise the back of my hand at an identity parade.' She started to visualise a line-up of severed hands.

The man sat down beside her. His sleeve cuffs were fraying and yellowed, and his fingernails beaked. He smelt of fermenting apples.

'My Mavis lives there.'

Greta turned.

'This year will be our forty-ninth wedding anniversary.'

'Forty-ninth!'

Somehow, congratulations didn't feel appropriate, but Greta couldn't think of what else to say.

'Thank you,' he said, with a gentle nod. He looked across the tracks, his eyes traversing some other scene.

Greta fumbled in her bag for her train ticket.

'She was a whiz at arm wrestling, my Mavis. Used to beat me every time.' He rubbed his arm as if he'd just lost a round to her. 'Not now, of course.' He turned his head away, pushing a finger into the corner of his eye.

Greta wished she could think of something comforting and meaningful to say.

'A pretty dangerous pastime, arm-wrestling,' she said. 'I've heard of people breaking bones and wrenching tendons.'

The man chuckled. 'That's what I loved . . . what I *love* about her. She's no pussy.'

Greta felt ticked off and entirely inadequate when measured against Mavis.

An approaching train rescued her.

The stationmaster stood up quickly, straightened his jacket, and like a soldier called to the line, put a trembling hand to his hat to greet the train driver.

CHAPTER 29

The train trip had been less than an hour each way, and yet by the time Greta disembarked at Charing Cross, she felt more drained than she had after any long-haul flight. She imagined members of a football team might feel the same way pulling into their home station after an unsuccessful bid at the world title. Flat. Disconsolate. Weary. On a day which had held so much promise.

At least players would have each other. Greta had no one with whom to share the heaviness in her head. She was the team. The goalkeeper, sweeper, midfielder, defender . . .

People were meant to be with others. Even the elderly stationmaster defined himself by his significant other. There was power in the plural — the couple, the family, the team, the town. Shared decisions, shared grief, shared joys and burdens. The worst thing about navigating the world solo was all the second-guessing. The knot of conversations in her head. The magnifying glass held too close.

She was not a recluse by choice. On the contrary, she longed to be with others; it was just that her awkwardness always got in the way, and so it became easier to simply retreat.

On occasion, when she did find herself with the opportunity to forge a connection, she was so out of practice that her ineptitude was even more pronounced. Catch-22.

And with Walter . . . well, with Walter it had been different. But he was one of a kind. Someone who'd been able to see beyond her fumbling foolishness. Someone who could put her at ease by just being himself.

'Well, it's easy to be Walter around you.'

He'd said that to her the day before he died. She'd put it down to him being confused. It implied that in some way she had helped him, when really it was the reverse.

178

Greta picked up the phone and rang room service, ordering a corned-beef sandwich.

She was annoyed with herself. She knew she should have pushed past her fears and met her aunt. But it was easier to be brave from a distance.

Her food arrived forty-five minutes later, sans silver cloche.

After a few mouthfuls, she pushed the plate aside and climbed into bed. She didn't even bother to remove her makeup or brush her teeth, despite knowing full well the detrimental impact this would have on both her complexion and dentition.

'Today you will learn to make pasta like an Italian person make pasta.'

Greta stood behind her stainless-steel bench and hoped she would not make a monkey of herself. It wasn't that she couldn't cook. She could! Walter's letter attested to her skill. It was the fact that she'd been paired with a cooking partner. Greta hated team activities. It was one thing to fail on her own, quite another to drag someone down with her.

'Hiya, I'm Brigid,' said the woman sharing Greta's bench.

Brigid, who looked about thirty, was dressed in fitted slacks and a long-sleeved silk blouse buttoned to the neck, despite the heat. Her hair was shiny, her perfume smelt expensive and her nails were carefully manicured.

Greta gave a tight wave.

It felt wrong to wave. They were standing too close.

'Welcome everyone!' said the instructor, a vivacious Italian woman with enormous brown eyes. 'My name is Giulia and I am here to teach you to cook a traditional Italian food.'

Greta felt very bland and Anglo-Saxon in comparison.

'In Italy,' Giulia continued, even her pauses sensual, 'when it is the middle of the day, shop shutters they come down; streets they go empty, and the only sound you hear is of the knife and fork.' She underlined her words with generous gestures. 'Everywhere, in villages, towns and cities, the much important business of eating happens.'

She caught Greta's eye and smiled widely.

'When there is good food, maybe for a businessman, his bad mood lifts. A family, it comes together. Lovers, they find the right words. A sick child gets strong. Food, it is a beautiful thing.'

Yes, thought Greta, food was so much more than mere nutrition.

It carried messages in its flavours. Afforded purpose and focus to a day. Could be an escape, a means of control, a declaration of love.

'We go round the room now for introductions. Tell us your name and maybe something about you.' She indicated for Greta to begin.

Greta felt the creep of a blush. She clenched her toes. Swallowed.

'I'm Greta Jellings,' she said, her voice chipmunk squeaky. 'I–I don't have a middle name.'

Giulia laughed. 'Neither do I. Nice to meet you, Greta.'

They continued around the room. Ewan was a Welsh policeman, who, besides cooking when time permitted, also sang in a barbershop quartet. There was grey-haired Cecile who'd gifted the experience to her somewhat disinterested goddaughter, Josy. Olivia was a weary-eyed mother of four, who was 'hopeless' at cooking, but revelling in the prospect of a few free hours to herself. Lance, an actor, had just been cast as an Italian chef in an upcoming sitcom and wanted to 'get authentic'. And Randolph was a retired law professor with newfound time on his hands. Deeba was a five-foot-three-inches Pakistani Home Economics teacher; Afra, a softly spoken woman in a full black burka, who'd won the class in a wager; and Brigid, 'a home executive' and *Master Chef* addict.

Everybody had added something of interest to their bios, except Greta. She wished she hadn't been forced to go first.

'Done much cooking before?' Brigid asked, as they returned to their work stations.

Greta eyed the ingredients on the benchtop for clues as to what skills would be demanded of her. 'Oh yes. Yes.'

That she could cook was a surprise really, considering the years of dry chicken, grey beef and waterlogged Brussels sprouts Nora dished up. It was Cyril Denopoulos who had first introduced her to the fabulousness of food. Poor Cyril, with his ears like a Fennec fox and his school shorts pulled clown-high. He and Greta would sit behind the school gym at break-time — Cyril eagerly swapping his spanakopita and babagounash pita pockets for Greta's cheddar cheese and tamarillo chutney sandwiches. Greta had once thought she and Cyril might marry. It was not so much her nine-year-old classmate she was in love with, as his mother. Whenever Greta went to play at Cyril's house, Mrs Denopoulos would squeeze Greta in a warm, garlicky hug, speak far too loudly, and laugh a lot. And she always sent Greta home with a tub of homemade halva.

Greta's equivocation now did not go unnoticed. Brigid's smile faltered.

'And you?' Greta asked quickly.

Brigid gave a forced laugh. 'Last week I made stuffed lobster tails for eleven of my husband's work colleagues. What was I thinking?' She lifted her hands in mock exasperation. 'And to follow, individual semifreddo bombs. What a nightmare!'

Greta felt momentarily buoyed. 'They didn't work out?'

'Oh, they were a great success.'

Greta fumbled with her apron strings.

'I can mix up the dough, if you like,' said Brigid, reaching for the flour.

Greta stood back. 'Okay. Thank you.'

Her partner ran a fuchsia fingernail along the recipe method.

Finally, she passed Greta a small ball of dough.

'Put your heart and your soul into the kneading,' Giulia said from the front. 'Food taste very different when it is made with love.'

Greta waited for the others to begin.

'See how mine is already starting to develop a sheen?' Brigid said, after a time.

Greta nodded enthusiastically.

'Want help with yours?'

'I think I can manage, thank you.'

'As you wish,' said Brigid. 'I just figured I've probably had more practice.'

Pearls of sweat started trickling down Greta's neck; kneading was a demanding job, especially when striving for a sheen.

'That's it,' said Brigid. 'Better.'

Greta had just finished rolling out her dough when the instructor came over.

'Gather round, people. Gather round.'

Greta lowered her rolling pin. She was back in Mrs Gribble's class, about to have her spelling mistakes paraded before the class.

Giulia put her hand under Greta's stretch of dough and lifted one end. 'See how thin? Is almost you can see through.'

Brigid gave the instructor a conspiratorial nod.

Giulia then slipped a recipe sheet under Greta's dough and lowered the dough again.

'My nonna, she always say, you must to be able to read a love letter through the dough. We have not a love letter this day, but I can read here the recipe very easy. *Bravissima*, Greta! Very, very right.'

The class clapped. Greta took a moment to grasp that she was being commended, not criticised. She smiled widely, then quickly frowned. It was not good to gloat.

A favourite Emerson quote popped into Greta's head. *'A great man is willing to be little.'*

Brigid held her pasta up to the light.

'Yes, good too,' said Giulia, moving on.

'The type of flour, *Tipo 00*, is so important, isn't it?' Brigid continued, to no one in particular.

After cutting her dough into small rectangles, Greta began pinching the middles, shaping them into butterflies.

'Make them more uniform.' Brigid said, placing one of hers in front of Greta's. 'Otherwise yours and mine won't cook at the same rate. And they all go in the same pot.'

'I think they'll be alright,' Greta said, emboldened by the recent praise.

'Well careless cooking is not very fair when we are working as a pair. I'm taking the time to shape mine evenly.'

Careless! Greta bit her lip.

The two continued on in silence.

After she'd finished shaping her pasta, Greta began on the pesto. Brigid had disappeared to the toilet, so Greta put all the ingredients in the blender and within seconds was rewarded with a brilliant green, fragrant paste.

'You began without me,' Brigid said, her voice edged with reproach.

Greta blushed.

'Where's the oil and butter?'

'In already. We're all good.'

'You put everything in together? But they are only meant to go in once the herbs have been finely chopped.' Brigid shook her head and muttered under her breath, 'Just my luck to be paired with a complete novice.'

Greta swallowed, lowered her shoulders, and stretched her neck. 'I can only assume,' she began, choking on some saliva, 'that if you really thought I was so incompetent, you'd not have the bad grace to say so.'

Brigid's mouth fell open.

Greta felt a flush of satisfaction. On the rare occasion, the right words found their way out of her mouth.

'Everything good?' asked Giulia, coming over to the table.

Brigid's eyes were shining. 'She put all the pesto ingredients in at once.'

'Is fine, is fine,' said the instructor with a gentle toss of her hand. 'It make a little difference.'

Greta and Brigid did not talk for the remainder of the session.

Later the group gathered around a lunch table laden with their labours — farfalle drizzled with brown sage butter, orrechiette tossed in basil pesto, crusty loaves of ciabatta and a delicate lamb's-lettuce salad.

It was a happy and loud gathering, Brigid the only person to look rather glum. Greta felt uneasy about their earlier interaction, but sometimes a person just had to be put in their place.

She preferred big gatherings. She could get lost in the busyness of it all, and listen to people without the weight of expectation, or a person's singular focus.

Whenever there was an unexpected lull in the conversation, though, Greta immediately felt the pressure to fill it.

'What was the bet?' she blurted out to the woman beside her, who was wearing a burka.

'Excuse me?'

'You said in your introduction that you won this class in a wager.'

'Oh.' The woman's voice smiled. 'That I'd be brave enough to leave my house.'

Greta's eyes widened.

'Salad?' offered the policeman.

Greta passed the bowl on without helping herself. 'Were you scared of being targeted because of your religion?'

'Oh no,' the woman said, with a laugh. 'I've got a thing about germs. I didn't used to leave my house much. For three years in fact.'

Greta couldn't think of what to say.

'It's a phobia,' the woman volunteered. 'But I'm managing it better now.'

Greta could never have imagined sharing such a personal truth with anyone, let alone a stranger. And yet, the woman's honesty was endearing. No pretence.

Pretence. Ha! For Nora, everything had been about pretence. How a person presented to society was paramount, even if it bore no resemblance to the underlying truth. Layers of lacquer applied year after year to approximate the acceptable and avoid derision or judgement.

Greta clenched her jaw. The black and white of Nora's world. Greta's world too.

How often did she make assumptions about people based on their appearance? Incorrect assumptions, as it turned out. She wished she could confront Nora now. Tell her what a burden it was to have to always be agreeable and pleasing. At times she could barely breathe for being so neatly and properly packaged.

'Food is a language everyone can speak, no?' Giulia said.

Yes, thought Greta, food transcended dialects and divisions, tapping into something universal, essential, emotional.

Emotions were messy. They could jumble straight lines and leave a person exposed and vulnerable. And yet, Greta mused, as in cooking, emotions added depth to life. A person needed an open highway between the soul and the cerebral to not only cook well, but love well and live well.

Nora's cooking had reflected how effectively her head was divorced from her heart, such a wide moat separating the two.

'If more people share a meal,' said Giulia, 'the world would be a very much better place.'

'I guess that's true,' Greta said, turning to her Muslim neighbour to seek her opinion.

It was disconcerting not to be able to see more than the woman's eyes, yet in some ways her absolute anonymity made it easier for Greta to talk to her, sort of like a Catholic confessional.

They chatted mostly to each other for the rest of the meal, and by the end of lunch had exchanged contact details and their favourite recipes. Greta learnt how to make Kousa Mahshi, a Middle Eastern dish of stuffed vegetables, and Knefeh, a syrup-soaked cheesecake with a semolina and pistachio crust. She in turn shared her recipes for mango chilli chicken and Easter fruit bread.

Afra's voice was warm, her voice all smile, except for when she told Greta that she'd lost her youngest child to leukaemia. Then the burka could not hide her pain.

Greta wished she were brave enough to give the woman a hug.

'I cannot change what has happened, so I must accept it.'

'I wish I had children.'

Greta recoiled from her own words. Never before had she articulated this out loud.

'There's still time. You are young, no?'

Greta felt the hurry of tears. 'Thirty-nine. I don't even have a partner.'

Afra rested a hand on Greta; her dark skin was soft and warm.

It was a relief to stop pretending. To say what she felt, without worrying she might be judged. Yes, she longed to be a mother.

Ewan, the Welsh policeman, his face now rather ruddy, asked for the wine.

Brigid reached for the bottle. As she did so her sleeve rode up to expose her forearm.

Greta squinted through her tears at the dark blue bruise encircling Brigid's wrist. Brigid quickly pulled down her cuff.

'You are very lovely class to teach,' said Giulia. 'Thank you for coming. Now go. Make a mess in your kitchen. And remember, you always to put your heart on top of your food.'

'Quite an image, but I'll drink to that,' Ewan said, downing the last of the wine.

'And not to forget there are containers to take home the leftovers.'

'You can have mine,' Brigid said to Greta back at their bench. 'My husband would never eat this.'

'Brigid, I'm—' But Brigid was already making her way through the swing doors.

CHAPTER 30

Greta wasn't thrilled about being shown to the same table for breakfast a second day in a row. Muriel Maloney, the pink-haired mortician, was again at the adjacent table, wedged behind the planter box. Fleeting moments with people were much easier to manage than repeated encounters. With more contact came the potential for people to discover who Greta really was. A disappointment. And this morning of all mornings she did not fancy the pressure to perform. She was tired and her stomach ached. It had been a long night — a night spent churning about the aunt Greta would never meet because of her own spinelessness.

Her breakfast neighbour was more enthusiastic.

'Top of the morning,' she said, peering at Greta through the fern fronds, her saloon-sultry voice out of place in a bright breakfast room.

'Hello again,' said Greta, giving a quick smile, then turning to the menu, despite already knowing what she wanted to order.

'Good day yesterday?'

'Yes.' Greta didn't want to encourage conversation.

But her 'yes' hung there so rudely, that she quickly added, 'thank you. And you?'

She was veering into hairdresser-appointment territory — that excruciating hour of stilted conversation. She always wondered what other women talked about with their hairstylists. Most around her seemed to prattle away with enviable ease. For Greta though, it was an endless struggle. So much so that she sometimes delayed getting her hair cut for months, just to avoid the ordeal.

'So, *what have you been up to, Greta?*' her hairdresser would open with. A seemingly casual enquiry loaded with expectation. Nothing in Greta's life was interesting enough to share.

'*Oh, you know. A bit of this, a bit of that.*' Non-specific words offering nowhere for the conversation to go.

Then in a desperate attempt to rescue a missed opportunity, Greta would try something like, *'Are you working late tonight?'*

'No.' Condescending smile. *'Thursday's my late night.'*

'Of course. How long is it now you've been working here?'

'Five years this August.'

The conversation would soon peter out and Greta would be left trying to calculate an opportune time to reach for her cooling cup of tea, while scrutinising her changing reflection in the mirror. Inevitably, her hair was the length she wanted, at least ten minutes before Ruby or Derrick or Dick finally downed their scissors. Ten minutes of apparently inconsequential snipping could make an alarming difference. And that was even before Greta's frizzy hair had dried, taking with it another crucial few millimetres of style. Yet despite this same scenario playing out so many times over the years, Greta never had been able to muster the courage to intervene. Again and again she chose to accept looking like a shorn spaniel, rather than speak up.

There was one hairdresser she had been able to talk to. Kirk. A garrulous fellow, always eager to share colourful anecdotes from his life. There was the time he'd languished in a Swedish prison after doctoring the birthdate on his passport. And the occasion his wife had flambéed duck for a dinner party with turpentine instead of kirsch. Then there was the story about how one of his clients stabbed a fellow book-club member with a cake fork after the woman kept revealing spoilers.

However, Greta's sessions with Kirk came to an abrupt halt one appointment when he suggested that AIDS and Ebola were Nature's way of eradicating 'the undesirables of this world.' Greta had got up and walked out . . .

Well, that is the way she wished it had happened. It was a scenario she sometimes still played out in her head. Even the bit where she'd had to walk back into the salon to return the hairdressing cape, her half-finished hairstyle defiantly on display.

But Greta had not been that courageous. In fact, she'd remained in her seat as if nothing was wrong, while Kirk finished cutting her hair. Then she'd paid and left, the man none the wiser as to why she would never book another appointment with him again.

'Pretty dry, to be honest.'

Greta frowned, lost in her thoughts.

It was the undertaker woman responding to her enquiry about the previous day.

'Oh. So, not very exciting then?' Greta said, her eyes still fixed on the menu.

Blood rushed to her face as she realised her faux pas. How could she possibly pair the word exciting with the sombre subject of death?

Muriel seemed unperturbed. 'To be honest, the technical stuff doesn't really light my fire. I'm more interested in making a connection with the cadaver, if you get my drift.'

Greta pushed back her chair.

'Getting to know the dead. What life they lived, what moved their soul. And, of course, what their loved ones want from a viewing. That's my monkey, that's my circus.'

Greta closed the menu.

'I'm more about meaning,' continued the woman, undeterred by Greta's obvious discomfort. 'I'd be happy to leave the science of pickling the body to someone else. That's the drudgery of the job.'

In an instant Greta was navigating the chapel down the road from the rest home where Nora had taken her last laboured breath. The suffocating smell of incense. The sail-shaped arrangement of flowers. The ornate mahogany coffin.

Ornate mahogany coffin. Greta again felt the pain of that decision.

Nora had not been an ornate sort of person, but the undertaker had pressured Greta into getting an expensive casket, the implication being that to choose one from the mid-to-low-pricing tier was to do her mother a disservice.

Greta wished she'd been able to stand firm and make a decision true to herself and Nora. If only she hadn't been so worried about appearing miserly. About appearing like an ungrateful daughter holding onto her inheritance.

A plain casket sans silver or brass would have been better aligned with Nora's life. Shiny mahogany with ostentatious handles was a mistake Greta could never undo. It was like that with deaths. And births. No second chances.

Poor Nora. How uncomfortable she'd looked submerged in pearly clouds of puckered satin, her hair concreted with lacquer, her cheeks rouged like some woman of the night.

'We spend a long time living,' said Muriel, through a mouthful of toast. 'Then we're in such a hurry to brush death under the carpet, closing a life midsentence.'

Greta sat back in her seat.

'I aim for an authentic, tangible closure,' the chatty woman went on. 'Not the hushed variety camouflaged in silence and waterproof mascara.' She pulled back a fern frond. It sprung out of her hand. 'You know, people usually soil themselves in the process of dying. It happens. It's normal.'

Greta's eyes darted around the room.

'I encourage family to help wash their loved one's body,' Muriel continued. 'It's a beautiful final act of service.' She snapped off the offending fern leaf and tossed it under the table. 'A very physical farewell. And when people touch death, stay with it, breath it in, they realise it's not a monster, but simply a part of life.'

The rest of the room faded out. Greta found herself nodding. It was so surprising to hear someone talk about a taboo topic with such ease and honesty.

Muriel took a gulp of her hot chocolate. 'Of all the times in a person's life, death is not the place for protocol. It should be all about release and freedom.'

So much of Greta's life had been ruled by protocol. She was forever concerned about doing the right thing and being seen to do it. But now, as she thought back to how she had farewelled Nora, Greta realised that she had let the purpose and essence of the occasion get subsumed by etiquette. By what others expected of her. She'd been too busy looking for approval in other people's eyes — the matron's, the undertaker's, the priest's — and had lost an important opportunity for truth.

She tried to imagine gently sponging Nora's body down. A strange thought, considering she had not seen her mother naked since she was a very small child — clothes just one of the many layers that had distanced mother and daughter.

Greta wondered how it would have felt to talk out loud to Nora and tell her things she'd not been able to say when Nora was alive? A venting, loving, questioning. A farewelling.

Greta sighed, smiled at her breakfast companion, then picked up the menu again. Perhaps she would stay and have poached eggs, after all.

Greta's week in London passed more quickly than she'd anticipated. The cabbie had been right; there was so much on offer. She doubted whether months, let alone her allotted ten days, would even suffice. She browsed through the food halls of Fortnum and Mason, feasting her eyes on perfectly crafted marzipan fruits, Opera Slice and gold-leafed Sachertorte. She stood for an hour in the queue for the London Eye, then got cold feet at the last minute and gave her ticket away. She watched the changing of the guard at Buckingham Palace in sweltering mid-morning heat, and oscillated between embarrassment and awe at an exhibition of *Underwear Through the Ages* at the Victoria and Albert Museum. She bought four different flavours of fudge at Covent Garden markets, and stood beside Princess Diana and Victoria Beckham at Madam Tussauds, this time wearing her red velvet wedges.

Stuffing her days full of activity left little time to think. Thinking was overrated. Greta sometimes wished she'd been born an earthworm, or a slug.

Her third-to-last day in London was earmarked for a meze master class. She expected the session to be much the same as the first cooking class, but it couldn't have been more different.

For one, the group was smaller — just four students in total — so everyone had their own bench. Greta breathed an internal sigh of relief. No cooking partners.

The instructor was a man this time. Tassos. An olive-skinned Greek with day-old stubble and mesmerising black eyes which, when cast Greta's way, left her with a funny feeling in her . . . undercarriage.

Tassos's class lacked any semblance of structure, so much so that Greta got the impression he was making things up as he went along.

'Why we don't add some oregano, eh?'

His casualness was unsettling, yet to Greta's surprise every dish turned out to be delicious, and Tassos's attentiveness more than made up for his deficits.

'Greta,' he'd say, rolling the R in a guttural growl. 'What you think about the taste. Is good no? Maybe more salt?'

At first she just agreed with whatever he proposed, but gradually, as the session progressed, she plucked up the courage to make a few of her own suggestions.

'A squeeze of lemon, I think?'

'Yes, you are right. Good idea!'

He gave her his full focus whenever he was talking to her. It was an intoxicating feeling.

On one occasion, after putting up her hand, Greta completely forgot what she'd wanted to ask, so lost was she in Tassos's molten eyes.

He just laughed and tapped her affectionately on the shoulder. 'The thought, it is run away?'

Greta eyed herself side-on in the glass splashback. Her blush was not discernible, but her silhouette was distinct. She pulled her shoulders back. She was quite well stacked really, even if she said so herself.

Greta left the class that afternoon with containers of taramasalata, stuffed vine leaves and delicious little meatballs. Also, an ill-defined excitement in her belly, or perhaps it wasn't her belly.

'Greta, you have a few moment?'

She turned. Tassos was standing at the top of the stairs.

'I'm need you to fill out a feedback form, please? I forget to give it to the class.'

'Of course,' she said, running back up the stairs.

'Slowly. Slowly. I'm do not want you to fall in front of my feet.'

She giggled at the not-too-unpleasant thought.

'Come. Is in my office.'

She followed Tassos into a small room crammed with cookbooks.

He closed the door and went over to the desk. 'Admin. Admin,' he said, shaking his head. 'Always admin.'

Greta could imagine this man would not easily be tied down to chores. He was too much of a free spirit.

'Here it is,' he said. As he pulled out a piece of paper from his jam-packed drawer, a small box was dislodged and dropped to the floor.

Greta picked it up instinctively, glancing casually at the rectangular blue box.

DUREX. She was holding a box of condoms!

'Oh . . . I . . . Oh . . .' She handed it to Tassos. Even her fingers looked like they were blushing.

He winked at her. 'Just four easy question,' he said, handing her the feedback form and a pen.

Greta stared at it, trying to order her flustered thoughts.

Please rate your satisfaction on a scale of 1–10

Did you enjoy the class?

10

Did the chef answer your questions satisfactorily?

10

Did the chef demonstrate steps in an easily understandable way?

10

Was the class well organised?

6̶ 10

Tassos was reading over her shoulder. He smelt good. Like a Latin lover. Or how Greta imagined a Latin lover would smell.

'Ten. Ten. Ten . . . Nearly six, but then it becomes ten too!'

'I thought the question was . . . I . . . you were great. Really.'

'And you too are very great, Greta,' he said, with a slow smile.

She looked away.

'You have time for some dessert?' he said, running his forefinger around the box of condoms. 'Greek dessert will score ten too.' He winked. 'I am guarantee.'

She started reversing towards the door. 'Oh, I'd love to say yes, Tassos, but I really must get going. Am late for another appointment. Thank you though. For the offer. It's very kind of you.'

She fiddled with the door handle. It was hard to open from behind her back.

Tassos shrugged. 'Maybe next time, Miss Greta.'

She nodded. Blushed. Stumbled. 'Better be on my way then.'

On the tube she went over the scene in Tassos's office again and again, wishing every time she'd thrown caution to the wind.

No one is watching, Grets. No one is watching.

But it was too late now. She couldn't very well go back. Could she?

And, as if on cue, Nora tuned in, filling Greta's head with stern admonitions.

'I've got a lot of leftovers from my cookery class,' Greta said to her regular breakfast neighbour the next day. 'Too much for me. Would you like some?'

'Hell, yeah,' said Muriel, yanking at another fern frond. The plant was looking significantly sparser since the start of the week.

'Why don't you pop up to my room later with your offering. We can have ourselves a little party.'

Greta swallowed; she only had herself to blame.

'Room eleven. I'll provide the booze.'

Greta cast around to see if anyone had heard. She didn't want people getting the wrong impression about her. Booze was not a word she would usually use.

Secretly though, the coarseness of Muriel's language sent scandalous sparks of delight through her. The sheer contravention of codes. The rebellion.

'What time?' she asked in a hushed tone, as if organising an illicit rendezvous.

'Just when it suits. Today's my beach day. I should be back about five.'

At 5.10 p.m. Greta knocked on Muriel's door.

It swung open immediately.

'Gosh, you gave me a fright!' Greta said, as Muriel put her head out, her hair wild, her face roasted red. She smelt of the sea and tanning oil.

'Go figure, girl! You're the one who knocked.'

Yes. How foolish Greta sounded.

'But good timing! I just this minute got back from the beach.'

'Sorry. I'm too early. You said five. I can come back la—' Greta stared. Muriel was wearing a skimpy, almost see-through sundress over bright orange swimming togs. Her skin, where it was untainted by tattoos, was lobster pink.

'You're very red.'

Muriel roared with laughter.

'What I mean . . . what I meant to say was that you've caught the sun quite significantly.'

'Of course I caught the sun, you dingbat! This has got to last me the whole goddamned year. Now are you going to stand in the corridor forever?'

Dingbat? Bizarrely the word felt more a badge of approval than an insult. It announced the familiarity of a friendship.

Greta stepped into the room.

As the door closed behind her, her heart started thumping in her throat. She'd been swept up by the energy and impulsiveness of Muriel Maloney, but now the awkwardness of having to interact without the protection of fern fronds loomed.

Many potential friendships reached this stage and then stopped. For Greta it was always easier to escape before rejection.

'Welcome to my parlour,' Muriel said with a sweep of her stubby arms.

Greta blushed. The word parlour felt wrong on so many levels.

'I see you don't need the sun to turn pink,' Muriel said with a cheeky smile.

No one had ever had the nerve to draw attention to Greta's blushing before. Her face grew hotter. Blushing about blushing. A Babushka, nesting-dolls moment.

She wanted to feel affronted. Turn and leave. But again, she felt less aggrieved than she'd have expected to. Articulating her debilitating condition with humour had instantly demoted it. Just a few careless words and her incapacitating habit was already shrinking in size.

Before she could think of what next to say, her host disappeared to the bathroom. 'Make yourself at home,' Muriel called out from behind the closing door. 'I've been desperate for a pee all afternoon. If the sea hadn't been so frickin' cold I'd have—' Her words were drowned out by the sound of cascading water.

Greta looked about for somewhere to put the containers of food she was still holding. The room was almost identical to hers, though any similarity had been camouflaged by mounds of clothes, books, magazines, shopping bags and empty crisp packets. Whatever would Nora have thought of such a mess? As for the hotel cleaners?

On the few occasions Nora and Greta had gone to a motel, Nora had insisted on a thorough clean of the unit before departing. *What will they think of us if we leave the place like a tip?*

Muriel's voice rose above the noise of the flushing toilet. 'I bought us some bubbly. It's in one of those shopping bags. You can open it.'

Greta rifled through the bags. Tampons. A tub of tiramisu. A box of waxing strips. Carton of orange juice. Motorcycling magazine . . .

It felt wrong to be rifling through someone else's shopping. But also intriguing. AAA batteries. A giant slab of white chocolate. A bottle of bubbly.

'C'mon slowcoach,' Muriel said, emerging from the bathroom. 'I'm gasping.'

'Better you do it,' Greta said, passing over the bottle.

Muriel popped the cork with effortless ease.

'Bugger,' she said opening the cupboard above the minibar. 'No clean glasses left. Oh well, teacups will have to do.'

'I've got glasses in my room,' Greta offered quickly. But Muriel was already pouring.

'It's cups I always run out of,' Greta added. 'I'm more of a tea person myself.'

Muriel looked at her askance. 'You don't make tea in your hotel room, do you?'

Greta's mouth went dry. 'Why?'

'Lordy, woman! Don't you know what people do in hotel kettles?'

Muriel's tone left Greta lightheaded.

'Boil their bloody underwear in them! Urinate in them when they're too lazy to get up for the loo. Make soup in them. Put used condoms in them.'

The saliva in Greta's mouth tasted suddenly foul. She sank onto Muriel's bed. How many cups of tea had she made on the trip so far? Too many to count. Paying sixteen dollars for a tray of tea at the Carlyle now felt like money well spent.

'Swallow this,' Muriel said, foisting a mug of bubbly on her. 'It'll help you forget.'

Greta obeyed, swallowing it in one go, as if to irrigate her insides.

'Far out!' Muriel said. 'I didn't pick you for a one-swig kind of girl.'

As Greta opened her mouth to explain, a huge burp escaped.

'Nor a belcher.'

The two women burst out laughing.

A few minutes later, Greta was still laughing so hard her belly ached.

'Now, let's see what you got in those containers of yours. I'm ravenous!'

Just before midnight, Greta made her way back to her room. She undressed in a daze and lay across her bed in her underwear, the full moon casting her room in a sapphire glow. Outside, clouds scudded across the navy night, a breeze tickled the trees, voices whooped and cheered and died away.

What an evening. The hilarity and craziness. Spilt champagne. Leaking tub of taramasalata. The unashamed excesses of her new friend, Muriel Maloney. Her unwitting wisdom too.

'*We can take a few lessons from the dead. For one, they're a lot calmer than we are.*'

Words shared casually, which Greta caught like bridal bouquets.

'*Sure, I'd like a lover. But being cool with who I am and what I do, that's as good as sex. Trust me. And the buzz lasts longer.*'

Raucous laughter. More champagne. The horror of an open brochure demonstrating the latest embalming techniques.

'*I can't be worried what others think. We might all be headed for the same place, but each of us has a different road map. This is my journey. Only I can walk it.*'

Addresses exchanged. Promises to visit.

'*I'm gonna get this Banksy quote for my next tattoo. Right here.*' Pointing to her left arm. '*Sorry, the lifestyle you ordered is currently out of stock.*'

An evening wrapped in a little bit of magic.

CHAPTER 31

Greta

Connections

Hey you,

Almost three weeks into your adventure. Can you believe it?

I bet Devonport, the pool shop and North Head feel like a lifetime away? Travel can do that. Transplant the mind into some parallel universe.

I'm a bit jealous. A lot jealous actually. Mostly about the food you will have cooked, which I won't get a chance to taste. And you getting to meet your aunt. I'm super chuffed Angus managed to track her down.

Acquisitions, achievements, all that stuff, are just one layer thick. It's the people in our lives who give it dimension and depth. Friends and family.

Family give us a place at the table, anchoring us to the bigger continuum of time. No guarantees though. Some families don't work. Mine for one. Anyway, I hope the meeting with your aunt went well.

Walt x

Too late! Greta folded away Walter's latest letter. She'd missed that opportunity. He would understand. He would.

She planned for her last day in London to be uneventful. It was foolhardy to gallivant around on the eve of her departure. New York had ended too abruptly. A buffer was important to allow time for packing and mental preparation. And for tidying her hotel room.

Deciding to start the day with a brief stroll, Greta headed out through the hotel gardens into Green Park. It was a glorious day. The world felt different when the sun was shining. It was in people's strides, the swoop of birds, the glinting spokes of bicycle wheels.

'*Daily Mail*, luv?'

Greta had stopped outside a newspaper kiosk.

She shook her head. The vendor had mistaken her pause; she was looking beyond him, into the mouth of Green Park tube station, at the concrete stairs disappearing into the ground.

Two hours later she once again stood on the platform of Sevenoaks station, her breathing faster than if she'd just run around the block, except all she'd done was alight from a train.

'Thought I recognised you,' said the stationmaster, walking over to her as other commuters cleared.

She smiled, his familiar face tempering the terror of her impulsiveness.

'Back to visit the old aunt?'

She nodded.

'Don't let them tell you she's asleep again,' he said, with a wink. 'She would want to be woken up. There'll be time enough for her to sleep when she'd dead.'

Greta bid him farewell and hurried along the now familiar route, as if the endpoint might disappear into a sinkhole before she reached it.

'All the way from New Zealand! Now that's pretty special,' said the matron animatedly, as she led Greta down a maze of corridors.

Greta peered through open doors — peep shows on the rigours of old age.

'My daughter holidayed in New Zealand with her boyfriend. Beautiful country, she tells me. They visited Hobbiton. Did white-water rafting. Bungy jumped off some ridiculously high bridge. Can't say I was delighted about that.'

An elderly woman sat crumpled in a wheelchair, her pale limbs poking out from her body at odd angles, her mouth leaking saliva.

'Mavis, Mavis, *give me your answer do*,' sang a nurse, as she combed the old lady's hair. '*I'm half crazy, all for the love of you. It shan't be a stylish marriage. I can't afford a carriage—*'

They passed a man with Einstein-white hair seated on a bench, fiddling with his pyjama pants. A Bus Stop sign was taped to the wall above him.

'Leave your catheter bag alone, Brian!' said the matron as they passed. 'You don't want it leaking everywhere.

'Bloody bus is late.'

The matron looked at her watch. 'Shouldn't be long, now.'

He sat back, seemingly satisfied.

Greta looked up and down the corridor, trying to work out the logistics of a bus.

'Our residents work best in an environment that is familiar to them. Many used to catch public transport.'

'So, no bus then?' Greta whispered. She was glad to have the problem solved, but also a little unsettled by the charade. When she grew old, she hoped people wouldn't try to trick her like that.

'Here we are then.' The matron had halted in front of an open door, the room beyond hidden behind a curve of curtain.

'Mimi, you've got a visitor,' the matron said, putting her head around the screen and beckoning Greta to follow.

Greta's heartbeats tripped over each other. She hesitated, then followed the matron into the room.

A brass plaque at the entrance. Large picture window opposite. University degree on the wall. Framed photographs too. A newspaper article pinned to a small corkboard. A leather swivel chair. Hospital bed. A . . .

'Get the fuck out of my office!' screeched an old woman, sitting hunched over a commode. 'Can't you see I'm busy?'

Greta shut her eyes and hurriedly reversed.

'Apologies, Mimi,' said the matron. 'Just wanted to let you know you have a visitor. A very special visitor.'

'Make an appointment like everyone else. I can't be seen to be giving favours.'

Greta stood in the corridor trembling. That voice. It could have been Nora's. Though Nora never swore. Ever.

'When did you last see your aunt?' asked the matron, no doubt in response to Greta's bewildered expression.

Greta shook her head. 'No. No. This is the first time. I . . . I didn't even know I had an aunt until a few weeks ago.'

The matron took Greta's hands in hers. 'You know Mimi has advanced dementia?'

Greta put a hand to her mouth.

'Unfortunately, her deterioration has become increasingly rapid. Such a bright mind, burnt out, like that.' She snapped her fingers. 'The disease is not discerning. One-time Businesswoman of the Year, to this.'

Businesswoman of the Year! Greta straightened. A trace of the extraordinary in her family. A thread of success running through her bloodline.

'We try to keep medication here to a minimum. Find ways around the hurdles.' She pointed to the brass plaque at the entrance. Wolfe and Co. 'Mimi likes to think she's still CEO of her company.'

Ten minutes later, the matron again knocked on Mimi's door. 'Your next appointment, madam. A Ms Jellings to see you.'

'Good. Good. Send her in.'

Greta stepped hesitantly into the room. Mimi was seated beside the window, her back to Greta, her legs angled to one side, lending her woolly pink slippers high-heeled elegance.

'Mimi?' Greta stuttered.

Her aunt turned.

Greta gasped, eyes wide. She leant forward, resting her hands on her thighs to support herself.

'Good morning,' said the woman slowly.

That voice. That face. That . . .

Fuzzy black dots were crowding Greta's vision. Then she was falling.

'Ms Jellings. Ms Jellings. Hello. Can you hear me?'

A face, blurred at the edges.

'Where am I?'

'Just rest here a minute, dear. You've—'

Her head hurt. 'Where am I?'

Someone was holding her feet in the air. Greta wrestled them free.

'There, there. It's all right. You fainted. Do you remember? You're here to visit your aunt.'

Greta was on the floor, covered by a blanket, a soft pillow under her head.

Then she remembered. The silver hair closely cropped and tapering to a widow's peak. Eyelids with pearly clusters in the corners. Wispy eyebrows that dived instead of ballooning. Thin lips folded around denture-perfect teeth. The turkey droop of skin, shiny red hands, shell-grey eyes. Even the dementia. All Nora.

But *not* Nora. Mimi. Her mother's sister. Her mother's identical twin sister.

'This is a bloody disgrace!' Mimi's voice boomed from somewhere down the corridor. Then she burst into the room. 'When can I get back into my office? Get that woman off my floor.'

'Mimi, this is your niece, Greta.'

Greta pulled herself up on one elbow. Everything ached.

'What was your mother's name?' whispered the matron.

'Nora.'

'Mimi, this is Nora's daughter. She's come to visit you all the way from New Zealand.'

Mimi's face faltered, the severity softening. Her mouth twitched. Then she let out a loud, tortured moan. 'Nora! My Nora! I won't let them take you away.'

She knelt down beside Greta and put a finger to her lips. 'Not a peep now. They won't find us.'

Big drops of water landed on Greta's face.

Mimi stroked Greta's arm. Her hands were cold. Instinctively Greta took them in hers, pulling her aunt towards her chest. Mimi folded over her, sobbing. 'Hush, Nora. I won't let them take you away.'

Greta closed her eyes and for a magical undreamt-of moment she was in her mother's arms. The few seconds stretched into an eternity, into every day she and Nora had shared. All the unhugged days of her childhood concertinaed into this one yearned-for embrace.

Someone passed wind.

'Haha!' Mimi boomed, crawling away from Greta. 'A bottie burp even better than the last.'

Everyone started to laugh. Even Greta.

'That's not very ladylike, Mimi,' said the matron, looping an arm through Greta's and helping her up.

'Not very ladylike,' Mimi said, imitating the matron. 'Nora can do even bigger bottie burps. Can't you, Nora the snorer?'

Mimi made a dash for the door. 'Catch me if you can.' Then she was disappearing down the corridor, two nurses in hot pursuit.

Greta's head throbbed as she sat in the matron's office sipping a cup of sweet black tea. The matron lifted off the icepack she'd been holding against the back of Greta's head.

'Quite a shock for you, I'm sure. We had no idea Mimi was an identical twin. Her medical records mention she was adopted from a home for unmarried mothers, at the age of five! That's very late for any child to be adopted. Now it makes more sense. Twins were far less appealing to prospective parents, the idea of the two having to be adopted as a package. I suspect after five unsuccessful years the decision was finally made to adopt the girls out individually.'

Adopted out. Unmarried mother. Sisters going to different families.

For the first time Greta understood the line written in perfect cursive script at the bottom of every page of Nora's diaries. *Where are you, M?* Greta's mind had conjured up so many different scenarios. None of them included her mother having an identical twin sister.

It also explained why Nora had not tried to track her sister down, even as a grownup. That would have meant acknowledging her history. Her thoroughly unrespectable history.

'Never allow a man into your pants before he's put a ring on your finger, Greta. Men will lure you with promises. False promises. But it will be just you and your bastard child who have to carry the disgrace around for the rest of your lives. Five minutes on your back, a lifetime of shame.'

'The name on all official documentation is Elma,' said the matron. 'But as her dementia worsened, she insisted on being called Mimi.'

Greta wondered whether Mimi had been her aunt's childhood nickname, or perhaps even her given name before she was adopted.

Greta's scalp was stinging and her mind spinning. It was too much. She'd found her last living relative, only to discover that dementia had got to her first. The realisation, too, that her family history was less contained than she'd ever believed, with roots reaching beyond the certainties she'd lived for so long. Her father had been the unknown, not her mother. Now everything was confused. The earth was round, not flat. Round, not flat.

She burst into tears.

'Oh, you poor love,' said the matron, patting Greta on the back. 'A lot to take in.'

Greta gave over to her emotions; crying in a matron's office felt permissible.

'You'll be wanting to speak with your cousins, I'm sure. I think Rachel will be here on Friday.'

Greta pulled back. 'Cousins?'

'Dear Lord!' exclaimed the matron. 'Of course, you wouldn't know about them either.'

Greta shook her head.

'Mimi has six children. They're scattered all over the globe. One in Toronto. Another in South America. Rachel and Liam are the only two left in Britain. Liam lives in the Lake District, so we don't see him very often, but Rachel is our stalwart. She's here every Friday.'

Six cousins! Her tiny family of three. Then two. Then one. Now eight!

'Rachel,' Greta repeated.

The matron smiled. 'Why don't you come back and meet her on Friday?'

'I can't!' Greta blurted out. It was impossible. 'I fly out tomorrow.' She couldn't even consider a disruption to The Plan. The Angus Plan. The Walter Plan.

'Oh dear,' said the matron. She opened her drawer. 'Rachel is away in Belgium until Thursday night. She's an entertainment lawyer. I can give her a call later. Pass on your contact details in New Zealand.

Perhaps you can write down where you're staying tonight, in case I need to reach you again after speaking with Rachel.'

Greta agreed.

'You'll just have to come back to England to meet the rest of your family,' the matron said, with a warm smile.

Come back. Meet the rest of your family. Yes. Greta would have to come back. But right now she needed to say goodbye to Mimi. For the first and likely last time.

They found her back in her room playing pick-up sticks.

Her eyes lit up when she saw Greta. 'Come play, Nora,' she whispered, her gnarled forefinger summoning Greta over.

Her voice caught Greta again. It was uncanny that two women who'd lived most of their lives apart, could have such similar voices. And come to such similar ends. The power of DNA.

'I have to go.'

Panic spread across Mimi's face.

Greta swallowed. Chewed her lip. Rested a hand on Mimi's.

'I mean, I just have to go to the bathroom. I'll be back soon.'

Mimi's face relaxed. She pulled at one of the coloured sticks, easing it out of the crisscrossed stack. 'That was close.'

Greta leant down and kissed Mimi on the head. Her hair smelt of talcum-powder.

Mimi looked up. 'Silly, silly girl.'

As Greta left the room, she thought she heard something. She turned, but Mimi was concentrating on easing another stick out from the pile.

Greta shook her head. She must have imagined it. For a moment she thought she'd heard someone say, 'Love you.'

CHAPTER 32

Greta ripped open the brown envelope, a tear zigzagging through the postage stamp. She chewed her lip. Majestic Lake Matheson was now split in two, as if an earthquake had yanked apart its shores. She'd ask for some tape from Reception and reconnect the edges. She couldn't afford to jinx her return to New Zealand.

She'd arrived back from Kent in the early evening having battled peak-hour concourses, crammed carriages and too many escalators. The mood amongst commuters was different from the morning. Londoners had succumbed to their day. Ties had been loosened, newspapers crumpled and notes of perfume no longer noticeable. Work-weary eyes replayed conversations, deals lost and won, boardroom banter. The collective focus had shifted. People were headed home.

Home. The hollowness of homesickness expanded within her. She was nearly three weeks into her holiday. Just three weeks. It felt so much longer.

To be fair, it had been better than she'd expected. It had. Only a few days earlier she'd again felt the spark of excitement while contemplating what Walter had in store for her next. Paris? Italy? Venice, if she could choose. But predictably, as the last day in London drew close, her delight dissipated and the unknown again loomed like a spectre before her. She wanted to go home.

It was a futile wish. She may as well have been in a cable car suspended halfway up a mountain. Escape was not an option. Unless of course she was a Bond girl prepared to scramble out of the car hundreds of metres above ground, swing from a loose cable and land on some craggy cliff face, while a milky-eyed hit man took aim, his shots inciting an avalanche, which Greta would manage to avoid by skiing at breakneck speed down . . .

No, Greta was locked into the trip. And not through anyone else's doing, but her own. It was the thought of wasting Walter's money, dishonouring his intentions, of squandering all Angus's effort.

Something else too. Deep within her. Even greater than the outside pressures keeping her on course. She wanted to keep going because . . . *she* wanted to. As unspecified as the future was, she wanted some ownership of it.

Thankfully, a letter was waiting for her at the front desk. At least Angus was dependable. Not having a plan was definitely more terrifying than a covert one.

She sat on the edge of her bed and withdrew the contents — a wad of typed instructions with the usual covering note from Angus.

She looked inside for the additional letter from Walter. Nothing.

She scanned the instructions, searching for the key word.

Mmm. Yup. Mmm. Uh-uh. No. No way! Not in a million years!

Fortunately, Angus answered his phone. Greta was in no mood for Cassandra.

'Greta.' His solid calmness momentarily stilled her panic. He sounded just next door, not oceans away. 'Good to hear from you.'

'Angus, I cannot,' she said. 'I absolutely cannot.'

There was the sound of static as he covered the mouthpiece and in a muffled voice, '—ease excuse—minute—overseas.'

He must have been with a client, but right now that was not Greta's concern.

'Frank tells me you had a good time in New York.'

'Angus, there is no way I am going to Rwanda.'

'Ah, yes. Rwanda.'

She wanted to reach down the phone and shake him like a piggybank, emptying him of all his casualness. She was not some lab rat to be forced through a series of hoops.

'Have you seen the movie? Have you? *Hotel Rwanda*! Well, I have. The machetes. The brutality.' Her voice wavered.

'Rwanda is a very safe country these days,' Angus said slowly. 'You have my word.'

'Your word. With all due respect, Angus, it will count for naught when my head lies severed from my body on some African plain.'

He chuckled.

The only time Greta did not struggle for the right words was when she was angry. Anger managed to create clarity in her head and push past all the other confounding considerations. All the self-consciousness and politeness.

'This is not something to laugh about.' She scratched her head irritably.

'Greta,' he said. 'If there is one destination I would give my eyeteeth to visit, it is Rwanda. Have you read Walter's letter? What he has planned for you?'

'There is nothing from Walter.'

'You sure?'

'Absolutely!' She tipped the brown envelope upside down again.

'Bother. I must have forgotten to include it. Look, the plan is you'll be trekking into the mountains of Virunga National Park to see the gorillas. It'll be a once-in-a- lifetime experience.'

'Only because my life will end there!'

Angus chortled.

'Look,' he said. 'I understand your anxieties, Greta. I do. They're to be expected.'

She flicked off her shoes and lay back against the pillows, holding the receiver in the crook of her neck.

'But I've done the research. Your fears are unfounded. I am certain Rwanda will be a highlight on this intrepid adventure of yours.'

She sat mutely. She was tired. It had been a long day.

'You still there?'

'Yes. Sorry. I don't mean to shoot the messenger. It's just that—'

'To be honest, I'm delighted to experience some of your fire and fury,' Angus said. 'A far cry from the tentative and timid woman who sat in my office a few months ago.'

She squirmed. She'd let herself down. Lost control.

'Sorry, Angus. I really am.'

'I like the new Greta,' he said, speaking over her. 'Or, should I say, Greta unleashed.'

Greta slams her bedroom door and locks it. The printer's tray on the wall shakes. Trinkets fall off. Her blown-glass mouse hits the floor, one of its ears snapping off.

'How dare you lock the door on me!' Nora hisses, rattling the handle furiously.

'How dare you lock the door on me,' Greta imitates.

'Haaaah!' Nora's fury oozes through the keyhole. 'If people could hear you now. Know what you are really like. I wonder what Mrs Mansfield would think of her favourite pupil.'

Greta is gripped with fear. Mrs Mansfield is the best teacher in the world. Her hero. She said Greta could be anything she wanted to be — an astronaut, movie star, even the captain of a cruise liner. Just so long as Greta believed it. But what if Mrs Mansfield gets to know of her badness? Those possibilities would surely be revised. They are only true so long as Mrs Mansfield says they are.

'Never in all my years did I imagine I'd hear such cheek coming from the mouth of my own daughter. As if my life hasn't been hard enough, Greta Jellings.'

Greta hunches her shoulders and slides to her bedroom floor.

'It's that father of yours coming out in you. That's what it is. You're just as selfish and headstrong as he was.'

Those words are tattooed onto Greta. It is her inescapable lot. Even if her mother washes her mouth out with soap, the bad bits will remain, because she is her father's daughter.

Over the years, Greta works hard to bury her wickedness beneath layers of goodness. She cleans the bath rim every night just in case Mrs Mansfield makes a surprise visit to the house. She does whatever people want of her, adapting to their demands like a chameleon switching between light and dark, leaf and bark. And as her childhood years pass, the original Greta — who dreamt in colour, and who was somewhat cheeky and inquisitorial and curious and confident — becomes buried beneath a mound of the other, more agreeable, Gretas. By her late teenage years, Greta has become more closely aligned with the template Nora has laid out for her.

'You will have seen from the information pack that I've arranged for you to join a guided tour.' Angus's voice burst into her reverie. 'You'll not be travelling around Rwanda on your own.'

'I haven't read it all,' Greta said, flicking through the five pages of instructions, visas, itineraries, flight tickets . . . She felt ashamed at her impulsiveness.

'A man by the name of Daniel will meet you at Kigali airport.'

She nodded.

Angus muffled his mouthpiece again, then came back on the line. 'Greta, I'm afraid I'm going to have to go. Take a look at the instructions and let me know if you still have concerns.'

'I will. Thank you, Angus. And . . . sorry.'

The line clicked.

Greta stared at the ceiling.

Rwanda. She was going to Rwanda.

'Just checking out,' Greta said to a young man standing talking to a colleague behind Reception. 'I need to get my passport from your safe.'

'Of course, madam. What is the name?'

'Jellings.'

As Greta waited, a tall, big-boned woman strode into the hotel and approached the desk. Probably a similar height to Greta. However, her stature was well camouflaged by her stylish clothes — a flowing silk jacket and beige palazzo pants.

'Can you tell me whether a Miss Jellings has checked out already?'

Greta shot a sideways glance at the stranger.

'One moment, I'll check for you.'

Greta's breathing picked up. Who was this woman?

'Your passport, Miss Jellings.'

'Greta Jellings?' the woman beside her exclaimed.

Greta's face grew hot. 'Yes.'

The woman enveloped Greta in a hug. 'I thought I'd missed you! I'm Rachel.'

Should Greta have known her? She stepped out of the embarrassing embrace. 'I think there's been some mistake . . . I'm afraid you've confused me with someone else. I've that sort of face.' (Greta had never met anyone who remotely resembled her.)

'I'm Mimi's daughter. The nursing home. They rung last night. I couldn't bear the thought of not meeting you. Brought my flight forward.' She looked down at Greta's luggage. 'Looks like I was just in time.'

Greta steadied herself against the counter. This was her cousin. Her first cousin! First as in the first cousin she'd ever known about, and first in lineage too. How she wished she hadn't chosen her comfy tracksuit pants for travelling.

'Sorry to spring myself on you like this, but it would have been such a shame to miss each other,' the woman said, tearing up.

Greta willed herself to say something appropriate. Meaningful. Impressive.

'You're very tall.'

The woman laughed. 'From the same stock, I guess,' she said, giving Greta a quick elevator assessment. 'Have you got time for a cup of tea?'

People in the lobby were looking.

'Ms Jellings, sorry to interrupt, but your taxi is here. I've told him to give you a few minutes.'

'We're family. It's the first time we've met,' Rachel said, making up for Greta's bewildered muteness.

'I know,' said the concierge. 'It's so exciting. Like that programme *Long Lost Family.*'

'Are you headed back to New Zealand today?' Rachel asked, blowing her nose with a hanky.

Greta shook her head. 'Rwanda.'

'Rwanda!'

Greta gave a nervous grimace.

'I've always wanted to go there,' her cousin said, running her hands through her hair. Nora had had the exact same mannerism.

'To Rwanda? Really?'

'Oh gosh, yes. It's on my bucket list.'

Greta unclenched her toes.

'I'm really sorry, Rachel. But I do have to leave in the next few minutes. I feel terrible. You've made a special trip. I don't know what the traffic to Heathrow will be like, but . . . perhaps we can email?' At least an email would allow Greta to control and revise her words.

'Absolutely! Look I'm just thrilled to have met you in person, albeit briefly. We'll have to plan a formal family reunion. Get you back here to meet the clan.'

She opened her arms. Greta hesitated, then stepped into another hug. The two women fitted perfectly, like matching pieces from a jigsaw puzzle.

CHAPTER 33

Greta's ears started to pop. She swallowed hard and looked out of her cabin window. The plane had broken through a clump of clouds and below was an undulating patchwork of reds and greens. It was what she'd been expecting. The ruralness. Yet also different from the image she'd held in her head. The vastness. Intense terracotta colour. The relentless blue of the sky.

Gradually the green gave way to almost all red — a clay-tile-and-tin-roof red interrupted only by the grey of dust dry trees.

She fastened her seatbelt and looked out of the window again. The vista had been transformed once more, this time by brick and concrete and lawn-lined avenues. A modern city sprawling up one hill and down the next. Kigali.

She was first in line to disembark, her belly a squelch and bubble of anticipation.

As the airline attendant turned the sturdy red lever and hauled open the cabin door, an oven-rush of heat hit Greta, instantly untying her. Her worries felt less valid in the heat.

'Welcome to Kigali,' said the attendant, her face all smile and shine.

Greta had been captivated by the cabin staff. Their tailored poise, generous spirit and easy laughter. The contour-swallowing blackness of their faces.

Kigali airport was not as overwhelming as Heathrow, nor JFK; but, reassuringly, as ordered and regulated, with snaking queues of people, polished linoleum floors and officials wielding stamps. It was certainly more sophisticated than she'd been expecting, especially after one of the cabin crew had used a manual click counter to confirm the number of passengers on board.

She wiped her palms on her pants, this time the heat, not fear, to blame.

It was only after she'd collected her luggage and was making her way through the roiling sea of faces in the Arrivals Hall that she felt the familiar hurry of her heartbeat. Would this Daniel person be there to meet her? How would she recognise him? Had Angus done his homework properly? What if the atmosphere turned suddenly sour; how easy would it be to get out? New York and London now seemed a doddle in comparison — the common language, culture, the cosmopolitan skin colours.

The airport trolley with one wonky wheel offered a shield against the newness.

Greta Jelly.

She did a double take.

The sign was meant for her. Surely.

She started to smile, with relief, and at the humour of it. She'd been called many things — old men favoured Gretchen, for some reason — but Greta *Jelly* was a first.

She steered her trolley towards the man holding a whiteboard.

'Hello. I'm Greta. Greta *Jellings*,' she said, enunciating her words carefully and pointing to her name on the whiteboard.

'Ah, Greta, you made it. Welcome.' He shook her hand. 'Daniel.'

'Daniel?' She paused. 'My guide Daniel?'

He smiled, his cheeks bunching into balls. 'The very one.'

'Oh,' she said, her thoughts tangling. 'It's just I was expecting you to be, uh . . . I thought you were going to be . . . Daniel is a white man's name, isn't it?'

White man's name. Really? What was she thinking? She'd never been good at pulling back once a thought had been released from the stalls.

A line of heat spread up her neck.

'This is not boot polish, I promise,' he said, with a chuckle.

Greta ploughed on. She pointed to the sign he was holding. 'Je-ll-ings, not Jelly. That's a wobbly pudding.' How condescending she sounded!

Daniel's brow creased slightly, then he burst out laughing. 'Hillaly made the sign for me. My eight-year-old daughter. She loves to help. She loves jelly too.'

Greta was relieved that her new host did not appear offended. He had a generous face with rounded features, as if a carpenter had sanded smooth any sharp edges.

Yet again she'd made presumptions.

'How was your flight?' asked Daniel with the focus of someone oblivious to the busyness around him.

'Oh, very good. Thank you for asking. The shortest one so far.'

'Yes, Angus tells me you have been on the go for some time.' He spoke English with effortless, colloquial ease.

'So, where to from here?' Greta asked, her nervousness driving to fill in gaps before they appeared.

Daniel took her trolley. 'I'm parked out front.'

Outside, Greta shielded her eyes from the bright sunlight and followed Daniel down a ramp lined with hibiscus bushes in full coral bloom. Everything was turned up high — the colours, the smiles, the heat, the sky.

He loaded her luggage into a battered green Jeep.

'Hop in,' he said, opening the front door for her.

The car smelt of perished leather and overripe bananas — oddly comforting after the fake fragrances of taxis and aeroplanes and expensive hotels.

Daniel climbed into the driver's seat and handed her a bottle of water.

'Thank you,' she said, almost grabbing it. 'I'm so thirsty.'

'There is plenty more where that came from,' he said, pointing to a block of bottles in the back seat. 'It gets hot here.' With that, he started the engine and they lurched down the road.

Greta sat mesmerised as Kigali unfolded before her. The road was teeming with vehicles, the pavement with people; yet, there was an overarching order to it all, confounding her notion of Third World chaos.

Terraced gardens rose up on either side, the staggered stonewall planters filled with frangipani trees and hibiscus bushes. Islands of lawn divided long, wide avenues. Black and white concrete blocks tessellated curbs. Cars and motorcycles circled a large fountain like orderly ants.

Daniel slowed for a traffic light.

A pool of pedestrians was waiting on the sidewalk. Some were carrying chic handbags, others balanced big bunches of bananas on their heads. Some wore jeans and a t-shirt, others traditional print, the bright-coloured swirls in sharp relief to their very black skin. A grey-haired man was raking the ring of sand around a tree. A woman sat on a bench breastfeeding . . . Then the Jeep was moving again.

Despite the heat and long flight, Greta felt so alive. As if a veil had been lifted. Every image, sound and smell acute, vivid, insistent.

Maybe that's what Walter had been getting at when he'd spoken of the wonders of travel. The way it pitched the novel against what had become stale and familiar. The way it could woo a person out of their own head.

Years of sameness had turned Greta's gaze inwards.

'So many mopeds!'

'Moto taxis,' Daniel corrected.

'You mean . . . people catch rides on them?'

'Sure. See that driver there? He is carrying an extra helmet on his arm ready for his next customer.'

As Daniel spoke, a woman on the roadside raised her hand. The moped swerved and pulled over. In a few seamless seconds the woman had hoisted herself onto the pillion seat, secured the spare helmet, and wrapped her arms around the driver's waist. Then off they went. Greta was quietly relieved that Daniel had collected her in a more conventional vehicle.

There was something about the city she couldn't quite place. Then it dawned.

'There's no litter.'

Daniel nodded. '*Umuganda*. We all collect litter on the last Saturday of every month. Everyone across the country gets involved.'

Greta was incredulous. She could conceive of someone orchestrating such an initiative in a single suburb perhaps, for a particular occasion. Maybe a Girl Guide drive, like those 'bob-a-job' days when she'd clean the neighbour's car or weed their front lawn for a coin. But collecting rubbish on a regular basis? An entire nation?

'Ya. Even our president, he participates,' added Daniel, taking a swig of water. 'For three hours once a month all traffic stops, stores shut and we clean up.'

Greta sank back into the springless slack of her seat. There was something quite unexpected about this little country in the heart of Africa.

'It's made easier,' he went on, 'because plastic bags are banned here. Rwanda, I believe, was the first country to achieve this.'

Yes, that was what was also missing — the ubiquitous plastic bag.

The Jeep swung into a driveway and came to a halt in front of a security boom. A man in camouflage gear stepped out.

Greta gripped her armrest as Daniel wound down his window and began conversing with the guard in a language she could not understand.

She eyed the gun slung over the man's shoulder. In New Zealand the

214

most dramatic thing she'd witnessed was a policeman using a Taser to subdue a vicious dog. Yet since she'd left home there'd been the border patrol officer at JFK airport, the guards at Buckingham Palace and now this soldier in Rwanda; all carrying serious weapons.

Her nose started to itch. She wiggled it. This was no time for sudden hand movements.

A second guard emerged from the guardhouse and moved slowly around the vehicle, sweeping a long stick with a mirror attached, under the car's chassis.

'What's going on?' Greta whispered, without moving her lips.

'A standard security check,' said Daniel. 'Nothing to worry about.'

Greta searched her memory for an appropriate prayer. She felt guilty about only praying when she needed something. One day she'd be penalised for it.

All she could retrieve from her fear-frozen brain was a song from her youth-group days. *He's Got The Whole World in His Hands.*

How she'd hated those Friday nights, which Nora forced her to attend. *'They are good kids from good homes, Greta.'*

Greta's dinner hamper receives the lowest bid at the 'dinner for two' night. Todd Druff was the only boy to bid for it at the auction, so she has to spend the entire evening with him, eating tuna quiche and oranges cut into smiley faces. Nora did not even include crisps.

Greta was up to the line, *He's got you and me, brother, in His hands,* when the security boom lifted and the guard waved them on.

The Jeep swung into the forecourt of a modern brick building. Daniel hauled up the handbrake. 'This will be your hotel for the next two nights,' he said, climbing out. 'Then we leave for the mountains.'

'Got it,' Greta said, trying to fake an easy-going demeanour.

A suited doorman with the whitest teeth she'd ever seen beamed at her as he relieved Daniel of her luggage.

'Good afternoon and welcome, madam.'

She curtsied.

Why on earth had she curtsied?

'Let us meet in the lobby at nine o'clock tomorrow morning,' Daniel said, climbing back inside the vehicle.

Greta didn't want him to go. This constant desertion by people charged with looking out for her was proving very stressful. What would it have been like to have a permanent partner in her life, she wondered? The guaranteed safety of someone, always. How was it that her life had turned out like this? Why did she have to be the one left swimming solo?

'*There's a lid to fit every can,*' was what Nora used to say. So, Greta grew up believing that somewhere out there was a man who would complete her. She just had to find him and then she'd be fine.

But she was thirty-nine and had not yet found that someone. No one bar Walter, who didn't count, being 'unavailable' in the life-time-commitment sense. Where was this superman who was supposed to supplement her deficits and be the solution to all her problems?

Superman . . . the thought brought a different memory to the surface.

'*Time to take off your super-cloak,*' *her father says to her as she climbs into bed.* '*Even supergirls need their sleep.*'

Greta pretends to take off the cloak and lay it on her bedside table. It's red and gold with silver tassels and emerald stars.

Whenever Greta is struggling with something, it is the first thing her father directs her to.

'*You'll work it out, young lady. You have all the power in that super-cloak of yours.*'

When did she stop believing in it, she wonders?

The doorman of the Kigali hotel was holding open the door for her and she scurried inside.

'If madam could please place her handbag and belt in the tray before walking through the scanner.'

Greta was standing in front of a device more suited to US Airport Security than a hotel. Safe country indeed! If she lived to tell the tale, she'd have words with Angus.

She stepped through the metal detector and made her way through the lobby to Reception.

Nothing so far fitted with what she had envisioned for a small Third World Nation recently emerged from one of the darkest periods in history. It was the manner of the people which caught her most by surprise. The Customs officer. The janitor in the airport toilets. The baggage handler. Cabin crew. Daniel . . . Everyone was so gracious, while also owning a quiet confidence and pride. But pride? Greta was perplexed. Hacking your neighbour to death with a machete was not something to be proud of. This was surely all just a veneer to beguile the tourists. Well, she knew better.

Greta awoke to the sound of birds in the bougainvillea outside her bedroom window and the bluest of skies. A sky which swallowed everything in its vastness.

Daniel was already waiting for her when she emerged from the breakfast room.

'And how are you this morning, Greta?'

'Glad to be alive.'

He chuckled. She was being absolutely serious.

'So, you have strength for this day?'

Greta blanched. *Strength for this day* was an alarming turn of phrase.

'Everybody thinks of the genocide when they think of Rwanda, no?' Daniel said, as they walked to the car.

His directness caught her off guard. She mumbled. Nothing sensible came out.

Despite the absence of any preamble or suitable segue, she was relieved to have that word out in the open. Genocide. Dancing around it was more frightening. For her, and surely for every other visitor to Rwanda, it was the elephant in the room.

'So today I must take you to the Kigali Genocide Memorial and explain a little of our history.'

Greta nodded cautiously.

'Some of it will not be easy,' he warned, as he opened the car door for her. 'But to understand this place and our people, to appreciate what is the richness of Rwanda, and where we have come from, it is important.'

Greta searched for her seatbelt. Securing it did little to lessen her disquiet. She'd been expecting a tour of local tourist spots, not a trip through the country's time of terror. Lounging beside the hotel pool held more appeal. Though she wouldn't be swimming; she'd noticed patches of black algae on the walls. The chlorine balance was clearly off.

'The museum will tell a better story than I can,' Daniel went on. 'Pictures have more power, no?'

Greta flicked her thumb against her forefinger until it hurt. She was annoyed. With him. With Walter. This was her holiday. Holiday. Why on earth had he chosen Rwanda?

'I've seen the movie,' she said. 'Well, from behind the safety of my sofa cushions.'

Daniel's brow creased.

'You know. *Hotel Rwanda.*'

'Ah, yes.'

She waited for him to say more. For him to suggest aborting the trip and instead take her to some craft market or art studio. At the very least, she expected him to try to convince her that the film was more Hollywood fantasy than reality.

He said nothing.

A small open van laden with mattresses overtook them, the driver apparently oblivious to his precarious load — fifteen odd mattresses stacked loosely in a listing Princess-and-the-Pea pile.

Daniel slowed, possibly to avoid any unexpected foam missiles. But then she saw that they were approaching a wide archway heralding the entrance to the Kigali Genocide Memorial.

'I'll wait for you here,' he said, parking in the shade of a flame tree in brilliant flower. 'There will be a short introductory film, then you are free to wander through the exhibitions and gardens. Be comfortable to take your time.'

Greta ran her tongue between her top lip and gum as she crossed the car park. It was barely mid-morning and already she could feel the heat of the red brick paving through her shoes.

What was she doing in this tiny landlocked country, about to revisit some of history's worst brutality? Only weeks earlier she'd been ordering pool chemicals in Auckland and making cups of tea for Jud Rutland.

She signed in at the desk and made her way to the small theatre, positioning herself three seats away from other tourists already seated. She wished she had the courage to sit beside them, but it was always the same, just like at the movies, a few chairs at least, her buffer.

She'd stopped going to the cinema by herself; the outings only made her feel more alone. Solitary moviegoers invited judgement, or worse, pity. These days she opted for DVDs, though now that they were being phased out, she'd have to learn how to master Ned's Flicks, or whatever it was called.

Two hours later, Greta again crossed the paved carpark. Despite Daniel being where she'd left him, the distance to the car felt further and the day dingier. She now knew the facts. Had a handle on the truth. The text-book details. How eight-hundred-thousand Tutsis had been massacred by Hutus in under a hundred days. How the ruling Belgians had stoked years of tension between the two tribes, favouring one over the other because their facial features more closely resembled those of the colonialists. How in 1994 the shooting down of a plane carrying the Rwandan president incited the first violence.

She could relay these facts to anyone who asked. But the rest — the images, the stories and the harrowing emotions she'd experienced inside that building — they'd fallen into a black hole in her head. She was glad for the respite, even though she knew it could only be temporary. It would all resurface in time and she wasn't sure she'd be able to deal with the deluge when it did.

She looked up. Heavy charcoal clouds had squashed themselves into the Kigali sky.

'All okay?' Daniel asked, lowering the newspaper he was reading. 'Much to take on board, no?'

She lifted her eyebrows in dazed acknowledgement.

'It must be time for lunch,' he said, his face breaking into a beam.

Smiling felt wrong. Eating too.

'I will take you to a traditional Kigali restaurant. There you will be able to sample our customary fare.'

There was a sudden clap of thunder and giant raindrops started exploding onto the windscreen as the clouds dumped their cargo.

Greta could barely hear Daniel above the noise of the rain on the roof. It was as if the sky was weeping and raging and trying to wash clean the earth.

Rwanda was like a child's fairy-tale — the beauty, the smells, the pain — everything so vivid, dramatic, exaggerated.

Torrents of muddy water gushed down the drains between the terraced banks, waterfalling into cambers, which only minutes earlier had been dry.

She inhaled the fresh fragrance filling the car — a bold confusion of grass clippings, steaming earth and tree-green sweetness — the cool air soothing some of the turmoil inside her head.

Daniel appeared unfazed as he manoeuvred the car through an almost opaque curtain of water.

'That's efficient drainage for you,' Greta exclaimed, marvelling at the way the huge man-made drains diverted torrential volumes of water.

She cringed at how her comment came out; she sounded like some sage town planner.

'Ya,' Daniel said, lifting his hands off the steering wheel. 'Erosion was once a big problem,' he said. 'Terracing the banks and installing big drainpipes has changed all that.'

He put her at ease the way he engaged so enthusiastically with her comments. She liked him. He was easy to be around. Though she did wish he'd keep both his hands on the steering wheel.

She pointed.

He chuckled.

The forecourt of a fuel station was packed with hundreds of moto-taxis sheltering from the deluge.

'Don't the garage owners get annoyed? I mean, anyone who wants fuel can't get near the pumps.'

Daniel turned to her, his expression one of surprise. 'The storm will pass. Everyone understands.'

She nodded, the comment capturing something essential about the place. Rwanda seemed both patient and profound. As if it had learnt an important life lesson.

They stopped for lunch at a restaurant more akin to a private home than a public eatery. The small brick building opened out onto a square of garden around which were dotted a clutch of tables. Inside the front room clay pots were arranged buffet style. As Daniel explained the contents, Greta helped herself to a little of each.

Isombe, a vegetarian dish of cassava leaves, eggplant, and spinach. Beans. Matooke or cooked green bananas. Ugali, a stiff maize porridge. Chapatti. A small pot of beef stew. A cauldron of peanut gravy.

Greta passed on the gravy.

'You don't like peanuts?'

Greta loved anything to do with peanuts. In fact, her favourite snack was a slice of white bread smeared thickly with peanut butter. But the peanut sauce in the cauldron was gum pink.

Reluctantly, she ladled a little onto her plate.

Once seated, Daniel picked up a chunk of the maize porridge with his fingers, indented it with his thumb, then used it to scoop up some stew.

Greta glanced around.

No one is watching, Grets.

She picked up her fork. Put it down again. Let her hand hover over her plate. Lowered it slowly towards the food . . .

Nora's horrified face appeared on the plate.

Greta shut her eyes and like a blind seagull dive-bombing the ocean, sunk her fingers into the warm, putty-like porridge.

Her first mouthful had the metallic aftertaste of hand-sanitiser, but she persisted. Eating with her fingers felt supremely satisfying.

'I see you enjoy your meat,' she said, chewing on a rubbery piece of steak. Daniel's plate was piled high with stew.

He mopped up some gravy with a piece of chapatti. 'Ya. It is a treat. My family we eat meat maybe once a month. It is very expensive.'

Greta felt herself flush. She would not be able to leave hers.

A memory surfaced of the time Nora took her to Warkworth for a long weekend. They'd stayed at a bed-and-breakfast run by a woman with a cluster of black whiskers on her chin, who'd over-catered for her two visitors.

'I'm full.'

'You can't leave it, Greta. You will offend our host.'

'But I've eaten a lot already.'

'Give me your backpack,' Nora says brusquely. The small daypack doubles as Greta's school bag. 'Scoop the rest into your serviette and we'll put it in the bag. Hurry now.'

Greta never is able to rid her bag of the smell of sausages and bacon.

The memory dislodged another avalanche of anger at Nora's misplaced priorities. What did it even mean to be true to oneself? Nora certainly hadn't known.

She eyed the pool of peanut sauce as she chewed through the rest of her stew. The pallid pink liquid was not something she could stow in her handbag, nor could she stomach eating it. Fortunately, Daniel commented on its spiciness.

'I'm sorry, but the sauce, it's . . . well, not really to my taste.'

Daniel didn't seem bothered at all. 'How did you find the memorial today?' he asked with a steady gaze.

She put down her glass. 'I don't think I can talk about it,' she said, her voice cracking. 'Not now. Sorry.'

Her blouse sleeve had dipped into the pink peanut sauce, and as she reached for a tissue in her handbag, gravy dripped down her front.

'Oh no! How clumsy. I . . .'

'I understand. When you are ready.'

Daniel didn't linger on her distress, nor focus on her fumbling.

She rummaged in her handbag for her sunglasses.

'So,' she said too loudly, her eyes now hidden. 'What have you got planned for my afternoon?'

'I will drop you back at the hotel after lunch.'

She was relieved. She needed time alone.

'Tomorrow we have an early start. It will be a long day. We begin our journey into the mountains.'

There was something very genuine and unaffected about Daniel. Greta wondered what his story was.

A loud barking moan interrupted their conversation. They spun round. A wide-faced boy, seated at the table behind them, was thumping his head on the table.

A glass on the table teetered, toppled and shattered on the slasto paving.

The boy's bellows grew louder.

An elderly man at the table stood up and started picking up the shards of glass, while a woman with the party used her serviette to mop up the spill and the drool leaking from the boy's mouth.

He shrieked again, rocking backwards and forwards.

The woman took his arm gently and began rubbing it in a steady circular motion. Slowly the boy settled.

The owner of the eatery emerged with a replacement drink and started chatting to the group, all the while patting the young boy on the back.

Daniel joined in the conversation. And though Greta couldn't understand what was being said, the mood was relaxed and convivial. There was even laughter.

The room, death quiet, is filled with people. Photographs of people pegged to strands of wire. Some of the faces are buckled, some creased, some pinned to the pages of identity booklets. Row upon row upon row of faces.

222

Greta doesn't know where to begin. Her progress through the room has to be considered and measured. She cannot gloss over one single image. If she does, she will be diminishing that life.

A barefoot child with toddler pudginess beams. If there were sound, the child would surely be giggling. Greta can't help but smile.

A man holds an ornate stick in his hand. It is some sort of ceremony, perhaps.

One woman sits with identity-document seriousness, an official stamp hiding some of her softness.

A family pose for a portrait, father in suit and bowtie, mother in a flowing dress of blue and white. The teen has gangly legs; the youngest, a girl, folded arms. A third child holds his arms straight as a soldier's. Greta tries to imagine what it would be like posing for a family photograph. She in the middle, Victor and Nora on either side of her.

A young woman smiles side-on in a self-conscious, coy kind of way.

A couple cradle their newborn.

An old man dances.

A bride beams.

In a corner of the room Greta spots a man seated on a chair a few feet from a photograph. His jacket, too wide for his frame, has sunk into the hollows around his shoulders. His proximity to the photograph leaves Greta uncomfortable; there is a code of behaviour for museums. An acceptable distance from which to observe exhibits. The man is too close.

Twenty minutes later, as she is leaving the room, Greta looks round. He is still there, his back still turned on the rest of the room. All of a sudden she understands.

Another room is filled with objects. Objects dropped in a hurry. A key on a ring of red beads. A tin mug. A tiny shoe, its glitter-speckled plastic as cold as the air-conditioned room. A wooden comb with strands of black hair caught in its teeth. A scythe. A machete.

It is the hair in the comb that gets Greta, even more than the weapons with blood-stained blades.

A washing line has been suspended across another space and pegged with clothes. A pretty floral skirt gathered at the waist. Greta loves gathered waists. She steps closer. Squints. Puts a hand to her mouth. Fine black splatters interrupt the busy floral pattern.

223

Beside the skirt hangs a pair of men's trousers. The central crease of one leg has been ripped where a thigh would have been.

Greta moves quickly on, leaving the remainder of the room unexplored.

As she moves through the next doorway she stops, turns, starts to retreat. But it is too late. The snapshot in her head has already been taken. Bleached bones and skulls stacked in small, steady piles.

Greta smooths out the damp pamphlet in her hand and scrutinises the map of the building. Only a few more rooms left.

She could retrace her steps. Or escape through a fire exit. But she doesn't. Like reading a book, she feels she must finish what she has begun.

In a room devoted to children murdered in the genocide, more photographs hang. But here the portraits have not been scaled down; they are life-size and annotated.

> Fabrice MURINZI MINEGA
> Age 8
> *Favourite sport: Swimming*
> *Favourite sweets: Chocolate.*
> *Best friend: His mum*
> *Behaviour: Gregarious*
> *Cause of death: Bludgeoned with a club.*

Greta's pace picks up. To her relief she sees that the next room contains personal written accounts. Just words. No photographs. She can cope with that.

'In my search for a hideout, I found Jérôme, his legs cut off. I could not leave him in this state. I tried to lift Jérôme up so that we could leave together, but the car of the commune stopped near me. It was full of machetes and other instruments of death. I lay Jérôme down on the ground and ran, because a man got out of the burgomaster's car to kill me.

He finished Jérôme off.

I saw this when I looked back to see if anyone had followed me. I will never forget the way Jérôme's face was filled with desperation. Whenever I think about it, I cry all day long.'

— Eric, 13

The fire-exit slams behind her.

Outside, Greta sucks in big gulps of hot, suffocating air. Tears stream down her face. She walks in a daze through the gardens.

There is a memorial wall running alongside the path. She stretches out her hand and touches the cool, grey marble, her fingertips tracing one of the many names engraved into it.

Ngarambe Benithe.

Beneath this name, *Ngarambe Bosco.*

Then *Ngarambe Charles.*

Ngarambe Console

Ngarambe Mukanyangezi

Ngarambe Oswald

Ngarambe Pierre

So many Ngarambes.

Greta sat up in the dark, her bedclothes damp with perspiration, her face wet with tears. The outline of her hotel room came slowly into focus.

She swung her legs over the edge of the bed, steadying herself on shaky arms.

The alarm clock fluoresced. 2.17am. The morning was still such a long way off.

She switched on the light. Too bright. She switched it off again. Circles of jagged green drove through the darkness. She shut her eyes. Another image appeared behind her eyelids, of thousands of bloated bodies floating down a river towards Uganda.

She opened her eyes again.

'So, what am I to do with these horrors, Walter?' she whispered into the darkness. 'What did you hope me to get from it all? What?'

CHAPTER 34

Kigali receded and a panorama of hills unfurled in front of them.

'We call it land of a thousand hills,' said Daniel, tossing a handful of nuts into his mouth.

Greta filled her lungs and breathed out slowly. She was glad to be leaving the city behind them. Beautiful scenery offered fewer challenges. The previous day had stripped away the layers she usually wrapped around her life. She felt exposed. Vulnerable. As if the emotions had drilled down to a deeper place. To the centre. To Greta unchecked.

Their progress was slowed by a milk tanker. Through her open window Greta could hear the metal urns clanging as they jostled against each other.

A cyclist interposed himself between the Jeep and the truck.

'Not an incline I'd want to cycle up,' Greta said, contemplating the seemingly endless ascent. 'He must be very fit.'

All of a sudden, the cyclist listed to the right.

Greta covered her eyes.

Daniel chuckled.

She squinted through her fingers. 'Never!'

The young man was now clinging to the back of the tanker and enjoying a free ride up the hill.

As the Jeep pulled out to pass the truck, the new passenger beamed in greeting.

'*Land of a thousand hills and a million smiles,*' Daniel said, waving back.

'I don't understand,' Greta said. 'Why is everyone so happy? I mean after all that's gone on here.'

Daniel was quiet. Had she offended him?

'We had two options,' he finally said. 'To die and decay. Or begin again. Under Paul Kagame we began again.' He lifted both hands off the wheel.

'The focus of everything we do is about rebuilding our community. About making Rwanda strong once more.'

'Yes, but there must still be so much sadness. And resentment. So much hatred.'

'There is forgiveness instead,' he said. 'Forgiveness offers something for victim and perpetrator. What you see when you look around is the power of compassion.' He wiped his mouth with his palm. 'In special reconciliation villages some people even live next door to those who may have murdered the rest of their family.'

Greta unscrewed a bottle of water and took a long drink.

'I'm sorry, Daniel, but I just cannot understand that. Living alongside someone who's slaughtered your loved ones?'

She tried to imagine coexisting with the gay-bashing thugs who'd kicked in Walter's skull and ruptured his spleen.

No, she could never forgive them.

A valley fell away in front of them, opening onto fields that stretched all the way to the horizon. Greta spotted what looked like a line of pink embroidery thread weaving through fields of sorghum. As they got closer, she saw that it was workers dressed in Nesquik-pink overalls, hoeing the land.

'Prisoners,' Daniel said, answering her gaze. 'Many are still serving time for crimes they committed during the genocide. They work their community's land. Always visible. Always seen to be giving back.'

If this was a charade, it was on a fairly grand scale.

'Are you Hutu or Tutsi, Daniel?'

His cheek twitched. 'There is no tribal identification now,' he said. 'It is illegal to use such terms.'

'Yes, but what were you at the time of the genocide?'

'I am Rwandan.'

Greta felt ashamed that she had persisted, like a journalist desperate for a story.

They passed three policemen leaning against their patrol car, one with a machine gun slung over his shoulder.

'They are speed trapping,' Daniel said. Then he was gesturing to the driver of an oncoming car, his right finger pointing upwards.

'We have a sort of sign language,' he said, repeating the signal for another approaching car. 'This means *cop at the top of the hill*.'

'I see,' Greta said, delighted to have finally found a flaw in Daniel's perfection. 'So even in Rwanda people try to foil the authorities.'

He gave a hearty laugh. 'If you get caught, you must pay the fine on the spot, or they take your car as payment, until you do.'

'Your car! But what if you don't have money on you?'

'Cash does not change hands anymore. Not when a government body is involved. Everything is done with our mobile phones. From paying taxes to traffic fines. Since this was introduced corruption has halved.'

Apps. Mobile phones. Banned plastic bags!

Daniel told her how almost everyone, even villagers, owned a mobile phone. How 4G cables surrounded the country, and drones delivered blood to victims of car accidents in remote rural regions. How a permit was required to cut down a tree, and three trees had to be planted for every one cut down. How all government offices closed at midday on a Friday to enable employees to participate in an exercise programme. How guns were permitted only in the police and army. How each village could decide upon the way their allotment of taxes was spent.

Greta was stunned. Such a tiny country with such a phenomenal drive to repair, progress, succeed.

The previous night had been the longest ever. She'd felt overwhelmed by what she'd seen at the memorial, by man's cruelty. Overwhelmed and helpless. She was a useless bystander with nothing to offer. A tourist who at the end of her holiday would get on a plane and leave this country behind.

Yet now, not even twenty-four hours later, she was feeling different. Buoyed. Hopeful.

Four days after Walter is discharged from hospital following the attack, he rings Greta to ask if she'd like to go with him to Tiritiri Matangi for the day.

'Where?'

'It's a small island just three kilometres offshore. A wildlife sanctuary. Can't believe you've never heard of it. You'll love it.'

'But are you up to an outing? Don't you think you should still be resting?'

'Any more rest and I'll be dead.'

And so they head out by ferry across the Hauraki Gulf.

It is a perfect day — blue skies, calm ocean, salt-sweet air. But Greta cannot relax. Walter's yellowing bruises lend his face a sallow hue, and his gait is painfully tentative. They walk the island slowly, her arm through his. He doesn't object. For the first time he looks the fifteen-years-older-than-her that he is.

The island is beautiful, the native forest, golden grasslands, the clusters of cabbage trees. They spot a plump kereru with its startling-green chest and bright beak, also wetas, geckos, a takahe and a saddleback. They climb the lighthouse steps carefully and take in a breathtaking vista of greenery tumbling towards the ocean. They enjoy a cup of tea and a date scone at the small kiosk . . .

'Tiritiri Matangi means "buffeted by the wind" in Māori,' he says, lying back on the beach beside the ferry terminal.

This translation conjures for Greta the fragile, battered Walter.

'Are you really okay?' she asks, turning to him.

He smiles. He is missing a front tooth. 'This place always makes me feel whole.'

It is then she realises that Walter had made a conscious decision to leave the horror behind. She must, too, even though she feels so helpless and angry seeing her friend still suffering.

'Nothing stays the same forever, Grets.'

It was evening when Greta and Daniel wove through mist-muted tea plantations, arriving at a small lodge nestling in the Ngungwe Forest. Dusk had transformed the green mountains into black silhouettes which receded into the distance like staggered stage props.

Greta climbed out of the car and stretched, the evening air swathing her in cool blue silence. A burst of breeze brought whispers and smells of a damp earth.

'Oh my!'

She closed her eyes, swept up by something bigger. In New York and London and Auckland, man bellowed from the skyscrapers, pulsed from the fluorescent lights and boasted from bright signboards. Engines roared. Suspension bridges soared. Satellites circled. Politicians talked. Prisoners rioted. Stock exchanges crashed. Divorce lawyers haggled. But in the mountains . . . in the mountains man was less significant. Far less significant.

Daniel's voice broke through her reverie.

'Someone will show you to your bungalow. At dinner I will introduce you to the rest of the group.'

Greta's heart sank. She'd been hoping that Angus had got it wrong. That the 'tour group' would comprise just her, with David as her guide.

How foolish! It probably wasn't even possible to have a tour party of one, unless you were some A-list celebrity.

CHAPTER 35

Greta made her way through the plantation along lantern-lit pathways. Lights were on at the lodge, brightening a small corner of the dawn. It was four-thirty in the morning and already bent bodies bearing conical baskets bobbed silently up and down rows of tea bushes.

Greta stifled a yawn. She'd not slept well. Reception had offered her a wake-up call, but she'd set her travel clock too; after all, computers could crash. Then she'd spent much of the night worrying the batteries in her clock would die.

An enormous brown bug on the ceiling hadn't helped, especially after it disappeared when she went to the loo. She pulled her bed away from the wall, shook out her bedding and checked her slippers. All to no avail. Catching rogue insects was definitely a prerequisite for an ideal life partner.

The image of that superwoman cape with silver tassels again flashed into her mind. She pushed away the thought.

Back home in Auckland, a stocky little man dressed in a blue boiler suit arrived each October to douse her house in pyrethrum. Pyrethrum, an entirely natural substance that kept most bugs at bay. Not that there were many harmful creatures in New Zealand, other than the very rare katipo spider. There were no deadly insects, or snakes, or bears, or crocodiles, or gorillas, or scorpions. Nor hippos either. Come to think of it, New Zealand was a little pocket of perfection. The most dangerous inhabitant was probably the human.

Spraying her house for insects was not entirely aligned with Greta's ethos, and she did feel conflicted whenever she found one in a state of rigor mortis on her windowsill. However, the discomfort this engendered was far less than the anguish she experienced spotting a spider abseiling down her headboard. Paying the pyrethrum man seventy-nine dollars once a year was definitely money well spent.

Dinner at the lodge the previous evening had been an odd affair, akin to some sort of reality TV show in which an eclectic bunch of contestants were thrown together under challenging circumstances. All that effort required to prove herself again.

The evening had started out with Greta trying to decide what to wear. First impressions were so important.

She oscillated between her intrepid-adventurer outfit and something more elegant, finally settling on the second option — her black cocktail dress and New York red wedges. She felt good in her new shoes. Superwoman good.

Something elegant turned out to be the wrong choice; the others were kitted out far more casually.

The 'others' comprised Lian and Quon, a Chinese couple from California; Dorte, a young Danish woman; Fergus, a widowed Australian pilot; and Edith and Hal, a couple from Britain.

Fergus, the pilot, was a burly, heavy-browed man with a wide, downturned mouth. Greta was familiar with his sort. Recently single and suspicious of every unmarried woman's motives, he made a point of loudly ring-fencing his personal space, affections and fortune. He mentioned his late wife, Sylvia, so many times that by the end of the evening Greta felt as if she'd been seated alongside her all night.

Dorte, a photographer in her late twenties, had Scandinavian-blonde hair and legs which eventually ended in a pair of eye-wateringly-short shorts. So much for defying stereotypes.

Greta noticed that Fergus did not mention his late wife quite as often when Dorte was in earshot.

Greta, on the other hand, found Dorte disconcertingly brusque.

'I have a spare pair of gloves, if you need them,' Greta offered. 'Daniel bought me two pairs in Kigali.'

'Glove?'

'Gardening gloves,' Greta said, beginning to blush. There was a brash confidence about Gen-Y youths. 'I'm told there'll be stinging nettles to contend with. Apparently they're a favourite snack for gorillas.'

She felt good about sharing this important piece of information. The group might consider her a valuable asset.

'It's a good idea to wear gloves, just in case you mistakenly grab onto a—'

'No, No. I don't need.'

Dorte was definitely not some stumbling, bumbling, woolly-worded woman. She was everything Greta was not.

Lian and Quon were more genial, with a steady supply of Chinese/Californian charm. 'We have wanted to do this for a very long time,' Lian said softly, dipping her head to one side. 'It is exciting to now be so close.'

Her husband, a man of few words, gave a solitary nod.

When Greta learnt that Quon was an actuary, conversation took a turn for the worse. That the man likely interacted with only the most intelligent of people left her tongue-tied and struggling to come up with anything urbane to say.

'And what work do you do?' Lian asked.

It was inevitable, the question. Just a matter of time.

She worked in a pool chemicals shop. No, she was not a chemist. No, not her own business. Yes, more of an administrator slash personal assistant. But a big client base. She did all the invoices and was sometimes even charged with placing product advertisements in the paper. Quite a challenge in terms of word limits and catchy phrases . . . She petered out.

The other couple, Edith and Hal Nibblit, arrived late, somewhat flustered and ill-tempered. Their connecting flight had been delayed and they'd had to arrange new transport into the mountains after missing their earlier ride. They owned an electrical business, and, while they loved to travel, struggled to get away because of the challenge of finding someone 'competent enough to manage the business in our absence'.

The second course, steamed tilapia on a bed of lemon rice, was just being served when Hal summoned the waiter.

'The wine has been chilled.'

'Yes, sir,' the waiter said, beaming.

'Red wine should never be chilled.'

'Good on a warm night, no?'

'No. Not good. Not good at all. You can't call yourself a top-class tourist destination and chill the red wine.'

The waiter's smile collapsed. 'You would like me to make it warm?'

'Not make it warm! I'd like you to get another bottle. Is all your red kept in the fridge?'

'I will check with the manager, sir.'

Hal turned to the rest of the table. 'Third World service, bloody First World prices.'

'The whole trip is overpriced, if you ask me,' piped up his wife, Edith. 'Just because they have a monopoly on the gorilla market.'

Greta looked down at her plate, avoiding the eyes of a second waiter still waiting on the table.

If Hal had wanted to be absolutely correct, thought Greta, he should not have ordered red wine to accompany a fish dish in the first place.

The next morning, Lian and Quon were already standing beside the Jeep when Greta approached.

'Hello, Grehtah,' said Lian. 'What a beautiful morning.'

Greta looked down at Lian's small feet. Everything about the woman was delicate, reserved, considered.

'Oh, it is,' said Greta, a little out of breath after the steep climb from her bungalow.

A pink band on the horizon was unravelling into dawn. It was breathtaking — the colours, the majesty, the peace of the place. Yet it left her with an ache in her chest, her aloneness more acute against such a beautiful backdrop. She had no one to share it with. The small place that had been her Devonport villa, filled with all her familiar things, had kept the loneliness contained.

Edith and Hal were again the last to arrive, protesting that their bungalow had no hairdryer, nor any Earl Grey tea bags.

'It beggars belief. I mean, this is a tea plantation,' Edith said, her eyes bulging in thyroidal exclamation.

Both were dressed in full safari regalia, pith helmets to boot.

With everyone finally assembled, Daniel briefed the group. Then they were piling into the Jeep and heading to the starting point in the Nyungwe Forest from where they would be trekking to see (hopefully) one of the troops of habituated chimpanzees.

It wasn't long before they left the open hills and were tramping through a hot and humid forest crammed with vegetation. Trees, hungry for light, stretched to the sky, their paths confounded by creeper and fern and air-rooted epiphyte. Every now and then a hole in the dense canopy opened onto a small balloon of blue; however, Greta kept her focus on her feet as she negotiated the slippery slopes and gnarly roots.

Gripping a carved wooden walking pole with one hand, she swatted away insects with the other. The repellent she'd slathered over herself was clearly not as effective as the package promised, and it wasn't long before her mind was navigating the corridors of some small rural hospital, where she saw herself on a cold, metal-framed bed, her body shaking with fever and rigors, as malaria consumed her brain.

Dying alone in Africa was not how she'd envisaged her life ending. On the plus side, any lack of numbers at her funeral could be comfortably explained away by Rwanda's distance from New Zealand. Greta fretted not infrequently about what the turnout would be to her funeral.

The spongy forest floor was alive with blue-backed caterpillars, orange toadstools, striped beetles, tiny crimson flowers . . . Greta had never seen anything like it, and gradually her focus started to shift from her fears to her surroundings.

Every now and then sun punctured the layers of green to land on the path in a slice of golden light. Walking through these warm pockets of gold felt weirdly spiritual.

Greta glanced at her mother's old watch. Bubbles of condensation now clung to the glass. It was this almost insignificant detail that brought home to her what she was doing — walking through a humid African jungle in pursuit of wild animals. Never would she have believed it had a clairvoyant read this in her palm.

So far, she'd been pushed forward by the momentum of The Plan, every experience letter-automated and surreal and not quite hers.

The realisation both terrified and thrilled her, for in that split second both the dangerousness of what she was doing, and her intrepidness, dawned. It was a moment of admonition, while also a rare nod to her nerve.

'Ants!' The word echoed down the human chain like falling domino blocks.

'Ants!'

'Ants!'

Ever since the Stuart twins had imprisoned Greta on top of an Argentine ant nest while playing war one summer, Greta had had a phobia about the tiny critters. She started stomping her boots.

'Doing the gumboot dance, Glenda?' Hal said, spittle escaping his moustached mouth.

'Greta,' she corrected, reluctantly tempering her footwork.

Fortunately, the groups attention moved to Dorte, who had ignored Greta's guidebook-advice about tucking her trousers into her socks. As the woman hopped around, furiously trying to rid herself of the biting ants, Fergus explained to anyone who'd listen that ants were a good source of protein for gorillas.

The group kept moving, and despite Dorte now nursing angry red ankles, she still refused to indulge in the trousers-in-socks fashion faux pas.

After a particularly steep climb, they all stopped to catch their breath.

Greta eyed the Kalashnikov — a Fergus fact — slung over the rangers' shoulders. Never mind the condensation on her watch. Being in reach of a semi-automatic weapon was a sobering reality check.

'So, you want to be a daredevil, do you?' says Nora, insisting Greta get down off the waist-high wall. 'Well not on my watch, my girl, unless you want a broken leg or twisted ankle. If God had wanted you to be able to travel above the ground, he'd have given you wings.'

If only Nora was here now to call her back inside.

Would she ever get back home, she wondered? Home. Ha! Travelling had supplanted her life with different concrete details, and her old existence almost seemed an abstract series of neural connections.

Samuel, the ranger, called everyone over. 'Our tracker has located one of the chimp families. Let us go quickly. Chimpanzees move very fast.'

Invigorated by the news, they picked up their pace.

'We must be quick,' he said, chivvying them on. 'Also quiet.'

Not fifty metres further, as they entered a small clearing, the forest hum was fractured by an ear-piercing screech.

Greta froze.

Another screech followed, and another, as the sounds built to a terrifying crescendo.

Habituated to humans indeed! Chimpanzees were clearly about to attack.

Greta's brain searched for what to do in such a scenario.

Stop, drop, roll? No, that was for a fire.

Drop, cover, hold? No, that was for an earthquake . . . but it would have to do.

She flung herself down to the forest floor, rolled under a giant fern frond and held her head in her hands.

236

As abruptly as the sound started, it stopped, but the blood was thumping so loudly in Greta's head, it took a few moments for her to realise.

'No, no. Don't you be worrying.'

She peeked out from the damp undergrowth to see the ranger's heavy brown boots moving towards her. He was beaming widely.

'It is nothing to be afraid of,' Samuel said, helping her up.

'You okay there, Grehtah?' asked Lian, rubbing Greta's back.

Greta dusted herself down and gave an embarrassed laugh. 'Just a little unnerved.'

'Panting hoots,' piped up Fergus.

Greta swung round. 'What?' Her irritability was more a measure of her fear than anything else.

'Panting hoots. The way chimps communicate to the rest of the troop when they've found fruit.'

The man had an answer for everything.

Rustling overhead made everyone look up.

'Woah!' Greta cried, as a chimp landed on a branch directly above her.

It bent so low that it looked like the chimp was going to slide right off, but at the last minute, the branch sprang back up, ricocheting the interloper onto another tree.

'Ahah,' Quon said with a grunt of satisfaction.

'More over there!' Dorte cried, focusing her long lens in a different direction.

Greta followed the woman's gaze.

In the crook of a tree, one leg nonchalantly crossed over the other, sat a chimp chewing on a bunch of brown berries. He tilted his head as he surveyed his audience, his expression that of a cheeky schoolboy.

Without warning, the tree-jumping chimp grabbed the bunch of berries off the second one and swung to the next tree.

Screeching in frustration, the robbed one gave chase.

'We keep following,' said Samuel, beckoning to the group. 'Chimpanzees are not like gorillas. They are always moving.'

'A mother with its baby,' Dorte said, pointing to a platform of branches.

'And still in bed,' chortled the ranger. 'Lazybones.'

'You know they make a new bed every single night,' said Fergus.

Greta was impressed. They were not simple constructions.

The mother wrapped an arm around her baby and eyed the humans cautiously. Greta leaned forward in an almost swoon. Lian clapped her hands. Dorte's camera whirred. Edith laughed.

'Chimps have ninety-eight percent human DNA,' said Fergus, severing the magic of the moment.

'Ssssh!'

Greta looked around to see who had finally put him in his place. She felt instantly sorry for Fergus. His collapsed face said it all.

The forest erupted again as four chimps swung through the space, somersaulting, fooling and shrieking. Their tomfoolery was infectious. Everyone in the group, even Hal, was laughing.

Two hours later, tired and hungry, they all climbed back into the Jeep.

'The mother and baby were my favourite,' said Lian, assuming her seat beside her husband. 'So special to see that.'

'Do you have children?' Greta asked, squeezing in beside her.

Lian's face fell.

Quon stiffened. 'We have one daughter. She practices law in Chicago.'

'Yes, a lawyer,' Lian repeated.

'You people tend to only have one child, don't you?' Edith said, turning round from the front.

Lian coloured. Quon pulled his head back as if assessing Edith from a distance. Greta could see his actuarial mind considering, dividing, concluding.

'And you Grehtah?' Lian asked quickly.

'Oh, no. No children. Poor me, I don't even have any siblings,' she said with faux humour.

Too late, she realised this was not an appropriate comment considering what had just been said about single children.

Greta swallowed. For her the penny always seemed to drop a few seconds after it did for everyone else.

She ploughed on. 'Though as an only child you do get all the attention. And hidings.'

Lian gave a faint smile.

'A psychic once told me I'd have a girl and a boy,' Greta said. 'The perfect pair, right?'

Edith rolled her eyes.

'I don't believe in psychics, myself,' Greta added hastily. 'Just a bit of

238

fun, you know. At a local fair. Poor woman had no one waiting in her queue. I felt sorry for her, and . . .' She turned to Lian. 'Anyway, what a day. What an amazing day.'

There was a tear lying in the curve of Lian's eyelid.

Greta chewed her lip. 'I'm so sorry, Lian. I think I've offended you.'

The small woman dipped her head and wiped her eyes. 'No. It is fine. Really.'

Quon turned to his wife. 'Enough.'

CHAPTER 36

Dinner the second night was a more relaxed affair. A day had been shared, the unit defined, and people were settling into the group's skin.

Besides the fact that they were sharing a four-day adventure, they all had something else in common too. Money. The trip was not something just anyone could afford. That bothered Greta. She, for one, would have been denied this experience had it not been for Walter's generosity.

Money was so confusing. She found it hard to be frivolous and channel the 'fairy-tale factor' after living such a hand-to-mouth childhood. Whether May Roberts wanted her skirt let out two inches, or Doreen Stuart needed a dress made for the Art Deco ball, determined whether there was food in Nora's fridge, hot water in winter and money to cover the school-camp fees. Consequently, unnecessary spending always made Greta uncomfortable.

Nora had been of the belief that money and privilege engendered soft character and 'moral flabbiness', and despite years of financial hardship, never once hinted at wanting more. In fact, she relentlessly endorsed the authenticity and honesty that came from being poor. Were someone to compliment her on a new dress or handbag, she was quick to say, with obvious pride, how little it had cost. Greta did the same now too.

Thoughts swirled and swelled. Till she'd met Walter, Greta had been an unchallenged blueprint of her mother. Walter's arrival confused things.

After he died, Greta's confusion started to wane, and Nora's opinions again took precedence. After all, what was two years of friendship when pitched against thirty-four years of family?

Then came the shock of Nora's diaries, which Greta discovered buried beneath a pile of lace-edged pillowcases in an old linen trunk.

Reading Nora's most private records left Greta wondering whether her mother's unwavering views had been more a way of coping with the circumstances she found herself in, than anything else. The diaries' revelations shook the very foundation upon which Greta had built her life. Who was she, other than a disciple of Nora's doctrines? It had been impossible to hear her own music when Nora's had been full volume for so long.

Walter's letters followed, and the trip and all its challenges, and Greta's confusion was again at full tilt.

'Pointless garnishing,' Edith said, picking a sprig of mint off her lamb. She turned to Greta. 'Don't know how I'm going to get those blasted curios through customs.'

'A fine time to think of that now,' interjected Hal, through a mouthful of potato.

'I assumed the products were export safe,' Edith said defensively. 'Pretty irresponsible to sell things that are not.'

That afternoon, on the way back to the lodge, Daniel had taken them to a women's co-operative. 'The proceeds go to families who have lost a breadwinner to AIDS.'

Greta's gums prickled. For her, AIDS was a password to other stories.

As she stepped into the small brick building that smelt of clay, cow dung and musty sweet straw, her heart was thudding in her throat and her skin raised in hundreds of tiny bumps. The room felt almost familiar, a history of loss on every shelf.

'Muraho,' said a wizened woman, her toothless smile creasing her eyes shut.

The cool, dark hut was filled with the most exquisite array of basketry wooden carvings, walking sticks, coasters and cards. Clay masks too. And clothing in bold geometric designs.

Greta hadn't bought a single memento since leaving Auckland — besides the shoes, of course. It was tricky not knowing the duration of her trip. She didn't want to be hauling too much extra weight around the globe. Already one of the wheels had fallen off her leopard-print luggage. For all she knew, she'd be travelling for several months yet.

She wasn't used to not having a plan. Or rather, not being in control of the plan. Perhaps that had been Walter's intention, to force her to take one day at a time.

'*For all the things you worry about, Grets, many will never materialise. Then there'll be things that don't even cross your mind, which do come to pass. So, you may as well just live in the moment and deal with what each day brings.'*

If she did buy something, for whom would it be?

Jud? There was no point getting anything for him. She didn't work at the shop any longer.

Lorraine? Greta no longer felt confident that she knew her friend's taste.

Angus? That would be awkward. Greta had no idea what he liked. Besides, they were not really friends.

This wasn't the person she'd envisaged she'd be — someone without a list of friends for whom to buy a gift.

Twenty minutes after the rest of the party had climbed back in the car, Edith was still bartering with the old shopkeeper. Everyone was tired and hungry. Finally, Edith emerged with two bulging brown-paper bags.

'That's Christmas sorted,' she'd said triumphantly. 'And for next to nothing.'

Greta fingered the small brown package in her own hand. Inside was a round, beaded box. Just the thing to hold Holly's rings and earrings.

Greta excused herself from the dinner table. The others were planning on moving to the deck for nightcaps, but she didn't want to risk getting bitten by mosquitoes. According to the guidebook, dusk and dawn were the most dangerous times of the day.

She'd done everything the book advised — smeared herself with insect repellent, worn light-coloured clothing, buttoned her long-sleeved shirt right up to the neck. She'd even ordered the soup at dinner, because lemon-grass was listed in the ingredients. However, there were no guarantees.

What's more, the horse might have already bolted. What had she been thinking, wearing a short-sleeved cocktail dress on the first night? She'd risked her life all in the name of making a good first impression.

She was tired. Tired of the chirruping in her head, tired of the endless analysing, reviewing, ruminating . . .

Another thought seized her. Perhaps she was tired because she'd already contracted malaria. Fatigue was one of the first symptoms.

She scurried along the path to the bungalows, swinging her torch left and right to out any sinister shapes. Tea bushes every time.

As she reached the first row of bungalows, she stopped.

What was that?

She switched off her torch.

The night was still. Even the crickets had suspended their song.

She switched her torch back on.

Then came the sound again. Clearer this time, without Greta's footsteps to confound it. A sort of whimpering.

Was it human or animal?

'Hellooo,' she whispered, as she started to reverse, sweeping the darkness with her torch as if it was a lightsaber.

The narrow tunnel of light landed on a dark shape on the bottom rung of Greta's cabin stairs.

She froze

'Who is it?' a soft voice called out.

'Lian? Is that you?'

Greta's torched illuminated Lian's pale face.

'Who's that?'

'It's me. Greta,' she said, switching off the blinding beam. 'I didn't mean to give you a fright. I was just headed back to my room and—'

Lian leapt up, wiping her nose on her sleeve. 'I . . . it's . . . oh . . .'

'What's wrong?'

Lian was standing very straight, her cheeks glistening with tears. When she didn't answer, Greta continued.

'The others are getting stuck into port and cigars on the veranda, so I thought I'd have an early night.'

Lian looked anxiously up towards the lodge.

'After all, we have an early start tomorrow.' Greta always seemed to feel the need to ramble on when faced with uncomfortable silences.

The little woman nodded.

'Would you like to come up to my cabin for a cup of tea?' Greta's voice was unnaturally loud against the still night. She needed to sound assured, give direction, inspire confidence.

'I'm fine. Thank you.'

This was a woman who didn't want to impose. Greta could relate.

Something brushed against Greta's leg. She shrieked. 'What was that?'

Lian's face broke into a grin. 'It is just the bush, Grehtah.'

A leggy stem of camellia was flapping in the breeze.

243

'So it is,' Greta said, trying to laugh off her outburst. She rummaged in her handbag for her room key. 'Come on up. We'll be sitting ducks for marauding mosquitoes if we stand here much longer.'

She started up the stairs. Lian followed obediently.

'That's quite an odd metaphor, isn't it?' Greta said. 'Using the verbs "sitting" and "stand" together. And having ducks and mosquitoes in the same sentence too.' She unlocked the door. 'It's surprising how the temperature drops up in the mountains. When I think of how hot Kigali was.'

Lian looked nonplussed by Greta's ramblings.

'Oh look! Someone's lit the fire. Turndown service, even in Africa!' Greta put down her bag. 'It's going to be a rude shock getting home after all this.'

'You don't travel much?'

'No. This is a first for me. All the luxury too.' She was anxious to distance herself from such extravagance.

She turned on the lights.

'Have a seat. I'll put the kettle on.'

Kettle? Greta faltered. But she didn't have time to indulge Muriel Maloney's cautions. She'd offered a cup tea and was now going to have to make one.

Lian perched on the edge of the couch like a small bird on a branch. Greta felt grotesque in comparison. She'd have to start watching what she was eating; her trousers were getting tight.

'Exciting to think we'll be seeing the gorillas soon.'

Lian nodded.

Greta handed her a mug of camomile tea. She was a firm believer in the power of camomile.

'I told you a lie today, Grehtah,' Lian said.

Greta sank onto the cowhide poof. 'I don't understand?'

'I lied to you when we were in the car.'

'Oh?' Greta said, thrown by this unexpected confession. Lian did not seem like the sort of person to lie. She was so pretty, and she had such delicate feet.

As the pause between them deepened, Greta started to feel somewhat offended by the woman's admission.

'When you asked me how many children I had.'

244

Greta nodded slowly.

'I said I have one daughter. Alice. But I also have a son.'

Greta took a sip of tea.

'I guess he just slipped your mind. I once forgot my own telephone number.'

In retrospect, this was not a good analogy.

Another long pause followed.

'Is the tea too hot?'

'It is good, thank you.'

'Lian—'

'Until last year, I had a son Eli.'

Greta's throat constricted. No wonder there'd been tears in the Jeep. 'I'm so sorry. How did he—'

'Last year. During mid-semester break. He is studying medicine,' Lian said, her eyes lighting up momentarily. 'Fifth year.'

'Medicine!' That made sense. Quon was a smart man.

'He made a very bad decision.'

Was the boy dead or doing time? Greta felt honoured to have been taken into the woman's confidence, but also confused.

She found herself thinking about Frank; and Rosa, the old lady she'd met at the New York deli; and Afra, the Muslim woman at the cookery class. Muriel Maloney too. The unexpected intimacy and depth of each of their stories. Their full and flawed existences openly shared. Was it just some odd coincidence?

People she'd met through the shop (bar Walter, that is) seemed different, more superficial, their lives and stories like a sunset carefully painted in oils. The colours correct. The shading and lines too. Correct, but not quite real.

Perhaps that was the true wonder of travel. The authenticity and freedom unleashed by anonymity. Was this what Walter had wanted for her when he'd urged her beyond the shallow end? Did he want her to discover that other people's lives were complex and challenging and imperfect too?

She closed her eyes, momentarily wallowing in the comfort of this.

Lian was staring into the fire.

Greta craned her neck forward. 'What happened to your son?'

'He is,' Lian said, dropping her voice to a whisper. 'You know . . .'

Greta's imagination started to run like a pulled thread, but Lian put an end to that with a single word.

'Homosexual.'

The way the word came out of Lian's mouth told of her embarassment. 'You mean . . . he's gay?'

Lian cast about anxiously in case someone else might have heard.

'But Lian, that can't be right—'

'It is!' she said, her posture still composed, but her darting eyes indicating her anguish. 'He told us. He said, *I am gay*.'

'No . . . I mean . . . it can't be right that you're so ashamed of your own son for who he is. That you deny his very existence.'

Lian put down her mug and stood up. 'I'm very sorry to have bothered you, Grehtah.'

Greta counted to ten, for once heeding Nora's advice. '*One day you will get yourself in trouble with that impulsive tongue of yours, Greta Jellings. Other people won't forgive your ill-conceived words as easily as I do.*'

She gazed into the fire, the richness that had been her life with Walter flooding back. His kindness and humanity. Humour and intelligence. All the vilification, hatred and suffering, too.

Here, not three metres from her, was prejudice dressed in petite court shoes and a tailored linen dress. Prejudice so strong it saw a mother deny her only son.

Instantly Nora sprang to mind. How dismissive she had been about Edgar Anderson, the young man with the earring who had worked at their local Four Square store. Nora always took her basket to the other cashier, even if the queue was longer.

'*I don't know how Roger can abide having that Edgar Anderson working for him. The boy's as gay as a coot.*'

'*Is gay bad?*'

'*Yes it is, Greta.*' *Her mother's face is flushed and her eyes angry.*

She thought back to four separate entries in her mother's diary.

Sometimes I wonder if Victor really loves me anymore. These days he rarely touches me. And when he does, it feels forced, like he is trying too hard. It is not like that with Steve and Lorna. Lorna says Steve can't keep his hands off her.

. . .

Today Victor came home from work so excited. I haven't seen him this animated in such a long time. Nattering on about this and that, and his new boss, Harry Adams. It left me oddly unsettled. I hope Vic isn't having an affair. I know a pretty young blonde was recently transferred to his department.

. . .

Harry Adams has been taken into custody. Lorna just rang to tell me. I can't believe it. Someone in our circle having a brush with the law. I thought it might be for fraud, but Vic says that you couldn't meet a more honest and upstanding man than Harry Adams. He's so upset; he barely ate any dinner. He says Harry hasn't committed any crime. I'll get the details from Lorna tomorrow. Vic is hopeless when it comes to getting the gossip.

. . .

I should have known. I think I did.

. . .

Greta swallowed. Yes. Of course.

'I must go,' Lian said, with a slight bow.

Prejudice so strong it saw a mother deny her only son. And a wife erase the existence of her husband, the father of her child.

Greta put up her hand. 'Two of the best people I have ever known were gay.'

Lian was already opening the door.

'Who are we to say what is acceptable under this immense night sky?' Greta continued.

Lian frowned. Shook her head. Stepped outside.

Greta's chest was heaving. She had offended her visitor. She felt bad about that. But liberated too. The past weeks had worked to peel away several layers. She was again that six-year-old girl with a superwoman cape. She knew what she liked and what she didn't. She hated baked beans. And she hated bigotry.

'I hope you and your son find each other again,' she said more softly. 'You know I'd swap places with you in a heartbeat. I've always wanted to be a mother.'

'Thank you for tea, Grehtah. I am sorry to have interrupted your evening.'

In the woman's politeness, Greta saw herself. Amenable at all costs.

Greta put a hand on Lian's arm. 'You know, being gay is just about two humans loving each other. It doesn't make a person any less than their fellow man.'

The woman faltered, then started down the stairs.

'I'm sure you still love your son,' Greta called after her. Then Lian disappeared into the night.

Greta stood on the small landing of her bungalow, leaning against the railing. The moon had shimmied behind a cloud, leaving just a silver memory of its light. However, the darkness was not oppressive, nor complete; the sky was embossed with stars, and the croaking frogs and clicking beetles lent their own light to the night.

Should she laugh or cry? She was bewildered and overwhelmed by what had transpired. With Lian. And within herself. The incident had opened a hidden door in her head. So much suddenly made sense.

She felt for the woman torn between her culture, marriage and a mother's instinct. Greta didn't know Lian's son, yet could easily conjure his struggles.

He'd have spent a childhood looking in from the sidelines. A 'different' boy, whose difference would become more pronounced the older he grew. He'd work hard to quash it.

Oh, the impossibility. The exhaustion. The desperation.

His self-loathing would threaten to stain every fragment of his life and frame every thought in his head. He'd be plagued by one recurring question. *Why me?* Perhaps he'd contemplate suicide. Then one day he'd lose the race. Or rather, win it. Succumbing finally to himself.

He'd be delirious with relief after all the years of charades. Nothing would have changed, and yet everything would have.

The next step would usher in fresh risk and terror as the young man articulated his secret out loud. He'd still live a careful, circumscribed life though, navigating highs and some horrible lows. Relationships would come and go. But it would be better than before.

However, his honesty would still have its limits, and a side of his life would forever be concealed from certain colleagues and acquaintances. And from his family.

Over time he'd start to hunger for that one safe base to which he could return whenever the outside world proved too much. That one safe place where he could be himself.

It would be a gamble, but a chance he'd finally decide to take. He would tell his parents and his sister.

Poor Eli.

Poor Walter.

Poor Victor Jellings.

The next morning they set out for Volcanoes National Park in the Virunga Mountains — a line of volcanoes bordering Rwanda, Uganda and the Democratic Republic of Congo.

Lian avoided Greta at breakfast and made sure that when the group departed for their next destination, she and Quon were seated in the very back of the vehicle.

Greta opted for the passenger seat beside Daniel. She was glad for the distance. Daniel demanded nothing of her, and her mind could coast freely as they drove along the banks of Lake Kivu, each bend in the eucalyptus-lined road offering another spectacular view of the great lake.

Passing through villages always elicited the same warm welcome, villagers stopping what they were doing to smile widely and wave.

'Abazungu! Abazungu!' 'White people! White people!' cried posses of giggling children as they chased the Jeep down the road.

When Daniel slowed to avoid a divot, Dorte threw a handful of coins out of her window.

'It is better we not do that,' Daniel said, glancing in his rear-view mirror at the children now scrabbling in the dirt. 'We do not wish to encourage begging. Later, I can stop at a market where you will be able to buy some tennis balls to give instead.'

Edith rolled her eyes. 'A little bit of gratitude would go a long way,' she said in a loud whisper.

'See,' Daniel said, shaking his head at two small boys standing on the side of the road. 'They are asking for our empty water bottles. We discourage this too, because such practice spreads disease.'

Greta was impressed by Daniel's quiet assertiveness. It was clear he felt a responsibility for his country's prosperity. Like Dorte, Greta had been tempted to hand out money, but now realised that her impulse to be charitable was perhaps confused with her own need to feel good. Tourists were transient, their vision limited. Rwanda was where Daniel and all the giggling children would continue to live.

She found herself wondering again about his story. He was warm and generous, but there was a reserve she could not get beyond. He held onto something very tightly.

'If it weren't for people like us, this country would be on its knees,' Edith said to Hal. 'Tourists are what keeps it afloat.'

Greta was mortified. Hal and Edith were the worst sort of tourists, with their colonial arrogance and belief that they had some sort of higher understanding.

Three women who'd been hoeing a fallow corner of field stood upright and waved, perspiration glistening on their foreheads. Life was clearly hard here, and yet no one looked impoverished. Everywhere, people were busy weeding, building, repairing, grinding, weaving, picking. Every square of land had been cultivated, every bank terraced and planted.

'So much energy and industry,' Greta said.

Daniel smiled. 'Akazi ni Akazi. Work is work. It gives purpose.'

Greta was suddenly gripped by anxiety. She was unemployed. She had no job to go back to.

The landscape started to change, banks of frayed banana trees giving way to an urban sprawl.

'What's the catch, Dan?' Fergus piped up from the back. 'It's all too good to be true, if you ask me. HIV rates down. Thousands of kilometres of fibre-optic cable encircling the country. Education and healthcare for all. Gender equality. C'mon, really? Is it the Chinese? Have they infiltrated this little corner of the globe too?'

In the silence that followed Fergus realised his faux pas. 'With all due respect,' he added quickly, turning to Lian and Quon. 'But hey, you're practically Yankees anyway.'

'No catch, just an honest leader,' Daniel said, diffusing the awkward-ness. 'Paul Kagane led us through difficult times. Made his vision ours. Today Rwanda is for sure one of the safest, most prosperous countries in Africa.'

'Yeah, but—'

Daniel put up his hand. 'Sorry, Fergus, I must interrupt you.' They had slowed and were turning into an empty parking lot.

'I bring you here to show you the opposite of what we have been talking about. It is important, please, that no one takes photographs.'

The car was suddenly silent. Even Edith and Hal.

Greta slunk a little lower in her seat. Being in the front no longer held as much appeal.

'Over there, you see the border with the DRC.'

'The what?'

'Democratic Republic of Congo,' Fergus said, pre-empting Daniel.

They looked across the empty car park to a row of prefab buildings and a solitary security boom manned by soldiers. Behind it, a human line stretched into the smog for as far as the eye could see.

Everything in the vista was deadened by dust — the colour of the people's clothes, their skin, their loads. Windowpanes, advertorials, and walls were all dressed in a dull film of dirt. Mangy dogs rummaged in upturned bins. A donkey lapped from a putrid puddle. Live chickens swung limply from baskets, suspended by their legs. A piglet screeched. A ghetto blaster thumped. This was the derelict disorder of Goma.

'Unfucking believable,' said Hal.

Dorte leant forward. 'For what do they queue?'

'To get into Rwanda. Mostly just a one-day trading pass. Many, of course, very much hope to leave the DRC for good.'

'I don't blame them.'

A flash of light filled the car.

Daniel swung round. For the first time Greta saw something akin to anger in his eyes. 'No photographs. It can make for us much trouble.'

Fergus lowered his lens.

'Someone's coming!' Greta hissed. A soldier was approaching.

She fixed on his heavy brown boots. That's what Judy had once suggested. *Focus on something benign, like the dental nurse's necklace . . .* It had been some time since Greta had felt the need to channel her therapist.

Daniel wound down his window. 'No one talk.'

The guard peered into the van. He smelt of cigarette smoke.

Daniel spoke rapidly in his native tongue. The soldier did not reply.

Daniel spoke some more.

Greta cursed Fergus as she envisaged herself languishing in some damp rat-infested Congolese cell.

Then Daniel started the engine and they were reversing back onto the road.

'All bark and no bite,' said Fergus with a chuckle. But Daniel was quiet for the rest of the journey.

CHAPTER 37

Greta woke early, her body charged with excitement. Or was it apprehension? No, it was definitely excitement.

Still in her pyjamas, she made herself tea, then, cup in hand, stepped out of her bungalow. The air was dawn fresh and awaiting the imprint of a new day. In front of her a mountain range stretched in staggered cones towards the horizon, haze-blue peaks piercing a diaphanous membrane of mist.

For a second time on this trip, the significance of Greta's life zoomed out to blend with a bigger backdrop. Her story was just one pixel on a vast canvas. It was oddly comforting, knowing that nothing mattered quite as much as she'd always believed it did. Not every decision had to be carefully weighed up. A wide-angled lens was more forgiving.

At the park's head office the group was treated to a welcome dance by local villagers, before receiving instructions about the upcoming trek from an imposing older man dressed in a khaki uniform and heavy brown boots.

Do not look a gorilla in the eye.

Make no sudden movements.

Keep your voices down.

If a gorilla charges, crouch. Do not run away.

Greta's newfound calm evaporated. So much for the significance of her life zooming out.

'My love for the gorilla began many years ago,' he said, his lined black face reflecting triangles of light, 'when I was working with Dian Fossey.'

Greta gasped. Dian Fossey! Standing not even five metres from her was a man who'd spent time with the famous primatologist whom she'd idolised since her teens.

Suddenly it made sense — Walter choosing Rwanda as a destination.

Greta is thirteen when she first reads Gorillas in the Mist, *falling instantly in love with Nyiramachabelli — 'the woman who lives alone on the mountain'.*

The more she delves into Fossey's life, the more it resonates with her. Fossey's parents had divorced when she was a young girl, and she too had been forbidden from keeping contact with her beloved father. Growing up in a house devoid of affection saw Fossey retreat into a world of animals, a pet goldfish her first real friend.

For Greta, the parallels are profound. She'd had Nutmeg, her hamster, and books, of course.

Fossey's story leaves Greta feeling less alone.

Years later, when a local movie house advertises Gorillas in the Mist *in a Golden Oldies promotion, Greta excitedly persuades Walter to join her.*

It is a terrible idea. Already unwell and unsteady on his legs, chemo-therapy no longer keeping his cancer at bay, Walter takes a tumble in the cinema, splitting open his forehead on a handrail. He sits slumped in a wheelchair while they wait for the ambulance, his gaunt yellow body trembling, his eyes skittish with fear. It is the last time Walter goes out in public. Six weeks later he is dead.

A few days after the cinema fiasco, Greta hires a DVD player, and together they watch the movie from Walt's bed. The odour of illness hangs in the air. His bedside table is cluttered with pills, used tissues and a bowl of discoloured custard. The curtains have been drawn against the harsh afternoon light . . .

For a short while, Greta and Walter escape, travelling into the majestic mountains of Rwanda. Halfway through the movie Greta turns to tell Walter something. He is asleep, his face collapsed against its bony scaf-folding. She traces the contours with her forefinger — his scale-dry lips, absent eyelashes, the prickly crust of stitches from the cinema fall. Never before has she felt so lonely.

Putting it together now, Greta realised that sometime between that night and his death, Walter must have mustered the energy to talk to Angus about putting Rwanda on the itinerary.

She smiled. He had been thinking about her right to the very end. The man didn't get more singular than that.

Another thought dawned. Her mood dived. Walter had fallen asleep before the end of the movie, so never did find out that Dian Fossey was murdered in her hut in the Rwandan hills!

She straightened. She could not allow herself to be romanced by Walter's grand ideas. She had to keep her eye on the prize. Staying alive.

Another ranger, Pacifique, was talking.

'They are offered work one day a week.' He was gesturing towards a line of local men and women dressed in bright blue overalls. 'Some of these people used to be poachers. Now they are participants in the gorilla protection programme. When you hire a porter, you are providing a salary for them and of course, their family. They benefit from your tourism and get to play an important role in the protection of these endangered animals, and in ensuring the future of their country.'

'Nah,' said Hal, sucking his teeth. 'No way I'm paying for someone to carry my water-bottle.'

'Me not also,' said Dorte.

Greta's eyes met the porter first in line — a sinewy man with the blackest of faces. Where his left arm should have been was a dent in his blue overall.

She nodded. 'Yes, can I get one? What I mean is, can someone please port for me. I mean, be my porter.'

Lian, Quon and Fergus opted to employ someone too.

'I am Innocence,' said the man, keenly shaking Greta's hand.

How to respond to that?

'His name,' explained Pacifique, with a wide smile. 'His name is Innocence.'

'Oh, Innocence!' Greta felt a blush envelop her. 'I'm Greta. My father was a fan of Greta Garbo. Do you know her? You get movies here, don't you?'

The bewildered porter looked to the ranger for a translation.

'My mother wanted to call me Theodora,' Greta went on. 'Fortunately my father insisted on Greta. Which is a relief, because I'm not that keen on Theodora. Though I'm sure I would have got used to it. I wouldn't really have known any different, I guess. Anyway, what I'm trying to say is, you can call me Greta.'

As Pacifique translated, Innocence's smile went up and down and up and down.

'Here, I'm talking about me. Tell me how you got your name.'

'Yes, Innocence,' the man said, smiling widely.

He handed her a hand-carved walking pole and gestured for her to pass him her daypack.

'No, no. I can carry it.'

'Innocence does not want your charity,' said the ranger. 'He wants a job.'

The porter slung her small pack over his shoulder and took Greta's hand.

Holding hands with a complete stranger felt very odd, but Innocence held firm. He was there to guide her and clearly that is what he was going to do.

They started walking and soon had left the open plains to make their way through thick bamboo forest. The excitement in the group settled into stolid focus as the humidity and tough topography captured everyone's concentration.

Greta was glad for her hiking boots. It was one of the few occasions her feet did not attract unnecessary attention; everyone's feet looked big in boots. Well, maybe not Lian's.

They'd been walking for almost two hours when Pacifique stopped and gathered them round. Greta took a swig from her drink bottle. It was nearly empty.

'The trackers, they tell me Agashya family is moving very fast. Another male, he is trying to break into the group, so the big chief, the silverback, he is keeping his family moving. Hopefully we can catch up.'

Greta hoped so too. Though just the thought of walking any faster, or much further, was exhausting in itself.

A barking roar reverberated across the valley.

Innocence momentarily released Greta's hand to raise a finger. 'You hear?'

She nodded nervously.

He thumped his chest with his fist. 'Is gorilla.'

'Gorilla?' The adventure was lifting off the brochure. She decided she was definitely someone who preferred adventures in retrospect, rather than real time.

'Ya,' one of the other porters said, with a chuckle. 'Not far.'

The group's pace picked up. The jungle deepened. The air grew thick and close. Shafts of bamboo towered. Mud sucked the spring from their steps. As any sort of recognisable path disappeared, the rangers took to slashing the virgin vegetation with pangas. The smell of raw crushed leaves rose off their blades. Greta winced as the image of a skull divided cleanly in two found its way into her head.

Then the land was plunging into a volcanic crater overgrown with vegetation, and they were clambering down the steepest of banks.

Those in front of Greta were swallowed by the undergrowth. All she could discern were fleeting glimpses of khaki, the corner of someone's white collar, a flash of blue. She gripped Innocence's hand tighter.

'This guy doesn't have a clue where he's going.' It was Hal, somewhere behind Greta.

'We should turn back,' panted Edith.

'That's a stupid idea. Could you find your way out of this fucking maze?'

'Don't get shitty with me. You chose this bloody tour.'

'Blame me, why don't you? Nothing new.'

'That's rich coming from you, asshole.'

'There you go again, with your insults.'

'Oh, go polish your halo.'

'Shut up, Edith.'

Greta was afraid, and the bickering couple behind her wasn't helping. She and a handful of other humans were battling the most challenging of environments without guarantee or safeguard. It was a different fear to any she'd experienced before. It felt real and warranted. Trekking through an African jungle *was* dangerous. She *could* actually come to real harm.

Deep down she'd always known that a spider on her headboard was unlikely to harm her, just as an aeroplane was unlikely to fall out of the sky. It was also improbable that when her house was plunged into darkness during a power outage, some escaped convict would break in and murder her. As for a fire alarm at the mall, it was just that — an alarm, not a death knell. Yet she'd always behaved as if the worst was about to happen. Only now, in the middle of the African jungle, in the face of real danger, did she appreciate that perhaps her behaviour on other occasions had been more out of habit than anything else. A circuit of learned thoughts.

It was thrilling and terrifying to feel real fear for the first time. To know that the stakes were truly high.

The group began scrambling up the opposite side of the crater from where they had entered.

Greta grabbed a stem of bamboo. It buckled. Innocence held firm.

Hal and Edith caught up. His face was puce, his brush-over hanging down like a confused ponytail. 'This is a bloody circus!'

Greta kept climbing. She could not allow naysayers to sabotage her dwindling stamina.

Perhaps Innocence sensed her anxiety, because he stopped, patted her on the back and smiled widely. His smile spoke of decades in the territory. It told of a comfortable contract between man and his land.

He pressed his dry, cracked palm into hers. It was all the reassurance she needed.

'Over there,' Fergus cried in an agitated whisper.

Greta followed his gaze.

Off to the right, not even ten metres away, was something akin to a giant boulder protruding from the undergrowth, its darkness in stark relief to the greenery.

Greta gasped. Nothing had prepared her for this.

Then everyone was jostling for a view.

Ahead, in the clearing, sat a silverback chewing on a stick of bamboo, his close-set eyes deep and pensive. He scratched his head, examined his digits, scratched his head again.

Greta marvelled at the size of his hand. It was huge and human-like. That anyone could ever want to turn it into an ashtray was unthinkable.

All of a sudden, the greenery behind the silverback shuddered and through it lumbered a smaller gorilla.

'Oh my god!' whispered Hal. 'It's got a baby.'

The ranger put a finger to his lips.

There was indeed a black fuzzy ball on top of the second gorilla's back.

'Edith, here! Bring my camera. Hurry!'

The silverback lifted its head, gazed at the group, then flopped forwards and started lumbering towards them.

Greta's mind went blank.

Dorte, the closest to the massive primate, stumbled backwards, bumping into Edith. Both women fell to the ground.

The ranger rapidly interposed himself and started making deep guttural grunts in the back of his throat.

The silverback stopped.

No one moved.

A burst of breeze rippled the long grass. An ant the size of a small pebble scurried up a stem of bamboo. A bird reeled in the sky.

The gorilla sank back onto its haunches, ripped out another bamboo stem and started to chomp on it.

The ranger gave the thumbs up.

People breathed. Shifted. Carefully repositioned themselves.

'The gorilla will do anything to defend its young,' said Pacifique calmly. 'Sometimes a poacher must slaughter twenty adults before he can capture one baby to sell to a zoo.'

The thought was too terrible to contemplate. Greta looked over at the mother, now settled in the grass. Such a gentle, sentient being.

The baby slid to the ground. A spindly little thing, with a mop of black hair and huge eyes ringed with charcoal skin, giving it a permanently astonished expression.

'Look,' whispered Lian, reaching for Greta.

The gesture caught Greta by surprise. She and Lian hadn't spoken since their altercation.

Lian dropped Greta's hand. Clearly she'd mistaken Greta for Quon. But the connection, although involuntary, had been made.

Greta touched Lian's arm. 'Incredible, isn't it?'

Lian looked at Greta, her gaze uncertain and guarded. 'Yes.'

Incredible, thought Greta. Miraculous. Magical. All these. And so much more.

Fergus manoeuvred in front of them, obscuring their view.

Greta was just about to say something when he turned, his eyes rimmed with red. 'My apologies, ladies,' he said, and crouched down.

Time collapsed. Five minutes passed, or was it forty-five, as the group stood mesmerised by the huge creatures whose every gesture and inflection was so uncannily human.

'The baby is teasing its mother,' Lian whispered.

Startled by a bird, the baby gorilla scrambled onto its mother's lap and nuzzled into her armpit.

Another barking roar rang out across the valley.

The silverback stopped chewing. Tilted his head. Then stood up and began beating its chest like King Kong.

'How awesome is that?' hissed Fergus. 'All four hundred pounds of gorilla up on his hind legs.'

Greta smiled. Four hundred pounds. That would be a good fact to recall when she relayed the story to Holly.

Despite her initial misgivings about him, Fergus was handy to have around with all his knowledge. She imagined he was a first-rate pilot.

The silverback tapped the female gorilla on the shoulder, and as if part of a well-rehearsed dance, the mother swept the baby onto her back, turned, and disappeared through the wall of greenery, followed close behind by her protector.

The ranger signalled for the group to follow and fifteen minutes later they again caught up with the gorillas.

The scene they were met with was akin to a large family picnic, the three gorillas having now joined the rest of their twenty-five-strong Agashya clan.

Young gorillas cartwheeled through the trees, adults contemplated their navels, others ate bugs, stripped branches or checked their offspring for fleas.

'Our one hour is up,' said Pacifique after what felt like just a few minutes. 'It is time for you to say goodbye.'

'I'd like to stay longer,' said Hal. 'It's been one hell of a hike to find these guys.'

'Just one hour for humans to be with the gorillas,' said the ranger, reiterating what had already been made very clear at the start of the day.

'I hear you,' said Hal. 'But an extra fifteen minutes won't be a problem, surely?'

The ranger shook his head, his expression congenial, but firm.

Hal's face reddened. Edith put a hand on his arm. 'Leave it, love. No point arguing with the natives.'

Hal flicked off her hand. 'I paid bloody good money to be here.'

The ranger signalled to the rest of the group to follow. 'My job is to protect these gorilla,' his said, rolling his Rs. 'This is the rule we tell you before you come, no? One hour.'

Edith nodded, her face all blotchy.

'The gorilla can get too much stress around humans. Also, he has the risk of our diseases. There are only eight-hundred-and-fifty left, so our rule is for careful conservation.'

'Yes. Yes. But all I'm saying—'

'Your money,' Pacifique continued. 'It protects these endangered animals.'

'And as the Japanese say,' Greta piped up. 'It is better to stop when you are two-thirds full.'

Edith glared at her.

'If you know what I mean,' Greta added. 'It protects against gluttony. In the broadest sense of the word. Not that I mean you are a—'

Pacifique burst out laughing. 'Ha,' he said, shaking his head. 'It protects against gluttony. Yes, this is true.'

CHAPTER 38

Greta felt exhilarated as they trekked out of the rainforest that afternoon. Her body was weary, her feet boot-sore, but she felt replete. All the therapy sessions in the world could not achieve what this extraordinary day just had.

She thought about people the world over living in small, cramped spaces and high-rise buildings. How barren a soul could become in a treeless, smog-filled city. Cities had the power to rob a man of wonder. It was no surprise there was so much aggression and crime in the concrete jungles. Town planners, property developers and politicians frequently forgot about the miracle of the natural world.

Halfway back to base, Hal tripped over a buttress root, spraining his ankle, so Innocence was seconded to help carry him out. An unenviable task; Hal was not the lightest of loads.

Innocence, however, did not give up on his primary charge and stopped regularly to check on her. 'You fine, Miss Greeta?'

Finally, as the late afternoon was drained of its warmth, the group arrived back at the conservation centre. It had been a day like no other.

'*Murakoze*,' Greta said, paying Innocence his ten-dollar fee. Then she wrapped her arms around him. The gesture surprised her as much as him. Less than a month ago she'd never have dreamt of doing anything so impetuous.

The other porters burst out laughing and began wolf whistling. Innocence averted his eyes bashfully.

'You are a top-notch porter,' Greta said, patting him on the shoulder, her hand recoiling as it sunk into the emptiness of his left sleeve.

Later, Daniel would tell her that Innocence had lost his left arm during the genocide. His left arm and his whole family.

'Top not?'

'Top-*notch*. Excellent. Good. Very professional.'

Pacifique translated.

Innocence pulled his shoulders back and beamed. 'Thank you, Miss Greeta.'

For a brief moment she visualised herself living in Rwanda forever, Innocence, her husband, a baby on her back. Cornmeal porridge for breakfast. Mangoes and bananas for lunch.

Two women walked past, one holding a live chicken by its feet.

On second thoughts, Greta decided, maybe not.

By the time Greta had helped herself to a little of everything at the buffet table that night, the rest of the group were already seated and the only chair left was between Hal and Fergus.

'A rose between two craggy thorns,' laughed Edith.

More like between two toads, thought Greta.

The mood at the table was jovial, despite Hal's ankle injury. People had been infected by the magic of the day.

'And when it started moving towards you, I thought, this — is — it. I did! I thought you were a goner.'

'So did I. It was a kind of King Kong moment. Him about to hoist you in the air.'

'I think hipflasks should be mandatory.'

'Portugal is going to be such a letdown after this.'

'Look at the baby. Isn't it just adorable!'

'Please send me that photo. Actually, we should create a Facebook group and share all our photos.'

Greta turned to Fergus who was uncharacteristically quiet. 'Bet you wish Sylvia had been here today,'

It didn't come out quite right. Greta had just been pre-empting the inevitable. Getting Sylvia's name out there first. Making it clear she understood the rules.

Fergus shrugged. 'Sylvia and I weren't very well matched. We'd been thinking of separating just before she got sick.'

Greta floundered with this new information. Was this the same man who mentioned his late wife at every available opportunity?

'She used to call me a pedantic know-it-all. Guess I am.' He gave a cynical laugh.

'Well,' Greta said slowly, 'it takes all types. I imagine you'd need to be pretty pedantic to be a pilot.'

He nodded, shrugged, sighed.

'This was her thing,' he continued. 'The gorillas. Rwanda. She'd always wanted to come here. I didn't. So we never did.'

Greta waited. There was nothing she could say to alter the outcome of the life Fergus was reliving at that moment. All she could do was listen.

'I wish I could remember facts like you do,' she said, after a time. 'I'm hopeless. In one ear and out the other.'

Fergus drained his glass. 'You can train your memory. I did. It didn't come naturally.'

'I find that hard to believe. You're a fund of information.'

His tight mouth curled up at the corners.

'Money was pretty scarce when I was growing up.' He looked up at the ceiling. 'I spent my childhood dreaming of winning big on *Double Your Money*. You know, the TV quiz show?'

Greta didn't know, but she nodded.

'Spent every afternoon of my high-school years in the library, memorising facts. Endless, useless facts.' He sniggered. 'When I won, I was going to blindfold my mum, lead her outside, and there, waiting for her in the yard, would be a brand-new Holden.'

Greta climbed into Fergus' dream. She saw his mother's eyes grow round. Saw her sink to the ground, laughing and crying. Saw an awkward blond-haired boy grin widely as all the pain peeled off.'

'So? Did you get onto a game show and make your fortune?'

'Yeah,' Fergus said, too loudly. 'When I was eighteen. Got knocked out in the second round!' He shook his head. 'Still remember the bloody question.'

Greta waited nervously, as if she were now the contestant about to be stumped.

'What do you call a group of bears?'

'That *is* hard,' she said. 'A troop? A growl? Hang on, hang on. Isn't it a posse?'

'A sleuth. A sleuth of bears.'

Later Greta sat out on the concrete porch in front of her bungalow. The smell of wood-smoke mingled with that of the rainforest, red earth, frangipani flowers, and citronella candle. The proverbial crickets and toads and other anonymous noises of the night competed with the lowing of a lone cow. The navy night sky was sprinkled with thousands of diamond chips leading her eye and thoughts towards infinity.

Lian and Quon. Their son, Eli.

Edith and Hal.

Dorte.

Fergus. And Sylvia.

Innocence.

Daniel.

Victor Jellings.

Each person trying to forge their own meaningful path on the planet.

She'd just made herself a cup of tea and climbed into bed, when there was a loud knock at the door. She looked at her watch. 10.30pm. Who on earth could that be?

She slipped on her dressing gown.

'Who is it?' she said, her ear to the door. She half expected Lian to reply.

'It's me. Fergus.'

Fergus?

'I'm already in my pyjamas. Is something wrong?'

'Sorry. I know it's late. I have something I thought might interest you.'

Greta chewed her lip. 'Tomorrow maybe?'

There was a long pause. 'Uh, sure.' He sounded disappointed.

She unlocked the door and pulled it slightly ajar, hiding her body behind it.

'Sorry,' he said with an embarrassed chuckle. 'But you seemed to be quite into your collective nouns and I thought you might be interested in this. I'm finished with it.' He was holding a small paperback. 'I always try to read something each night to better my knowledge. Often just useless facts. Ha! Throwback from my quizzing days.'

Greta opened the door wider, momentarily forgetting about being in her pyjamas. Books had that effect on her, even one with as dry a title as *The Definitive Compendium of Collective Nouns*.

'Thank you, Fergus. That's very kind of you. I'd love to take a look at it.'

She reached for it. He held on.

'Only if you can tell me what a group of toads is called.'

'I think I know that one. A wart. A wart of toads?'

He shook his head, looking supremely satisfied with himself 'A knot of toads.'

He relinquished the book.

'Aha. Well, thank you, Fergus.'

'Talking of toads, how do you feel about kissing one?'

Greta worked her way around his words. What? Surely not! Really?

Nora started up. *'Greta, you know nothing about this man. It takes a long time to know someone properly, believe you me. Sex should never be entered into lightly. Never! You have no idea where his what-you-may-call-it has been? For all you know he—'*

Walter shrugged. *'No one is watching, Grets. Try on a few different Gretas. Have some fun.'*

She thought about her missed opportunity with Tassos.

Greta opened the door fully. 'Come in, Fergus. It's cold out.'

CHAPTER 39

Greta stared at the windmill silhouette cast by the ceiling fan. Fergus was snoring beside her. A relentless, repetitive cycle: four snores rising to a crescendo, followed by a long, is-he-still-breathing? pause, then back to the beginning.

It felt very strange to have someone in her bed. The smell. The sounds. The unexpected movements. How was she ever going to get to sleep? And what if she did drift off and ended up sleeptalking?

She bit her lip shyly as she thought about what had transpired. Fergus was surely a very good pilot. It was a little odd, though, that just after they'd . . . well . . . done it, he asked if she would photograph the moles on his back with his mobile phone. 'To check for irregularities. Over 13,000 melanomas are diagnosed each year in Australia, you know.'

Checking Fergus for melanomas did not rate highly on Greta's list of romantic manoeuvres. On the plus side, with Fergus focused so intently on his own body issues, he was less likely to notice her cellulite.

By 2am Greta had had enough of this two-in-a-bed business. She leant up on her elbow and hovered over Fergus, trying to pluck up the courage to wake him.

His eyes flicked open. 'Sylvia!'

Greta sprung backwards.

'It's me! Me! Greta,' she cried.

He looked about, clearly disoriented.

'I'm really sorry to disturb you, Fergus, but I think you might want to go back to your own cabin now.'

'What?'

'If you wouldn't mind. The thing is, I can't sleep. It's the . . . snoring.'

'Jesus!' he said, hauling himself out of bed. 'This is worse than bloody jetlag.'

266

As he pulled on his clothes, Greta threw in a few more apologies.

He harrumphed to the door. Turned. Came back to get *The Definitive Book of Collective Nouns*. Then left.

'Well, there you have it, Walter,' Greta said, with a sigh. 'Not sure whether that Greta was quite the right fit.'

She was wide awake now and in need of a cup of tea. So, she put on the kettle, rekindled the fire, and then sat curled up on the couch with her hot drink reflecting on all that had been happening.

Where was her father, she wondered? In some graveyard, buried under a favourite tree, or scattered in the ocean? She hoped he hadn't departed the world all alone, unclaimed in some hospital bed.

Oh, that he were still alive.

Her heart hiccoughed. Nora's diary had put an end to that notion.

March 4, 2006.

Greta would have been twenty-eight years old. Twenty-eight and oblivious to the fact that she'd just lost her father. For a second time. For forever, this time.

How had Nora known? Had she secretly kept in touch with her homosexual husband? With the man who'd steeped so much shame on her. Had Victor asked someone to notify his wife? (There was never a mention anywhere of a divorce.)

So many questions without answers. Answers which had died when Nora did.

Greta now held a clearer picture in her head of the father she'd only known for six years. Since embarking upon the trip, his picture had gained colour and detail, as if clues gathered over the years had finally coalesced. As if all they'd needed was the space to arrive.

How mysterious and surprising the human brain could be.

She had no memory of her father sharing a beer with the blokes, but could see him chatting to Nora's clients in the kitchen as he drank copious cups of sweet black tea.

She sees him on a Saturday morning polishing his work shoes, while she sits beside him listening to 'Penelope', her dad's portable radio.

Afterwards, while his shoes dry in the sun, he sets up the ironing board and irons his shirts and a garment Nora has finished sewing for someone. How Greta loves to watch his face — the way it tightens as he edges the tip of the iron into tight crevices, then loosens again as he takes bigger sweeps.

Later, Greta pretends to iron her dolls clothes, caressing them in the same way, the 'silks', and 'linens', and tight cotton pleats.

Penelope's aerial is very temperamental, and if her father doesn't angle it correctly, the radio hisses and crackles.

'What does "temperamental" mean, Papa?'

But most of the time Penelope's music is lovely, and Victor sings along to the tunes. He knows all the words.

'Tell me how you met Mama?' It is her favourite story.

'Well, it was a cold autumn night and the wind was howling something terrible. Something terrible. So, a few of us went down to the local dance hall to get warm.'

'Because dancing kept you warm, didn't it?'

'Yes, because dancing kept us warm.'

'And?'

'And, as usual, I knew most of the lovely ladies in attendance.'

'But this time there was someone new. It was Mama, hey?'

'Straw.' He always says straw when she ends a sentence with hey.

'Don't be silly, Papa. It was Mama, wasn't it?'

'It was. It was. A gorgeous woman, so elegantly turned out, and with such a lovely laugh.'

'She was beautiful!'

'So beautiful, Greta. Statuesque, with a perfect posture, despite her height. She spun around the room in her sage-green silk like a—'

'Like a movie star!'

'Yes, like Anna in The King and I.*'*

'And then you got married. Didn't you? And you danced the first waltz at the wedding and Mama looked like a princess in cream chiffon, and her veil had to be carried by two bridesmaids, and . . .'

'And after our first year of marriage a bonny baby came along with the biggest hazel-green eyes and fine wisps of auburn-flecked hair.'

Did he feel complete, Greta wondered? For a time, at least?

After he left, there was a hiatus in the gold-rimmed pages of Nora's diary. No entry for a month. Empty, clean, cream pages. So empty they felt full.

When the writing began again, it still sounded like her mother.

Handsome, charismatic Harry Adams. I should have known. I think I did.

But then after that, the words were all Nora. Clipped and restrained like a lighthouse-keeper's logbook. Even the shape of the words was different.

Gone. Both her father and mother in one weekend. A hole punched out, leaving a small tunnel through Greta's life like in the pages of *The Very Hungry Caterpillar*.

After a time, letters started to arrive. Letters in brightly coloured envelopes addressed to Greta, with postmarks from some fabulously foreign place. York.

Unread, they still kept on coming, until they didn't.

When Rutland Senior appeared on the scene, Nora had been navigating shame for nine years. She was back in control. Had seen it all. Fallen a few times and stood right back up again.

She stopped Rutland's flattery at the gate. *We will have none of that, thank you very much*. Flattery did not pay the bills.

But Nora was a beautiful woman, with her high cheekbones and large grey eyes, and the man persisted.

Finally, she gave in, allowing him to wine and dine her, though never to dance.

And after a time, as Nora knew it would, the novelty faded. Rutland retreated to the marriage Nora had known nothing about, and she retreated to her sewing room. But not before negotiating a paid position for her daughter at his shop.

As Greta pieced the story together in the middle of the Virunga Mountains, filling blank pages in her mother's diary, and blank spaces in her memory, her mind found something cohesive and comprehensible.

To think she'd always thought it her fault that her father had left.

CHAPTER 40

Greta

Woody's Words

This is Walter Haywood tuning in on Radio Rwanda.

Greta smiled. She'd nearly kissed the wrinkled man who'd knocked on her bungalow door with a letter in his hands.

You have one up on me now, Grets. I've never been to Africa. So make sure you enjoy it for us both, won't you? I'm told the landscape can swallow a person whole.

She nodded. There was no partial immersion in this place. Africa demanded a person's undivided attention, and soaked into every corner of the soul.

I had a friend from Kenya. Woody. I know you would have liked him.

Greta tried to still the sheet of paper shaking in her hands. She was being included in the relationship. At last! She closed her eyes. 'Thank you, Walter.'

He gave me a sense of the vast continent I never got to visit. His face was as open as a wide-open plain. His laughter, an African sky. And his passion for life as powerful as an afternoon thunderstorm.

Greta swallowed. Lines written by someone clearly still very much in love.

He offered to show me Africa. Rwanda specifically. You see he was in awe of the tiny country, which had risen from its ruins and moved beyond its past.

We didn't get to go, but I never forgot Woody's words. They helped free me. You see, before I met him, I'd been bound to my past.

'Walt, I already know about Woody.'

I learnt from him that you cannot erase what has been; it will always be there and will always call to you. If you keep looking back, it is forever

270

in front of you. But if you turn your head to face forward, the past stays behind you, where it belongs.

I hope you discover this truth too.

Walt x

CHAPTER 41

After breakfast Greta said goodbye to the group. Hal and Edith were trying to change flights. Dorte was chatting to a tall, tanned journalist from Brazil. And Fergus and Quon were on the front deck discussing the future of hybrid cars.

Fergus gave Greta a peck on the cheek.

She blushed deeply. Hopefully Quon didn't put two and two together.

'I'm not at my best when woken from a deep sleep,' Fergus whispered into her ear. He pulled out the little paperback book from his pocket. 'This is yours, I believe.'

'No, no. Really.'

'I thought of another one to add to the list,' he said, opening it on the title page.

There, written in blue ballpoint pen was:

To Greta from Fergus x

A snore of pilots.

Greta chewed her lip and looked down at her feet. 'Thank you.'

She found Lian sitting alone in the lounge reading.

'It has been lovely getting to know you, Grehtah,' Lian said, taking both Greta's hands in hers.

Neither had mentioned Lian's son again, yet he was there in the small sliver of space between them, connecting and distancing them. Greta wondered if a mother's unconditional love would triumph, or whether prejudice would win the day. She thought of gorillas fighting to the death to protect their young.

'An interesting group of people,' she said to Daniel, as they began their drive back to Kigali.

He smiled.

'I bet you meet all sorts in this job.'

'All sorts, ya.'

'Some must drive you mad,' she persisted. 'Mrs Gladwell was my most annoying customer. Dion Parkle too. How do you manage to remain so good humoured?'

He offered her some dried banana from a packet. 'You know the word ubuntu?'

She shook her head.

'It means, "I am who I am, because of you." Everybody we meet changes us a little, no?'

Greta thought about the group. Seven lives had unexpectedly intersected. She wondered whether anyone's path had been altered as a result. Whether anyone's cosmic plan had been reconfigured.

'What you do today, impacts me,' Daniel said. 'And what I do, impacts you. We are all connected. That is humanity.'

Yes, thought Greta, that is humanity.

'Daniel, were you in Rwanda during the genocide?'

His jaw pushed out against the smooth black skin of his cheek.

'I don't mean to pry. I just—'

'Yes.'

Greta gulped.

'My parents and brother, they died in the genocide. I escaped with my baby sister, Agnes, to Uganda. She was four years old.'

Greta had had her suspicions, but it was still shocking to hear them confirmed.

She thought about Daniel's wording, how in recounting such a personal story he still avoided emotive language. His parents had *died*, not been *murdered* or *massacred*. Everything Daniel did, even the words he chose, were forward looking. She once again felt guilty for allowing her curiosity to persist beyond the parameters he'd carefully erected.

'I'm sorry. It must have been awful.'

'We are nearly at the border,' he said.

She was confused. Which border?

'But Agnes is thirsty. So, when darkness falls, we run to a garage to use the tap.'

His use of the present tense was disconcerting, as if he'd climbed right into the memory.

'While we are there, I see a band of men coming over the hill. They are armed with axes and pangas and bricks and spades. I believe Agnes and I will die, like the rest of our family. We scramble under a truck parked on the side of the road, and with Agnes pressed against my belly, I pull us up off the ground. We hang there between the axles. Soon the feet and ankles of the mob are near. They circle, stand, lean. They eat and drink and loot the garage. Their laughter is loud. They are this close.' He held a hand to the side of his face.

'I can smell death, like the black diesel dripping from the truck. I feel it too, like the blisters on my hands, which bubble and burst. We stay in this way for maybe one hour. Or longer. It is too long, but my arms and feet, they find a strength I have never known before. And my baby sister, she stays as still as a corpse, not the wriggling four-year-old she is. Even she knows how close death can be.'

Greta's hands were trembling in her lap.

'I close my eyes when urine leaks from Agnes onto the dust and trickles out from under the truck. But the men are too drunk to notice. Eventually they move on.

'We collapse onto the road. I find feeling again in my legs and arms and we continue on to Uganda.'

Daniel stopped, his face contorting as if watching something terrible unfold on a screen.

'When I get there, I think I will never go back.'

When *I* get there. The *I* hung in the air where just moments earlier there had been *we*. Greta knew she would never be able to ask what had happened to Agnes.

'I live in Uganda, but Rwanda, she keeps calling. Always calling. And so, after five years, I return.'

'You are Tutsi then.'

'I am Rwandan.'

Greta's body started shuddering with sobs.

'No, no,' said Daniel. 'You must not cry, Greta. You must not cry.'

But she couldn't stop. She was crying for Daniel, so genial and wise, and surely scarred. For Agnes remaining so still under the truck. She was crying for the bodies piled in mass graves, and the bleached bones

274

scattered unclaimed across the land. For Fergus and his wife Sylvia. For Lian and her estranged son. For Walter and Woody. She was crying for Nora, who'd once loved to dance. And Victor, now frozen in time, a collage of bedtime stories, teases and tricks.

'You cannot change what has already happened,' Daniel said, his eyes on the road ahead. 'Only what you choose to take with you.'

Greta's tears abated and her thoughts drifted to the juddering Jeep, the whisper and sway of banana trees, the murmurs of a tepid breeze. It was a good place to be, in the now. Not revisiting any yesterdays, nor worrying about tomorrows.

And then, just like that, they were back in Kigali, in the midst of the mopeds, markets and mayhem.

'I must pick you up for the airport at around midday tomorrow.'

Daniel's words should have wound themselves around Greta's innards and tugged. Her pulse should have picked up and the tenor of her breathing changed. Yet she felt surprisingly calm about another flight, another city, another adventure.

'Where am I headed?'

He smiled.

'You can tell me.'

'I'm not supposed to say. There should be a letter waiting for you at the hotel.'

'Don't be a spoil sport, Daniel!'

'Johannesburg. That's all I know.'

Johannesburg. Greta had transited through the city en route to Rwanda. She was going to get to explore South Africa! Cape Town was meant to be one of the most beautiful cities in the world. She didn't know much about Johannesburg, apart from the staggering crime.

'Welcome back to Kigali,' said the woman at Reception.

Greta signed in with the confidence of a seasoned traveller. 'There should be a letter waiting for me.'

The woman looked in the cubbyholes, scanned the counter, disappeared behind it, popped back up, opened a folder, closed it, asked a colleague . . .

'Nothing, I'm sorry.'

'Are you sure?' Greta's innards clenched. 'A thick brown envelope?'

'Perhaps it will come tomorrow.'

Tomorrow would be too late.

It was inevitable. Too good to be true. She should have seen it coming. A letter delayed, lost, or, worse, not even posted. Angus had already forgotten to include Walter's introductory letter to Rwanda.

Another thought seized her. What if Angus had had a heart attack? He didn't look that healthy, and she'd seen an ashtray in his office. How would she get money? Complete the itinerary? How would she get home?

She hurried towards the lifts. She'd have to call him. But it was night-time in New Zealand, and she didn't have his home number. She could try and Google the White Pages, though that would be a long shot. Lawyers' residences were likely often unlisted.

'Madam?'

She spun round. It was the woman from Reception.

'It was hidden under our staff roster.'

CHAPTER 42

'Please fasten your seatbelt.'

Greta stared out of the small oval window.

'Madam? Your seatbelt.'

Greta laid the opened envelope on her lap and secured the strap.

'Sorry. I was daydreaming.'

She was thinking about Rwanda. Its raw, untempered beauty. The generous smiles, sweet smells of the forest, the sigh-blue expanse of sky. She didn't want to leave. Didn't want to return to a concrete, skyscraper world.

The flight attendant's mouth was moving.

'—and unfortunately our delay in departure will make your connection time very tight.'

Missing her connection wouldn't be such a bad thing.

She caught herself. How could she be thinking such a thing? Greta Jellings was slave to The Plan.

'When you disembark in Johannesburg, a member of staff will be available to assist you in getting to your next flight as quickly as possible.'

'Thank you.'

Greta had to admit to feeling a little disappointed that she wasn't going to have some time to explore South Africa after all.

'Air New Zealand has been notified.'

New Zealand. How familiar it sounded. And how foreign.

She pulled out the letter again.

Walter's increasingly uneven hand had been exaggerated by the fine, air-letter paper; his pen had poked holes through it where he'd pressed too hard. Parts of the script were almost illegible — the slumped Ws, slow Ss, tremor-skewed Ps. She could see him hunched over in his bed, trying to finish it as the clock counted down.

Greta

<u>*Southbound*</u>

*When you read this, you'll have been away for just under five weeks.
And survived. I never doubted you wld.*

Wld? It was very unlike Walter to use abbreviations.

Next stop. NZ.

The first time she'd read that line, those two upper case letters had
exploded onto the page like a hand grenade.

NZ. Her first reaction had been disbelief. Then relief. She was going
home.

I didn't want the trip to become a test of indurance.

Endurance, Walter! Endurance.

*but rather an opportunity to look through some different doors. Five
weeks is a good amount of time to be away. Before homesickness sets in.*

Hope you don't feel duped.

This sentence dropped below the ruled line, as if losing its footing,
then clambered back up.

*I had to keep the length of the trip a secret, to force you off the deep
end. Otherwise, you'd simply have kept your old life on hold.*

She tried to swallow. Her mouth was dry. She was going home. She was
happy. She was. But her relief felt qualified. It was just that . . . well,
she'd been getting into the adventure. It didn't feel complete. Or, rather,
she didn't feel complete.

A freight train of responsibilities now bore down on her. She'd have
to find a place to rent. One that would allow her to keep a pet chicken.
She'd need to find a job. Touch base with Lorraine and Rory. And Holly.
She hadn't sent any postcards. Perhaps, deep down, she'd been hoping
she wouldn't be going back to her old life.

Home, but not quite.

Come on, Walter! She was in no mood for riddles. She was angry
with him. Well, not angry. How could she be? The trip had been a gift.
A generous gift. And Walter was dead. She was being petulant.

And yet, if she was absolutely honest, she did feel duped. She'd been
led to believe she'd be away for months. Even a year. She'd mentally
prepared for that. Not for five feeble weeks.

New Zealand. But not the

This time the sentence slipped two lines down, and did not recover.

278

New Zealand you know.

The scrawl nosedived into the corner of the page, before heading up the right margin in small, almost indecipherable script. She turned the letter on its side.

The South Island of New Zealand, to a little wine-growing valley in Central Otago.

The South Island! Greta had never ventured across the Cook Strait.

A friend of mine has a house there. It's shut up for most of the year, because he works in Geneva. He visits when his schedule permits. It's yours to enjoy for as long as you wish. I want you to

The letter ended there, as if someone had pressed *pause*

To what, Walter?

But Greta knew it wasn't a pause; it was permanent.

In her mind's eye she could see the pen rolling off the bed onto the hospital floor, and Walter sinking back into his pillows, no energy left to pick it up. That moment finally arriving when he could no longer succumb to worldly worries, to unfinished business, an unfinished letter. A cerebral letting go, ahead of the physical one.

'Our Rwandan special,' said the flight attendant, handing Greta a tall cocktail decorated with fresh pineapple and a curl of coconut.

She took a long sip, the drink sucking up some of the heat and hassle of her day. 'Thank you. Just what the doctor ordered.'

The attendant's smile shrank. 'You need a doctor?'

'No, no. It's an expression. Sort of like receiving a prescription for the right medication. Though I'm not on any medication. I did used to take Spironolactone for polycystic ovaries, but I haven't been on that for some time. It's, well, it is sort of hard to explain. Really, I just meant that this cocktail is exactly what I felt like.'

The attendant looked confused.

'All good. Really. Thank you. It's delicious.'

Greta scanned the information sheet from Angus — the flight details, contact numbers for a Queenstown shuttle service, the address of the house in the Gibbston Valley. Also, an additional handwritten note from Angus.

Greta, this was the last letter Walter managed to write. As you can see, he didn't finish it, but you get the gist, I'm sure. I'll be in touch once you've settled into your new abode. It will be easier to talk when we are in the same country, albeit on different islands. Please call when you have found your feet. I don't think there is a telephone at the house, so you may need to use a phonebox, if such things still exist. Alternatively, pick up a cheap mobile phone somewhere. I'll await your call.

Last letter. Walter's last letter. The end. She'd lost him all over again.

Greta's gums prickled. She'd let herself be lulled into thinking this was a story Walter was writing. *Greta* by Walter Haywood. A story he would finish with, 'She lived happily ever after.' Ha! Instead, the story stopped midsentence. She was on her own.

Was this Walter's way of finishing that conversation they'd started on the side of the North-western motorway?

'I don't know what I did before I met you,' she says, as she lowers the jack.

'You changed the tyre on your own. I simply talked you through it,' he says, leaning against the bonnet to catch his breath.

'Yes, but—'

'Greta, you don't back yourself enough. You're a very capable woman.'

A car hoots as it speeds past, two passengers leaning out like rowdy schoolboys to hurl insults.

Walter gives them the finger.

'Walter!'

'What?' he says, with a slow smile.

'And if they stopped? You've been beaten up before. I couldn't bear it if—'

'You can't live your life in fear, Grets.' He climbs into her car. His is parked behind hers with its hazard lights on. He reclines her passenger seat and lies back. He looks uncomfortable.

'Are you alright, Walt?'

'Just a bit of cramp. Probably wind.'

She feels the grip of panic pull around her. She's known for most of their friendship that it would be finite. Terminal.

'Most people are flying by the seat of their pants,' he says breathlessly. 'You are the most qualified and capable person to live your own life. Don't be scared. Just do it. It doesn't matter if you make mistakes. Confidence doesn't grow out of the safe and certain, but from sometimes coming a cropper.'

Greta feels a spike of anger towards her mother. Nora had never afforded Greta the freedom to make mistakes. Her control had robbed Greta of the opportunity to grow, restricting her to a miniature version of what she could have become.

'But I'm scared. Sacred of the next step.'

'Me too.'

She swings around, meeting Walter's gaze.

'I'm scared too,' he says. 'Thank you for being here.'

Greta's eye started to twitch. It had been a while since it had done that. She was six years old again and had just lost the firm grip of her father's hand.

She stared at the safety pamphlet in front of her. She was in an exit row. The pamphlet outlined in detail how to open the emergency door.

DO NOT PRACTICE THIS NOW OR IT COULD DELAY OUR DEPARTURE was printed at the top.

'I wasn't going to,' she said to no one in particular.

CHAPTER 43

'Gotta be the best approach in the world,' said Lochiel McAlister.

Greta leaned awkwardly across her fellow passenger to look out of the aeroplane window. The university student's shoulders were broad and his legs long, and no matter which position he assumed, his limbs, scarred by many 'mountain-biking mishaps', spilled into her space. Saying that, they were muscular, tanned legs, and Greta didn't really mind being squashed up against them.

The view was worth the moment of awkwardness; they were flying through a corridor of snowy peaks — peaks that dived down schist slopes to a turquoise ribbon of river below. The colour of the water was astonishing, harnessing the greys and greens of the riverbed and the astounding blue of the sky.

'You're real fortunate to have all this on your doorstep,' crooned Lochiel, his Glaswegian accent wrapping itself musically around the words. 'It's pure barry.'

Fortunate. Greta supposed she was. She'd never thought of it that way. New Zealand was just New Zealand. Where she'd been born. Where she'd lived her whole life. Other places always sounded more exotic.

She waited impatiently to get off the plane. Not because she was back in New Zealand, but because she'd been in the air and transit lounges for over thirty hours and was exhausted. All she wanted to do was take a shower and lie down on a big double bed.

'Hope the ski job works out,' she said, as Lochiel lifted down her cabin luggage for her.

'Cheers' he said, giving her a wink.

Greta's face felt instantly hot. She lurched forward into the man standing in front of her.

'Hold your horses, love. We're not moving yet.'

'Sorry. I'm so sorry . . .'

It was another five minutes before they could disembark. Five interminable minutes with Greta wedged between the two men.

It had been some time since her last bout of blushing. Come to think of it, she'd barely blushed in Rwanda. Except for saying goodbye to Fergus.

The queue started to move.

She stepped out of the plane, stopping at the top of the stairs.

The noon sky held a ball of white sun in its embrace.

She breathed in deeply, then grabbed the handrail and started down the stairs.

A sound reverberated across the valley. *Tk-tk-tk-tk-tk-tk*. A helicopter in an adjacent airfield was lifting up, its glistening blades slicing up the sky. It hovered momentarily, then, like an ice-skater navigating an arena, tilted and pulled away.

'Welcome home,' said the woman behind the desk, stamping Greta's passport.

Greta opened her mouth to explain that she actually lived in Auckland. That this was not . . .

'Thank you.'

She felt an unexpected rush of delight. Home. Yes, New Zealand was her home. It felt bigger than before.

'Any pinecones, fresh fruit or seeds?' asked the man at Customs.

Greta burst out laughing. The officer's expression sobered her.

'No. Nothing like that,' she said, quickly.

Never mind declaring drugs or firearms. In New Zealand it was pinecones and seeds. Ha! It felt good to be home.

'Here we are,' said the shuttle driver, pulling up in front of a farm-style gate. 'The Clochán' was written in oxidised brass letters across the top plank.

They'd driven for about forty minutes and, bar a few pleasantries, Greta had sat silently, the countryside capturing all her attention.

One half of the valley was wrapped in shadow, the other outed in gold. Wintered weeping willows held stiff postures despite the breeze, and creamy tufts of tussock grass broke through the sweeps of snow like miniature Truffula trees. Quaint signs advertised art galleries, a fromagerie and vineyards. So many vineyards — the vines marching up and down slopes to rustic cellar doors. Smoke spiralled from chimneys. Sheep dotted snowy fields. A lake, glass-still, reflected mountains and sky so seamlessly it was hard to tell where the upside-down image ended and reality began.

The road was straighter than any Auckland road. The vehicles were different too. Cumbersome campervans and utes stacked with mountain bikes and snow skis. Also quite a few cars with dented doors.

A rabbit shot across the road.

'Look out! A rabbit!'

'You're not from here, are you?' said the driver, with a wry smile.

She shook her head, but proffered nothing more. Even she knew that Aucklanders didn't have the best reputation down south.

'Go on in, love. I'll bring your bags,' said the driver, unlatching the gate.

Greta walked towards the stone-and-corrugated-iron cottage perched on the hillside. To her right, the land fell away in a gentle slope of winter-bare vines, climbing again steeply towards the sky.

She found the key for the heavy oak door as per Angus's instructions.

It felt odd opening the door. This was not her house. And yet it felt familiar. Not a hotel room, but a home with a history.

Greta's first week in the house on the hill was idyllic. No one knew she was there, except for Angus (and Emerson, the owner who lived overseas). She didn't have to engage with anyone, be anywhere or behave in any particular way. It was wonderful and peaceful and perfect. She went to bed early, slept late, and sat out on the small stone porch under the pergola, reading, daydreaming and eating cheese from the local fromagerie. She successfully reconnected the battery of the old Citroën in the garage without electrocuting herself, though rarely ventured out, except to get provisions. And when she did, she travelled incognito with her bug-eye sunglasses and a thick woollen beanie. Not that anyone would have known her anyway.

There was something supremely appealing about living a life away from the madding crowd. A Dian Fossey, Boo Radley kind of life — people who, like her, had found human interaction hard.

After her second solitary week, though, the appeal of such a life started to pall. Greta felt a shot of warmth when the postie waved from her van. Also, when a man from a local power company dropped by to inform her of a planned outage. On both occasions the rest of Greta's afternoon felt fuller.

She thought back to Fossey and the glamorous ball gown found hanging in her closet in her small African hut.

She thought about the tiny treasures Boo Radley had left in the knothole of a tree for Scout to find.

Perhaps Fossey and Radley had also wanted something more. While they too shied away from human interaction, maybe they'd also hungered for it.

'Good to hear from you, Greta.'

The relief in Angus's voice was obvious.

'I was beginning to wonder whether you'd fallen off the edge of the earth. In fact, I was just contemplating getting one of the locals to check up on you.'

Greta apologised, offering the rather weak excuse that there were no phone booths in the area.

They chatted for a short time about the highlights of her trip, then Angus cleared his throat. 'So, what are your plans, moving forward?'

Plans? Greta chewed a hangnail. She had no plans.

'I'm just getting my head around things,' she said quickly. 'Got a few balls in the air. Working out the finer details.' She felt like a politician juggling empty words.

'Excellent,' Angus said, each syllable carrying a different level of enthusiasm.

The way he said it bothered her, as if there were other words hiding behind it.

'Am I still okay to stay here?' she asked, her voice petering out.

'Absolutely. Emerson is more than happy for you to remain in the house. He only flies out in January, I think.'

She ran through the months. September, October, November, December — four months.

January sounded like an end date. Walter's letter had led her to believe she could stay in the house for as long as she liked.

'That's—'

'Greta, something has come up we need to address.'

She closed her eyes.

A string of pips brought her back. She fed more coins into the slot.

'I've received correspondence from Walter's estranged sister, Clare. Or, rather, from the lawyer acting on her behalf. She is contesting Walter's father's will.'

Greta pressed the receiver to her ear to prevent any words escaping through the gap.

'A bit of a bind, I am sorry. Rather unexpected after this period of time. But it is what it is.' He sneezed. 'So, until the matter has been resolved, Walter's inheritance, and therefore a significant portion of his funds, are frozen.'

Greta slid down the glass wall of the booth. The concrete floor was cold and smelt of stale urine. She stood up again.

'You there?'

She nodded.

'Greta?'

'Yes. I'm here.' She picked mindlessly at a pink blob on the front of the phone box. Chewing gum! She rubbed her fingers furiously, trying to wipe off some stranger's frozen saliva.

'Now, I don't want you to panic. Emerson is more than happy to have you in the house. As I say, he's only flying out in December.'

'I thought you said January.'

'Yes, January.'

That cut-off date again.

'I'm not sure what your financial position is, Greta, but I'm assuming you have some savings to tide you over until you find another job, or whatever it is you plan to do next?'

'Of course,' she said, giving a what-do-you-take-me-for chuckle, her mind already spinning in myriad directions.

Dreams are all very well, but they don't pay the bills.

Thank goodness she'd heeded her mother's advice. At least she had the rainy day fund.

'While I do not want to get your hopes up,' Angus continued, 'I think it's unlikely Walter's sister stands much of a chance. It is well over six months since probate was granted. Though one can never say never.'

The pips again. Greta fed her last coin into the slot.

'Don't apologise,' she said briskly, trying to salvage her self-esteem. 'It's been fun. More than I could have wished for. Really.'

Then a terrifying thought hit. Would she have to pay back the holiday?

That would be impossible. Where would she get money like that? The hotel in New York alone was . . .

The screen was counting down her last minute.

'I shan't overstay my welcome, don't worry. I just need—' her voice crept up a few octaves. She cleared her throat. 'Just need some time to get things in order.'

'Good. Good. Let's talk again soon, shall we? In the meantime, enjoy the winter wonderland.'

Greta dropped her head onto the phone box, staying there for some time till her forehead was achingly cold.

She jerked her head backwards. Someone was knocking on the glass. A man with an Irish-red beard wanted to use the phone.

She stepped out into the icy evening.

'Also out of data?' he said, with a grin.

She nodded absentmindedly.

'Bloody miracle there are still some of these prehistoric booths around,' he added, edging past her. He smelt of beer and body odour.

How foolish she'd been. Lured from the safety of her Auckland existence in search of some elusive goal. She shook her head. 'Stupid, stupid me!'

She kicked a power pole, but unlike in the movies, she crumpled to the kerb in agony.

'Sh . . . shit!'

She limped down the main street to the car, her toes all the more painful because her feet were so cold. She didn't have a suitable pair of winter shoes, bar her trainers, which were now wet from the slushy snow. She should have bought a pair of boots in New York. She'd even spied a gorgeous pair in *Sassy & Sensual*. However, it was swelteringly hot at the time and the idea had seemed ludicrous.

Perhaps it was just as well she hadn't bought boots; after all, she now had a credit card bill to settle.

It was a Thursday evening and people had spilled out of restaurants onto Arrowtown's sidewalks, their laughter melting cold corners of the night. Street lamps illuminated circles of the old mining town — historic edifices, cobblestone alleyways, sunken pubs. Greta felt disconnected from the convivial mood and quaintness of the place, the tears falling onto her cheeks instantly robbed of warmth by the icy wind.

CHAPTER 44

Angus looked up from his desk, his face all surprise.

'Greta! You should have told me you were coming. When did you get in?'

'I came straight from the airport.' She put down her leopard-print luggage. 'Is it a bad time?'

'No. No. Come in. Take a seat. Can I get you a cup of tea?'

'Yes, thank you. I'm gasping.'

He smiled. It was a knowing sort of smile.

'Give me a minute. I'll put on the jug. Cassandra is out to lunch. Gosh, you look so tanned and well.'

Greta looked around the windowless office. Nothing had changed from her last visit. The piles of paper were as high, the dust as thick.

The sameness and familiarity should have been comforting, and yet if felt unsettlingly stale.

'So, you're back,' Angus said, returning with two mugs of tea. 'I thought you might have stayed down south a bit longer.'

She tossed her head from side to side. 'I need to get back to work.' Her rainy-day fund had covered the flight home and would suffice for a few frugal months.

'Yes. What a bother. I'm still hopeful this whole unnecessary business will be sorted in your favour. It might just be a bit protracted, that's all.'

'Anyway,' Greta said, reaching for her tea. The rim was marked with someone else's lipstick. She turned the mug around and took a sip from the other side. 'I just wanted to thank you for all you've done. You know, helping with the trip and all.'

Surprisingly, she felt strong. Focused. As if the sheer necessity to survive had cleared away the fluff.

Angus put up his hand. 'It's been a pleasure. Really. I hope it was worth it. Was it?'

Was it worth it?

'Oh, yes. Yes. Really.'

Angus opened his top drawer. 'Seeing you're here.' He rummaged for a moment before pulling out a white envelope, then a crumpled crimson one. 'Will save me having to post these to you in a fortnight.'

She frowned.

'Walt's final epistle. To be opened a month after your return. And this one. It's the letter I forgot to include in advance of your Rwandan leg. Sorry about that.'

'But I thought you'd already sent me Walter's last letter. Remember, he didn't get to finish it.'

'This one was written well before all the others,' Angus said, sliding it across his desk to her. 'He expressly asked that it be given to you four weeks after your return to New Zealand.'

Greta blinked. So, the letters kept coming, finding her wherever she was, in New York, London, Rwanda, Auckland . . .

Auckland. She was back. What had begun several months before with that very first call from Cassandra was over.

'So . . . where to from here?' Angus asked.

'Oh, you know,' Greta said, trying to keep a check on the panic building inside of her. 'Find a job. Place to live. That sort of thing. I'm staying with friends while I sort my life out.'

Staying with friends. It sounded so normal. So regular. But Lorraine had paused a moment too long when Greta had rung to ask if she could stay until she'd found accommodation and a job. A moment that had stretched into awkward hesitation.

Greta recoiled at the idea of imposing. She'd bought a giant Toblerone and bottle of whisky for them at the airport in the hope this would help.

'Of course, Greta. We'd love to see you. How long do you think you'll be with us? It's just that we have friends visiting from Canada later in the month, though I'm sure you'll be well sorted by then.' More of a statement than a question. 'I'll get Rory to retrieve your car from our neighbour's paddock.'

'Neighbour's paddock?'

'It was getting in the way when we needed to back out the boat.'

Jud's daughter was at the front desk when Greta walked in to Blue Sun Spas, Pools and Pipes. Tiffany stopped mid-chew and gaped at Greta, her green gum lodged on one of her molars.

'Well I never!' shouted Jud from the back of the shop. 'Look what the wind just blew in!' He hurried over and kissed Greta on both cheeks. He'd never kissed her before.

'So, are you back?'

'I just popped in to say hello. Yes. Great holiday. An excellent time. Excellent. The High Line. Gorillas. And I have an aunt. My mother's long-lost sister. The cooking was fun too. I now know how to make pasta properly. Jud, I need a job. You don't know anyone who—'

Her former boss looked at her quizzically, then fell to his knees. 'There is a god after all. Yes! The job is yours, girl. Right now, if you want it.'

Greta could not compute what he was saying. She was focused on Jud being so close to her feet.

He hauled himself up. 'That other woman, Sandra. Bad news, let me tell you. Forever at the dentist. A root canal here. Two crowns there. Full polish. I mean, there are only so many things you can do to teeth!'

'Said she was allergic to Dad's aftershave,' Tiffany added, with a snigger.

'I know! Can you believe it?' Jud said, spittle spraying out of his mouth. 'Sneezed every time I went near her. I told her to take a bloody antihistamine, but she said she didn't do drugs. That was the last straw.'

'*Well then, Sandra, maybe this is where we part ways,*' Tiffany said, imitating her father's voice.

Jud nodded vigorously. 'Yeah. I mean, *I* was allergic to *her*.' He looked down at Greta's feet. At her red wedges. 'Great shoes, Greta.'

Greta was caught between a smile and a blush. She slid one foot behind the other out of habit.

Tiffany jumped up from the desk as if she'd been unshackled. Greta had never seen the girl so animated before. She eyed Greta's shoes. 'So, are you coming back to work here?'

'Yes, she is. Aren't you?' said Jud excitedly. 'When can you start?'

Greta's heart swooped, all her anxieties whited out in less than a minute.

'I just need to get myself sorted. Find a place to stay. How does next week sound?'

Tiffany's face fell. 'But it's only Wednesday.'

'Now, don't go pressuring her, Tiffs. Monday will be fine. Absolutely fine. I've got to go ring Charlene. She'll be ecstatic.'

And that was that. Greta had her job back.

Once she'd left the shop, she drove on to Devonport, all four windows open to rid her car of the sour farm smell. She'd have to scatter dry teabags around to suck up the smell of pigs and paddocks.

As she turned into her former avenue, blood started thudding in her ears. She'd been gone barely two months, yet already the road looked different. Blossoms were in bud, trees promising green. She slowed as she passed number 43. The curtain in the front room was drawn and the outside light on, despite it being the middle of the day. The grass along the fenceline was leggy, and the bower of roses over her gate a messy tangle.

A woman walking her dog stared. Greta felt her cheeks warm; she probably looked suspicious, idling there in her car. She sped up, realising too late that she had driven right past Holly's place.

She could have rounded the block, but if the dog-walking woman saw her again, her suspicions would be confirmed.

Greta decided to come back another day.

Instantly, the ring of angst around her chest loosened. There was no rush. She could say hello to Holly any time.

That night, she rang her former landlady.

'Valenka, it's Greta.'

'Greta! You are well?'

'I am, thank you. Back in Auckland.'

'Auckland? So, the big holiday is not so big.'

'It was just enough time. You can pack a lot into seven weeks.'

Valenka did not reply. Greta could imagine her raising her pencilled-in eyebrows.

'The thing is, I'm looking for a place to stay.'

'Your house is gone now. You know that. One year lease the new man sign. One year. Maybe it would have be better you pay the rent for a seven-week holiday. No? Now you lose it.'

Greta chewed her lip. 'Do you have anything else?'

Valenka made a series of grunting noises. 'Nothing now. Big demand. Big demand. Four or five group come for every rental I'm advertise.

Maybe I have a one bedda in Belmont in a month. But the price is bigger. Fifty more a week because it is closer to Takapuna.'

Greta closed her eyes. Hopefully Lorraine would have her for the month.

'I'll take it.'

'I meet you Tuesday. You can sign the paper.'

'Thank you, Valenka. Does it have a garden?'

'A small concrete yard. It will fit your spa.'

Marilyn Monroe could not come back to a concrete yard.

'The thing is Valenka—'

'See you Tuesday.'

And just like that, Greta was back. To familiar street names. Auckland traffic. Her small cubicle of space. Her desk.

She placed her pens and pencils, nibs down, in the green ceramic holder. Rearranged the scattered drawing pins, pinning them into the corner of the corkboard. She flipped through the undertaker's calendar to get to the correct month. Somebody had drawn in black biro on the August picture — a cartoon corpse lying in the August casket. Greta turned the calendar towards the wall.

She wiped the film of fingerprints off the credit card machine, restacked the lever arch files, placed the dustbin in line with the front leg of her desk, and pulled off seven pieces of chewing gum stuck to the underside of the desk, after which she sanitised her hands.

Then she got up and opened the front door of the shop, positioning a canister of chlorine against the glass to stop the door from blowing closed. A car-exhaust breeze blew in.

She sat down at her desk again and peeled off her jumper.

'Cup of tea?' Jud said, putting his head around her door.

'Oh yes, please.'

His face twitched. 'You forgotten how to make your old boss a cuppa?'

Greta jumped up, colour filling her face. 'Don't know what I was thinking. I mean. Right. I'll put the kettle on.'

He chuckled. 'All good times must come to an end, eh? Holiday's over, love.'

Holiday's over. Holiday's over. Holiday's over.

Greta pushed open the little window in the tearoom. It hadn't been opened in forever. A disturbed spider ran down the pane. She took a piece of paper and gently flicked it outside.

'You going through the change early, or what?' Jud asked plonking himself down on the small grey couch. 'Just like my missus, opening every bloody door and window. It's goddamned freezing.'

Greta looked at him, while trying to catch the words whizzing around inside her head.

'Why so serious, Miss Jellings?'

'Sorry?'

'Left your humour in the African jungle, did you?'

'No. No.'

She dropped a teabag into one of the mugs and poured in the boiling water.

'Things aren't that tight,' Jud said, looking over her shoulder. 'We can each have our own bag.'

'Jud, I really am sorry to inconvenience you like this.'

'Look, it was good for us. Hell, we learnt to appreciate what a wonder you are.' He picked up a magazine, appraising the scantily clad model on the cover. 'One of Tiffany's magazines,' he said, feigning disapproval.

'Jud?'

He looked up. She handed him the mug of tea, the bag still floating in it.

'The thing is, I can't work here any longer.'

'Pass me a teaspoon, won't you?' he said, focused on the teabag. 'And the milk. Gosh, you are out of practice.'

Greta started backing out of the tearoom. 'Sorry.'

'Greta?'

She darted back to her cubicle, scooped up her handbag and pushed her chair in under the desk.

'Greta?'

She hesitated. Turned the calendar round, and picking up a black biro, hurriedly revised Tiffany's sketch, drawing the August casket open and the cartoon corpse climbing out with high-heeled shoes on.

Then she scurried out of the shop.

Outside she bumped into the friendly courier driver.

'Nice to see you back,' he said, his face opening into a broad grin.

She shook her head. 'I'm not back. Just here to tie up loose ends.'

CHAPTER 45

'You look amazing! I love your hair,' Holly said stepping out of the hug to appraise Greta from a distance.

Greta did not want to let go.

'I didn't dare brave a foreign hairdresser,' Greta said, scooping her brown curls behind her ear. 'So, it's had time to grow a bit.'

Holly eyed Greta's leopard-print luggage and frowned. 'Have you just got in?'

'No. No. A few days ago. I—'

Her friend looked nonplussed. 'Come in.'

Greta didn't move. 'I have a favour to ask.'

'A favour?' Holly pretended to look solemn. 'Sounds serious.'

'Can I . . . stay here for a few days?'

Holly sucked her lower lip. 'Mmh.'

Greta held her breath.

'Yes. Yes. And did I already say, yes?'

Greta breathed out, although her stomach was still in a tight knot. To stay with Holly would be a gamble. In many ways it would have been easier to remain at Lorraine and Rory's. Less to lose.

She could have got into the habit of not rinsing her breakfast dishes in Lorraine's sink, before putting them into the dishwasher. 'It makes such a mess, all the little bits of food and water splashing everywhere, and it wastes water.'

She could learn to hang her wet towel over Lorraine's heated towel rail, and not over the bedroom chair, 'because the damp damages the wood and that chair was not cheap.'

But like Jud's last cup of tea, it was Lorraine's final comment, which had opened up a highway between Greta's head and her heart.

'I know I'm being a little bit cheeky,' Lorraine said on Greta's second evening there. 'But Rory and I thought that, seeing as you are staying, we might as well use the opportunity to head away for a few weeks. You wouldn't mind looking after the house and dogs again, would you?'

Greta had wrung her hands, looked down, shifted uncomfortably.

'I'm sorry, Lorraine, but actually it won't suit. The thing is, something's come up and I'll be leaving first thing in the morning.'

And she'd driven to Devonport at 6 a.m. the next day so as not to make a lie of her excuse. The city lights were still twinkling, and mist was levitating above the still harbour waters.

Being up at that hour, on the periphery of time, felt like an adventure in itself. It reminded Greta of when her family had headed off to the beach on their one and only family holiday. *Her father behind the wheel, peering into the dawn. Her mother pouring tea from the flask to accompany a breakfast of cold sausages and hardboiled eggs.*

A perfect memory. One perfect memory.

'This is so exciting,' Holly said, ushering Greta inside.

'Really. I mean, I don't want to impose. I– It's just–'

'It's so good to see you, Grets.'

Greta smiled. She felt . . . happy.

'Now I better get ready for work or I'm going to be late. Make yourself at home. I'll sort the pull-out bed later when I get home. Tonight we can talk. I can't wait to hear all about your adventures.'

Greta made herself a cup of tea and wandered about Holly's house in a daze. She stopped in the front room. Morning sunshine was streaming through the bay window inviting her to curl up on the couch, which she did. Then she pulled out the crumpled crimson letter Angus had forgotten to post in advance of her trip to Rwanda.

Greta

Expanding horizons

Hope London's been fun. I reckon it's one of those places everyone needs to visit at least once in their lives. An amazing mix of the old and new, tradition and innovation. People complain about big cities. They can be unpleasant places, but to me, cities are also monuments to the remarkableness of humans. Eight million people in one place, moving through their day — up escalators, down stairs, across the countryside. Coffee machine's buzzing, Laundromats whirring, elevators dinging.

Teachers teaching, ballerinas practising, electricians tunnelling, art curators contemplating, police cars cruising, food kitchens feeding, charities fundraising, traffic lights turning, washing billowing, musicians playing. The lights on in evening windows. The topiaries, parks and ponds. Babies delivered. Corpses collected . . . Whenever I find I'm losing faith in mankind, I remind myself that there is a lot we do well. And each one of us is in some way a small component of it all. Each of us adds to the whole.

Anyway, enough philosophising. Where to now, you ask?

I've chosen the next destination for several reasons. The main one being that it does not spring to mind when you think of a poster place for a holiday. Its difference is the main point, the challenge. And of course, your affection for Dian Fossey. Rwanda was also the favourite place of a friend of mine.

I'm so often rewarded when I step outside of what's comfortable and expected. I hope Rwanda offers you that same satisfaction, Grets.

It was strange reading the letter after the fact. Rwanda had come and gone. Greta felt a bulge of pride at that. At having gone to Africa without a letter to lean on. Perhaps she was foolish to think it an achievement, but to her it was. She'd been left to work out Rwanda sans Walter's wisdom. And she'd survived. It was more than that, though. The place, the people and the experience had left their imprint. She felt different for having been. In a matter of ten days parts of Nora's narrative, which ran like an endless newsreel in Greta's head, had started to falter and fade.

Over the years, Nora's praise had been given and withheld at whim; Greta's self-esteem ever dependant on the direction her mother's tide took. But in Rwanda, Greta found an anchor against the elusiveness of self-belief. An anchor in her own actions. Actions could not be so easily undone. And Greta had done Rwanda.

After reading Walter's letter, she fell asleep on Holly's couch, which smelt of Mario and hessian and a home. It was the deepest sleep she'd had in a very long time.

By the time Holly returned from work that evening, the house had been vacuumed, the curtains drawn, and a dish of *melanzane parmigiana* was bubbling in the oven.

'I'm never going to let you leave,' Holly joked, as they sat on the couch after dinner, sharing a packet of marshmallows. Two girls eating marshmallows together — the image so close to what Greta imagined girlfriends did.

'. . . and when Fergus, the pilot guy, said that he and his wife were just about to split up before she got sick, I felt so sad for him. He looked full of regret.'

'Oh my God. That's heartbreaking.'

Holly looked at her watch. 'Yikes! Look at the time. I'll have to blame you when my boss catches me sleeping on the job tomorrow.'

Greta jumped up to do the dishes.

'Leave them. I can do them in the morning.'

But Greta could not leave them. Holly had to keep on liking her.

As she lay on the pull-out bed that night, she felt the same thrill she'd felt as a child playing house, sheets suspended between sofas becoming something more.

Relaying her adventures to Holly had instigated something important. Like an accountant balancing the books, or a shopkeeper doing a stock-take, recounting the events of past weeks had seen them gathered into a whole. A satisfying summation. A rounding off. An epilogue.

Greta was on the toilet when her airport shuttle arrived. She'd been four times already since waking up, her stomach bubbling with nerves.

'Grets, your ride is here!' Holly called from the kitchen.

Greta had been in Devonport for five perfect and exhausting days.

It was a tiring business ensuring a friendship remained flawless.

She handed her leopard-print luggage to the driver.

'Let me know when you get there,' Holly said, giving Greta a hug.

The driver slid the door shut, locking Greta in, and Auckland out.

With a farewell hoot, they headed off, Greta waving and waving till the van turned the corner.

She sank back into her seat. Talkback radio was on, but she didn't tune in. There was something still nagging at her. Marilyn Monroe.

A hollow lump of longing expanded in her throat. It would be too hard to see her beloved hen and then say goodbye all over again. She'd have to wait a bit longer before they could be reunited.

'Domestic or international, Ms Jellings?'

'Domestic, thank you,' Greta said, with a slow smile.

CHAPTER 46

Walking back into the corrugated-iron cottage in the Gibbston Valley felt like coming home. It was the familiarity of the chipped stone paving, the matted spiderweb suspended across the eaves, the frayed maroon cushion moulded to the outdoor wicker chair. The mountains felt familiar too. When the pilot had tilted the plane to afford a better view, and Greta had gripped her seat for dear life, the view had suddenly thrilled her — tall, wide peaks glinting white in the generous splashes of sunshine.

She'd never sought charity before. Not ever. However, the offer had been there for her to use the house till January and she was in no position to ignore such bounty. She thought of Frank. His directness. Every word carrying the weight of its meaning. No second chances. An offer was an offer.

She put down her bags. She was back, but this time on her own terms. On her own . . . no map or person to guide, advise, rebuke, or praise her. She filled the kettle, her hands trembling as she turned on the switch. The unknown stretched before her. A new unknown. However, there, in amongst the angst, something else stirred again. That feeling of excitement.

Greta parked the Citroën at the entrance to Arrowtown and walked along the road lined by old miners' cottages. They all looked the same. She'd seen the sign in one of the windows before she'd left. But which one?

The exercise was probably pointless anyway; the position would surely have been filled by now.

The pavement was still icy and she had to tread carefully to avoid slipping. Despite two pairs of socks, her feet were frozen. The extra bulk made her trainers bulge — an unwise decision in retrospect, considering she was hoping to make a good impression.

Did she really think it would be that easy? A glimpsed job advertisement from a fortnight back, the answer to her future?

Then she saw it, the red sign hanging from a wrought iron bracket. Mel's Bed & Breakfast.

And the notice. It was still in the window!

Housekeeping help needed. Enquire within.

Greta took a deep breath, unlatched the front gate and made her way up the pathway.

A stout, florid-faced woman with a nobble of nose opened the door.

'Hello. I'm coming about the advertisement in your window,' Greta said, slouching to minimise her height. 'For housekeeping help. I'm Greta. Greta Jellings.' She put out her hand, then quickly retracted it, in case the gesture was too forward. 'I was wondering if . . . I mean I've never formally cleaned before, though I did previously run the office at a spa shop. Jud Rutland. He was my boss. He always commended me on my organisational skills.'

Greta wished she had not brought Jud into it. What if the woman asked for a reference? Jud could be spiteful.

'I am a very house-proud person. *A healthy house is a healthy mind.* That's what Nora used to say. Nora was my mum, but she preferred to be called by her real name. It's complicated. To do with my father leaving. But that's another—'

The woman held up her hand. 'Back up, hon. Just back up.'

It was a relief to have someone stop her. Greta's brakes had failed.

'Catch your breath, Gretchen, and come on in. It's minus four this morning and if you stand out there much longer you'll turn to ice. Although all that talking might melt you instead.' She gave a boisterous laugh.

'It's Greta,' Greta said, following the woman down the hallway.

The house was warm and smelt of grilled bacon.

The woman pushed open a swing door. There was a rush of golden light, then the door swung back.

Greta stopped it with her hand. Was she meant to follow?

She hovered.

The door came at her again.

'Lost you already,' said the woman, bursting into another bout of loud, own-the-room laughter. 'This way.'

Greta stepped into a bright white kitchen. There was a potbelly stove in the corner and a huge AGA cooker up against one wall. She had always wanted an AGA. There was something so hunter-gatherer-honest about that sort of stove.

Above it hung a wooden pot rack from which was suspended a clutter of copper pots and pans.

A farmhouse table dominated the room. Ten place settings and an old tin teapot in the centre filled with dried lavender.

'Push aside a plate and grab a perch, Gretchen. My guests have just finished breakfast.'

'Greta.'

'What? Oh, Greta. And here I was thinking you had the same name as my idol, Gretchen Reuben. Do you listen to her podcasts? That woman has a world of wisdom at her fingertips, I tell you. This morning she was offering advice on how to avoid procrastinating. She was talking to me. A direct line, I tell you.' Another boom of laughter.

Greta blushed. She was a disappointment already. If only her name had been Gretchen.

'Sit, hon, you're making me nervous.'

Greta pulled out a chair and sat down. On the plate in front of her were the remnants of a waffle and some smudges of maple syrup. Greta could detect maple syrup a mile away.

'So, you've worked in a spa? Now that could be useful. I need some pampering.' The woman spread her left hand. She was missing two fingers. 'Would you give me a discount?' Another wave of laughter.

'No, no,' Greta said, shaking her head.

An image burst into Greta's head of an axe coming down in some Canadian conifer forest. Two fingers rolling off a tree stump and landing in a pile of bloodied pine needles. Greta grimaced.

'Too bad. Manicuring eight fingers must surely be less time-consuming.'

'No, I mean not that sort of spa. I worked at a shop selling spa pools and chemicals. You know, chlorine and salt and—'

The woman's grin faded. 'Ah well, I guess these eyebrows will have to remain untended. I might let you have a go at them anyway.'

Greta tried not to stare at the woman's heavily overgrown monobrow.

'So, a spa shop, eh?'

'I used to pluck my mother's eyebrows,' Greta said quickly. 'And the hairs on her chin.'

This round of laughter lasted longer than all the others, finally petering out like a car running out of fuel.

'Main thing,' said the woman, her face now a shiny red, 'is that you're used to dealing with the public, because that's what this job is all about, Gretchen. Dealing with people. Tricky creatures. There's also all the mundane stuff too, of course — stripping beds, vacuuming, cleaning toilets.

'There are four double bedrooms, all with en-suites. I pay seventeen-eighty an hour and provide a midday meal.'

She told Greta that the last cleaner, a French girl, had left without giving notice. 'Said she was tired of doing all the shitty jobs. Can you believe it? And at my busiest time too. I've been run off my fat little feet.'

The woman was not even a size six. Greta shifted her feet further under the table.

'I've had to put my fencing lessons on hold,' the woman added, bending her knees, holding up her three-fingered hand behind her head, the other pointed straight out at Greta. 'On guard!'

Greta hovered between disbelief and delight. There was a comforting craziness to the place.

'So, when can you start? I mean there are beds to be made this very minute if you are so inclined.'

Greta tilted her head. Held her forefinger up in a sort of question mark. Had she just been offered a job? It was not what she'd envisioned for her first ever job interview. With Rutland senior, it was less an interview than him casting his lascivious eye over her.

'I'm good to go if you are,' said the woman. 'A trial for a week. How about it?'

It was so spontaneous. Greta felt completely unprepared. She was not even in the right clothes for cleaning. But she needed the work. What's more, she was itching to declutter the pot rack; it had lost its farmhouse charm under all the excess. As for the skirting boards . . .

'Well, Gretchen, what's it to be?'

Greta nodded. 'Yes. I can. I mean, I will. Yes.'

And without further ado, Greta began work at Mel's Bed & Breakfast.

'More steak pie?'

Greta shook her head. 'With all these big lunches, my clothes are getting tight. It used to just be a cheese sandwich for me.'

Not gaining weight was something Greta had to work at. It would be different if she'd secured a lover. There was a little leeway then, she imagined. With her lengthy limbs, unfeminine height, and oversized feet, the least she could do was watch her weight.

Between one and two in the afternoon was her and Mel's reprieve. The rooms had been made up and new check-ins not until two.

'Never agree to an early check-in, Gretchen,' Mel had cautioned. 'Guard the boundaries with your life, or you'll become a slave to the tourist.'

She insisted Greta sit down with her to a cooked lunch every day, the table set with silver cutlery, a crystal jug filled with fresh water, and all the condiments put out — HP sauce, mayonnaise, horseradish cream, ketchup and two types of mustard, even if there was little chance of any being added to an omelette or piece of pan-fried fish.

At first Greta was reluctant to partake in this daily ritual. Eating in front of others was an uncomfortable, focused affair, with the ever-present pressure to make conversation. Fortunately, it turned out that Mel did most of the talking. What's more, eating at work meant Greta's grocery bill could be halved — an important consideration with her rainy-day fund rapidly running out and no further word from Angus in three weeks.

As she eased into the routine she started to look forward to the hour of ring-fenced calmness, a change from the shop where she often gobbled down lunch at her desk.

'People will take as much of you as you're prepared to give,' Mel warned. 'Climbing off the treadmill is not the sole prerogative of retirees. Time for yourself should be stitched into every day. It's a matter of necessity.'

Necessity, or self-indulgence?

Greta knew what Nora's take on it would have been, her mother's outlook injecting guilt into this small new pleasure.

She sighed. The power of Nora. The power of words. Words could dominate a life and dent a person's happiness. Like *cheeky*, and *bad*, and *insect*, and *faggot*.

Over lunch every day, Mel dispensed much advice, which Greta promptly added to an ever-growing mental manual. Other people appeared to have all the answers, and Mel more than most. Especially after a glass or two of pinot noir.

Each evening, after Greta got home from work, she would sit out on the porch of her cottage and decompress. From her seat she could see a small ripple of silver halfway up the opposite hill — the corrugated-iron roof of a shepherd's hut tucked into the crease of land. A mere speck on Mount Malcolm, which, when the sun caught it, glistened like a nose piercing.

Mount Malcolm.

Mount Edward.

Mount Scott.

Greta mused how people were in the habit of naming peaks, as if mountains could be owned.

The South Island scenery, with its high summits, plunging gorges, and enormous boulders, left her feeling Lilliputian. Though not the same smallness she'd experienced in Auckland. The vastness of the landscape was more a reminder of how impermanent man was. The thought did not terrify her. Rather, she found it oddly comforting, the way it downscaled things man held to be important, such as money and prestige and small, svelte waists. It was a wisdom she'd first glimpsed in Rwanda amongst the timeless Virunga Mountains. Mountains that straddled centuries.

Her mind wandered to macheted corpses and slain soldiers scattered across battlefields. To a man burnt at the stake for reenvisaging the solar system. And another deemed a criminal for loving a man. To women fondled and forced and denied the vote. To Romans marching on Gaul. To planes flying into twin towers . . .

Grasses now grew on those battlefields, wildflowers the only reminder of the crimson colour that had once seeped into the earth. Roman columns had crumbled. A left-wing government was voted back in. Women went to the polls. And a Callery Pear bloomed again.

Perhaps, Greta thought as she sipped a glass of Indian tonic water minus the gin, she was getting the hang of all this. Just perhaps.

CHAPTER 47

Walter's last letter had been sitting on her dressing table for twenty-six days when Greta finally allowed herself to pick it up. It had only been twenty-six days since she'd arrived back in the valley. However, if she included her short stay in Auckland, she'd been back in New Zealand for over a month.

Greta
In Closing

Leaving the unopened letter propped against the mirror for so long had not been easy. It was like putting a Christmas present under the tree a month early. She couldn't even shake the letter to get a sense of what was inside.

As D-day approached, her excitement built, as if an old-fashioned trunk call had been booked. As if she'd been given a definite date for Walter's return.

She brewed herself a pot of orange pekoe tea and sat down with a plate of digestive biscuits and Walter's letter. Walter's final letter.

Hey you!

She smiled. 'Straw.'

Hope you've had a good day.

'Not great. But I don't mean to complain.'

By now the trip will be receding in your mind and as best as I try to project where you might be, or what you might be doing, I can't. This next leg of the journey is all yours. Though, of course, I'm curious.

'Perhaps you'd be disappointed if you could see me now.'

She lowered the letter. Drank her tea. Mindlessly ate three biscuits, ignoring the crumbs falling into her lap.

She'd fooled herself into believing her life had changed, when really very little had. She was not on some new trajectory, but rather in a familiar holding pattern. She worked a job which guaranteed a survivable salary but did not excite her. She was answerable to a friendly, if flawed, boss. She was living in someone else's house, and, while not paying any rent, was not at liberty to put her stamp on it in any significant way. As for the long arms of her childhood . . . Nora's words continued to rule.

Greta's body slackened. She was tired.

This, being my last letter, is about tying up loose ends. About not leaving anything out. I realise it wouldn't be fair not to fill in some of the gaps. You are, after all, my closest friend.

Greta's skin prickled. Reading those five words was even better than a marriage proposal (she imagined).

So here goes.

I trained as an architect. Frank's probably already told you that. I really wanted to be an actor.

I did know, but also didn't, that I was gay, from about the age of fifteen. It felt like the vilest of curses and something I railed against for a long time, thinking I could get the better of it. That it was a decision. Up to me.

I couldn't. Get the better of it. It was me. So, I tried to delete me in a car beside a beach.

Even that didn't work. All that was left was to escape. To run away from those I'd disappointed.

In New York I met Woody, the man who would become my friend, my lover, my life partner.

Greta was speared by an arrow of jealousy.

You would have liked each other, of that I am certain.

'I guess we could have all been friends.'

New York was new and different. Woody too. He had the blackest of faces and the whitest of teeth. It was in his foreignness that I found the freedom to be me. His trust in what I still had to become. That's what I tried to offer you with the trip.

She nodded slowly.

I could have chosen any number of destinations, Grets. Any place that would have taken you away from the ties which kept you bound to a life I don't think was really yours.

Yes. That feeling of moving through the wrong life.

The opportunity for a blank slate.

Woody got AIDS. It was terrifying. Prejudice distilled to its purest.

Love, the thing which had rescued me, suddenly became the thing which could kill me. A relentless diarrhoea, which could dissolve two humans in a bedpan of fear.

And then he was gone.

Gone. The word looked so empty on the page. The hollowness of the 'g', the circle of nothingness inside the 'o'.

When I finally pulled myself together, it felt as if nine beautiful years had died too. I was again the boy playing sick on the sideline of the rugby pitch, disappointing my parents. How far reaching is childhood.

'I know.'

Then the guilt hit me. They have a name for it. 'Survivor guilt.' People all around me had died from this terrifying disease, and I, worthless as I was, had for some reason been spared.

So, it almost came as a relief when I finally tested positive.

Greta stopped reading. Looked up. At the rim of curtain bulging backwards where a hook had become detached. At the tassels on the rug splayed unevenly. At the fire grate leaning to the left.

By then there were new drugs, which could hold the disease at bay and force me to keep on living.

It was then that I realised I owed it to Woody, and all the others who'd been taken, to live my life as best I could.

To live my life as best I could. The line bounced against the walls of Greta's mind.

I only came back to New Zealand when I learnt about my liver. Liver cancer is more common in those with HIV.

I came back not so much to die at home, for home is not necessarily where you are born. No, I came back more to reassure myself that I could be anywhere and still hold onto the Walter I had found.

And that is what I wish for you, Greta. That when you find a track which feels true, you keep on it regardless of the hurdles you encounter. Regardless of where it is headed. Regardless of where you are.

Go well, my dear, dear friend.

Walt x

CHAPTER 48

'Sick?' bellowed Mel down the line. 'But—'

'I know. I'm sorry. But even if I were up to it, Mel, I wouldn't want to pass it on to you or the guests.'

'There are different schools of thought. Some say it's better to sweat out a virus. You could wear a mask and just do the beds—'

Greta felt like a truant. She wasn't sick.

You can't shirk your responsibilities on a whim. There are people relying on you. You're just like your father. Impulsive and selfish, with no thought for the consequences of your actions.

Normally Nora's words whittled away at her, but today, as they played on repeat, they had the opposite effect, galvanising Greta. Her father had been a good person. He had.

'I'm sorry, Mel, I won't be coming in.'

There was a stunned pause. 'I have to go, Greta. I can't keep chatting when there's work to be done. This will mean having to cancel my fencing lesson too.'

People will take from you what you are prepared to give.

Greta replaced the receiver, any residual guilt slipping off her like a silk nightie. She collected her change and headed out of the booth, scurrying down the road in the direction of the shops.

The assistant behind the counter at the fabric store was extraordinarily tall.

Greta stared. She couldn't help herself. It was the woman's tailored turquoise blouse, brown skirt and twist of chintz around her waist. Greta had grown up in a seamstress's home; she could recognise custom-made chic when she saw it.

The lady looked as if she'd just stepped off a *Vogue* shoot. Greta imagined her name was something like Sadie or Sasha.

'I'd like half a metre of that navy velvet in the window please.'

'Just half a metre?'

Greta blushed, embarrassed by her small-enough-to-be-a-bother request.

'Let me see if I have some on the shelf,' said the woman, scanning the bolts behind her. 'Otherwise I'll get it out of the window.'

'Oh, don't destroy your display for me.'

'What's it for? Perhaps I have something similar. Are you making an evening bag?'

Greta's blush deepened. 'No. I. It's . . . to cover a pair of shoes.'

Since purchasing her charcoal-coloured flats in New York, Greta had worn them almost every day and in all sorts of weather. They'd become quite scuffed and the velvet had started to wear thin over the toes and heels.

The woman looked down at Greta's feet, her eyes widening.

Greta cringed.

'Lovely shoes! May I ask where you bought them?'

It took Greta a moment to compute the woman's response. She was admiring Greta's feet. Well, not exactly her feet, but her shoes.

She tilted her right foot at an angle. 'New York.'

The woman's face fell.

Greta immediately regretted being so honest; she sounded like some precocious jetsetter.

As the woman moved out from behind the counter, Greta took the opportunity to check out her footwear.

She glanced back up quickly.

The woman's cheeks had pinked.

Below her elegant calf-length skirt, were sneakers. A pair of man-sized sneakers.

'It's so hard to find suitable shoes our size, isn't it?' she said to Greta.

Our size. Greta was reeling. The instant camaraderie. Shared pain. How she'd longed to be included in someone's 'our'.

Ninety minutes later, with the occasional interruption from a customer, the fabric in the window had been cut and the two women's contact details exchanged.

'Let me know how you get on,' Piper Kelsey said.

'I will. Fingers crossed it works out.'

Her heart was still hitting against her ribs as she drove home, exhilaration dictating the beat. She felt as if she'd finally guessed the correct code for some secret door and it had just swung open. Most of her life had been spent striving to be accepted by The Norm, her greatest wish to blend in. It was overwhelming to now discover that an outlier could be cool and valued too. It was a Princess-Diana-handshake moment. The small, but massive gesture had affirmed for Woody and Walter and millions of others that they did indeed belong. And in a similar, of course much smaller way, Piper Kelsey's 'our' had pulled Greta into a fold.

In the wee hours of the next morning she stood up, her shoulders stiff and lower back aching, and she slipped her feet into a pair of rather elegant navy ballet flats.

They were not perfect. The fabric over the left heal had creased, the inner seams were noticeable, and a small nick in the fabric on the left shoe had left an unsightly scar on the vamp. She managed to camouflage it by adding a small velvet bow to each shoe, with the unexpected bonus of this shortening the shoe's apparent length.

She twirled around the lounge. She'd refurbished a pair of shoes all by herself (and a little help from YouTube).

YOU ARE INVITED TO TONI BIAGONNI'S BIRTHDAY PARTY
WHEN: SATURDAY 12TH JANUARY
TIME: 10AM
THEME: MAD HATTER'S TEA PARTY. BEST BONNET WINS A PRIZE.
RSVP: MRS BIAGONNI 447-3150

The thrill of the days leading up to Toni's ninth birthday party. The pink dress with a giant mauve frill Nora has made from offcuts. All Greta's sketches of different hat designs, each more elaborate than the last.

She finally settles on a green-and-gold top hat with silver stars bursting from the top.

On the big day, however, the cardboard buckles, the stars slump over the edge and the brim peels off. Greta has to hold the hat in place to prevent it slipping off her head like some ill-fitting pageant crown.

Not even the caramel-coated popcorn, which Nora never buys, nor Mrs Biagonni's ginger crunch, can make up for Greta's disappointment and envy. Laura Woo wins the giant bag of candyfloss, sparkly plastic bracelet and new Barbie doll for her hat.

Throughout her childhood Greta suffers many such creative disasters, her ideas always grander than the reality of their completion. There is the go-cart, which loses its wheels on Kildare Avenue. The bivouac-style cubbyhouse, which blows over in the first August wind. And her own sad section of Nora's vegetable patch. Then, of course, there are all the shoes she tries to revise, like the sandshoes she paints with watercolours — watercolours that run in the rain.

Realising dreams was an impossible business. But this project, refurbishing her New York shoes, had been a success.

Greta admired her handiwork between mouthfuls of muesli. Muesli was an immensely satisfying snack in the middle of the night.

She thought of all the chidings Nora had dished out over the years, and was again gripped by resentment. Her mother's exacting perfectionism had put the kibosh on anything involving the possibility of failure. How deftly her mother had cut Greta down to size, tailoring her to fit the Nora pattern.

'No. No more!' Greta shouted out loud.

It felt satisfying to articulate her anger out loud.

And yet . . . she took another spoonful of cereal . . . and yet, this very project had worked out because of her mother. Because of how Nora had taught her to handle fabric, draw up a pattern, be meticulous.

Yes, her mother had been both a boon and a burden.

Life was complex.

In a rest home in Kent, Greta had travelled back further than her thirty-nine years, learning more of her mother's story. It was strange to now think of Nora having once been a child too. A child who had been deserted by her unmarried mother and then separated from her twin sister. A young woman who married a man, only to be shamed by him when he left her for another man.

Greta dropped her head onto the kitchen table.

I want you to call me Nora. Not Mama.

Perhaps Nora knew it was best for Greta not to love any person too much. Perhaps she was just protecting her child from the heartache of loss.

Greta thought about a saying the French had: '*Tout comprendre ces't tout pardonere.*' 'To understand is to forgive.'

310

She was trying to forgive. She was.

Staving off her mother's superstitions, Greta picked up the navy shoes and put them upside down on the kitchen table, then, pouring some methylated spirits onto a cloth, wiped the soles clean, before dabbing them dry with a paper towel. Finally, she picked up a permanent marker and in her best handwriting wrote *Nora* on one sole and *Victor* on the other.

'You should get sick more often,' Mel said at lunch a few days later. 'You've come back to work with so much energy. I heard you whistling earlier. Though I'd never have picked you for one to whistle the "Colonel Bogey March". Took me back to days with my poppa, it did.'

So that's what the tune was called. It had arrived in Greta's head from nowhere — something her father used to whistle while pottering in his shed. To think it had hidden in the recesses of her mind for so many years.

Other extraordinary things had been happening in her head too, as if layers of insulation had started lifting off to expose parts of Greta she'd forgotten belonged to her.

'*Hitler has only got one ball,*' Mel sang.
Göring has got two, but they're small,
Himmler has something sim'lar
But poor old Goebbels has no balls at all.'

Greta sat agog, her cheeks burning, her temples thumping. That she had been whistling this within earshot of the guests, too!

Just when she thought she was getting a handle on herself, resolving some of the riddles of her existence, becoming more mainstream, she went clumsily back to the beginning. Being Greta was hard. Sometimes too hard.

After work she drove to Cromwell to show Piper Kelsey her revamped shoes.

'Stunning!' Piper exclaimed. 'I love the addition of the bows.'

'What size are you?' Greta asked, stepping out of the navy flats.

'Ten. Sometimes ten-and-a-half.'

Greta was familiar with that sort of qualification.

'Try them on.'

'I couldn't.'

'Go on.'

Piper untied the laces of her left sneaker and like a tentative child slipped her foot slowly into the shoe.

She looked up, her eyes glistening with delight and disbelief.

Greta felt a rush of gratification, how she imagined a doctor would feel discovering a cure for a patient's lethal disease.

Piper yanked off her right sneaker without undoing the laces (this bothered Greta in a Nora sort of way) and put on Greta's other shoe. Then she walked towards the full-length mirror, and back. Towards the mirror, and back.

'I'm still looking for something small to put in the centre of each bow,' Greta said, infected by Piper's elation. 'It needs a little motif to finish it off.'

'Got just the thing,' Piper said, darting over to a glass cabinet crammed with cards of buttons.

'Perfect,' Greta said, detaching a pea-sized bauble from a set of six.

Greta looked at her watch. 'I'd better pay for them and be on my way. I need to get hold of my lawyer before he leaves work.' She felt rather important referring to her lawyer.

'If I kill you, I get to keep these, right?'

Greta laughed. She wished she could give them to her new friend, but that was beyond the reach of her generosity.

'Do you remember the name of the shop in New York where you bought them? Perhaps they sell them online.'

'I'm so bad with names,' Greta stuttered. 'A small place on some side street. Sorry.'

Driving home from Cromwell, Greta took in the landscape — the vineyards with their satisfying symmetry were now in spring leaf, the orchards, an explosion of pink and white blossom. Windmills spun sluggishly against the coral sky. Snowy peaks seeped into the steep brown slopes. Blue lupins freckled fields. Every month had seen the countryside transform more dramatically than she'd ever experienced in Auckland.

She slowed to read the chalk-white words written on a winery blackboard.

WISDOM BEGINS IN WONDER. SOCRATES

Yes, Greta thought. To be in awe was to acknowledge that life was complex, and often beyond the reaches of understanding or control.

She had spent so much time inside her head, yet more and more she was realising that the best of life lay outside of herself, across just such a twilight-blushing vista. She didn't have to solve all of its mysteries on her own, like some scientist trying to crack a code. Nor did she require a letter to help her navigate the way. Nature held many of the answers. Disarmingly simple answers.

She thought of the film she'd seen about emperor penguins. How they bunched together against the Antarctic cold, regularly rotating their positions to give each bird a turn within the warm core of the colony.

She thought of the dung beetle in Rwanda struggling up a mound of earth, its progress beset by so many setbacks.

She thought how drought and fire and rib-protruding hunger were also a part of Nature's palette. A tsunami could hit, while across the ocean the sun might shine and palm trees sway in an island breeze. A baby foal might slip into the world, while another fight to find its way out of the womb and fail.

Life was ugly and beautiful, and random and assured. It was terrifying and electrifying. And always filled with hope.

She smiled. Yes, always filled with hope.

CHAPTER 49

Greta pulled into her driveway. The Clochán's gate was open. She never left it open. As she drove into the garage she chided herself for being so careless. She must have been distracted earlier when heading out to get groceries.

She put her key in the front door.

It was already unlocked and opened on its own.

Blood drained from Greta's gums. She had definitely not left the door unlocked.

She hurried back to the Citroën, every sound amplified — her footsteps on the gravel, her breathing, the chaffing of her trousers.

The old vehicle usually took a few goes to start, and the noise would likely alert an intruder if they were still in the house. Then there was the gate to deal with. The gate she had just closed.

She sat in the car, paralysed. For the first time ever, she wished she owned a mobile phone. Well, a working mobile phone. If she got out of this situation unscathed she would definitely buy one. She would.

She looked ahead. Squinted. A space now gaped on the garage bench where the microwave had lived since her arrival. So, the house *had* been burgled!

Greta glanced in her rear-view mirror, making ready to reverse.

A man was standing behind the car.

She screamed and fumbled with the ignition.

He was tall and thin, with a brown birthmark covering his right eye like Falconnetti's eye-patch. (The villain from *Rich Man, Poor Man* — Nora's favourite mini-series — still terrified Greta.)

The man behind the car was holding a suitcase. A suitcase probably filled with her belongings. The cheek of it!

The thought loosened her mind, which had been locked on pause.

She scrolled through various emboldening quotations.

Best form of defence is attack. Inhale courage, exhale fear. Peace is not the absence of conflict, but the ability to handle conflict by peaceful means.

The man smiled. Was it the smile of a psychopath about to decapitate his victim?

What to do?

She should defer to Nature. Hadn't she recently come to that realisation?

A lion would attack (but a springbok run). A vulture would circle (but an eagle dive down). A gorilla would beat its chest and bellow (but a leopard move stealthily).

So much for Nature's disarmingly simple answers!

She opened the window a crack.

'I'm not sure what you think you are doing here, but I want you to leave right now.'

She jammed the window shut again.

The man pulled back his head, as if she'd thrown a punch.

Emboldened, she edged down the window again.

'The police are on their way. Best you leave before it gets ugly.'

He put down the suitcase. This was either a good sign, or a bad one.

A bad one, as it turned out. Next thing he was at her window.

She screamed so loudly the man blanched.

'I've got a gun in here,' she cried, waving her handbag.

He mouthed something as he backed away.

'Don't even—' Greta stopped and worked her way around the words she'd lip-read. *My house.* My house? My house!

She felt nauseous. Rolled the window down a little further. 'Are you . . . you're not . . . you're not Emerson, are you?'

He nodded.

At that moment Greta would have preferred him to be a burglar.

She gulped. Closed her eyes. Opened them again.

He was still there.

She climbed slowly out of the car.

'I wasn't expecting you,' she finally managed, unsticking her top lip from her teeth. 'Angus said January.' Then under her breath, 'Or December.'

It was the first week of December.

Say something.

'I tried to get hold of him the other day,' Greta went on. 'You see, I don't have a mobile. Though that is going to change. Yes. I see now it would be handy to have one in an emergency.'

Please say something.

She made an odd barking whimper, willing tears to come; tears would have been useful right then. They didn't oblige.

'You're Walter's friend, right?' the man said, his robust voice not matching his lanky frame. 'I didn't realise you were still here.'

Greta willed a sinkhole to open up. The ground remained firm.

'Did Angus not tell you?'

'I thought he said you'd gone back to Auckland.'

She had, but she'd come back. Angus should have—

Greta knew her face would be the darkest shade of red imaginable. 'I'll just gather my things. Be gone in a couple of hours.'

'Don't leave on account of me. Not on account of me. Really. I'm happy the old girl has company.'

Greta straightened. 'I'm only thirty . . . thirty-nine.'

'Oh, I wasn't referring to you.' He lifted his hand in apology. 'Not you. I was meaning the house. The old girl . . . as in the house.'

Greta had never seen a man blush before.

They both hesitated.

She looked down. Emerson was wearing one red sock, one blue. And the smartest pair of suede loafers.

'This is just awful. I don't know what to say. I'm so sorry about the confusion.'

Every time Greta thought she'd finally found herself, had some of the answers to life, was at peace with the world and her foibles, something happened to take her right back to the beginning. Life was like a game of snakes and ladders, and there seemed to be so many more snakes than ladders on her board.

She dropped her handbag on the console table.

Emerson jumped back.

'The gun?'

'Oh no. Never,' she said. 'I was just calling your bluff.'

His eyebrows settled.

He picked up the suitcase now in the hall. 'I'll get my bag out of the way. Which room are you in?'

Greta pointed to the main bedroom. 'I can move to the smaller—'

But Emerson was already walking down the passage to the small single room at the other end of the house.

There was half a dish of moussaka left over in the fridge. At least Greta had something to offer him for dinner, the man whose house she'd been occupying as if it were her own.

She warmed a portion for each of them in the oven, despite the fact that it would have been quicker in the microwave (which, she noted, Emerson must have moved back into the kitchen). She also opened a bottle of pinot noir given to her as a gift by one of Mel's guests.

The moussaka tasted even better than it had the first time round, the flavours having had a chance to intensify. Conversation, however, was less satisfying. There were a lot of protracted pauses.

Despite this, Greta felt a ripple of delight spread through her. It was the way Emerson was eating her food. With focus and quiet gusto.

'Very good. Very good indeed,' he said, wiping his plate clean with a piece of bread.

It had been a long time since anyone had complimented Greta on her cooking. A long time since she'd cooked for a guest. Of course, she hadn't cooked with Emerson in mind. Nor was he a guest, not to put too fine a point on it! She was the guest.

Ironically, his awkwardness made hers a little easier — the sum of their gaucheness something not so gauche after all.

'How did you know Walter?' she ventured, after an especially long pause. Walter was their only reference point. It was because of him that they were in this odd predicament.

Emerson told her that he worked in the Office of Public Health in Switzerland. In the 80s he'd flown to New York to present a paper on tackling the spread of HIV. At the conference he'd met Woody. And through Woody, Walter.

'When Walter and I discovered we were both from New Zealand our friendship was cemented. Yes, cemented.'

Greta could see Emerson would have been Walter's type. Unaffected. A thinker. And a humanitarian.

Had they been lovers, she wondered? She blushed at the thought.

'Is the race flowing okay?' Emerson asked.

Greta was puzzled. Was this slang for 'Is your life on track?' How much had Walter and Angus told him about her?

'Oh, in fits and starts,' she said. 'You know how it is.'

'That's annoying. There's no good reason for it not to be running smoothly. No reason at all.'

She straightened. Set her jaw.

'I'll call someone in the morning. Get it sorted.'

Now she was completely baffled.

Finally he clarified the misunderstanding. The race was the stream, which ran across the back of the property and supplied the house with water.

Emerson's dialogue was disconcerting. His jerkiness. The absence of predictable segues. The way he frequently repeated parts of a preceding sentence.

'I had no idea our water came from a stream. I mean *your* water.'

Emerson stood up, almost knocking over his chair, and left the room.

Clearly she'd offended him. Regardless, it was rather rude to not excuse himself and just expect her to clear up.

She caught herself. Clear up was the very least she could do. After all, had the roles been reversed, she would have been furious to find some random man living in her house. It was all Angus's fault. She'd have words with him when next they spoke. He could have given her some warning.

She decided she'd pack her belongings and ask Mel if she could stay in the outbuildings, until she'd found alternative accommodation.

'Every good meal should be rounded off with a few blocks of dark chocolate,' Emerson said, returning to the room. 'Yes, dark chocolate.'

Greta was at the sink.

He held out a slab of Swiss chocolate.

'Thought I'd misplaced it. It had slipped to the bottom of my bag. The very bottom.'

Greta's heart skipped a beat. Swiss chocolate. 70% cocoa. What fine taste this man had.

Emerson tried to dissuade Greta from moving out, reassuring her that he preferred having someone in the house during his long spells away.

But Greta was done with being the recipient of well-meant directives. She needed to steer her own way. Find a place to call her own. Somewhere she could hang out her undies over the bathtub, start the day with a slice of cake, if she so wished, and sit out on the porch without being obliged to make polite conversation. She also needed to find a job she could be passionate about.

What's more, as kind as Emerson's offer was, she didn't imagine it would be easy sharing a house with him, even intermittently. He was rather untidy. And absent-minded. That he held down some high-flying position in Switzerland, a country which prided itself on order and regulation, was an anathema to her. Clearly his bright and creative mind was focused more on ideas and solutions, than on whether his socks matched, or whether the milk bottle had been left out of the fridge all morning.

Despite his shortcomings, he seemed to be a kind and generous man, insisting that, at the very least, she remain living at The Clochán until she'd found a suitable place to live.

He smelt good too, his eau-de-cologne a subtle fusion of sandalwood, smoky salt and . . . rain.

She scoured the rental market every night after work, but it still took Greta over three weeks to find something within her budget, and a place that would house a hen. Finally, after looking through far too many undesirable abodes, she chanced upon a tiny, two-bedroom cottage on the back road of the valley. It was more of a hut than a cottage really, having once been accommodation for seasonal grape pickers, before falling into disuse when the vineyard owner built bigger premises.

The timber building bordered on being ramshackle. The cistern ran relentlessly, only one of the hotplates worked and the small patch of garden out front was all weed. However, the rent was within Greta's means, Marilyn Monroe was welcome, and, most importantly, the place had *soul*.

'Anything you do to it will be an improvement,' said the owner apologetically.

On her first night there, Greta perched on a small milking stool and looked out over the rows of vines stretching across the hill like a long, green sigh. Her arms were aching from lugging her possessions up the driveway, her head throbbed and her fingernails had been bitten to the quick. But she was content. The same contentment she'd experienced after learning to drive. That feeling of being on the brink of selfhood and independence.

Being the driver of her life was perhaps the wrong metaphor for her present situation. Emerson's Citroën was no longer at her disposal, and it was too expensive to ship her own car down from the North Island. This wasn't an insurmountable problem, it simply meant her days had to start earlier and end later to accommodate the infrequent bus schedule.

With at least an hour to wait each evening before her ride home, Greta took to frequenting the small town library. It was a pleasant place to pass the time, and, more importantly, the ideal place to do some rather important research.

CHAPTER 50

Greta was sitting out on her small front deck enjoying a glass of Indian tonic water, when she spotted Emerson's car winding up the hill, a trailer in tow.

'Finally!' she cried, running down the drive to meet him. Her furniture had been in storage for the longest time.

Emerson had kindly offered to have the container delivered to The Clochán, which was easier to find than her new dwelling. What's more, he was usually home during the day so would be there to receive the delivery.

'Careful! Don't hurt your back,' she cried, as they teetered under the load of Nora's rosewood armoire. 'Bit more to the left. That's it. Little more to the right. Perfect.'

Well, it was not actually perfect. The antique cupboard occupied nearly half of the space Greta had assigned for the living room. It would take some getting used to again.

'That's some piece of furniture,' said Emerson, his brow dripping with perspiration.

'Can I get you a cold drink before we unload the rest?'

'Won't say no, I won't.'

'If I'm absolutely honest,' Greta said, filling two glasses with water. 'I've never really liked it.'

'The armoire?'

She nodded. 'Those splayed legs. The dark wood. I used to be terrified of it as a kid. Thought a monster lived inside.'

'So why keep it?'

'It was my mother's prized piece. An heirloom she inherited from her mother. Or, rather, her adoptive mother. She'd never forgive me if she thought I didn't like it.'

'But your mother's dead, isn't she?'

'Yes,' Greta said, ruffled by his line of questioning and rather tactless use of the word 'dead'. He didn't understand. It was complicated.

'So?'

Greta handed him his drink. 'There's a lot of meaning and emotion invested in a piece of family furniture, you know.'

She walked into the small second bedroom.

A solitary light bulb hung from the ceiling, the curtains were faded and the rail was coming away from the wall. The walls were in desperate need of a coat of paint, and the cupboard door had come off. It would take some doing to get it ready for Holly.

That her friend was coming to stay after tramping the Routeburn Track left Greta delirious with excitement. Holly was making a special trip to see her. However, beneath Greta's excitement was the inevitable apprehension. Could their friendship survive a week of living in such close and humble quarters, Greta's very small life on show? What if Holly got bored? What if she wanted to go to a restaurant that Greta couldn't afford?

She had racked her brain for a plausible excuse. 'That's unfortunately the weekend Mel has asked me to hold the fort.' Or, 'I've not been very well of late and . . .'

Deep down, though, Greta knew that any such excuse would sound the end of their friendship. This was an opportunity. A fork in the road. And the thought of going back to Before filled her with dread.

She had to give up the pretence of perfection. Just be Greta. It was time to take the next step.

'What's left in the trailer?' Greta asked, heading outside.

Emerson took a swig of water and followed her.

'My flowerpot holder,' she cried, clapping her hands. 'I'd forgotten all about it. And my books!' She wrapped her arms around the huge cardboard box. 'It feels like Christmas.'

Sitting on wooden pallets for a few weeks had not been much of a hardship. After all, she was striving for a simpler life. But there was something unexpectedly comforting about being surrounded by her possessions again. Possessions which transformed her hut into a home.

'Thank you, Emerson,' she said, once her two armchairs had been unloaded. 'I couldn't have done this on my own.'

He blushed. A bright into-the-roots-of-his-hair, estuary-at-high-tide blush.

Greta could have kissed him. This was the second time she'd seen him colour. How fabulous.

'I'd better be off then,' he mumbled. 'It's getting late. Yes, late.'

'Emerson?'

He turned.

'Would you mind very much if I asked one more small favour of you?'

'Sure,' he said, a little warily.

'I'd like to move that again.'

His eyes grew wide. 'The armoire!'

'I'm sorry.'

'Which way?'

'Uh . . .'

Your mother is dead. Your mother is dead.

'Out back, please.'

'Out back! Are you sure?'

'It'll make an excellent storage cupboard for my gardening tools and chicken food.'

'But you don't even have chickens.'

'I do. Have a chicken. Though that's another story,' Greta said, grasping her end of the armoire impatiently.

And so they manoeuvred the cumbersome piece out onto the back porch, under the cover of the eaves.

Back inside, the room felt so much more spacious. And calmer.

Greta refilled their glasses.

'What's this?'

She turned. Emerson was holding a piece of paper.

'Oh nothing,' she said, putting down the glasses on the bench and grabbing it off him. 'Just some doodling.'

'You like shoes?'

She felt exposed. Foolish.

'Shoes are important,' she mumbled. 'Footwear. People don't realise.'

Emerson tilted his head to one side.

'Some silly scribbling,' she said, shoving it into her pocket. He wouldn't understand.

They both hovered. He was unwittingly blocking her way. She

couldn't very well edge around him to open the front door, not without looking rude.

'A comfortable shoe is worth its weight in gold,' he said.

Was he making fun of her?

He looked serious enough.

'Yes. Comfortable, while still being stylish,' she ventured.

'A tricky relationship that,' he said, sitting down. 'The marriage of comfort and style.'

Greta felt a surge of excitement. 'I'll let you in on a secret,' she said recklessly. 'I'm making a shoe.'

'You. Making a shoe? Goodness.' He pulled his lip down at one side, his obvious doubt puncturing her elation. She should never have confided in him. The project might be a folly, but it was hers.

She pulled her shoulders back. 'For centuries, shoes were made by hand using everyday household tools. Even kitchen cutlery!'

'Indeed,' he said.

'Shoemaking is no different from plumbing,' Greta continued. 'Or law, for that matter. Just another profession protecting its exclusivity. Well, anyone can make a shoe, Emerson. Anyone! It's not that hard. And it's certainly not the sole prerogative of some secretly-trained artisan.' She swallowed.

He smiled. 'Sole prerogative.'

She glowered at him.

'Get the pun?'

'Yes!'

'Glass of water?'

'What?' she barked.

'I was just after that glass of water.'

She flushed and passed him his refilled glass. 'Sorry.'

He downed it in one go.

'I've been using the computer at the library to watch some excellent instructive YouTube videos.' She bent down and pulled out a shoebox from under the sink. 'It all begins with a good last.' She lifted the lid. 'I made this mould by casting my foot in a box of alginate gel.'

Emerson peered inside. 'I have a last.'

'This is no joke, Emerson. I'm serious.'

'So am I. I have my own last. And a Lina. Yes, a Lina.'

324

'A Lina?'

'Lina is my shoemaker in Fiesole, just outside of Florence. A remarkable woman. Quite remarkable.'

Greta was reeling.

'She makes all my business shoes from a wooden last not dissimilar to this.'

Greta looked down at Emerson's feet. He was wearing his loafers with a neat white trim. 'You have your own shoemaker?'

It was as if he'd just told her that he was the President of the United States. A truth almost impossible to comprehend, but also so incredibly exciting (current President excluded).

Why were all the good men gay?

She didn't know for sure, but felt certain he was. A friend of Walter's + a passion for fine footwear + unmarried. It was not a complicated equation.

'So what's the next step?' he asked. 'If you'll excuse another pun.'

'You are on top form,' she said, grinning.

He blushed again.

Greta felt an urge to slip her hand into his. She resisted.

'The next step,' she said, trying to focus, 'is covering the last with masking tape. Then drawing on the design of the shoe, removing the tape, tracing the pattern onto a sheet of leather and cutting accordingly. I'm going for an avocado green.'

She felt excited just describing the process. She took a breath.

'You have to add a folding allowance, and some for the inner seam. I'm still trying to work out where the vamp will meet the toe line.'

'Impressive. Very impressive. But what I meant by next step was, what's the next step in your business plan?'

'Business plan?' She'd said nothing about a business.

Emerson pointed to the list of names scribbled down the side of an A4 sheet of paper.

Sole Mates

Sizeable Soles

Fabulous Feet

Foot First

Ample Ends

The room was quiet except for the wind slapping against the side of the small wooden building.

'I want to make beautiful shoes for women with big feet.'

As she articulated her dream, it came into full view, like a ship breaking through a curtain of mist.

'Everyone deserves to feel fabulous. And it's impossible to feel fabulous when you are wearing flippers. Unless of course, you are going scuba diving, which is not what I—'

'I understand,' Emerson said. 'I understand.'

He opened the front door. 'For the record, I like Fabulous Feet. Got a nice ring to it.'

She shook her head. 'No, it's not right.'

It felt strange to disagree with him in such a forthright fashion. Strange, but also good to know and speak her mind.

His eyebrows pinched together. 'Which is your favourite then?'

'None of these,' she said, scrunching up the paper. 'But I have the perfect name.'

'You do?'

'As of just a few moments ago.'

She ran her fingers through her hair — an easier exercise than in Auckland where the humidity kept it in a permanent frizz.

'The Next Step. I'm going to call it The Next Step.'

CHAPTER 51

'It's going to be a drawn-out case, I'm afraid,' Angus said. 'Nothing moves fast when it comes to the courts.'

'We're talking about Walter's sister,' Greta said. 'She has more right to the money than I do. I just need time to pay back the holiday. That hotel in New York will have cost a fortune—'

'Greta, take yourself out of the equation.' Angus was clearly in no mood to negotiate. 'This is about whether Walter deserved an equal share of his family's inheritance. That's all. How he wished to spend the money he inherited was entirely up to him.'

She nodded. 'It's just that I wouldn't want to be muscling in on his family's fortune.'

Angus did not reply. She'd noticed that about him. Whenever her words were unnecessary or repetitive, he simply withdrew from the conversation. It was hard to keep talking without the encouragement of *aha* or *mmh*. Lawyers were clever that way.

'So, how are things going down there?' he asked, changing tack. 'I might have to come down and visit sometime.'

Greta gulped. This was becoming a bit of a habit. Visitors.

'The work at Mel's keeps me afloat while I dabble in other things. And guess what? Marilyn Monroe is heading this way soon.'

'She is?'

Greta nodded. 'I can't wait. Holly has booked her onto some pet bus.' Greta giggled. The thought of Marilyn Monroe travelling by bus.

'Well I never,' Angus chuckled. 'Anyway, I'd better let you go before you run out of coins.'

'I'm not calling from a phone box, Angus. I bought a mobile phone.'

'Greta Jellings!'

She laughed.

'You sound happy.'

Happy. Such a glib word. Such an all-consuming, twenty-first-century goal.

But yes, she was happy. Not in the golden destination sort of way peddled by magazines, real estate agents, travel brochures and clothing stores. No. It was more a sense of contentment. Of being in sync with herself and her surrounds. Of being worthy of friendship. She folded down her fingers one by one — Holly, Piper, Mel, Emerson, Angus. She felt in a small way integral to their lives, like one of those paper dolls on a chain of nursery-school bunting.

'Yes, I am.'

Was she jinxing it by saying so?

Angus paused, as he was wont to do. It was a good space. Too momentous to fill in a hurry. She was happy.

'We'll keep in touch, Greta.'

'Thank you, Angus, for everything. I couldn't have done it without you. Or Walter. Or Emerson. Emerson has been amazing.'

She relaxed her shoulders. She had been hunching them.

'Pity all the good men are gay.'

Angus laughed. 'Emerson's no—'

The line went dead.

Greta looked at her phone screen. It was an empty grey. She had to remember to charge it.

Greta spent the weekend constructing a pen for Marilyn Monroe. She could imagine her hen's indignation at being confined. However, it would just be temporary, until she'd learnt the new boundaries and Greta had had a chance to create a suitable cover for the vegetable patch. She relied on her produce now. There could be no room for indulging one of Marilyn Monroe's degustation ventures.

She polished an old hubcap for a water bowl, bought some tamarind-flavoured sunflower seeds (Marilyn Monroe's favourite), and got a bale of hay delivered, along with a thirty-kilogram bag of chicken feed.

'Lot of food you got here,' said the man from the supply store, heaving the bag off his truck.

Thirty kilograms did look a lot more than Greta had envisioned.

'How many chickens you keep then?' he asked, looking around.

'Just enough' Greta said quickly, without even colouring. For the first time ever, she'd successfully sidestepped humiliation.

'You can leave it here, thank you,' she said, pointing to a space beside Nora's armoire.

'Need a hand to shift that inside? You won't be wanting such a precious piece of furniture rubbing up against the likes of chicken food.'

Greta graciously declined.

That evening, as she sat in her sitting room sipping soda with a dash of lime, she was beset by a flurry of concerns. Would Marilyn Monroe even remember her? What if the two-day bus trip proved too arduous? As for the dry southern climate, Marilyn Monroe was an Auckland bird. Greta didn't even know how old her hen was. For all she knew Marilyn Monroe was nearing the end of her life. Hens didn't live much beyond ten, although Greta had heard of one living into its twenties.

So much had changed in Greta's life. Mostly for the good. However, she hoped Marilyn Monroe would be one of the enduring constants.

Greta was dosing in her armchair when the sound of a car horn woke her. She squinted at her watch. 8.10 pm. She'd fallen asleep before dinner.

She peered out of the window, at the vines cast in a saffron glow. Someone was opening the gate. Emerson, silhouetted against the setting sun. She could recognise his gangly frame from a mile away.

As a rule, she was not a fan of spontaneous drop-ins, but with him it was different.

She tucked her hair behind her ears, pinched her cheeks to give them some colour and opened the front door. A cool gust swept in.

Emerson had left his car at the gate and was walking towards her with a crate in his arms. A small wooden crate.

'Is it . . . ?' she cried, running down to greet him. 'Is it my Marilyn Monroe?'

He was smiling. He looked particularly handsome in the evening light, his smile using up all the slack in his face. Despite his leanness, Emerson had no angles, just congenial corners. Even his balding scalp softened his thicket of sandy blonde hair. He was dressed simply, in a white business shirt unbuttoned at the collar, sleeves rolled up to the elbow, and a pair of dark blue denim jeans. His olive skin conferred him with a robust healthiness, and helped camouflage the birthmark staining his face.

329

'Is she okay? I hope she's okay.'

'She's fine,' he said, putting an eye to one of the holes peppering the crate. 'Now, let's get you out of here,' he said, his voice all paternal.

He'd make a good father, thought Greta.

'Let me do it!' she cried. 'Sorry. Thank you.'

This was her hen. Her pet. Her history.

Emerson lowered the box and took a step back.

She sank down on the cool grass.

'This was attached,' Emerson said, handing her a plain white envelope.

Greta took it. It was probably the bill for cartage.

'Aren't you going to open it?'

She would have been happy to open it later, but with Emerson pestering her, she tore it open. There was a bright yellow card inside.

'No. The crate. Aren't you going to open the crate?'

'Oh, yes!'

As Greta leant forward and unlatched the wooden door, the yellow card fell to the grass.

Written in bold black felt-tip was the shortest of messages:

Surprise!!!

> **Lots of love,**
>
> **Holly x**

And there, standing in a frozen pose, at the entrance, was Marilyn Monroe, her left eye obscured by her crimson fascinator, her right glancing suspiciously at the newly opened gap in her confinement.

Greta gasped.

Emerson crouched down beside her.

Marilyn Monroe ruffled her feathers, a shiver rippling up her body. Then she ran, full tilt, into Greta's lap.

Greta closed her eyes and breathed in the smell of sawdust and sweet earthiness. She fingered her hen's silky white feathers, and answered the soft tut tut tutting. 'Yes, yes, I've missed you too.' Her beautiful bird felt so satisfyingly substantial.

Then Marilyn Monroe was wriggling free. Retreating.

It all happened so fast. The hen backing up to the crate, her wings arched oddly like some satellite dish, as one . . . two . . . three . . . four balls of yellow fluff scurried out of the wooden box into their mother's soft white embrace.

CHAPTER 52

Darkness dropped over the hillside in a matter of minutes, chasing Greta and Emerson back to the house. Marylyn Monroe and her brood were finally settled into their new coop for the night.

Greta and Emerson hovered at the back door.

It would be rude not to invite him in, but it was getting late and—

'Fancy a quick cup of peppermint tea?' she said, slipping off her sandals.

'Sure. Thank you.'

He followed her inside.

Greta looked pointedly at his shoes. He didn't take the hint.

'Have a seat. I'll put the kettle on.'

Heat rushed to her cheeks. The laundry basket was standing in the middle of the room, her crimson bra draped over the side.

Emerson quickly looked the other way.

'Champagne!' he blurted out. 'I brought a bottle. To celebrate Marilyn Monroe's arrival. Yes, her arrival. I'll go and get it, shall I? It's in the car.'

In his haste, he left the front door open, channelling the valley's entire population of flying insects towards the light. Greta pulled the door shut and leant back against it. Too many surprises. Too much spontaneity. The day was losing its shape. She was losing control.

She took three deep breaths.

By the time Emerson returned, she'd laid out a plate of cheese and crackers. What on earth had he been up to? He was very easily distracted, that man.

'Here we go,' he said, pushing open the door.

'Oh my! Such a special bottle.' She'd never tasted Moët before. Not even in Business Class.

'Only the very best for . . . for Marilyn Monroe.'

'I'll have to find suitable bras for the occasion.'

Emerson's cheek twitched.

'I mean glasses! I'll have to find suitable glasses.'

Greta buried her head in the kitchen cupboard long enough for her colour to subside.

'It's lovely out,' Emerson said, popping the cork. 'We could . . . I mean . . . if you want . . . we could sit outside.'

Yes, thought Greta, that would be easier. The cover of darkness, the chairs facing the mountain, rather than each other.

They stepped outside, their flutes filled to the brim. Greta gave a little gasp. In just fifteen minutes the night had grown into its skin, and a thin scoop of moon now hollowed out a crescent of sky.

Emerson lifted his glass. 'To one remarkable, yes, remarkable lady.'

'To Marilyn Monroe,' Greta said quickly, taking a small sip. 'And to her new brood,' she added. 'Whom I hereby christen: Judi Dench, Whoopi Goldberg, Susan Sarandon and . . . and Lorde.'

'An entire tribe of remarkable women!'

Greta laughed. She took a bigger swig. 'Thank you, Emerson.'

He did not reply.

She couldn't turn to look at him; he was standing right beside her. Out of the corner of her eye, she saw a smile crumpling his cheek.

Then he had downed his glass and was stepping back towards the house, snuffing out the flutter of excitement in her chest.

It *was* late. He was probably tired. What had she been expecting anyway?

No expectation, no disappointment.

She breathed in the night's harvest-sweet smell.

'Can I top you up?'

She spun round. He was on the deck again, holding the bottle of bubbly.

Greta opened her mouth to reply. A burp escaped. 'Oh, excuse me!'

Here they were drinking champagne like a sophisticated couple, Emerson smelling of sandalwood and spice (just how she imagined 007 would smell) and she'd burped.

He refilled her glass, either politely ignoring her indiscretion or oblivious to it.

'To another remarkable lady,' he said, lifting his glass to hers.

Greta giggled. Shrugged. Looked away.

'And a lovable friend.'

Lovable? *If people only knew what you are really like.*

She glanced up at Emerson, expecting to out the tease, but all she found were his kind brown eyes, canopied under creased lids. In them she saw a reflection of herself for the first time. Complex. Human. Apparently loveable. And very much in love.

Count to ten before you do or say anything you might regret, Greta. You are such an impulsive child.

She leant towards him.

He sucked in a breath of surprise.

It did not deter her.

Time slowed, every millisecond recorded: The fumbling as he put down his glass. The warmth of his skin. The graze of his stubble against her chin.

She pressed her lips to his.

I'm gay, Greta. I'm gay, Greta. I'm gay.

But he didn't say that. Instead she felt his trembling hand slip into the small of her back and pull her closer.

The next morning Greta awoke with a champagne-thick headache and aching cheeks. Had she been smiling in her sleep?

She put a hand to her lips and blushed.

Marilyn Monroe's distant clucking intruded.

Ha! How long it had been since she'd heard that delightfully annoying sound? Some things never changed. Thank goodness!

She slipped on her dressing gown and padded barefoot to the back door.

Outside, the sun was toying with the dew, illuminating beads of moisture as if switching on hundreds of tiny light bulbs. A slice of oyster-coloured cloud banded Mount Malcolm's midriff. Across the valley, a tractor rumbled to life, but within minutes its low growl had been absorbed into the day.

Greta hobbled across the deck, dodging rusty nail heads.

She opened the doors of her mother's armoire to a strong smell of hessian sacking and chicken feed. The enormous bag was still sealed.

Greta bent down to open the drawer. She was after a Stanley knife and something to use as a food scoop.

The drawer had barely budged, when it jammed on its rail.

She yanked and rattled the handle, cursing its stubbornness. However, her curses were half-hearted. Nothing could really intrude on her mood.

Marilyn Monroe's demands grew louder and more persistent.

'I'm coming. I'm coming,' Greta called, positioning one foot on the side of the armoire and taking a firm grasp of the handle.

On the count of three she heaved.

The drawer hesitated, then gave way, sending Greta flying off the deck, the wooden cavity and its contents airborne.

She fell back on the damp grass. 'Well, that's one way to do it,' she said, laughing, and looking up at the morning sky. It was a gentle blue, not yet distilled by the day.

She kept forgetting how much magic there was above eye level.

After a few minutes, she sat up and, on all fours, set about collecting the scattered contents of the drawer. Pair of pliers. Ball of string. Stanley knife. Trowel.

She stopped. Her eyes narrowed. There was something mauve lying on the deck.

She scrambled over to it.

An envelope. An unopened mauve envelope peppered with tatty holes where fish moths had obviously been busy.

The postmark was illegible; however, the yellowed stamp still held onto the picture of a black man in a sharp satin suit playing the saxophone.

Greta ran her fingers around the envelope's worn border and lifted it to her nose. There was no remnant of a postie's satchel, nor the sweetness of mandarin peels. Just musty wood, dust and furniture oil.

How?

She looked up, as if expecting to see a peregrine falcon, or a messenger owl. But all she saw was the blue Gibbston sky.

She closed her eyes.

They stand beside the feijoa hedge, mother and daughter staring at the envelope as if it is a hand grenade, then Nora's expression grows dark and thunderous.

'Don't let me ever catch you meddling with one of these again,' *she shouts, walloping Greta with her fluffy grey slipper and leading her inside. 'Do you hear me, Greta Jellings? Never!'*

Later that night, Greta creeps out into the garden.

There, still lying on the ground, is the letter addressed to her.

She picks it up and with trembling hands hides it under her pyjama top, the damp paper cool against her skin.

As she tiptoes back into the house, the floorboards creak.

'Who's there? Greta, is that you?'

Quickly she kneels beside the creepy cupboard in the entrance hall and forces the hydrangea-coloured envelope through the gap between the drawer and wall of the armoire.

'What are you doing there in the dark?'

'I've got a sore tummy. It's really sore. I don't feel very well.'

'I'll warm a hotty for you. You hop back into bed, my girl.'

So there the envelope remained. Forgotten about for more than thirty years.

A 'cluck' brought Greta to her senses.

'Apologies, Marilyn Monroe. You've been more than patient.'

Greta sat on the narrow porch in front of her house and opened the disintegrating envelope.

My darling Gretabug,

Today I met someone in a bookstore whom I know you will love. Her name is 'Eloise'. She reminds me so much of you. Six years old. Sassy. And superwoman smart. A little bit naughty too. Actually, very naughty. She lives in one of the grandest hotels here in New York along with her nanny, her pet dog, and the tiniest turtle called Skipperdee. She calls room service at the drop of a hat, plays plenty of pranks on boring old grownups, and roller-skates, yes roller-skates, down the very posh corridors! Eloise has oodles of confidence, can talk the hindleg off a donkey, and, like you, will surely grow up to be an amazing woman.

One day, when you are older, and your mum says it's okay, you will perhaps visit me here. Then we will stay for a few days at the very swanky Plaza Hotel, call room service at the drop of a hat, eat double (no, make that triple) scoops of ice cream, ride the elevators from the basement to the very top, then back to the bottom again. And we'll roller-skate, if not down the posh corridors, then definitely down the very fancy Fifth Avenue.

I miss you this much ... (arms as wide as I can stretch). Hope you are wearing your superwoman cape.

The biggest hug coming your way. Can you feel it yet?

One for your mum too.

All my love,

Papa xxx

PS: I've posted the story of Eloise to you today. Let me know when she arrives and what you think of her. I am sure that you, Madeline and Eloise will soon be the very best of friends.

Greta scrutinised the address.

Greenwich Village. New York.

She'd been there! Walked through Washington Square Park en route to the 9/11 Memorial. Sat on a bench under the sycamore trees. Heard the twinkling laughter of children in the playground. Felt the cool spray of water from the fountain.

She folded the fragile piece of paper and slipped it carefully back into its envelope.

For the first time, her father was not bound by a blank frame, nor an orbit of nothingness. She could see him sitting on a bench under a giant sycamore tree. He had a cheese blintze in one hand, a book in the other. Children laughed in the distance, and the sun captured a fine rainbow in the spray.

Greta looked out across the Central Otago landscape. Thoughts came and went, some leading her down deep holes, others passing like clouds scudding across the sky. And all the time the sun crept steadily up the front porch, until it had reached her chair, bathing her feet in a warm stripe of gold.

'Coffee, my . . . my dear?'

She turned. Emerson was standing in the doorway, his face still crumpled by sleep, a shy smile playing on his lips, and two steaming mugs of coffee in his hands.

Notes

p. 55: The extracts come from Chapter Nine of *The Wind in the Willows* by Kenneth Grahame, Methuen, 1908.

p. 107: 'She was not afraid / of mice — / she loved winter, / snow, and ice. / To the tiger in the zoo / Madeline just said, / "Pooh-pooh"'. Excerpt(s) from *Madeline* by Ludwig Bemelmans, copyright 1939 by Ludwig Bemelmans; copyright renewed © 1967 by Madeleine Bemelmans and Barbara Bemelmans Marciano. Used by permission of Viking Children's Books, an imprint of Penguin Young Readers Group, a division of Penguin Random House LLC. All rights reserved.

'Chocolate-brown leather banquettes, nickel-trimmed black glass tabletops, a dramatic black granite bar and a 24-carat gold leaf-covered ceiling.' Quote from The Carlyle, New York City's website. http://www.rosewoodhotels.com/en/the-carlyle-new-york/dining/bemelmans-bar

p. 108: 'Red Velvet' cocktail description appears in 'Bemelmans' Famous' on The Carlyle, New York City's website. https://www.rosewoodhotels.com/en/the-carlyle-new-york/dining/bemelmans-bar/bemelmans-bar-menu.pdf

p. 163: The quote 'When a man is tired of London, he's tired of life' is from Samuel Johnson.

p. 198: '[Mavis, Mavis], give me your answer do. I'm half crazy, all for the love of you. It shan't be a stylish marriage. I can't afford a carriage,' song lyrics from 'Daisy Bell' by Harry Dacre, 1892.

p. 215: 'He's got you and me, brother, in His hands,' lyrics from the hymn 'He's Got the Whole World in His Hands', Master Sergeant Obie Edwin Philpot, Spirituals Triumphant, Old and New, 1027.

p. 224 and 225: Quotes taken from the Kigali Genocide Memorial's permanent exhibition. Reproduced with permission from Aegis Trust/Kigali Genocide Memorial. For more information about the trust and memorial visit: www.aegistrust.org / www.kgm.rw

p. 311: 'Hitler has only got one ball, / Goring has two, but they're small, / Himmler has something sim'lar / But poor old Goebbels has no balls at all,' from 'Colonel Bogey March', music composed by Lieutenant F.J Ricketts, lyrics attributed to Toby O'Brien, 1939.

Acknowledgements

Every time I write a book, I am reminded of what a collective process it is. I'm so grateful to everyone who has lined the route to publication, offering encouragement, guidance and the occasional firm word when I was tempted to turn back.

Special thanks to:

Luigi, Nadia and Andrew, for believing in Greta right from the start, and for always believing in me.

My dearest late mum and dad, who nurtured my love of the human story, and whose hard work and sacrifice made it possible for me to travel.

Peter, best brother ever, for treating me to my first trip to New York. And what a treat it was!

Jaqueline Cangro, Jock Matthews and Amali Fonseka, for such sage input.

Hannah Ferguson, for being so excited about that very first draft.

Nadine Rubin Nathan, agent extraordinaire, for finding Greta the very best of homes.

Louise Russell and Samantha Guillen, who from the start just 'got' Greta, and brought such enthusiasm, insight and acuity to the editorial process. And the rest of the stellar team at Bateman Books for doing all that has to be done to launch a book into the world.

Keely O'Shannessy, for capturing the essence of Greta's story with such a striking cover.

'Harriet', for flying into our lives one wintery morning, and laying a perfect egg almost every day thereafter.

Kira and Mia, devoted canine companions, for doing the long shift in my office every day.

And last, but by no means least, my loyal readers, who waited so patiently for novel number three. All your lovely comments have kept me excited about this writing journey.